Gold Web

Gold Web

A Klondike Mystery

Vicki Delany

DUNDURN
TORONTO

Editor: Cheryl Hawley
Design: Courtney Horner
Printer: Webcom

Library and Archives Canada Cataloguing in Publication

Delany, Vicki, 1951-, author
    Gold web : a Klondike mystery / by Vicki Delany.

Issued in print and electronic formats.
ISBN 978-1-4597-0772-6

    1. Klondike River Valley (Yukon)--Gold discoveries--Fiction.
I. Title.

PS8557.E4239G66 2013   C813'.6   C2013-902955-9
C2013-902956-7

1   2   3   4   5   17   16   15   14   13

Conseil des Arts du Canada   Canada Council for the Arts   Canada   ONTARIO ARTS COUNCIL
CONSEIL DES ARTS DE L'ONTARIO

We acknowledge the support of the **Canada Council for the Arts** and the **Ontario Arts Council** for our publishing program. We also acknowledge the financial support of the **Government of Canada** through the **Canada Book Fund** and **Livres Canada Books**, and the **Government of Ontario** through the **Ontario Book Publishing Tax Credit** and the **Ontario Media Development Corporation**.

Care has been taken to trace the ownership of copyright material used in this book. The author and the publisher welcome any information enabling them to rectify any references or credits in subsequent editions.

J. Kirk Howard, President

The publisher is not responsible for websites or their content unless they are owned by the publisher.

Printed and bound in Canada.

VISIT US AT
Dundurn.com | @dundurnpress | Facebook.com/dundurnpress | Pinterest.com/dundurnpress

Dundurn	Gazelle Book Services Limited	Dundurn
3 Church Street, Suite 500	White Cross Mills	2250 Military Road
Toronto, Ontario, Canada	High Town, Lancaster, England	Tonawanda, NY
M5E 1M2	LA1 4XS	U.S.A. 14150

For Caroline, Julia, and Alex

Chapter One

The last thing he saw in this world was my shocked face.

He stared directly into my eyes. Red blood and white foam bubbled around his lips as he struggled to speak. "MacGillivray."

"I am Mrs. MacGillivray. Help is coming," I said.

He gasped, his breath sounding rough and wet in his chest.

"Try not to move." I didn't know why I was whispering. Somehow it seemed appropriate.

"Culloden." He breathed the single word with great effort. Then, with a final burst of blood, his head dropped to one side, his eyes rolled back, and he lay still.

The man had appeared out of nowhere, heading straight for me. He reached out his arms as he approached, and then he simply crumpled to my feet. Instinctively, I'd dropped to the ground beside him and gathered him into my arms.

His face was recently shaven, showing an excess of old acne scars, his eyes a light grey. The bags under those eyes were dark and deep. Lines radiated out from his mouth, and his nose appeared to have been broken several times over the years. His unkempt beard and thin, unwashed hair were heavily streaked with grey. Blood saturated his filthy jacket and many-times-mended shirt.

I had never seen him before, yet he knew my name.

I uncurled my arms from his back and laid him as gently onto the ground as I was able. I closed my eyes for a moment and took a single deep breath. I lifted my hand in front of my own face. Wet red streaks glistened in the dim light of the alley. I felt liquid soaking into the folds of my dress.

I'd been on my way home for supper in the company of ...

"Angus," I bellowed, unceremoniously shoving the body aside. "Angus, where are you?" I struggled to my feet, heart pounding, arms flailing, feet slipping in the blood seeping into the dirt of the alley. My son had been with me, full of chatter about the antics of one of his friends. I had not been paying the slightest bit of attention, instead thinking of the evening to come. I was most certainly paying attention now.

"Angus," I called again.

I was alone. Alone with a dead man. It was unnaturally quiet: in Dawson City, Yukon Territory, in the summer of 1898, there were always people around, even in a back alley at suppertime. I wiped my wet hands on the hips of my dress in a fashion that would have had Miss Wheatley denying me tea. I started down the alley. It was still daylight — this was, after all, the Yukon in July.

A blond head popped around a corner, and I almost screamed. Instead I said, quite sharply, "What on earth? Didn't you hear me calling?"

"Of course I heard you calling, Mother," he replied, not at all put out. "That's why I came back. He's gotten away."

"Gotten away?" I sucked in a breath. "I would most certainly hope he's gotten away." My twelve-year-old son had charged down a deserted alley in pursuit of person or persons unknown who had recently murdered a man.

Angus brushed past me and dropped to the ground beside the body. I stood above him and we were silent for a few moments. The man lay on his back, empty eyes staring into the sky. His right side was matted with blood and a pool had formed beneath him.

"Footpads," I said, "in Dawson. I never."

"Do you recognize him, Mother?"

"No."

"Did he say anything to you?"

I hesitated. "He seemed to know my name."

"I'll wait here. You'd best go for the Mounties."

"What's going on there?" a voice called from the dry goods shop. We were in the narrow alley at the rear of the Savoy Saloon and Dance Hall, of which I am the proprietor. One half of the proprietorship, I should say. As is my custom, I was heading home for something to eat and to change into evening wear before returning to the Savoy to supervise the night's activities.

Someone had to fetch the police. Someone should remain with the body. Stray dogs, starving feral beasts, were known to creep into town on occasion, and although I had been told there are no rats in the Yukon, I don't quite believe it. There are always rats. I hate the things with a passion.

I couldn't leave this man, whoever he might be, to the attention of wild dogs and non-existent rats. Yet I didn't want to leave my son alone in case the attackers returned.

Two fellows turned the corner of the alley. They were walking slowly, and one was telling the other that an unnamed woman was a "poor excuse for a whore but better than ..." His mouth snapped shut at the sight of me, and he whipped off his cap. "Mrs. MacGillivray, what a pleasure." I felt his eyes run down my body. For once I knew it was not in admiration of my female charms.

"Mrs. MacGillivray," the second man cried, "are you injured? Has that scoundrel attacked you? By heavens, if he weren't dead I'd kill him myself."

"I am unharmed. No one attacked me. Angus and I arrived after the deed was done. Someone, however, needs to fetch the police." I studied the two men. They alternately smiled stupidly at me and moved closer to get a good look at the body on the ground.

"I said, what's all the commotion out there?" My across-alley neighbour, wife of the owner of the dry-goods shop, peeked out her door. A scowling-faced woman with a nose like a hatchet and a tick in her right eye, she could barely restrain from spitting whenever she encountered me. The premises next to the shop was a mortuary. The body would not have to be moved very far.

No one answered her question.

"Go for the Mounties, Mother," Angus said, his voice firm.

Angus had changed recently. He'd headed off into the wilderness on a North-West Mounted Police mission, and I suspected he now considered himself to be a man. At the conclusion of the mission he'd wept in my arms, but that was not something either of us mentioned. He had to grow up someday. But did it have to be so soon?

"Very well." I straightened my hat and set off on a mission of my own. I am not unknown in the streets of Dawson, and no matter where I might be I make it my business not to be unnoticeable. The moment I exited the alley onto King Street people stopped whatever they were doing to stare at me. I began to regret not sending one of the men for the Mounties. I was, unfortunately, clad in a two-piece, white day dress. Most unsuitable, I'd always known, for the dusty streets of this mining town, but the fabric was so delightful I could scarcely resist purchasing it. Besides, I had the services of an excellent laundress, and I make it a point of honour to sometimes do what is not entirely practical.

Now that I was in somewhat better light, and recovering from the initial shock of the man's appearance and sudden demise, I could see that the bottom of the blouse and the lap and side panel of my skirt were red with blood. I checked my hands and shuddered. Blood was rapidly drying in the crevices of the skin and around my fingernails. I hurried through the streets, not stopping at cries of my name or gasped inquiries as to my health.

It wasn't far to the NWMP town detachment on Queen Street. I gathered my skirts in my fists, galloped up the stairs (once again feeling the force of Miss Wheatley's disapproval — a lady never hurries) and threw open the door. The three men inside turned and stared at me, as their mouths dropped open.

"Mrs. MacGillivray," the youngest of them cried. "Save us! What's happened?" He crossed the small room in two strides, grabbed me, and attempted to wrestle me into a vacant chair.

"Unhand me." I swatted at the over-eager arms. "This is not my blood."

"So I assumed," Corporal Richard Sterling said, "or you would not be standing straight, nor have such colour in your cheeks. Nevertheless, you do present quite a sight, madam."

"The alley behind the Savoy. A man has been attacked. Killed. Angus is with him ... with the body. You'd better come."

Richard grabbed his hat. "McAllen, you're with me. FitzHenry, watch the office."

"But ..." FitzHenry, the one who had attempted to minster to my wounds, protested.

"Fiona, go home," Richard said, ignoring the constable's protests.

"Don't you want to know what happened?"

He headed out the door. "Of course I want to know what happened. I'll call on you later to get the story." He turned to face me, his boot on the top step. "If I may be so bold as to say so, you need to change and have a bath. The way you look will frighten small children."

And then he was gone, Constable McAllen following.

I looked at FitzHenry. Tall and gangly, with a prominent Adam's apple and arms and legs he had trouble keeping under control, I wondered if he was old enough to shave. He flushed blood red under my examination and dropped his eyes to an intense study of the floorboards. They had not been in place for more than a couple of months and already shoddy workmanship was evident in the uneven tread, popping nails, and gaps between the planks. It was no worse than any other building in Dawson. The town had grown so fast, hacked out of sheer wilderness, it was a wonder walls weren't falling down all around us.

"Good evening, Constable," I said, preparing to make my departure.

"Mrs. MacGillivray, ma'am," he coughed. The colour rose even higher in his cheeks. I wondered if he were about to burst spontaneously into flames.

"Yes?"

"You might not want ... I mean, you might want ... I mean ..."

"What do you mean?" I snapped, with more irritation than was polite.

"Nothing, ma'am. Sorry, ma'am."

"Very well. Good day." I stalked off, head held high.

When I got home, having received more open stares on the street than even I am accustomed to, I knew what Constable FitzHenry had been referring to. I might not want, he no doubt meant to say, to be seen in public with blood splattered all over my face.

Chapter Two

I screamed at my reflection in the mirror, which was missing the top right corner, and began scrubbing frantically. Fortunately my arrival had been expected, and Mrs. Mann, our landlady, had laid out hot water and towels so I might freshen up.

I'd come in the front door and gone directly to my rooms, not passing through the kitchen where Mrs. Mann was banging pots and pans.

A light knock on the door.

"Come in," I said.

The door opened and Mrs. Mann stood there. "Will Angus …" Her jaw dropped to the floor. "Mrs. MacGillivray, what on earth have you been up to this time?"

"I came across the scene of an accident," I replied, not wanting to discuss details. "Help me off with this dress. Will you be able to get it clean?"

Her fingers worked at the row of tiny buttons running down the back of the blouse. She wasn't quite finished when I yanked it off, sending pearl buttons flying everywhere. With a disapproving "tsk," Mrs. Mann took the blouse while I slipped out of the skirt.

"The blood isn't dried yet. If I put it to soak immediately, the stains should come out."

"Good."

"Supper's not finished."

"I'll do the cooking while you tend to the dress."

She eyed me most suspiciously. As well she might. I have many and varied talents but skill in the kitchen is not one of them.

"That blood is drying even as we speak," I said. "Get to it. The supper will have to wait. Now that I think of it, you'll have to send something for me later. I have to get back to the Savoy immediately. Angus is assisting the police."

"Not again!"

"Sadly, yes. Once again."

Chapter Three

Angus MacGillivray wanted nothing more in this world than to be an officer in the North-West Mounted Police. To serve his Queen, his country, his fellow men. His mother, he knew, intended that he become a gentleman. Whatever that might be. She insisted on proper grammar at all times, had taught him a bit of Greek and Latin, how to address a duke and a prince, seating arrangements at a formal dinner party. Not that they had met any dukes or princes in Dawson, and they'd never had a dinner party. If company dropped in, they could barely squeeze six around the rough-hewed kitchen table at Mrs. Mann's boarding house. The tiny, overcrowded house didn't have a dining room.

Angus's mother had made her way through life by herself, orphaned as a child and later alone after the death of his father, discarded by his heartless paternal relatives. She'd succeeded because she spoke like an English aristocrat, was perfectly groomed at all times, dressed well, and conducted herself with absolute deportment. It didn't hurt, he knew, that she was considered to be the most beautiful woman in Dawson, if not the whole territory.

But his mother was a woman, and Angus MacGillivray would be a man someday. He didn't think it mattered much to his future prospects if he could recite Homer in the original Greek, play the violin (which, thank heavens, they'd left behind in the flight from Toronto), execute a proper bow in the presence of royalty, or wield a fish fork.

No, Angus MacGillivray was destined for great things. Two more years until the twentieth century would arrive. Time to throw off the shackles of the old world and embrace the new.

He'd only be fourteen years old in two more years. Sometimes he feared he'd never grow up.

A good-sized crowd had gathered behind the Savoy. Nothing like a bit of excitement in Dawson to draw the multitudes. The sight of Fiona MacGillivray, running through the streets with her virginal white dress soaked in blood from neck to hem and flecks of blood and brains (the story grew in the telling) dotted across her perfect, yet horror-struck, face, was excitement indeed.

Angus stood protectively over the body, not letting anyone venture too close.

"Search the pockets," someone said, stepping forward as if to do just that. Angus planted himself firmly in the way. Despite secret boxing lessons with Sergeant Lancaster, a former champion, he was scarcely a match for a full-grown man. And he knew it. But he had been given this responsibility, and he was not going to back down.

"The Mounties have been summoned," he said, trying to deepen his voice, for about the tenth time. "Leave him until then."

"Mounties," a man spat. "Help themselves to the man's poke they will."

Angus bristled, but before he could protest he heard a welcome booming voice from the back door of the Savoy. Ray Walker, his mother's business partner, stepped into the alley, slapping the sturdy billy club he kept behind the bar into his hand. Ray was shorter than Angus, with scarcely an ounce of excess flesh on him, but he was a street fighter from the slums and shipyards of Glasgow and a match for almost any man in town.

"I'd suggest we do what young Angus says," Walker said, in his indecipherable Glaswegian accent, "and wait for the police. Bar's open, if anyone's interested."

More and more men, and a few less-respectable women, were arriving every minute. Dawson boasted more than its share of drifters. Tens of thousands of people had headed north into the wilderness, on foot, on hearing word of the gold strike at Bonanza Creek. Many, if not most, had not the slightest idea what mining entailed or how remote the Klondike was. When they arrived, after months of hardship, to find that nuggets were not lying on the ground like windfall apples and that placer mining was nothing but darned hard work, a great many of them spent their days wandering from one side of town to the other, their nights crowded into the plethora of saloons, gambling dens, and dance halls. Waiting for the police to arrive was better than another stroll to the end of the street.

When he heard the voice he'd been hoping for, Angus felt the weight of responsibility lift from his shoulders.

"You men have nothing to do today? Get on your way. If you want entertainment the dance halls'll be opening soon. There's nothing to see here. George O'Reilly, haven't you done enough chopping wood down at the fort? I don't want to see any more of you."

The assembled men shifted and shuffled to let the police through, but no one did as they'd been told and left. Not even Ray's reminder of the bar so tantalizingly close was enough to distract them from a bloody body. Those at the back pushed forward trying to get a better look.

Corporal Sterling and Constable McAllen emerged from the crowd. They stood quiet for a moment, simply looking. Sterling dropped to his haunches. He held his fingers against the side of the man's neck, although there could be no doubt he was dead. Sterling pushed himself back to his feet, wiping his hand on his trousers. He spotted the undertaker, standing in the shadows behind Angus. "Mr. Dion, convenient to have you here. You can take him away now, if you please. I'll be in to talk to you further once I've checked around here. Send someone to fetch the doctor, will you?"

Dion grunted, and he and his assistant pushed their cart forward. They loaded the body and wheeled it, arms and legs flapping, the few yards to their place of business. The puddle of blood, seeping into the dust of the alley, remained behind. No one moved.

"Angus, do you know anything about this?" Sterling asked in a low voice.

"We were passing, Mother and I, when —"

"Enough. Tell me inside. Did anyone here recognize that fellow?" he called to the crowd.

Men muttered and shook their heads.

"In that case, didn't I tell you people to be on your way?"

Show over, the men at the back began to peel away. One by one the others followed.

"Do you have a shovel, Walker?" Sterling asked.

"Aye, for when it snows."

"Fetch it. Constable, dig that mess under. Then head to Fort Herchmer and get Inspector McKnight."

"What do you want me to do, sir?" Angus asked. He'd have been embarrassed to know he sounded like a puppy eager to perform tricks.

"Did you recognize that man?"

"No. I don't think I've ever seen him before. Mother said he knew her name."

"Let's go inside and talk. Too many ears around here."

Ray Walker emerged from the Savoy carrying a shovel with a bent handle. He passed it to McAllen, who was looking a mite green around the gills. "Make sure ye do a fine job now, lad. Bad for business, ye ken, folks tracking blood across yon floorboards."

McAllen swallowed.

"I might as well interview Angus here," Sterling said. "Can we use a private room, Walker?"

"I suppose I can trust the two o' ye in Fiona's office."

The dance hall, at the back of the Savoy, was empty of customers at this time of day but would not be for much longer. The nightly show was scheduled to begin at eight o'clock and the room would be filled to overflowing with foot-stomping, cheering, belching cheechakos and sourdoughs. The room had no windows, the only light came from the front rooms and the kerosene lamps, which emitted a smoky, yellow glow. The second-floor balconies were dark. Helen Saunderson, the Savoy's maid of all work, was sprinkling fresh sawdust on the floor while Murray the bartender arranged benches in rows in front of the stage. Four of the dancers were standing together, chatting. They were dressed in their street clothes prior to heading to the dressing room to change into costume. They broke off as the men came in.

"A man murdered only steps from our door," Betsy sighed in delicious horror. "Oh, young Angus," she gave him a bawdy wink, "you'd best be walking us girls home tonight."

Angus felt himself changing colour. He tripped over a cracked floorboard.

Ray growled. "That's enough o' that, Betsy. Don't let her hear you talking like that."

They had not the slightest doubt who "her" was.

"Nothing but another drunken layabout," Irene yawned. Irene Davidson, stage name of Lady Irénée, was the most popular dance hall girl in all of Dawson. Ray Walker put his arm possessively around her. She giggled and snuggled in close.

Irene and Ray were courting. Angus knew his mother wasn't at all happy about that, although she refused to discuss the reason why.

"No one said anything about murder," Corporal Sterling snapped. "And I don't want any of you spreading rumours."

The girls twittered demurely.

"She said it was safe to work here," said a pretty girl standing slightly behind the others. She was new and younger than most. "My father won't be pleased to hear there's been a killing."

"No one was killed here," Irene reminded her. "And don't you start saying he was. We can't do much about what happens outside our doors."

"Mrs. MacGillivray might be delayed tonight," Ray said. "Isn't it time ta start getting changed?"

"Delayed? Whyever would I be delayed?"

Angus loved watching people react to his mother. She swept into the room, dressed in a red silk evening gown with plunging neckline and bare shoulders, black hair perfectly arranged beneath a stunning hat, jewellery sparking in what little light filled the room. Her face and hands were scrubbed clean and a touch of rouge applied to her lips and cheeks. He had no doubt she'd been hiding in the wings, waiting for the suitable moment to make a grand entrance.

"Good evening, Corporal. I was delighted to see that the alley is once again clean and tidy. Angus, your supper is waiting at home. Ladies, I believe we have a show to put on."

Only Richard Sterling and Ray Walker never seemed to be nonplussed when Fiona put on a display. "Supper will have to wait, I'm afraid," the corporal said. "I want to know who that man was and what you and Angus have to do with all of this."

"Nothing. We have nothing to do with it. Angus and I were unfortunate enough to be passing by shortly after he was set upon by footpads. That's all."

"Let's go upstairs, shall we. You can tell me about it. I've sent for Inspector McKnight."

"Most unfortunate."

Sterling struggled not to grin.

"You got back awfully soon, Mother," Angus said. "Didn't you have your supper?"

"I could scarcely eat while you were under interrogation, now could I? Mrs. Mann will be bringing me a package later."

Chapter Four

One end of the upper floor of the Savoy was used as accommodation for any of the male staff temporarily without lodging, as well as a place for big gamblers to take a nap rather than having to leave the building and possibly neglecting to return. Fiona's office was at the other end of the hall.

It was a practical room, used for nothing but business. Her desk was placed under the window, pens and pencils and paper laid out neatly on the green blotter. A single visitor's chair faced the desk, looking out over Front Street, and a cabinet had been pushed up against the wall. No drapes hung across the windows and no pictures were on display, only a cracked mirror so Fiona could check her appearance before heading downstairs. A green and orange sofa, which had seen far better days, provided the office's only feminine touch.

It was in this room, Richard Sterling suspected, where Fiona could be herself. Practical, sensible, down to earth. All the rest: the dresses, the jewels (most of which were fake), the voice, the gestures were strictly for public consumption.

Fiona threw herself into her chair, leaving Angus and Sterling to stand.

"Richard, I have never seen that man before. And, as you know, I remember the face of everyone who comes through the doors of the Savoy. Angus, did you know him?"

Angus shook his head.

"One of the dancers had been here, in my office, earlier in the afternoon. She left her shawl behind, and I took it to the dressing room on my way out." Fiona smiled at her son. "Angus was kind enough to offer to escort me home. As we were in the back, we simply exited through that door, intending to cut through the alley." She threw up her hands. "He came out of nowhere. Straight toward us. And ..." she looked at Angus, "fell into me. It was only then I realized he was wounded. I knelt beside him, intending to offer assistance, but it immediately became obvious he was beyond help. Then he expired. In my arms." She shuddered.

"Angus?" Sterling asked.

"He was being chased. I saw him. A man was after him. Soon as he saw us, Mother and me, he darted away. I ... uh ... I went after him."

Fiona groaned.

"And?"

"Sorry, sir, but he disappeared. By the time I came out onto the street he was gone. I didn't know which way to go. I went north, but only as far as Second Street. No sign of him there, and I remembered Mother was all alone. If he returned ... well, I thought I'd better get back to Mother."

The boy was too brave, sometimes, for his own good, Sterling thought. Just as well he hadn't cornered a man who'd thought nothing of knifing a fellow in broad daylight. He'd say nothing about it in front of Fiona, but have a word with Angus later about fools rushing in.

"Would you recognize this man again if you saw him?"

Angus chewed his lip. "I don't think so, sir. He was just a shape, you know. Running away."

"Are you sure it was only one man?"

Angus thought. "I saw one. But I can't swear he didn't have an accomplice running ahead."

"Clothes?"

"Ordinary working man's clothes. Dark trousers, jacket. A cap."

"Mrs. MacGillivray, did the deceased say anything to you?"

"No. Well, my name. He said my name."

"But you didn't recognize him?"

A smile touched the edge of her mouth. She lowered her head and arranged her skirts. "I am not unknown in this town, Corporal Sterling."

"He said nothing else?"

She hesitated. There was more, he knew it. She ran her long fingers across the silk on her lap. It rustled gently. "Nothing. He said my name, and then he died."

The heavy tread of boots sounded on the stairs. Inspector McKnight burst in, moustache bristling, eyes gigantic behind the thick lens of his glasses.

"We might as well set up a detachment in this office. When I was informed that a dead man had been found in the alley behind a dance hall I scarcely needed to bother inquire as to what dance hall. Do you bring trouble upon yourself, Mrs. MacGillivray?"

"Sir," Angus straightened in protest, "my mother ..."

"Yes, yes." McKnight waved a hand. "Your mother is never responsible for anything that goes on here. What is it this time? A man's been stabbed, the constable said."

"Looks that way, sir," Sterling said. "The body's at the undertaker's and the doctor's been summoned. Angus saw a man running away."

"Will you look at the time?" Fiona rose to her feet like a river of shimmering red. She tucked her pocket watch into the folds of her skirt. "Almost eight o'clock. Now that I've answered all your questions, I need to get downstairs and ensure all is ready for the evening's show. If you gentlemen manage to sort this business out, please do join us. Angus, once you've assisted the police, go home." She rounded her desk and made little shooing gestures as if she were chasing chickens into the coop. "I suppose, Corporal, you'll want to join the doctor when he makes his examination. Most unpleasant. You will, of course, not be taking my son to witness that."

"No," McKnight said, "that won't be necessary."

Angus was smart enough not to even try to protest.

Quickly and efficiently she cleared the room. She locked the office door behind her. Sterling had a great many more questions to ask of her, but now that McKnight had arrived it was up to the inspector to ask them. As he didn't seem so inclined, there were other things they could be doing. Such as examining the body.

* * *

As I've previously observed, there's apparently nothing that will keep the crowds away from the Savoy. We've had dead bodies on the stage, a hostage taking, a suicide, a kidnapping, yet we continue to be the most popular dance hall in town.

We might, truth be told, be the most popular dance hall in town *because* of those things, rather than *despite* them.

Tonight was no exception. Once I got the police out of my office — rather neatly done, if I do say so myself — and descended the stairs, eight o'clock was approaching.

Precisely at eight p.m., give or take a few minutes, up and down Front Street all the dance halls send out musicians and callers to announce the beginning of the evening's entertainment. It makes an unholy hullabaloo as callers bellow out the attractions to be found within, and every orchestra strikes up a different piece. More than one musician in this town is remarkably short on musical aptitude.

Yet that hullaballoo is music to my ears, as crowds pour into the bar, the gambling room, and the dance hall, every one of them eager to spend their money as fast as they can.

Ray and I are more than happy to oblige them.

I went through to the back to watch the beginning of the stage show. Six nights of the week we put on four straight hours of entertainment: show girls, comedy routines, scenes from Shakespeare. Tonight the performance opened with a magician who went by the sobriquet of Roland the Magnificent. He was a new act, and I wanted to ensure I was getting my money's worth. Roland, if that was indeed his name, wasn't much of a magician. He did a few card tricks, pulled coins from the décolletage of a giggling Betsy, messed about with coloured scarves, but he was highly amusing and played to the crowd so beautifully some of the old timers forgot they were only enduring the opening performance while waiting for the girls to prance across the stage. Roland the Magnificent got fewer boos than male performers usually did, and, satisfied with my decision to hire him, I made my way through the gambling room — also echoing with the sound of money — to the bar.

When Ray and I bought the building, less than a year ago in the autumn of 1897, it had been nothing but a two-storey shell, erected so quickly some of the wood was still green. It boasted a rickety staircase, loose floorboards, a slanting floor, crooked windows, and doors that didn't close properly. The first thing we did was to have the front and back doors fixed and sturdy locks installed in order to secure the precious supply of whisky. The condition of the structure we could do nothing about, not that we much cared — no other building in town was any better — but we set about decorating the place in an attempt to turn it into the sort of establishment that would impress miners and labourers. We hung red-and-gold wallpaper on two and a half of the walls, and when that ran out covered the white-washed remainder with mirrors and paintings. A portrait of Her Imperial Majesty, in all her aging glory, hung in pride of place behind the long mahogany bar. We'd stuck a Union Jack into one side of the frame and, in an attempt to please the sizeable number of Americans who made up our custom, a Stars and Stripes into the other.

Two nudes, one fair-haired, one dark, graced the walls on either side of the Queen. A large mirror in a heavy guilt frame filled the wall beside the stairs. It had been dropped in the hanging, and a substantial crack ran from one corner to the other.

In Dawson, one made do.

According to the law, we were expected to provide a source of fresh drinking water, and a large barrel to that effect stood at the end of the bar, beside the scales where Ray and his men weighted the gold dust used in place of money. Every establishment in town dealt in gold. Once a month we carefully lifted the floorboards beneath the scales, usually turning up a welcome extra bit of profit. The saloon was always dimly lit, even in the middle of the extended northern day, as the room was long, the windows small, the glass poor. Kerosene lamps provided additional illumination, along with smoke and a noxious odour that clung inexorably to the interior of my nose. A small kitchen, which also served as a closet, was situated behind the bar. There Helen Saunderson could whip up a meal of toast and beans and bacon in the event that a big spender at the tables began making noises about going in search of something to eat.

I smiled when I entered the room. I loved every creaking, smoky, stinky corner of this place. Particularly when it was packed to overflowing and men continued to attempt to stuff themselves inside.

Ray and I had met in Skagway, each of us heading to the Klondike in search of our fortune. We decided to join forces. We were two halves of a highly efficient whole, and it was unlikely either of us acting alone would have been able to run the *FINEST, MOST MODERN ESTABLISHMENT IN LONDON, ENGLAND, TRANSPORTED TO DAWSON* as the banner hanging over the street so proudly proclaimed.

Patrons were lined up three deep at the bar. Ray and his men were a blur of motion, pouring drinks, wiping up spills, collecting coins, weighing gold dust. Barney, an old drunk and one of the few who'd been near when gold was first found and thus arrived at the Creeks in time to dig up a fortune, occupied his usual place perched on a stool in the centre of the long mahogany counter. Barney might have made his fortune, but he'd lost it almost as fast as it had been made, and these days he earned his drink spinning tales to new arrivals, those we called cheechakos, eager to hear all about the legend of the Klondike as they consumed my whisky.

Barney waved me over. I was rather fond of the old soak and went to say hello. Before I could reach him, a man stepped in front of me. He was perfectly dressed in striped trousers, shiny black waistcoat, and fluffy white cravat. A gold ring sat on his index finger, so large it covered the entirety of the first joint. His moustache was thin and neatly-trimmed, and his black hair shone with an excess of carefully applied grease.

"Madam." He offered me a formal bow. You don't see that in Dawson much. "It is a pleasure."

I smiled and held out my hand. He bent low, and touched it with his lips. "You are the proprietress?" he asked. He was young and quite handsome with good teeth, a long straight nose, and a clear complexion. His accent was formal and slightly off, indicating he'd learned English in school rather than at his mother's knee.

"I am Mrs. MacGillivray."

"Allow me to introduce myself. Count Nicholas Ivanovich Prozorovsky, at your service."

A count. And not penniless by the look of him. How nice. Not even a King of the Klondike could spend money like minor Russian aristocracy.

"I hope you're enjoying yourself, sir. Please do check our dance hall. We have the best show in town. And our gambling tables are fully equipped."

"I have a mind to try my luck at poker. Do you offer such a game?"

"Certainly, Count Prozorovsky. You should have no trouble finding men eager to play with you."

"Please, you must call me Nicky. This is America, no? Where all men are equal."

"This is America, no. This is Canada. Where we honour our Queen." If Count Nicholas Ivanovich Prozorovsky had truly wanted to be called Nicky, he would have introduced himself as such.

He laughed. "A matter of semantics perhaps, or a shift of a borderline."

I never talk politics with the customers. "Do enjoy your evening, sir." I began to move away.

"Might I request the honour of your company over a late supper?" he asked.

I never dine with them either.

At that moment, I spotted my son crossing the floor, carrying a brown paper package that no doubt contained my evening meal. "As it happens here comes my supper now."

Angus stuffed the bag into my arms. "Here you go, bye."

Count Nicholas Ivanovich Prozorovsky sniffed and thrust a small coin at Angus. "Have you no manners, boy?" he said. "Take this lady's supper to a quiet table and lay it out. If you can do a decent job of it, I'll give you another coin."

"Huh?" Angus said.

"Count Prozorovsky, you are speaking to my son," I said.

He bowed deeply to Angus and tucked the money away. "My apologies, young gentleman." He turned to me. "You will forgive my impudence, please. An easy mistake to make. Surely this boy is your stepson; you are far too young to have a child of this age, no?"

I was tiring rapidly of the count and his tedious old-world manners. I accepted the package from Angus. "Thank you, dear." Angus made no move to leave. He stood firm while drinkers milled about him. Offended at being mistaken for a messenger boy or a servant, he was going to ensure the count left first.

"A pleasure to meet you, sir," I said. "Please enjoy our hospitality. Come, Angus."

I left the disappointed count and, with Angus in my wake, navigated the crowd, nodding to customers I did not know, exchanging words of greetings to those I did.

"Whew!" I said when we reached the relative quiet of the space under the stairs. "Thank you for bringing this, my dear." I accepted a kiss on the cheek and watched him make his way across the room and out the door.

I settled myself at my desk with a contented sigh and opened the parcel containing the food. Mrs. Mann had made sandwiches out of the remains of last night's moose dinner. The texture of the meat might indicate that the creature had died of a highly advanced age, but the bread was fresh and she had not spared the application of sweet butter.

My mind returned to the man in the alley. The man who had died with my name on his lips. My feeling of contentment disappeared.

I am not entirely an uncaring person. I simply had not had time to spare him much further thought, what with wanting to scrub his blood from my person, dress for the evening, dash back to the Savoy to interrupt the police questioning of Angus, open the dance hall, check on Roland the Magnificent, and charm the customers.

All of that and it was scarcely nine o'clock.

I have a good memory for faces, a talent that has served me well, but try as I might I could not recall seeing the nameless man before. That he knew my name was not surprising — more surprising had he not known who I was. Surely it was nothing but a coincidence that he was set upon by assailants at the moment Angus and I exited the Savoy, taking a short-cut though the alley. Perhaps he, knowing he was about to expire, headed for me as he might for the arms of his mother or his nanny.

Culloden?

His dying word was not, as I had told the police, my name, but rather it had been Culloden.

The bloodiest of all battles. The end of the Jacobite Rebellion and the death of dreams of an independent Scotland. It might be possible that the man's name was Culloden, but so sacred was the battlefield to the Scots I had never known that word to be a name. Was he perhaps from that area, dreaming of his home-land as he saw the gates of heaven swinging open and the long, thin finger of Saint Peter beckoning?

MacGillivray. Culloden.

When I was young, I walked the Black Cullins of Skye with my father, and I never tired of hearing how the MacGillivrays had fought to the last for the Bonnie Prince and Scotland, losing their all for the cause.

And would do so again, down through the generations.

That battle had been fought, and lost, in 1745. A long time ago, yet to some men, such as my father, it might have been yesterday. To me it was nothing but an old story, exciting to listen to on a cold, damp winter's night seated around the peat fire in our whitewashed croft or while tramping the bare brown and purple hills.

My parents were murdered when I was but a few days short of my eleventh birthday. Fleeing their killer, I left Skye in the company of a group of Travellers and have never returned to my stark beautiful homeland. I think of my parents — Fiona and Angus MacGillivray — often, but I haven't thought of Culloden or the honour of the MacGillivrays since.

How strange that a dying man would link those names together.

I did not tell anyone, not Angus, certainly not the police, what the man's last word had been. I decided it had no meaning.

My past has never been entirely, shall we say, respectable. Or even legal. I've built a new life here in the Yukon for Angus and me on a foundation of not-quite-the-entire truth.

I drummed my fingers on the desk.

To be totally honest, I must admit that I've built our new life on a foundation of almost total fabrication.

I fear that any questions about my origins, no matter how innocent they may at first appear, might start weakening that foundation.

I looked at the food laid out in front of me. I'd taken one bite. I wrapped up the remains of the sandwich and tucked it into the top drawer. Perhaps I'd have an appetite later.

I am not a religious woman, but I closed my eyes and said a silent prayer for the man, whoever he might be, who had died with my name on his lips.

Chapter Five

"Stabbed, no doubt about it." The doctor peeled off his gloves as he stepped away from the body laid out on the table in the back room of the mortuary. "Three times, at least. The first two got him in the side, lots of blood but not fatal, but the last slipped in between the ribs and struck the heart."

"A good-sized knife then?" Richard Sterling asked.

"It had to be a long enough blade. And a sharp one."

"Anything else you can tell us?" Inspector McKnight said.

"He was in his late forties, probably. Well nourished, at least as well as anyone of us up here. Not many teeth left and what he had are rotting, must have had a lot of pain from them. Nothing unusual."

"Thank you, Doctor."

The police took their leave and walked through town, heading toward Fort Herchmer, the NWMP post. "The first thing we need to do is find out who this fellow is. Was," McKnight said.

"Agreed."

"I'm not happy. The superintendent is not happy. The commissioner will be not happy when he hears. Not only was a man murdered in the streets in the middle of the day, but the culprit got away."

"Five dollars in bills and some gold dust were in his pockets,"

Sterling said. "Not a lot of money, but men have been killed for less. Yet he wasn't robbed."

"That might have been the intent, though. And when Mrs. MacGillivray and her son appeared they ran off."

"I don't know. The back alleys of Dawson are not quiet places, particularly behind the dance halls and so close to the river. People are coming and going all the time. Mrs. MacGillivray and Angus thought nothing of cutting down the alley."

"A falling out between ne'er-do-wells," McKnight said, his voice lifting.

"I don't mean ..."

"Yes, that's what it was. Altogether too many vagabonds and layabouts in this town. Some petty argument between fellows with nothing better to do and someone draws a knife. Tsk tsk. The respectable citizenry have nothing to fear. Find the man responsible, American probably, altogether too many of them in town as well. We'll hang him, and any of his accomplices, and prove Her Majesty's forces are fully in command of this territory."

"I ..."

"What are you waiting for, Sterling? Get on with it. I want to see the scoundrels in the dock as soon as possible."

Sterling stood on the boardwalk watching the inspector walk away, highly pleased with himself. McKnight was probably right and it shouldn't be too difficult to find the dead man's friend. Probably still wearing his bloody clothes and hoisting a few drinks in an attempt to forget what he'd done.

Still, never a good idea to rush to judgement.

He turned and, after nearly colliding with a plump matron, made his way back to the town detachment office. He'd get McAllen and FitzHenry visiting the dance halls, asking if anyone knew the dead man and who his friends might be.

Sterling himself should pay another call on Fiona MacGillivray. She was holding something back, although what she could tell him about the death of a total stranger he didn't know.

He smiled to himself and straightened his hat.

He stopped in at the office first, to give his men their orders.

Constable FitzHenry was out, but McAllen was behind the desk, reading reports.

"You're wanted, Corporal," the young officer said, before Sterling could so much as open his mouth.

"As soon as possible." McAllen lowered his voice, his eyes wide. "By Inspector Starnes himself. You're to go to his house, not his office. Immediately. Come alone, the message said."

* * *

The Savoy Saloon and Dance Hall is open twenty hours a day, six days a week. We are somewhat unusual in that as most of the other places keep their doors open around the clock, save for compulsory closing to honour the Lord's Day. I decided from the beginning I wanted to keep my eye on the place as much as possible. We could afford to shut our doors for a few hours after six a.m. when the percentage girls — those employed to dance with the men after the stage show ends at midnight — go home. The rule isn't set in stone, and particularly if a big spender is on a losing streak in the gambling hall, we will stay open.

Even I can't function well on less than four hours sleep a night. It's my custom to go home at six after paying the girls for their night's work. The stage performers get a set wage, but the percentage girls earn twenty-five cents for every dollar-a-minute dance. A small disk, which they place in their stockings, records each dance. By the end of the evening the legs of some of the more popular girls resemble those of African elephants.

Ray and the bartenders escort the last of the punters — some willing, some not — out the door, I settle up with the girls, we close, and I go home to bed. I manage to get about three hours sleep before rising to have a quick breakfast, then returning to the Savoy at ten o'clock when another round of eager men pour through the doors. I shut myself in my office, open the big ledger to do the accounts, and take the previous night's take to the bank. Then it's back home for whatever household chores need attending to, a bit of shopping perhaps, or helping Angus with his education (although I am running out of things to teach the boy) if he is not working down at Mr. Mann's shop on the waterfront. A nap, if I'm lucky, and back to the Savoy at four as evening custom begins to build. Home again at six to change into evening gown, gulp down supper, and attempt to be back at seven when the dancers and performers and musicians begin arriving.

It's an exhausting schedule, but I'm well aware that this gold rush won't last forever — there's talk of there not being all that much gold after all, and most of it already taken — and I intend to ensure I make as much money as I can while I can.

The morning after the unnamed man's unfortunate demise in my arms, I left the Savoy for the bank, bearing a satisfyingly heavy bag. There are not many cities in the world where a woman could walk, unaccompanied and openly, through the streets, bearing a sack stuffed with cash and gold. Particularly as part of her regular routine, known to almost everyone in the vicinity. Dawson was perhaps the most peaceful, safest place I had ever lived. Not only did the NWMP keep the stamp of law and order firmly on the town, but should anyone attempt to break the law we were surrounded by nothing but wilderness, leaving the miscreants precious little opportunity to affect an escape.

Yet thoughts of the man yesterday, set upon by ruffians, intruded into my usual calm, and I hesitated at the front door.

Murray, one of the bartenders, was serving a couple of customers, and the one I always thought of as Not-Murray was in the storage room. I could hear the roulette wheel turning, and Jake say "No more bets." I considered waiting for Not-Murray to return and asking one of them to accompany me.

"Mornin' Mrs. Mac." Helen Saunderson bustled up the boardwalk. It had rained in the night, fortunately not too much, and the hem of her brown calico dress was not too terribly dirty. After a good rain the streets of this town, built on a flood plain at the convergence of two rivers, could be thick with mud high enough to reach a horse's knees. "Gonna be a lovely day, ain't it?" Helen stood beside me watching the ebb and flow of people. I felt like a fool, afraid to walk down the street.

Nothing but the usual lines of men heading for the Creeks, respectable women going about their family's business, listless cheechakos looking for something — anything — interesting. Half-starved horses pulled wagons, men carried loads, stray dogs dodged around legs, human and equine.

I tightened my grip on the bag and walked the short distance — less than a block — to the bank, exchanging greetings with others.

The lineup at the Commerce Bank snaked along Front Street, men pushing and shoving, trying to edge themselves forward. I myself never wait in line. Almost as one, the men stood to attention as I passed, touching their caps or saying good morning.

"Wow, 'o's that then?" I heard one chap, plucked straight from the filthy alleys of Whitechapel, say to his companion. "A duchess or som'think?"

The bank itself was not at all impressive, but it was an improvement over the tent it had occupied a short while ago. I sailed through the doors.

To my considerable surprise a woman stood in front of the teller's window. Not that there are not a good number of women in Dawson, but few of them own businesses and thus have reason to frequent the bank. I stood behind her, as close as I could get without obviously snooping. Fortunately, she was quite short.

Over her shoulder I could see the teller counting money, a nice stack of bills by the look of it. He made notes in his ledger and signed a withdrawal slip with a whisk of his pen. He passed the money underneath the bars of his wicket along with the slip of paper. "*Merci, madame.* I 'ope you enjoy our fair town."

She wore a practical, handsome costume of sage-green bodice and plum skirt. The collar of the shirt was high, the leg-of-mutton sleeves perfectly cut to flare out above her elbows and fit snugly below. The hem of the skirt was trimmed in matching green ribbon and the entire ensemble was spotlessly clean. Not an easy look to achieve in the muddy streets of Dawson.

"I'm sure I will," she replied. Her accent was flat, very American. She wore beige gloves. She gathered up her money, tucked it into her reticule, and turned. Her eyes opened at the sight of me, standing a mite closer than was proper. Lovely eyes they were, as pale blue as ice on the distant glaciers in winter, large and lined with thick black lashes. Her face was a tiny pale heart accented by pink cheeks and plump red lips. Blond curls peeked out from beneath a plum bonnet and small pearls decorated ears the shape of perfect sea shells.

She dipped her chin. "Good day."

I nodded in reply, and she slipped away. I heard the men behind me buzzing with questions. I had questions of my own.

"Who was that?" I asked as I hefted my bag onto the counter.

"An American lady," the teller said, opening the wicket door to grab the bag. His shirt cuffs badly needed the services of a laundry maid. He chatted as he counted. "Miss Eleanor Jennings, of Chicago. She is 'ere to open a photography studio."

"Photography?"

"*Oui*. Most unusual, *non*? A lady photographer. But in Dawson ladies do as they wish, *non*?"

"Indeed," I replied, accepting the deposit slip he'd completed. I checked to ensure the amount matched my accounting and put the slip into my own reticule. "Good day."

"Good day, Madame MacGillivray."

When I got outside, after exchanging greetings with the men lined up behind me, I looked up and down the street. I couldn't see the American woman, which was not much of a surprise as she was so tiny — perhaps not more than five feet tall — she would be swallowed up by a crowd of two.

A photographer. Several photographers had set up shops and were doing a roaring trade taking photographs of cheechakos posing as prospectors and selling scenic pictures to those wanting to send an image of the Yukon to their families back home.

I myself avoided them like I would a drunken gambler anxious to slobber his thanks across my face. I never posed for photographs, and if I were unlucky enough to be unwittingly captured in one I attempted, and usually succeeded, in convincing the photographer not to develop the image. On occasion I had had to buy the cursed thing and destroy it myself.

Influential people in London and Toronto might still be searching for me. Men can be highly vengeful, I've found, when a woman has taken advantage of them. What with people carrying the camera devices into the streets and taking photographs with ease, along with the incredible thirst of the Outside for news of the Klondike, I might be on one side of the world, yet my image could be reproduced in a newspaper on the other a mere weeks later.

Most distressing.

Sometimes I did not care for these modern inventions.

I vowed to stay well out of the way of Miss Eleanor Jennings of Chicago.

Chapter Six

"There you are, my boy, I was told I could find you here."

Angus glanced up from behind a stack of canned peaches. Most mornings, he worked at Mr. Mann's shop down by the waterfront. Angus hated working in the shop. His mother insisted he help bring in some money, but he suspected her real intention was to keep him out of trouble. He'd heard rumour of a school starting up in August. He figured he was too old for school, but his mother put great store in education.

"Me, sir?" he said accepting the hand thrust across the counter. The man had a strong grip.

"You're Angus, right? Mrs. McGillivray's son?"

"Yes, sir. But I don't know where my mother is." He went back to stacking peaches. More than a few men tried to make Angus's acquaintance thinking he'd provide a shortcut to his mother's affections.

"I'm not looking for her. I wanted to meet you, that's all. My name's Roland. They call me Roland the Magnificent." He had a strong English accent.

"They do?"

Roland laughed heartily. It was a nice laugh, deep and rolling and genuine. A laugh that didn't take its owner too seriously. "I understand your confusion. Nothing particularly magnificent about me, is there?"

"No, sir. I mean ..."

Roland laughed again.

He was an older man, perhaps about the age of Inspector McKnight, clean-shaven with a round belly, and no more than a few strands of greasy grey hair. His nose had red streaks running across it and was large, lumpy, and pitted. "Magnificent," he said, "is my stage name. I'm an entertainer. A magician. I've the good fortune to be employed by your mother at the Savoy."

"A magician!"

Roland grinned. "And so, as I'm hoping to have lengthy employment with your mother, I thought I'd take the opportunity to make your acquaintance. The ladies at the Savoy talk about you, you know. A fine lad, they say."

Angus blushed.

"You wants to buys or to sell?" Mr. Mann had come up behind Angus. "Peaches. Good price."

Roland eyed the merchandise. "How much for one can?"

"Fifty cents."

"Fifty cents! For a can of peaches?"

"Try to buy elsewhere." Mr. Mann shrugged.

Mr. Mann's shop was situated in a white canvas tent in one of the rows packed cheek to jowl along the riverbank. A rough plank was laid across the front of the tent to serve as counter. He also had a second tent, piled high with merchandise. He dealt mainly in hardware and mining equipment, but would take anything — from ladies' undergarments to oil paintings of bucolic landscapes to plates featuring the Queen's portrait – that might turn a profit. Last winter, with the town on the verge of starvation, the government decreed that henceforth everyone entering the territory must bring an entire year's supply of goods with them. On reaching Dawson City, after months spent on the trail with the required ton of food and possessions, many took one look at the town and immediately set about attempting to secure passage home. They had to do something with all the things they'd brought, and Mr. Mann and shopkeepers like him were happy to take the goods off their hands. For a fraction, in most cases, of what the would-be-prospector had paid for them in Seattle or San Francisco or Vancouver. It was amazing what some people considered essentials – Angus had sold a bronze statue of a dog earlier in the day.

Mr. Mann crossed his arms and stared at Roland the Magnificent. *Do business or be on your way*, the posture said. Mr. Mann did not engage in idle chat, and he had no patience with those who did.

"Just what I been looking for." A woman swept down on a pile of working men's caps stacked on the counter. She began sorting through them and, with a meaningful look at Angus, Mr. Mann went to assist her.

"It's been nice to meet you, sir," Angus said, "but I have to get back to work."

"How about you show me around town when you're finished for the day? I've only just arrived and could use a guide. In exchange, I'll buy you a meal, and I might be persuaded show you a trick or two."

"Sure. I finish at one o'clock."

"One o'clock it is." Roland the Magnificent tipped his hat and sauntered away. He did not purchase any peaches.

Angus thought it would be great fun to be a magician. Perhaps he could get Roland to teach him a couple of card tricks he could use to impress his friends.

"I said, how much are the peaches?" Angus blinked and saw a red-faced man standing in front of him. "Are you deaf, boy, or plain stupid?"

"One dollar," Angus said. "Per can."

"Humph. Seems like a lot. Still, the wife wants peaches. I'll take two."

* * *

"He arrived on the *Victoria* three days ago," Constable McAllen said to Richard Sterling. "One of the dockworkers recognized the photograph. But the boat's left, so I can't check. Too bad we don't have a telegraph."

"You don't know where he was staying?"

McAllen shook his head. "There must be hundreds, thousands, of boarding houses, hotels, rooms to rent, in town. We don't have the manpower to get around to them all. He might have simply erected a tent at the edge of town."

Sterling studied the picture in his hand. They'd had Mr. Hegg, owner of a photography studio, bring his camera to the mortuary and take a picture of the deceased. Something they could show around town in an attempt to discover the identity of the man. The picture wasn't very good. Mr. Hegg had to explode a small amount of magnesium powder mixture to create a light bright enough to photograph by. The subject was, after all, dead. His eyes were closed, his face scrunched in pain or fear, and his jaw had been forced shut. The body had been well into rigor mortise by the time Sterling got the idea of sending for the photographer and Hegg, and all of his equipment, had arrived.

Still, it was better than a poorly executed drawing and Sterling wondered what other benefits photography might bring to policing.

"Well, keep trying," he said to the constable. "Someone has to know him if he's been in town for three days."

"The dockhand only said he thought it was the *Victoria*. Might not have been."

"Do what you can," Sterling said. He took his hat down from the shelf. There weren't many routes into Dawson. No one exactly wandered into town. They came by boat from St. Michael in Alaska on steamships such as the *Victoria*, or they walked from Skagway or Dyea, up the Chilkoot, over the border at the summit, where the Mounties recorded their arrival and checked they had the required year's supplies, and then by makeshift boat or raft down the Yukon River. That route was as crowded with newcomers these days as the bar at the Savoy at eleven-thirty on a Saturday night.

Leaving the office, Sterling headed for the riverfront, intending to meet up with Angus MacGillivray. The lad finished working for Mr. Mann at one. Sterling would offer to treat him to lunch and see if the boy remembered anything more about what happened in the alley yesterday. Sterling wanted to speak to Fiona again, but thought it better to find her in her office early in the evening. She could be like a bear with a sore head and an empty stomach if anyone interrupted her afternoon schedule.

Near the corner of York and Second Streets, two men were perched on top of a ladder, paint cans at their feet, putting the finishing touches on an elaborate sign advertising E. Jennings, Photographer, in cursive of brilliant scarlet. A tiny blond woman stood at the bottom of the ladder, looking up, waving wildly, shouting directions in a piercing American accent.

He stopped and watched. Mr. Hegg hadn't been at all pleased at being called out to take photographs of a dead man. He was busy, he'd said, with *paying* customers. Sterling suspected Hegg could have done a better job if he'd taken the time to get settled properly rather than ducking under his black cloth, igniting the magnesium, snapping the picture, and then bolting.

If they needed the services of a photographer again, perhaps this E. Jennings might be more obliging.

"Higher on the right," the lady called. "No, that's too high. Now you need to lift the left side more. I said left, that's not the left, you fool."

The ladder began to sway as one of the men leaned to his left to do as he'd been instructed. The other yelled at him to be still, pulled right, and the ladder shifted back.

"Look out," Sterling shouted. The men grabbed for the sign. One of them lifted his foot and brought it down on the side of the paint can. It tottered at the edge for a moment, and fell.

Sterling reached the lady in a couple of long strides, grabbed her arm, and pulled her out of the way. Paint as bright red as his uniform tunic sprayed everywhere. If she hadn't moved, the lady's purple skirt would have been drenched.

She whirled around and faced him. Pale blue eyes flashed fire in a white face. "Unhand me, sir."

He lifted both his hands. "Pardon me, madam, but you were in danger of being covered in paint."

"I'm perfectly capable of protecting myself, thank you," she said, biting the words. "Without being manhandled."

Scarcely manhandled, but he let it go and stepped back.

She turned her wrath on the men descending gingerly from the ladder, smothering grins. "You did that on purpose. I've a mind to dock your pay."

"I don't recommend it, lady," one of the painters said. "Word gets 'round you don't pay, ain't no one gonna work for you." He held out his hand. "And word gets 'round fast in Dawson. One dollar."

She dug in her pocket and pulled out an American bill. She wore close-fitting beige gloves. She slapped the money into the man's palm. They collected their ladder and their hammers and brushes and left, chuckling.

The empty can lay on its side, scarlet paint soaking into the boardwalk. The woman lifted one tiny booted foot and kicked it. "Fools." She forced her face into a smile. "Pardon me, Officer. You were, I'm sure, attempting to help."

He held out his hand. "Corporal Richard Sterling, North-West Mounted Police."

Her small gloved hand felt soft and cool in his. "Eleanor Jennings." She waved to indicate the shop. "Proprietor."

"You're the photographer?"

"I am. I've only just arrived. I haven't managed to unpack most of my equipment yet, but I'm excited to begin. May I take your photograph, Corporal?" Her teeth were white and perfect and her lips red. Bouncing blond curls escaped from her bonnet.

"Another time, perhaps."

"No charge."

"Another time, perhaps," he repeated.

She tilted her head back, cocked it slightly to one side. Her blue eyes danced in the sunlight. "I can only hope so."

He touched the rim of his hat and continued on his way, his heart thudding so loudly in his chest it was a wonder people weren't staring at him.

* * *

The waterfront was a mass of confusion. Nothing out of the ordinary in that. Since the ice had broken up in May, thousands, tens of thousands, of people had poured up the Yukon River to collapse in exhausted relief onto the floodplain where the Yukon met the Klondike. The climb up the Chilkoot Trail or over the White Pass was only the beginning of the journey. At Lake Bennett they had to board boats for the perilous five-hundred-mile journey downriver and over rapids. As no shipyard waited for them at the bottom of the mountain, men built their boats themselves, in varying degrees of serviceability. More than a few — boats as well as men — hadn't survived. All of June the armada came, everything from canoes to rowboats to flat-bottom scows made of whipsawed green wood with sheets or the sides of tents serving as sails. Boats were lined up as many as ten deep along the Dawson riverfront and men leapt from one craft to another to reach shore. Once the ice broke on the river and the easier path from the ocean opened, steamships joined the throng.

Where there were people and goods, there could always be found buyers and sellers. Almost instantly the mudflats became a sea of tents trading everything one could possibly imagine. And much, Richard Sterling sometimes thought, one couldn't.

Mr. Mann owned one of the largest of the stores. Sterling made his way there, mud squelching under his boots. Angus was helping a man with the purchase of snowshoes. Sterling wondered if the fellow'd last long enough to get any use out of them. Still only July and the steamships were packed with would-be prospectors heading out of the territory, shaking their heads in wonder at the madness that had consumed them for so long only to be extinguished at the first glimpse of the town.

Angus placed the money he'd received for the snowshoes in the tin box used for that purpose. He saw Sterling watching him and grinned.

"Almost lunch time," Sterling said. "Do you have to meet Sergeant Lancaster this afternoon?"

"No, sir. Not today." A boxing legend in his own mind, Sergeant Lancaster gave the boy lessons several times a week. Unbeknownst to his mother, who would no doubt forbid it if she found out — so between them, Mr. Mann, Sterling, Lancaster, and Angus ensured she did not find out.

Dawson was a peaceful town, law-abiding under the strong hand and watchful eye of the North-West Mounted Police. A twelve-year-old lad'd have little need to use his fists here. But,

Sterling knew full well, not every place was like Dawson and Angus was growing quickly.

"Ready, boy?" said a booming voice behind Sterling. He turned. It was a man, middle-aged, short with a cheerful round belly that even the rigours of the trail hadn't managed to diminish.

"Yup," Angus said. He untied the apron he wore to work, tossed it onto a wooden box stamped peas, and rounded the counter. "Bye, Mr. Mann," he shouted.

Mr. Mann was sorting through a pile of used clothes. He lifted a hand in acknowledgement but did not look up.

"This is Roland, sir," Angus said to Sterling. "Roland the Magnificent. He's a magician."

"Is that so?"

"A few simple card tricks," Roland said, shrugging his shoulders modestly. "The sobriquet is part of the act."

Sterling chuckled and held out his hand.

"Did you want me for something, sir?" Angus asked. "Mr. Mag ... uh ... Mr. Roland wants me to show him around town. He's new."

"I have questions for you about yesterday. But they'll keep. While you're here, Mr. ...?"

Roland's laugh was a deep rumble, infectious almost. "My surname is Montague-Smyth, I'm always sorry to say. I much prefer to be called Mr. Magnificent." He laughed again, and Sterling felt himself smiling in response. "Call me Roland, everyone does. You too, boy."

"I have a photograph," Sterling said, trying to get his mind back to the business at hand. "Of a man, a dead man, we're trying to identify. Would you mind if I show it to you?"

"Not at all."

"A photograph," Angus said in delight. "That's a capital idea!" He leaned forward. "He looks dead all right."

Sterling handed the small square of paper to Roland. The man glanced at it and gave his head a shake. "Sorry, can't say I've ever seen him."

"Let me see." Mr. Mann had come up to the counter. Roland passed him the photograph. Mr. Mann studied it for a long time. "Poor," he said at last. "But I may have seen him."

"Where? When?"

"Here. Around here. Bowery Street. It gets busy. Hard to remember everyone who passes by. But this man did, I think. Yesterday? Day before?" He gave the photograph back and as he did so, glanced down the row of tents, toward the river. "He did not buy anything. Looked but did not buy. Went that way."

"Thank you, Jürgen," Sterling said.

"Always happy to help zee police."

"Know where I can buy a rifle?" A man pushed his way between them.

"Mr. O'Neil had yesterday. Two rows over," Mr. Mann said.

"You can't use it," Sterling said. "Firearms are not allowed in town."

The man's cheek was thick with a wad of chewing tobacco and his clothes were crusted with mud and dried sweat. He smelled like he regularly slept in a mule barn. He spat a lump of tobacco onto the ground, barely missing the toe of Sterling's boot. "So I heard. Didn't believe it myself. Hard to believe men'll be so lily-livered as to let the po-lice tell them they can't defend themselves." His eyes were lumps of black coal in a face that had not seen soap or water for a long time.

"You don't need defending in Dawson," Sterling said. "The North-West Mounted Police will ensure your safety."

The man spat again. This time the lump of brown muck landed on the boot. He looked Sterling in the eye. Sterling was conscious of Angus beside him, of Roland and Mr. Mann watching. Sensing a commotion, the crowd stopped drifting. Well over half the people flooding into the territory were Americans. Some of them didn't seem to realize they were in another country, with different laws and a different way of doing things. Sterling shifted so his right leg was planted a fraction behind the left and found his balance. He let his arms fall to his side and flexed his fingers.

"Un-man us, more likely." The American turned away with a broken laugh. "Won't be your territory for much longer, Fly Bull. You can't fight for it, you can't keep it."

They watched him push his way through the crowd of onlookers. Then, with a collective sigh of relief mixed with a good helping of disappointment, everyone returned to their own business.

"You sure showed him, Corporal," Angus said his voice high with admiration.

"I doubt I showed him anything at all, son. Now I know to keep an eye on him, though. If he dislikes Canada so much, I wouldn't be averse to handing him a blue ticket."

As resources were so strained and the territory so far from any assistance — not even a telegraph — the police pretty much made up the law as they went along. Only two penalties were handed out to law breakers: a sentence to be served chopping wood for the ravenous stoves, or a blue ticket expelling the miscreant, permanently, from the Yukon.

Work finished, Angus scampered off, Roland the Magnificent trailing along behind. Sterling watched them, feeling a touch of melancholy. Angus was a boy, eager to become a man. The height of his mother already, he'd pass her soon, but he was still all uncontrollable legs and arms, knotty knees and elbows. Sterling could only hope the wild enthusiasm and unbridled zest for new experiences wouldn't leave the boy for a long while yet.

Chapter Seven

"Murder in Dawson. My readers will be anxious to hear every detail."

"They are not going to hear it from me."

"Come on, Fiona. You can remain anonymous. Hum ... let me think. Well-regarded, black-haired beauty was startled.... No, a delicate English rose was forced to confront the depths of mans' inhumanity ..."

"Graham, you can write whatever drivel you desire as long as you keep my name, and any identifying characteristics, out of it. I will not be providing you with a quote. And if you dare to speak to Angus, I'll ..."

He laughed. "Speechless for once, my dear. That I will get down on paper."

Graham Donohue tucked his arm into mine. Graham was a newspaperman, quite a successful one. He'd been sent to the Klondike by his paper, the *San Francisco Standard*, to report on events in the world's most exciting city (this year, at any rate). I care for newspapermen as much as I care for photographers, but as long as my picture never accompanied any of Graham's over-wrought epistles to the Outside I had little to which to object. He usually could be persuaded to replace my name with some sort of euphemism. Raven-Haired Beauty was among my favourites.

"Time to be off," I said.

Knowing my schedule, Graham had arrived in time to escort me to the Savoy for the evening. Graham fancied me, I knew, and aside from constant attempts to assist me to "relax" on the couch in my office, I suspected he might have thoughts of a more permanent relationship. That I resisted. I had not come this far in order to find a man to marry, and I had no intention of giving up my freedom. Not yet, at least. Although I worried sometimes about Angus, growing up in this wild town without a father. I had hoped Graham would provide a manly example to Angus, but the boy intensely disliked the American reporter for reasons I did not understand. Angus got on well with Richard Sterling, worshipped the corporal I sometimes thought. That I wasn't too pleased about, as I suspected Angus had ambitions to be a Mountie. I had loftier goals for my son. Still, it was better than seeing him running wild through the streets with a pack of boys and falling under the influence of the sort of men who hung around the Savoy day and night.

"May I say you look particularly lovely this evening, Fiona," Graham said. As he did every night. Nevertheless, I never tired of hearing it, and I nodded my head ever so slightly in acknowledgement.

Tonight I was dressed in my best gown of scarlet silk, although I had worn it the previous evening. I was, in fact, forced to wear this dress far too often. Miners and gamblers and men who were common labourers or farmhands a few short months ago wouldn't be shocked to see me in the same outfit several times a week. But I knew.

Dawson was proving to be hard on the wardrobe. I'd brought my best gown, a genuine Worth gifted to me in a suite at the real Savoy by a lord of the realm, all the way from London. During one unfortunate encounter, the dress had been ruined. Some of it had been salvaged and patched the lower part of Mrs. Mann's church dress. My pale-green satin gown with high neckline only hinting at the delights beneath was now not even suitable for rags. After my unwilling expedition into the wilderness wearing it, even Mrs. Mann, who could usually salvage something out of almost nothing, pronounced it fit only to heat the kitchen stove.

I offered Graham my arm, and together we walked through the streets toward the Savoy. He was looking rather nice himself in a moderately clean white shirt and brown trousers that had been dusted off recently. His jacket was threadbare at the elbows and a couple of buttons on his waistcoat were in danger of breaking free, but such was the lot of an unmarried man in a town with a disproportionally low number of women.

It had been a hot day with no wind, and despite the approach of evening, heat clung to the still air. My hair sat heavily on my head. Mrs. Mann had managed to save some of the genuine ostrich feathers that had adorned the Worth, and they were used to top the hat I wore this evening.

The streets were full, as they were day and night, and beside me I felt Graham preen as we passed men of his acquaintance.

We walked down York Street. As we approached the corner of Second Avenue, Graham said, "Seems there's a new photographer in town. Wonder if he'd be interested in taking some pictures for my paper."

We studied a large sign hanging over a shop front, dipping noticeably to the right. *E. JENNINGS, PHOTOGRAPHER*, was written in ornate scarlet script, the paint so fresh it shone. A woman stood in the open door, watching the passing throng. Her dress was an unadorned blue calico over which she wore a long white apron. A bonnet was tied under her pointed chin with a blue satin ribbon. The garb might be plain and inexpensive, but it fit her beautifully.

"It's not a he, but a she," I said.

Graham's ears almost stood up. "Really." He tightened his grip on my arm. "Let's meet her."

"We haven't been introduced."

"No one cares about that, Fiona." Indeed, in Dawson one largely dispensed with the civilized formalities. I knew that, but other than drag Graham away, provided he'd be willing to be dragged, I could do little but follow in his wake. He still had hold of my arm.

"The lady from the bank," Miss Jennings said, recognizing me.

"I am Mrs. Fiona MacGillivray and this is a countryman of yours, Mr. Graham Donohue."

"Pleased to make your acquaintance, Mr. Donohue," she said, extending a gloved hand so small it was like that of a child. "Miss Eleanor Jennings, of Chicago."

"San Francisco," Graham said. Graham is not a large man, neither bulky nor tall, but he could look over Miss Jennings' head easily. As could I.

The interior of her shop — I suppose she would call it her studio — was uncommonly bright. A big window faced south, letting in light. We could see lamps and camera equipment and a plain white screen I presumed she used as a backdrop. A few props were arranged about: a mining pan, some picks and axes, a couple of empty crates.

"Don't think I've ever met a lady photographer before," Graham said, showing her his best smile.

"Now you have," she replied.

"I must be getting to the Savoy," I said.

They ignored me. I do not care to be ignored.

"My newspaper would be interested in getting some photographs to accompany my dispatches. I'm going out to Bonanza Creek next week, Miss Jennings. Would you be interested in coming with me? Plenty of good opportunity for photos at the Creeks."

This was the first I'd heard of any trip to the Creeks. Graham had only just returned from our expedition into the wilderness. He'd told me he'd be staying close to town until he recovered from the ordeal.

Not that he'd had much of an ordeal. That had all been mine. I glared at him.

"I might be interested," Miss Jennings said. "But first I need to get my measure of the town." She turned her blue eyes on me. She had to tip her head back to look into my face. "I've been told people in Dawson will be more accepting of a female in my profession than they might be in Chicago, where I sometimes had trouble attracting respectable customers. Is that your impression also, Mrs. MacGillivray?"

"Sure," Graham answered. "Fiona here's a businesswoman herself. She owns the Savoy Saloon and Dance Hall."

She clapped her hands in pleasure. "How fortuitous. I've a mind to photograph women in particular. I'll bet some of your employees would love to have their pictures taken!" She tilted her head to one side and studied me. I shifted uncomfortably. I do not care for the attentions of women. They're too difficult to manipulate.

"As for you yourself, Mrs. MacGillivray, I'd be delighted if I could photograph you. I'll do it for free, if I can use the result to advertise my business."

I wrenched my arm out of Graham's grip. "Most certainly not. I never permit my image to be captured. I must be off now. Good day, madam. Graham, are you coming?"

"In a minute, Fiona."

I marched off. Behind me I heard Graham say, "How about if I come 'round tomorrow? Say ten-ish? We can talk more then."

I rounded the corner into Front Street. I could see the Savoy ahead. A satisfying stream of men entering. Even more satisfying, no one leaving.

I smiled to myself, but the sense of self-satisfaction died as I felt a cold shiver run down my spine and the small hairs at the back of my neck lift. I slowed my pace and glanced around. A small woman dressed in a tattered brown homespun dress, hair pulled sharply into a knot under an ugly straw hat, stood in the shadows of a building on the opposite side of the street. A man was beside her, large arms crossed over beefy chest. Neither of them were smiling. When she saw she had my attention, the woman crossed the street, not bothering to check for oncoming traffic, nor to lift her skirts out of the dirt. The man followed, half a pace behind.

"MacGillivray," she said.

"What do you want, Joey?" I asked. I addressed her, but kept my eyes on the man. He was a mean-looking creature and in this case appearances were not deceiving. She was Joey LeBlanc, the most notorious madam in town; he was called Mr. Black, and he was her enforcer. Mr. Black could be counted on to ensure that customers paid and the whores were kept docile. One way or the other.

"To wish you a good evening," Joey said, not smiling.

I swished my skirts and walked away, holding my head high. Sharply pointed daggers pounded into my back. Joey LeBlanc did not wish me well at any time. At Angus's pleading, I'd taken one of her unfortunate employees under my wing and helped the girl get out of town. Joey did not intend to let me forget that as far as she was concerned we had unfinished business.

I didn't allow myself to worry about Joey. Much. She might want to get her revenge on me, but she couldn't afford to do anything to draw police attention to herself or the cribs she controlled under the barely-approving eye of the law.

The first person I saw on entering the Savoy was the Russian count I'd met the previous evening. *Now he*, I thought, *would simply adore having his picture taken*. Tonight he had a diamond stick pin piercing his cravat, and the starched tips of his wing collar stood at perfect attention. The part in his oiled hair was as straight as my roulette table.

He approached me with a stiff bow. "Good evening, Madame MacGillivray. How lovely you look."

I gave him a radiant smile while noticing that Ray and Murray were behind the bar; Not-Murray was heading for the back with a bottle of Champagne; Irene was pretending to be enchanted by the attentions of a scruffy old miner without a tooth in his head (who everyone knew owned one of the most productive claims on the creek); our bouncer, Joe Hamilton, whose breath I could smell from ten feet away, was watching me with adoring eyes; Helen Saunderson was heading for the broom closet bearing a mop and a pail that didn't stand close inspection; Barney was telling his stories to a couple of cheechakos with faces as shiny as their boots; someone in the gambling room was shouting in anger; and Roland the Magnificent was leaning against the wall under the stairs, watching everything.

"When the dancing begins later," Count Whatever-His-Name-Is said, "may I have the honour of being your partner?"

"I do not dance, sir."

"You do not dine, you do not dance. What does a gentleman have to do, madame, to spend time in your company?"

Not-Murray came out of the gambling hall. He spoke to Joe Hamilton and both men went into the back, moving fast. I heard a shout, and then a roar, and they were back, dragging a struggling man between them. The drinkers stood politely aside to give them room, and the malefactor was unceremoniously tossed into the street.

"Most ... unusual ... establishment you have here," the count said.

I smiled. "That I do. Do you have plans to play poker tonight, sir?"

"I enjoy a hand on occasion."

"After the show begins I'd be happy to watch you play."

He beamed like a ten-year-old being told he could stay up to watch guests arrive and dipped his head in a short bow. I snapped my fingers at Murray, pointed to the count's rapidly emptying glass, lifted my skirts, and walked away.

You may note that I did not offer the count a drink on the house, nor did I offer to do more than watch him play poker. I wanted to get him to the tables somehow. He looked like a big loser.

"You're ready for your performance?" I asked Roland the Magnificent. He was dressed, as the previous evening, in a suit with white shirt and tie, black coat with tails and black velvet lapels, and a clean bowler hat. When he performed he put on an aristocratic accent that put me in mind of the Prince of Wales, but his normal voice spoke of a good education without being too posh.

"I had the pleasure of making your son's acquaintance this afternoon."

"Did you indeed?"

"I asked the lad to show me around town. Not much to see, is there?"

"No."

"One pass down Front Street and that was about it for the sights. You'll be pleased to know that he refused to take me to what I hear they call Paradise Alley."

I smiled.

"He's a fine lad, Angus."

"Yes," I said.

"Wants to be a policeman. Like that gentleman arriving now."

I looked to where Roland was pointing. Richard Sterling stood in the doorway. He glanced around, letting his eyes become accustomed to the weak light of the saloon. Spotting me, he headed for us.

"Good evening, Fiona. Roland."

"Good evening, Richard. Roland, you will be on first tonight, as usual. Perhaps you need to check your props and ensure everything is in order?"

"A good idea." He touched the top of his hat and left us.

"Nice fellow," Richard said.

"Although not much of a magician."

"I need to talk to you about that business yesterday."

I waved my hand in the air. "Nothing to discuss. I have no idea who that man was or who might have attacked him." I checked my watch. "Look at the time. Almost eight. I'd best …"

"Your people are quite capable of doing their jobs and putting on the show without your supervision, Mrs. MacGillivray. Shall we go upstairs to your office? The sooner I ask my questions, the sooner you can get back to work."

I swallowed a sharp retort. The corporal was watching me, but he did not have a smile on his lips, and the warm affection I sometimes saw in his eyes was not there.

"Very well," I said, "if I must." I turned and led the way up the creaky stairs to my office.

I had long ago hardened my heart against emotional involvement with any man. Living on my wits since the age of eleven, nothing but disaster had struck when I relaxed my defences. I trusted few people in this world. Angus, of course, who would love me no matter what. Ray Walker, I trusted with our business. I had friends here in Dawson, an experience that was somewhat new to me, but no one I would permit to know the details of my life or of my secrets.

Only Richard Sterling came close. And when I sometimes looked into his warm brown eyes or saw the edges of his mouth turn up in a rare private smile, I thought that if I were looking for a man this is the one I would choose.

But I was not looking for a man, and so those thoughts would be allowed to go no further.

A few times I'd almost thought he'd been on the verge of saying something to me. Something that could never be taken back. But the moment always passed, and we slipped away from the edge of the precipice back to the strict bounds of formality.

I settled myself behind my desk and made a steeple of my fingers over which I watched the big, handsome Mountie lower himself into the visitor's chair. He did not relax but rather perched on the edge. He pulled a notebook and the stub of a pencil out of the breast pocket of his red tunic.

"You never saw that man before last night?"

"That is what I said."

"Just checking."

"Very well. I have never seen him before in my life."

"What did he say to you?"

"My name. My surname. MacGillivray. Then he sighed and expired. I was highly startled, as you can understand. Angus had run off, heaven knew where, in pursuit of the scoundrel who had set upon the unfortunate gentleman. My thoughts bounced between the man dying in my arms, and my son who, in his determination to see justice done, might well have been confronting, at that very moment, an armed and dangerous criminal."

Richard's eyes narrowed, and I mentally gave myself a good sharp slap. What on earth was I doing, babbling on? I was not inexperienced in the arts of deception. I have been questioned by police officers more senior than he at other times and in other places and been in far more danger.

I had become accustomed to considering Richard Sterling my friend. On one memorable occasion, even my rescuer. I must not forget that he was first and foremost an officer of the law.

The Yukon, which served to toughen up everyone else, was making me soft. Making a living legally was causing me to let my guard slip.

"It was most distressing," I concluded. My office window was open. Down below the orchestra stuck up a tune. I almost jumped out of my skin.

"Why do you say one man? Did you see him?"

"No, I did not. Angus said there was one. I think that's what Angus said at any rate. Wasn't it?"

He didn't answer.

"Do you know who he was? The deceased?" I asked, raising my voice to be heard above the cacophony below.

"Why don't you close that window, Mrs. MacGillivray?" Richard said. "A man can hardly hear himself think."

It was not, I decided, a good sign that he was speaking so formally. I leapt up and wrenched the window down. It stuck for a moment before falling with a resounding crash.

"The men and I have been asking around. We had a photograph taken."

"A photograph? Of a dead man? Oh, dear."

"Much better than relying on a drawing. The future of policing, Mrs. MacGillivray, lies in science, I believe. Science, in combination with common sense. Have you heard about this art of fingerprinting? Everyone, they say, has unique and individual fingerprints, and they always leave a trace of them behind."

"I've heard something to that effect. I don't see that it will be of much use, however. You have this man's fingers, thus his fingerprints, but that means nothing if he committed a crime in London, say." *Shut up you fool,* I ordered myself. Why did I mention London?

"True. We've been showing the photograph around. Looks like he came to town on the *Victoria*, which docked Saturday afternoon. I was down at Bowery Street earlier. A couple of shop owners recognized the image, but no one could give me a name or an idea of where he was staying. He didn't seem to be up to much, they said, wandering around, checking things out. Unless we get lucky, we'll have trouble finding out where he was staying. I simply don't have the manpower to look into every nook and cranny."

Down below, the musicians stopped playing and they trooped back inside. I listened to them crossing the floor of the saloon, heading for the back. An excited murmur followed as the men gathered for the stage show.

"Mrs. MacGillivray," Richard said, a snap in his voice, "am I boring you?"

"Certainly not. I am hanging onto your every word. As fascinating as all of this is, I do not understand what business it is of mine. I was unfortunate enough to be in the vicinity when this gentleman fled his assailant and attempted to find help. Nothing more."

"One of the shopkeepers I spoke to said he had an English accent. Another said it was Irish. What was your impression?"

I thought. "He did say MacGillivray correctly. But as that was the only word he said, it's difficult for me to venture a guess as to his accent." Culloden, I did not venture to mention, he had pronounced properly. Cull-augh-den, not Cull-o-den as I had heard the ill-informed say.

"He said your name?"

"Yes."

"Nothing else?"

"Nothing." I swallowed and glanced over his right ear. I knew better than to look him straight in the eye. A sure sign, I'd been taught, of someone lying.

Silence stretched through the room. From below, we could hear men's excited voices, a burst of laughter.

"If there's nothing more ..."

"Yet you claim you'd never seen him before?"

"Claim! I don't claim anything." I stared into Richard's eyes. "I told you I'd never seen him before. I'd venture to guess quite a number of people you might not recognize happen to know your name, Corporal."

"You're probably right about that, Mrs. MacGillivray."

I thought he might press me further; instead he rose to his feet in a sudden movement. He put his broad-brimmed hat back on his head. "Think about it further, please. If you remember anything be sure and let me know."

"Of course."

He touched the brim of his hat and left my office.

My stomach performed summersaults.

Chapter Eight

Richard Sterling didn't know what to think about Fiona's story. If she were a man, he'd be certain she was lying. The way her eyes shifted around the room, looking at everything but his face. But she wasn't a man — that was certain — and he didn't know how a delicate, well-brought-up lady such as Fiona MacGillivray should act when confronted with the ruthlessness of a police investigation. No matter how he might try to make it easy on her, a police interrogation was brutal. It had to be, if they were to get the truth out of people.

He stopped halfway down the stairs, thinking over the recent conversation.

No doubt the encounter in the alley last night — the man expiring in her very arms, dress and hands streaked with his life-blood, the presence of her son, the police questions — would be upsetting to the delicate female constitution. She could not be expected to react as any man might. Sterling sometimes thought it wouldn't be a bad idea to allow women to serve as special constables. They'd know the workings of the female mind more than any man could.

But no decent man would allow his unmarried daughter or widowed mother to work amongst the criminal classes.

So, in the absence of a female constable to tell him what Fiona was thinking, he'd have to try to figure it out himself.

He turned at the sound of a light step on the stairs above him.

"Oh, Richard. Are you still here? Forget something?"

"No, ma'am. Just thinking."

She smiled. Not her personal smile, the one that made his heart lift, but her professional one. The one she used on the drinkers and gamblers, dancers and musicians. She peered at him from under thick black lashes, the edges of her mouth lifting. She cocked her head slightly to one side and said, "If you're not in a hurry to get back to work, why don't you stay for a while and enjoy the show?"

And he knew she'd been lying.

He'd suspected for some time that her expensive gowns, fashionable hats, and gracious manners concealed a layer of steel. That underneath the perfect accent, classical education, excellent breeding, and vivacious charm, her mind was constantly moving, always calculating.

Why she would want to lie to him about a stranger found dead in an alley, he had no idea. But she had lied.

Perhaps because she could.

Perhaps because she knew something.

He made his way down the rest of the stairs. As he reached the bottom, Fiona following, the door to the street swung open.

One by one the men in the room fell silent. In the gambling hall, Jake, the head croupier, cried, "No more bets." In the back room the chorus line broke into song.

A lady walked into the bar. She wore a plain costume of plum skirt and green blouse with a small pillbox hat atop fair hair braided and scraped back into a tight knot. Her head was high, her shoulders set, her blue eyes determined. It wasn't totally out of order to see a lady enter a saloon, but it was unusual to see one who was not an employee of the establishment or, in some of the less respectable places, one looking for custom of her own.

"Oh, dear," Fiona muttered. She pushed past Sterling and headed for the newcomer. Men separated to let her through. Sterling followed.

"Miss Jennings, this is a pleasure," Fiona said in a voice bright, cheerful, and totally false. "Welcome to my establishment. How may I be of assistance?"

Eleanor Jennings smiled. "I hoped to be here before the show began, but I was delayed chatting to the delightful Mr. Donohue." She held a small pile of cards in her hand and smelled of good soap. "I've set up a photography studio," she said, raising her voice so it would carry. She was a tiny thing, but she had a powerful voice. "I intend to specialize in photographs of women. I'd like to introduce myself to your dancers. But I'll be available for anyone who would like a portrait." She turned to the table nearest the door. Four men sat around it, still covered in the dust from the Creeks, glasses clenched in dirty hands. She handed them each a square of paper. "My card, gentlemen."

"I'll take one o' those," a man yelled, and a chorus started up. Miss Jennings moved through the room, handing out her card to every outstretched hand.

"A good businesswoman," Sterling said to Fiona.

"Humph," she replied.

Once that task had been completed, Miss Jennings made her way back to where Sterling and Fiona stood watching. A good number of the drinkers edged closer, listening in.

"How about I bring my camera around tomorrow, before the show begins? I'll take a photograph of your dancers, on the stage perhaps. In a group. You can use it for advertisement."

"I don't ..." Fiona began.

"No charge. That way I can introduce myself to the ladies and meet those who might want to have a studio portrait taken."

Sterling saw hesitation cross Fiona's face. Clearly she didn't want the photographer around, but she was a sensible enough businesswoman to know the suggested picture would be a good opportunity.

"Are you taking appointments, madam?" A well-dressed and well-spoken man interrupted. "I'd love to have my portrait captured. A small token of my regard to send home to my mother, the dowager countess."

Jennings whipped out a notebook. Small, clean, unmarked, it looked brand new. "Eleven o'clock tomorrow?"

"Perfect." He then turned to Fiona. "I don't believe I've met your police friend."

Fiona made the introductions. The man, it turned out, was a Russian count. He made sure everyone was aware of that fact before insisting he wanted to fit into the new world and thus they must call him Nicky.

The small group was soon joined by Roland the Magnificent.

"Another stupendous performance. I was sorry not to see you standing at the back, Mrs. MacGillivray. You would have been highly impressed, I'm sure." The twinkle in his eye went a long way toward taking the pomposity out of his braggadocio. "Good heavens, sir, you seem to have lost something." Roland reached out one hand and plucked Sterling's pencil off the brim of his hat.

"What on earth?" Everyone laughed, and Sterling found himself grinning as he took his pencil back.

"You must be the photographer lady," Roland said to Eleanor.

"I am," she replied. "Can I put you down for an appointment tomorrow? One o'clock is free."

"Another time, perhaps. Now, if you'll excuse me, I see a gap opening at the bar. Once more, into the breach." He melted into the crowd.

"How about you get your ladies to come in at seven tomorrow evening?" Eleanor said to Fiona. "Would that be acceptable?"

"I suppose."

"Great." She turned her lovely blue eyes onto Sterling. A single blond curl escaped from the confines of the knot and caressed her cheek. "And you, Corporal. When would you be able to come for your portrait? Full dress uniform, I hope."

"I'll have to think it over."

"Not for long." Her eyes danced. "I expect to be busy soon."

He shifted in his boots, and his collar felt very tight. He glanced at Fiona. She did not look happy. "If you remember anything, Mrs. MacGillivray, about what we discussed, be sure and let us know. Now, I must be on my way. Good night."

"I'm done here," Eleanor said, holding up her empty gloved hands as evidence. "I've handed out all my cards. Would you care to walk me home, Corporal?"

"It would be my pleasure, ma'am," he said, refraining from wiping his palms on his trousers.

Chapter Nine

Over breakfast, an unappetizing mush of soggy oatmeal, I made the mistake of mentioning the photographer's visit scheduled for that evening.

"How grand, Mother," Angus exclaimed as his eyes lit up.

Mr. Mann mumbled into his bowl about unnecessary fripperies. Mrs. Mann hesitated in the act of pouring my coffee and said, somewhat wistfully, "I'd enjoy having my photograph taken."

Mr. Mann almost sprayed oatmeal across the table.

"I'll come," Angus said, "and watch."

I couldn't think of an excuse quickly enough to keep him away, and so I changed the subject. "No fresh milk today, Mrs. Mann?"

"None to be found. You'll have to make do with this." She pushed an opened can toward me.

Dawson produced gold. Gold and nothing else. No farms, thus no fresh vegetables, eggs, or milk. Everything had to be carried in over the Pass or shipped the long way around up the Arctic Ocean to St. Michael in Alaska and up the Yukon River. A man had arrived a short while ago with a cow in tow, and I'd ordered Mrs. Mann to spare no expense in ensuring I had fresh milk for my coffee and Angus had milk to lavish on his oatmeal. No doubt the demand had exceeded the supply, and we were once again reduced to consuming the canned stuff.

"Keep trying," I said. "An egg would be nice also." My friend Mouse O'Brien had gone to the outrageous extravagance of serving an egg to each of the guests at his recent wedding. That had come close to decimating the egg supply for the entire territory.

"Do you think this photographer fellow would teach me some of what he knows, Mother?" Angus asked.

"First of all, it's a lady. A Miss Jennings."

"A lady!" Mrs. Mann gasped. "How extraordinary. The things ladies do these days."

Mr. Mann's expression indicated that he had the same thoughts as his wife. Although not in quite so approving a manner.

"Photography isn't something you can simply start to do, Angus. Not like writing." Angus had taken on employment as assistant to one Miss Martha Witherspoon, who fancied herself an author. Miss Witherspoon had soon married Mouse O'Brien, at the aforementioned wedding, and her career as a scribe — and thus Angus's — abruptly ended. "All of that equipment, the camera, the chemicals, the studio. Plus I understand developing an image onto paper once it's been captured onto the plate is rather a complicated undertaking."

"Still," he said, "I'd like to watch. Are the ladies excited about having their picture taken, Mother?"

Excited wasn't the word I'd choose.

Irene had closed the show at midnight as she always does, doing a slow provocative dance while unravelling yards and yards of brightly coloured chiffon from her body to drift gently to the floor behind her. No one ever leaves early; they're all hoping that one day the last length of cloth will accidently come loose. Not that they'd see much if it did. Underneath she wore her regular, none-too-clean shift and many-times mended stockings.

Still, the men continue to live in hope.

Which is a good thing — none of them would be here, in the Klondike, if not for foolish hope.

I'd slipped into the dressing room while Irene was taking her bows and collecting flowers and gold nuggets tossed onto the stage at her lumpy, misshapen feet.

"Attention, ladies," I called, clapping my hands together as if I were headmistress in a girls' school. The acrid sent of sweat, cheap perfume heavily applied, burning kerosene, stage paint, and clothes badly in need of the attentions of a good laundress filled the small room. Garments, ranging from Maxie's mud-spattered bloomers to common-or-garden homespun street dresses to a pink feather boa to Irene's gown that wouldn't be out of place at a regimental ball in London, were draped across every possible surface. The women, in various stages of undress, stopped chattering and turned to face me. I waited a moment, not only for Irene to arrive, bearing her collection of flowers and (most importantly) gold nuggets, but to take the measure of them all.

Some of the girls looked frightened, as if I were about to announce they were being let go. Betsy, who I tolerated at the best of times, tried to disappear behind a substantially more robust woman. A few regarded me with wide-eyed interest, expecting perhaps I would announce wage increases all around. (As if!)

The newest dancer went by the name of Colleen. She was unusually demure and shy for a Dawson stage performer. But she was young and pretty and could hold a tune and thus I'd hired her in place of a girl who'd gotten herself married to a man who didn't approve of his wife working in a dance hall. Colleen kept close to the walls, wanting to take the measure of me, I suspected, before putting herself forward.

When Irene had dumped her loot onto a table, stopped fussing, and also waited for me to proceed, I did so.

"Tomorrow evening, we will have a very special opportunity. Mr. Walker and I have decided it would be terribly modern to advertise this establishment through photography."

A buzz began at the back of the room. "What'd she say?" one of the older women bellowed. She was instantly shushed. I folded my hands in front of me and waited for the noise to die down.

I could hear the men shoving benches against the walls, clearing room for the dancing, and the musicians taking their place on the stage. A man shouted, another one laughed, and one said, "What's keepin' 'em?" The interior walls of the Savoy are none too thick. In the boxes above, a foot began to stomp, and others joined in. The floors and ceilings of the Savoy are none too thick either, and I hoped the boxes and their patrons would not be making a sudden, unexpected descent into the ladies' dressing room.

"We have therefore," I continued, "arranged for a photographer to come to the Savoy tomorrow evening. She will be taking a photograph of those who wish to participate. No one will be compelled to do so." I'd eat the fake flowers on my hat if anyone of them declined.

The women burst into excited chatter. I lifted my hand, and waited for the hullabaloo to die down. "I believe I am still speaking."

"Sorry, ma'am. Pardon, Mrs. MacGillivray," they muttered. I knew, from listening at closed doors, they called me Mrs. MacPruneFace behind my back. If any one of them said that to my face, they'd be seeking employment elsewhere.

"Be ready tomorrow promptly at seven o'clock. Anyone arriving late will not be allowed in. If you would like to wear your stage costumes for the photograph, that would be ideal. But be sure and look ... suitable for the quality of clientele we wish to attract."

Maxie put up her hand.

"Yes?"

"C'n I bring my sister, Mrs. Mac? She's real pretty."

"My name is Mrs. MacGillivray. I'd suggest you remember that in future. You cannot bring your sister, as she is not in my employ. Any other questions?"

They all began speaking at once.

"No?" I said. "Very good. Carry on."

I swept out of the room, carried forth on a wave of high-pitched chatter and almost visible excitement.

I had no doubt the shops would be emptied of rouge tomorrow.

"Excited?" I said in answer to Angus's question over the breakfast table. "Perhaps a small bit."

*   *   *

Angus arrived at the Savoy at six-thirty. I couldn't help but notice he'd put on his cleanest shirt, scrubbed his face until it shone, and added a touch of oil to his neatly combed hair. He was accompanied by Mrs. Mann, matronly presentable in her church dress and hat, and Mr. Mann who had discarded his shopkeeper's apron and checked shirt for a coat and tie. His hair and moustache were so freshly trimmed that tiny pieces of hair clung to his face.

I'd ordered the dancers to be in position by seven o'clock. At least half of them were here already. Hair had been washed and arranged, hats puffed, rouge applied in excessive amounts, corsets pulled in a few extra inches, highly impractical shoes donned. I almost choked on the scent emanating from Betsy. Did she think the photograph would pick up her perfume if it were of sufficient strength?

The women looked like a flock of South American birds. They were followed, as the parrots had no doubt also been, by scavengers looking for droppings. Where women dressed to impress, men wanted to be impressed.

Not yet seven o'clock and the front room of the Savoy was almost full to bursting.

I chased the women off, telling them to wait in the dance hall. Mrs. Mann was examining the room with wide interested eyes while her husband tried to block her view of the nudes hanging behind the bar.

I'd said nothing to the male employees about the photograph, but clearly word had spread, and they'd also gone to some trouble to clean themselves up. Faces were washed, moustaches trimmed, teeth cleaned, hands scrubbed. Joe Hamilton appeared to be wearing a borrowed jacket, so large was it across the shoulders. Not-Murray had a diamond stick pin through his tie, a gold watch chain across his chest, and a large shiny buckle attached to his belt. Murray was resplendent in a brand-new pair of suspenders.

Richard Sterling walked in. He, I was pleased to see, was not wearing his full dress uniform, but he also had had a haircut. His jacket had been dusted off, and his boots shone with fresh polish. I felt a tiny fission of disappointment. Was Richard also so eager for his photograph to be taken? Or did he want to impress the photographer? Young Constable McAllen accompanied him.

Ray Walker had made no effort to dress up. He stood behind the bar, in the unusual situation of a full house yet no one clamouring to be served, a rag in one hand, shaking his head.

Aside from Ray, only one other employee of the Savoy was in their regular attire — me. I would hope I am ready at any time to be recorded for posterity. That, however, will not be allowed to happen. I had no intention of standing anywhere in range of Miss Jennings' cursed instrument.

I was herding the girls to the back and ordering Joe Hamilton to keep the customers from following them, when the door swung open once again.

Irene Davidson stood there. She placed her right hand on the door frame and paused, drawing everyone's attention. The sunlight streaming in from behind traced an aura around her body. Her black-and-scarlet gown clung to her generous curves. I swear I could hear men suck in their breath and Ray Walker swallow from across the room.

Irene stepped forward and the spell was broken.

Until now I'd had no intention of actually paying for any photographs. Miss Jennings had said she'd take a picture of the dancers for free as a way of drumming up individual business. Now, I reconsidered. Not for nothing was Lady Irénée the most popular dance hall girl in Dawson. No one would call her beautiful. She was too hefty to be fashionable, and she'd learned her manners (and her accent) on a farm in the Midwest. But she had an aura about her almost as visible as that cast momentarily by the sun, and men were drawn to her as a moth to a flame — if I may be allowed to mix my metaphors.

If that appeal would translate to a photograph, I might pay for a portrait of Irene myself. Something we could use on a poster to advertise the Savoy.

Although, I reflected as a three-hundred-pound man trod on my toe, we didn't really need to advertise at all. Somehow, they kept on coming.

I gave the man a sniff, glared down the length of my nose, and he slunk away, muttering fulsome apologies.

If he'd bumped me on purpose, I'd have him thrown out. That's if I could find a bartender or bouncer to do so. Ray, chest puffed up, back straight, was escorting Irene into the back. His men had rushed to the doors heading into the dance hall as if the place had caught fire.

Fortunately there was still one person with the presence of mind to observe what was going on. I saw Barney's hand slide toward the glass of the fellow standing beside him, whose attention was consumed by Irene's entrance.

"Barney," I bellowed, "don't you dare!"

Not at all bothered by being caught in the act, he gave me a crooked grin and shrugged. His hand returned to his own (empty) glass. "Snookem Jim's a good pal of mine," he said to his bar-mate, fingering his glass. "I can tell you some stories, friend."

Ray came back, his men reluctantly following, and I went into the dance hall to supervise the ladies.

The girls looked like exotic birds, but they chattered like a flock of crows.

"Do you want me to pose like this, Mrs. MacGillivray?" said Maxie, thrusting her bosom forth in an uncanny resemblance to the bow of a ship.

"A scene from *Macbeth* perhaps?" Ellie, who played the Thane of Cawdor to Irene's MacDuff in the dramatic climax, assumed a swordsman's stance.

"I think something more ladylike," said Betsy, who possessed only a passing familiarity with the concept at the best of times. Placing her hands under her chin she fluttered her eyelashes.

The girls practiced their poses singly or huddled together discussing what would be best.

Colleen, the new young dancer, climbed the stage and stood there alone. Smack dab in centre front. Smart woman, I thought. She'd left the others to fuss and quietly staked out the most likely spot.

Of the men, only Angus, Mr. Mann, and Richard Sterling were permitted to stay. Even Constable McAllen had been banished to the saloon. Not that I expected anything improper to be conducted, but I feared the picture would never get taken in the crush of males either anxious to see their favourite girl pose or to get into the picture themselves. Perhaps both.

Eleanor Jennings arrived promptly at seven o'clock, carrying a large wooden case. She wore an unadorned skirt and blouse in shades of green with a long white apron tied tightly around her small waist. I suspected the apron served to keep her clothes protected from the photography equipment and harsh chemicals. She was not wearing a hat. Her fair hair was tightly plaited and secured at the back into a circle the size of a dinner plate. She wore no jewellery save for a thin gold hoop through each ear. Angus and Richard Sterling rushed to assist her. She gave Richard a soft smile before turning her attention to my son. She held out a small gloved hand. "I don't believe we've met, but I know who you are. Angus, right?"

He blushed and stammered and shifted his feet. I rolled my eyes to the heavens. "Do you think you could clear some room for me, right here?" She gestured to the benches lined up in front of the stage awaiting the commencement of the show. "So I can move about."

Angus rushed to do her bidding. Mr. Mann and Richard gave him a hand.

She approached me. "Mrs. MacGillivray, let me thank you for giving me this opportunity."

"My pleasure."

Miss Jennings turned to the wide-eyed women watching us. She lifted her voice to be heard at the back. "Ladies, it's very nice of you to come to work early to accommodate me. First, if I may introduce myself, I am Miss Eleanor Jennings of Chicago and

I am here to open a photography studio. If you'd like to come to my premises tomorrow to discuss what options are available and make an appointment, here is my card. Mr. MacGillivray, would you be so kind?"

Angus almost fell over his excessively large feet leaping across a couple of scattered benches to get to her. With a radiant smile she handed him a stack of cards. He began passing them out. The girls snatched them out of his hand as though they were tickets to fame and fortune.

Miss Jennings studied the room. "The light is very poor in here. Is there another room we can use?"

I thought of the crush of men outside. "Not if we want to be able to move."

"It will have to suffice then."

Angus finished handing out the cards. "Can you fetch more lamps, young man?" she asked him.

He dashed off, accompanied by Mrs. Mann.

"Now," Miss Jennings continued, "I know you have a show to put on, so I'll be quick about it." She began unpacking the case. The tripod came out first. She unfolded and secured the legs, and placed them on the floor. The camera was next, a square brown box with a bronze tube fastened to the front and a back resembling an accordion. That device was attached to the tripod. Next came a flat square package wrapped in cardboard, which she placed on the bench closest to her, and a black cloth. Some of the dancers pressed in closer to get a better look. Angus and Mrs. Mann returned, bringing three more kerosene lamps. Miss Jennings directed them to place the lamps on the stage.

When they were lit, she placed her hands on her hips and studied the room. "Insufficient. Illumination is the essence of photography. I'll have to create light of my own." She dove into her box and came up with two glass vials and a metal tray with a long handle.

"What's that?" Angus asked.

"Magnesium and a mixture of antimony sulphide and potassium chlorate," she explained. "When combined and lit, it creates a strong flash of light, so as to illuminate a scene that does not have adequate lighting. It can be dangerous in untrained hands, young man, so keep your distance. Now, if you girls will gather on the stage. Mrs. MacGillivray, stand in the front."

"No, thank you. I will remain here and supervise the placement of the ladies."

She looked at me with something approaching surprise and then said, "Very well. Miss Davidson, stand in the centre, beside that lady right there." She pointed to Colleen. "The rest of you gather around."

I hadn't seen a rush like that since the last time we'd opened the Savoy doors after the enforced Sunday closing. The girls bolted for the stage, pushing and shoving. Maxie stuck an elbow in Betsy's side, and Betsy almost backhanded her. Ruby took a tumble when Janie shoved her off the stairs, saving herself only by grabbing Ellie's sleeve, which came away with a shriek of ripping fabric. Ellie screeched and pushed Ruby in the chest. Ruby fell to the floor, landing on her wide, well-padded bottom with a howl of indignation.

"Ladies, ladies," I said, "a bit of decorum please. We do have guests. Ruby, stop complaining. If you are hurt, then you may go home. Immediately. Otherwise get up." Angus held out his hand and helped the dancer lumber to her feet. She rubbed her rear end with both hands as she climbed onto the stage. She tried to wiggle in front of Betsy, who'd secured a prime spot, but Betsy stomped hard on her instep. Ruby gave her a glare that would freeze a gambler's icy heart but retreated.

I rolled my eyes once again. I had a difficult night ahead of me: the resentment and fighting would carry into the performance.

"Are people always so ... eager to have their photograph taken," I asked Miss Jennings who stood in front of the stage, head cocked to one side.

"No broken bones or blood drawn," she said making a box of her hands and peering through it. "I'd consider this positively calm. I assume you want Miss Davidson front and centre."

"I do." I was paying Irene the astronomical sum of two hundred dollars a week. I intended to get every penny of my money's worth.

I wasn't surprised that for someone who'd only recently arrived in town, Miss Jennings was remarkably well informed. A woman on her own, trying to succeed in business? No one knew better than I the importance of knowing everyone and everything.

Miss Jennings directed the girls as if she were putting on a tableau. I suppose photography is much like a tableau. Everyone must be positioned exactly right to make the most favourable impression. Irene stood, as ordered, in the centre, tall and proud. She stretched her neck, lifted her head, shifted slightly to one side, hip thrust forward. The girls were fanned out around her, the prettiest and best dressed in front, the others arranged by height and weight to make a pleasing composition. Betsy and Maxie, grumbling heartily, were sent to the back. Colleen remained in the second-best position at Irene's right.

Miss Jennings stood silently for several minutes studying the scene. All fell quiet, the only sound being the muffled hub-bub from the gambling room on the other side of the closed doors. The girls began to shift, and she snapped at them. "Miss Davidson, if you please, fluff your skirts a bit more. Thank you. You there, in the blue. Stand where I told you to." Maxie slunk back into place, accompanied by Betsy's chuckles.

Angus hovered at Miss Jennings' elbow. Richard Sterling came to stand beside me, well behind the range of the camera. "You don't want to be in the photograph, Fiona?"

"I'm not the attraction here," I said with a considerable amount of modesty. "We wish to attract custom because of the quality of our dancers and performers."

"Is that the only reason?"

I looked at him. "Of course it is. What are you implying?"

"Just asking."

I busied myself checking my watch.

Miss Jennings opened the cardboard box and took out a square of glass, about five inches by seven. This she placed into a slot in the centre of the camera.

Angus edged closer.

"Would you like to look?" she asked.

He nodded, and she gestured for him to proceed. He clasped his hands firmly behind his back so as not to disturb anything, bent down, and peered into the back of the box.

"But it's upside down!"

She laughed. "That it is. Upside down and the colours are reversed. What we call a negative image."

Miss Jennings unstoppered her two glass vials and poured a tiny amount of powder onto a piece of paper, taking great care putting the cork back in each bottle in turn and instructing Angus to place them on a bench a good distance away. She took the metal tray with the long (exceedingly long) handle and poured the powder mixture onto the surface. An instrument, looking somewhat like a miniature gun, was attached to the tray, which she held high over her head with her right hand. Angus came close and she ordered him to stand back.

She tossed the black cloth across her head and shoulders and bent forward. She made some minor adjustments to the little wheels at the back of the instrument. "Now everyone, stand perfectly still. There will be a noise and a flash of light, but it's important that you don't move." The girls froze. Ellie clamped her eyes firmly shut. With her right hand, Miss Jennings fiddled with the metal tray, and at the exact moment the powder exploded, she pulled the cap off the bronze eye at the front of the instrument with her left. We held our breath. The cap was replaced and the sudden bright light faded, leaving a good deal of smoke behind. "Don't move," she shouted, "I'll take one more." She repeated the process. The glass plate was flipped to the other side, the powder was lit, the cap removed, held for less than a second, and then replaced.

Miss Jennings straightened up and tossed off the black cloth. Blond tendrils escaped from her mussed coil of hair. Her gloves were streaked gray with traces of the powder. Grey smoke curled though the room and tickled my throat. A couple of the girls coughed. "All done," she announced.

The women burst into excited babble.

"When will we be able to see it?"

"C'n I have my picture taken?"

"Will you be making copies so I can send one to my mother?"

I clapped my hands. "Ladies, ladies. We have a show to put on in precisely fifteen minutes." All through the photography session, I'd been aware that the crowd was building in the gambling hall and the saloon. I'd told Ray to tell the musicians and Roland to remain outside until we were finished. They'd be late getting set up, but I figured the audience would forgive us this once. "Off you go now, backstage. If you're not in costume, you had best get to it."

They scampered off until only Irene remained. She descended the stage as the Queen might come down off her throne. The silk of her gown murmured as it moved. "Thank you, Miss Jennings. I hope we did you justice."

Miss Jennings stopped fiddling with her equipment. The edges of her mouth turned up. "Miss Davidson, how could it not, with you in the centre."

Oh, dear, I thought.

"I'd love to do a private portrait. Free of charge, if you'd be willing to pose for me."

"That would be great. When?"

"Why don't you stop by my studio sometime tomorrow morning, and we can discuss the details. You have my card?"

"I'll see you tomorrow." Irene drifted away.

I gritted my teeth.

"Can I help you, ma'am?" Angus said. "I can carry your things if you like."

"That would be wonderful, young man, thank you. It gets heavy sometimes." Miss Jennings turned to me. "Mrs. MacGillivray, I'll send word once I've processed the photographs. I'm sure you'll love them."

"I'm sure I will," I said. I wanted to send Angus to open the doors, but he was intent on studying Miss Jennings' camera.

I'd have to do it myself.

"That was amazing, Fiona," Mrs. Mann said as she and her husband followed me out. "Jürgen, we must arrange to have Miss Jennings take a photograph of us."

He muttered something in German that might have been "over my dead body."

We were almost trampled in the rush as men streamed through the doors.

Chapter Ten

Richard Sterling stood at the back of the gambling hall, watching. A game of faro was in progress and the stakes were getting high. Over the clattering of the roulette wheel, the muttering of the poker players, and the talk coming from the bar, he could hear Ellie belting out a lively song. She didn't have much of a voice, Ellie, and no one would call her young, but the men seemed to like her. And that was all that mattered to Fiona MacGillivray and Ray Walker.

Roland, who appeared at the beginning of the stage entertainment to warm up the men for what they'd really come to see — women singing and dancing and pretending to be acting — was intent on the poker game. He held his cards in one hand and fingered his pile of chips absentmindedly with the other. Sterling came up behind him and had a peek at the cards. Not bad, three queens. He kept his face impassive. No one else would be allowed to stand behind a card player, but Jake would not chase a Mountie away.

The man to Roland's right had a full house. Jacks over nines. He was dressed in working man's clothes. Layers of old grime under fresh mud and dust. His hands were marked by thick callouses and criss-crossed by badly healed scars. He'd made an attempt to wash up, but stubborn dirt clung to the folds and crevices of his skin. Strands of greasy black hair hung over his eyes.

The Russian was the third player. His small eyes darted nervously around the room, and he drummed a pattern on the table with his left hand. Sterling couldn't see the man's cards from where he stood, but the count might as well have hung a sign around his neck letting everyone know they weren't good.

The Russian was losing big. Sterling wasn't particularly surprised — the man was a dreadful player. His face recorded every thought that passed through his head. He'd ordered one of the bartenders to keep his glass topped up.

Roland and the other player, by contrast, barely sipped at the whisky resting at their elbows.

Sterling was off duty and could have headed back to the fort for his supper, but he'd lingered after the photography session. Miss Jennings, accompanied by an eager Angus, had departed, and the dancers had begun to prepare for the night's entertainment.

Sterling wasn't inclined to gamble, and couldn't afford it at any rate. His father had been a failed farmer and a dirt-poor hell-and-brimstone preacher. Father and son had departed on bad terms, surrounded by words that could never be taken back. But if one lesson of his father's had stayed with him, it was the evils of gambling.

He didn't mind the hardscrabble miners who'd spent the last twenty, thirty years alone in the wilderness searching for gold, and when they at last struck it rich, pretty much spent it as fast as they could on women, liquor, and cards. For most of those men, there was no place in the Outside for people such as them.

It did bother him sometimes to see men step off their makeshift boats, expecting to find gold lying on the ground like windfall apples, turning to the roulette wheel or poker table for consolation when they realized all their dreams were for naught. Those who'd left dirty-faced children, pregnant wives, hardscrabble farms or back-breaking factory jobs behind to try and make something of themselves, to provide for those families. Instead they spent their time throwing away what little they did manage to earn in a night at the Monte Carlo or the Horseshoe or the Savoy, or any one of the number of dance halls and casinos that had spring up along Front Street.

But he wasn't anyone's father, or even their preacher. If a man wanted to squander a months' wages or the last of the money he had to spend on food on a spin of the wheel, Richard Sterling wasn't here to lecture him.

Sterling had his back to the door leading into the dance hall, but he didn't have to see to know when Fiona MacGillivray entered the room. Everyone but the hardiest gambler sat a bit straighter, adjusted his hat or tie, dusted off his sleeves.

He felt the air move, heard fabric rustle, smelled good soap, and she was beside him.

"Quite a fuss, that photography business," he said.

She sighed. "I can't bear to watch any longer. Either the girls are strutting like peacocks because they were in the front of the photograph, or pouting and sulking because they feel slighted. They're tripping each other, stepping on toes, blocking sightlines. It's a disaster. The audience absolutely loves it." She threw up her hands, and he laughed. Some of the tension in his shoulders melted away.

"Mr. Turner?" the dealer said.

"I'm out, getting too rich for my blood." The badly dressed man at the poker table threw down his cards.

"Call," Roland the Magnificent said.

The Russian laid down his cards. He had a pair of nines. Roland laughed as he displayed his hand. He swept up the pot. Several hundred dollars.

Turner swore heartily.

"Watch it," Sterling said. "Consider this a warning. I hear that again, you'll be down at the fort for use of vile language."

Turner rose to his feet. His chair crashed to the floor. He stood with his feet apart. Hands clenched. Face reddening. "Sure you're not sending signals to that fellow? You've got a mighty nice view of my cards."

Sterling repressed a sigh. "You've lost. Don't make anything of it, friend."

"I'll make something of it if I want."

Sterling was conscious of Fiona's breath beside him. The roulette wheel clattered to a halt. Jake, the head croupier, came out from behind the faro table. Conversation in the room stopped. Men clutched their cards, or protected their chips, and watched.

In the dance hall, Ellie shouted, "Lay on MacDuff, and darned be he who first cries, hold enough."

Unfortunate timing for that particular line, Sterling thought. He wasn't armed; the police didn't carry firearms in the normal course of their duties. But neither did the citizenry. The man was about his age, big with what appeared to be a good set of muscles under his tattered and filthy clothes. Sterling never considered himself to be much of a street fighter, although he knew how to hold his own if he had to.

"Do you have a name, sir?" said a voice beside him.

"Stay out of this, Mrs. MacGillivray," Sterling said. "Please."

The man looked at her. He blinked, and then his shoulders relaxed fractionally as he said, "John Turner."

"Mr. Turner, the stage show is well underway, but I believe seats are still available. We will be open for dancing shortly."

"I'll dance with you. Now."

"There is no music."

"I'll hum."

The watching men began to murmur. Was the man stupid, or just a braggart? Mrs. MacGillivray was very popular in this town, and the men didn't like the tone Turner was taking.

He stepped toward Fiona. She didn't move. Sterling placed himself between them. He saw Jake signalling to one of his men to get Joe Hamilton, the bouncer.

"You're a right pretty lady," Turner said. "Speak nicely, too. So I'll take your advice. Have a drink maybe, come by for the dancing later." He turned suddenly and faced the watching room. He held his hands open. "No trouble. I have a couple of dollars left, anyone wants to join me in a drink. You, Yellow Stripe, I'll be seeing you later." He sauntered out of the room, heading into the saloon.

Joe Hamilton stood in the doorway, glancing at Fiona for orders. She waved her hand. Let him go.

On stage, a woman cried, "You bitch." Richard Sterling wasn't a Shakespearean scholar, but his mother had ensured he and his sisters had some knowledge of literature. He didn't recall that line being in *Macbeth*.

The men returned to their cards, their chips, and their whisky. The roulette wheel began to spin. The croupier called out, "Place your bets, gentlemen."

"You should have let us handle it," Sterling said. "That's why you have employees. Not to mention that I am with the police."

"There would have been a fight and someone's nose broken and blood on the floor." Fiona smiled and he found himself smiling back although he intended to be cross with her.

"That's a girl!" A man in the dance hall roared.

"Speaking of blood on the floor, I suspect the Battle of Dunsinane is about to get rather fierce if I don't step in." She made no move to leave.

"Fiona," he said, his voice dropping, "you do sometimes place yourself in more danger than is wise."

"So I have been told. I'll try to remember your advice. Good evening, Corporal."

"Good evening, ma'am."

* * *

The box was heavier than it looked and Angus was having trouble keeping up with Miss Jennings. She was small, but she could sure walk fast. She came to a stop at the street corner, waiting for a cart to pass. The cart was pulled by a horse so thin Angus could count every rib. The animal struggled against the mud gripping the wheels as the driver yelled and flailed his whip. The cart reached the duckboard, placed across the street to provide some passage over the muck, and the wheels stuck fast. The driver screamed louder and the horse strained. Three men waded into the road, got behind the cart, laid their shoulders to the boards and shoved. With a groan, and the suck of sludge, the cart wheels began to turn. At last they jolted onto the duckboard, and the journey continued.

"If that man gave his horse a bit of food now and again, the animal might be of some use," Miss Jennings said, watching the vehicle lumber away.

"No fodder," Angus said. "No hay, no grass, and most of the trees are pines or spruce. Not that there are all that many trees anyway."

The town of Dawson waged war relentlessly against the forest. Every tree for miles around had been chopped down, to clear the growing town site, to provide lumber for construction and wood for burning. Even on the far side of the river, tents crawled up the mountainside where a short time ago trees had grown and animals had lived. Over the long quiet winter Angus sometimes heard wolves howling and had seen tracks of moose in the deep snow. Come spring and summer, nothing remained but what man brought in.

They crossed the street and arrived at Miss Jennings' photography studio. She'd taken, she informed him, the rooms above as her residence. She unlocked the door and held it open for Angus. He staggered in and gratefully placed the camera case where she indicated. The room was full with what would be clutter in anyone else's home. He assumed she used the jumble of odds and ends for props. Mining equipment, shiny and unused, snowshoes, a fur hat, a lady's cape and a long pink boa, empty wooden boxes stamped with the names of foodstuffs.

"You won't need some of that, ma'am," he said, indicating a pick, without a speck of dust on it, leaning up against a table. "No one has any illusions left about the glory of gold mining, not once they get here."

"Perhaps you can be of help to me, Angus. What sort of pictures do you think people want?"

"Of themselves. Pictures to send back home to their wives and children. Showing they're okay."

"May I take your photograph?"

"I don't have anyone to send it to. My father died before I was born. My mother doesn't communicate with his family, and her own parents are dead."

"Something to keep for yourself perhaps. To show your grandchildren some day."

Grandchildren. What an impossible notion. *Still,* Angus thought, *it would be nice to have a photograph*. His mother had two pictures she'd brought from England. A formal portrait of him as a baby and another in which he was a fat thing dressed in a sailor suit on a day's outing in High Park.

"I don't have any money."

"In thanks for your assistance today."

If Miss Jennings hoped to make a living at this she shouldn't be so quick to give her services away for free. The Savoy dancers and then Miss Davidson. Now him. Maybe, he thought, she was a rich lady indulging her hobby.

"Sure. I can give it to my mother as a present. She'd like that."

"Your mother doesn't want to have her photograph taken. She has an interesting face. Excellent bone structure. Striking colouring." She tilted her head to one side and studied Angus to a degree that made him uncomfortable. "Quite different from yours. Resemble your father do you?"

"So she tells me. She doesn't have a picture of him. My father was blond, like me. Tall."

"Perhaps you could have a word with her. I know I could do her justice."

"Don't bother trying to change my mother's mind. Once she makes her mind up, nothing will change it."

"Tell me about Corporal Sterling. Is he friends with your mother? Close friends, I mean?"

"I guess so."

"I'm surprised at the number of Mounties I've seen about town. Quite a strong police presence, it seems. And a substantial fort. What do you suppose they're afraid of?"

"Afraid of? Nothing. They're keeping the peace, that's all. Some people say they have a machine gun up at the Pass. That's to keep Soapy Smith and any other American criminals out of Canada. Soapy's losing control, though, even in Skagway. The townspeople are tired of him controlling the town and driving business away."

"What makes you say that?"

"My mother told me."

"Your mother knows what's going on? Politics, the police?"

"Sure. She has to. She calls it keeping her ears to the ground. We were in Skagway for a while. Just a couple of days, and she realized Soapy wouldn't let her run her business her way, so we came to Dawson."

"I suppose she hears a lot of things in the Savoy. News, rumour."

"Oh, yes. She tells me men say things around her some-times that they shouldn't. Because she's a woman they think she doesn't understand."

"Your mother's an Englishwoman?"

"People think she's English because of the way she speaks. But she's Scottish, originally. She's from Skye. That's in north-ern Scotland."

Miss Jennings' eyebrows lifted. "Scottish, is that so? I have biscuits in a tin somewhere, would you like one?"

"Great, thanks! Why are you asking about my mother?"

"No reason. I'd like to make friends, that's all." She pulled a battered cake tin out from under an assortment of men's hats. "I'd also like to make friends with Miss Davidson. Tell me about her."

"She's stepping out with Ray Walker," Angus mumbled around a mouthful of a surprisingly good cookie. It was packed full of raisins. Angus loved raisins. "Mother doesn't approve, but I don't know why." He shoved the last of the cookie into his mouth. "I'm sorry, Miss Jennings, but I'd better be going home. Mrs. Mann will have my supper ready." Angus looked around the room. "I can help you, if you like. With your cameras and stuff, I mean. I'd like to learn about photography."

Miss Jennings smiled. "That would be an excellent idea indeed, Angus. You can be my assistant, and I will pay you a good sum."

His face fell.

"You don't want to be paid?"

"It's not that. I work at Mr. Mann's shop, down by the waterfront, every morning. Ma — I mean, Mother — says I'm old enough to contribute to the family income."

"Then I shall arrange my schedule so I do private portraits in the morning, and in the afternoons, when you are able to escort me, we will go outside. Take photographs of the streetscape and capture people unawares as they go about their business. Daylight lasts so long here, I won't have to rush to get the pictures I want."

"Does it matter? You have that magnesium to make light."

"Daylight is far preferable to artificial light, Angus. It makes a more natural photograph. Besides, I didn't bring much of the flash powder chemicals, so I'd like to save it for when I need it."

"When do you want me to start? Tomorrow?"

"Tomorrow would be perfect."

He headed for the door. He stopped with his hand stretched toward the knob. "Hey, I've an idea. If you want business, the police use photographers sometimes. A man was killed the other day and they had Mr. Hegg come to the mortuary and take his picture. So they could show it around and try to find out who he was. Mr. Hegg wasn't happy, said he didn't want that sort of work. Maybe you could do it?"

"An excellent plan. You haven't even begun your first day of employment, Angus, and already you've proved your worth. Perhaps you could put in a word for me with Corporal Sterling."

"Sure."

Angus left, feeling quite proud of himself.

Chapter Eleven

At the conclusion of the stage show, I marched into the dressing room and gave the girls a stern talking to. I reminded them that they were professionals (stretching the truth somewhat) and were expected to conduct themselves accordingly. Betsy, as is her habit, tried to argue that she wasn't the one who'd been out of line. I cut her off and reminded her that her employment here was at my favour. She, and all of them, were welcome to seek prospects elsewhere at any time.

Following my lecture, the dancing segment of the evening went quite smoothly.

Irene spent most of the night in the upstairs boxes, in the company of the grizzled old sourdough I'd noticed her with on previous occasions. As the headliner, she was free to concentrate her attentions on one man, if she so desired, and considering he was ordering bottle after bottle of the best Champagne, I was happy to leave the two of them to it.

Getting on toward morning, I noticed a man sitting in the round table in the centre of the saloon. I hadn't seen him before — nothing unusual about that, our clientele turned over with head-spinning speed. He was drinking heavily, his bulbous red nose testified that this wasn't the first time, not dancing or engaging much in conversation with the men sharing his table. He was, instead, watching Colleen. Every time she came into the bar after a dance to "let" her escort buy himself a drink (included in the dollar a minute dance), the man scowled mightily and knocked back an extra-large swig of whisky. She peeked at him out of the corner of her eyes, but did not approach. He was considerably older than she, well into his late fifties I'd guess.

If he was her husband or a jealous lover, I didn't want him causing trouble once he'd drunk enough to object to her smiling and being charming to our customers. I pulled her aside when her latest dance partner had staggered outside in search of the privy (also known as the back alley or street corner).

"Colleen, there's a man in the front room, sitting at the centre table. An older fellow. Do you know him?"

"You mean my dad?"

"Your father?"

She nibbled on her lip with tiny white teeth and nodded. "He's not causing any trouble, is he, Mrs. MacGillivray?" Her voice was small and low.

"No," I said. "But I don't care for the way he watches you. Or rather watches your companions. Your father is aware that dancing with the men is part of the job, is he not?"

"Yes, ma'am."

"Good." I stopped as a thought struck me. "Your father isn't … uh … expecting you to leave with any of these gentlemen at the end of the night, is he?"

"Why would I do that?" Her expression was as innocent as her words. I studied her. I could see no artifice there. Her face was round, a bit of baby fat clinging still, her cheeks pink from the dancing, her blue eyes wide and liquid, her brown hair tortured into bouncing ringlets (now drooping considerably in the heat of the enclosed room). She was pleasingly plump with a high, generous bosom and long legs. "It might be best," I said, "if your father doesn't sit there every night. Doesn't he have a job to go to in the morning?"

She studied the floor. "He's got a bad back. Can't get work."

The man in question waylaid Not-Murray, waving his empty glass in the bartender's face.

Not the first man, father or husband, who decided it would be easier to put the woman to work.

None of my concern.

"Thank you, Colleen. Please ensure your father doesn't cause trouble. Now, that gentleman over there appears to be attempting to attract your attention."

"Yes, ma'am. Thank you, ma'am." She pasted on a shy smile and went to join the gangly young fellow waving a dollar bill at her with an excessive amount of enthusiasm.

The next time I walked through the saloon, Colleen's father was no longer at his post.

When I carried the money bag upstairs at the end of the night (otherwise known as 6:00 a.m.), I was highly satisfied with the weight of it.

* * *

"I have a new job, Mother," Angus said the following morning. He'd come to my room to wish me a good day. I was sitting at what passed for my dressing table attempting to arrange my hair in front of what passed for my mirror. Difficult to do without the services of a lady's maid. I thought of Miss Jennings' tight plaits and shuddered. "Hold this, will you, Angus." He gripped a length of hair and I shoved a pin through it. It was highly unlikely any of the boys at Angus's former school would ever in their lives help a lady with her hair. Angus was learning a great many things young gentlemen of his class were not expected to learn. I didn't always know if that was a good thing.

I studded the mess of hair in the mirror. Today would definitely be a day for a good hat.

"I have a new job, Mother," he said.

"Pass me the cream hat, will you, dear. Hold the pins ready. A new job? You have responsibilities to Mr. Mann."

"I'll work in the shop in the morning. In the afternoon," in the mirror, I saw him puff up his chest with pride, "I will be a photographic assistant."

"Miss Jennings?"

"Yup. She needs someone to carry her equipment when she leaves the studio and to show her around town and introduce her to people. I'll be able to learn from her. Being a photographer would be a splendid occupation. Don't you think so, Mother?"

Hardly. More like a fancy tradesman. I did not say so. I'd learned never to pour cold water on Angus's enthusiasm. It usually served only to stoke the flames. If I may, again, mix my metaphors.

"Have you heard anything further about the police investigation? Into the sudden demise of that unfortunate gentleman on Tuesday?" I studied my reflection. It would do.

"They're showing the photograph of him, taken post-mortem, around town. That's all I know. Perhaps I'll stop by the detachment later, try to find out."

"It's none of your business. Stay out of it."

"Of course it's our business, Mother. The man died in your arms."

"Saying my name, yes I know, but ..."

"Saying your name ..."

"I told you that."

"What if he wasn't saying your name?"

"I know what I heard, Angus."

"What if he was telling you *his* name?"

"What?"

"You naturally assumed he said MacGillivray, addressing you. But suppose he wasn't." Angus's voice began to rise in excitement. His words tripped all over themselves in their haste to be heard. "Suppose that was his name, and he was trying to tell you it, so he wouldn't go an unmarked grave. Oh, my gosh, Mother. Suppose that wasn't his name either, but the name of his attacker. With his last breath, he was giving you a clue! I have to get to Corporal Sterling right away."

"Calm down, dear. There are no other people by the name of MacGillivray in town."

"You don't know everyone, Mother, although you think you do. If he, this other MacGillivray, didn't frequent the dance halls you'd have no reason to hear of him." Angus stroked his chin in thought. "He might be a relation of ours."

"Humph. If he is any relation of mine … I mean, of your father, he's unlikely to be a cold-blooded killer."

"Which brings us back to my original thought. He was telling you his name. Because he had been searching for us!"

Oh, dear. This was getting rather out of hand. "Surely not, Angus. If he were searching for us, I am not exactly difficult to locate." I threw cold water onto his enthusiasm. "He could have walked through the doors of the Savoy at any time and announced himself." I stood up. "Time to be off. Mr. Mann doesn't like you to be late." I presented my cheek for a kiss.

My son ignored me. "He was on the way to the Savoy, Mother, when he was set upon by ruffians. I have to tell the police right away. Mr. Mann always says it's okay if I miss work on police business."

He dashed out the door. I had, predictably, stoked the flames. "Now," I said to myself in the mirror, "you've gone and done it."

I not been married to Angus's father. His name had not
been MacGillivray. That was my parents' name. I was proud to
give my son the name of my own father, whom I had adored
— Angus MacGillivray. To the best of my knowledge, Angus's
father was not dead. Although if I ever caught up with him he
would wish he was. I had loved Angus's father — tall, blond,
blue-eyed, heart-breakingly handsome — deeply and passion-
ately. He told me he loved me equally.

He abandoned me the moment he found out I was in the
family way.

Good enough to seduce, but not good enough to marry.

I felt a stab of pain and glanced down. I'd picked up an
excess hat pin and stuck it into the flesh of my index finger. A
single drop of bright red blood appeared. I sucked it away.

I never thought it would hurt if I strung Angus a story about
his father and our wedding and the tragic demise of my great
love only a few short months later and then his heartless family
throwing me and my sweet wee babe into the streets.

I didn't think, as my beloved boy began to turn into a man, I
would ever be confronted by the web of lies I'd woven. We were
far from England and everyone who had known me back then. If
this man, the man who'd died, indeed was looking for me, either
because my name was MacGillivray or because his was — or
perhaps both — might the truth come out?

Nonsense. I arranged a tendril of hair to fall lightly across
my neck. My father was an only child. Even on Skye I had no
MacGillivray relatives. No one would be searching for me, or
finding me, all these years later.

The man had died with my name on his lips, no doubt only
because he recognized me as the well-known owner of the Savoy.
No other reason.

Why then had he said Culloden?

Chapter Twelve

"Yup, that's the man. I wondered where he'd gotten to."

The woman was probably only in her twenties, but already life's mark was stamped upon her. Her belly was huge and round and she rested her hand under it, trying to take some of the weight. Her hair was thin beneath a tattered bonnet and her dress and apron stained with dirt and grease. Black circles beneath her eyes dragged down her face. The fingers of her right hand were twisted and the skin a mass of puckered pink flesh. Old burns.

"My man's away at the Creeks," she said. "I take in boarders."

The house behind her was in no worse condition than most.

"May we come in?" Richard Sterling said.

"No need. We ain't got a parlour and no furniture neither."

He resigned himself to standing in the street.

Constable McAllen had located the house, by the tedious yet effective process of showing the photograph of the dead man around the docks until at last he found someone who remembered seeing him with someone whose name they knew, and that person, once located, had mentioned Mrs. Wallace's boarding house.

"His name was Jim Stewart?" Sterling repeated what she'd said.

"Yup."

"Did he tell you anything about himself?"

She shrugged. "I give 'em a room and two meals a day. I don't have no call to talk to 'em."

"He must have talked sometimes. Such as when he was having those meals. You have other boarders, don't you?"

"Yeah."

"Did they talk amongst themselves? Did you overhear anything?"

The edges of her mouth turned up. It looked as if she'd forgotten that they could do so. "Sure they talked. About how they're gonna make their fortune. About all the presents they'll buy me when they come back from the Creeks." She spat on the ground at Sterling's feet. "My man's gone to the Creeks. He ain't come back with nothin' but," she rubbed her belly, "more work to do.

"The man you're interested in, he didn't talk much at all. Listened though, he were a good listener."

"What do you mean by that?"

She shrugged. "Seemed to be payin' attention, is all. He had a way of putting his head to one side, so you thought he were listening to what a body had to say."

"You talked to him then, although he didn't say much in return."

"Sometimes. When I were puttin' the food on the table. Couldn't understand much when he were talkin' mind."

"Why's that?"

"He had an accent, real strong."

"Where was this accent from?"

She shrugged once again. "England, I recon? Look Corporal, I got work to get to. Bread ain't cookin' itself."

"I'm going to have to have a look at his room. Do you still have his belongings?"

"Room's paid up till end o' the week. I won't be throwing his stuff out till then." She stepped back. "Last door on the right."

Sterling entered, McAllen following. The house consisted of one long hallway with a series of doors leading off. No front room or parlour. No carpets, no furniture. The place smelled of

bacon grease, cheap tallow candles, and unwashed clothes. The
room the woman had indicated was unlocked and Sterling let
himself in. No window. A small bed covered by a scrap of blanket
— stinking to high heaven — was pushed up against the wall.
The trunk beside it took up most of the rest of the space. A single
pair of trousers hung by the suspenders to a hook on the wall.

Sterling opened the trunk. Winter clothes, bags of dried
food, a few books. "I wonder where the rest of his things are.
He had to have brought a lot more than this. Man can't get into
Canada without a thousand pounds of goods."

"There are ways," McAllen said, "of getting around the border. If you don't have the supplies."

"Or don't want your arrival recorded." Sterling picked up a
book. An illustrated history of Scotland, well thumbed. It fell
open to a page on the Battle of Culloden. An illustrated plate
showed a kilted Highlander, strong and defiant, wearing a blue
cap, carrying a sword in his right hand, a shield in his left. He
faced a line of uniformed troops armed with muskets.

They'd left the door open and heard footsteps in the hall followed by a man's voice.

Sterling stuck his head out the door. "You there, mind if I
have a word."

"Sure." The fellow was dressed in a dark suit with a white
apron tied over it. A waiter at a better restaurant, probably.

"Did you know Mr. Jim Stewart? Who had this room?"

"Seen him around. What's he done?"

"Did he tell you much about himself? Where he's from,
where he's working, that sort of thing."

"Not really. I'm a waiter at the Richmond Hotel, and I take
my meals at work. I don't have much to do with the other boarders. But I did say hello a couple of times when we passed in the
hall. He seemed like a nice enough fellow. What's he done?"

"Mrs. Wallace said he had a strong accent. Do you know what kind?"

"Scotch. I've heard a lot worse, believe me. That bartender at the Savoy? Might as well be speaking Hindu for all anyone can understand him."

"Did he have a job?"

"Not that he ever mentioned. Sorry, Corporal. That's about it. We discussed the weather, and I told him a couple of the best places to visit because he was new to town. I suggested going to the Savoy one night for a drink when I got off work, but we never did. Why'd you say you're asking about him again?"

"Thanks for your trouble," Sterling said.

"Anytime." The waiter went to his room and shut the door behind him.

Mrs. Wallace had disappeared.

"Seems like he kept himself to himself," McAllen said.

"Yes, it does. But we have a name at least." Sterling balanced the book in his hand. "And we know where he came from, although I doubt that's worth much. If he didn't try to make friends with the men, perhaps he was more interested in the companionship of women, if you know what I mean. Get down to Paradise Alley when the ladies are awake and start asking around."

McAllen muffled a groan.

"Mrs. Wallace," Sterling called. She appeared at the back door, wiping her hands on her apron. Sweat was streaming down her face, her hair was damp, and she carried a piece of kindling. She'd been working over the fire in the yard, heating water prior to doing the laundry.

"I'll be sending someone around from the fort with a cart to take Mr. Stewart's trunk," Sterling said. "Evidence, I'm afraid."

Her face fell. She'd been intending to sell the man's belongings. "What ya going to do with 'em after? Keep it for yourselves, I suppose."

"We'll give anything useful to the church. They'll know of men needing clothes and supplies."

"I need supplies. My man could use the clothes."

"We'll see ourselves out. Thank you, Mrs. Wallace."

She muttered and went back to her fire. Sterling didn't fell particularly sorry for her. She had a roof over her head, money coming in, and a working husband. Plenty of women were a lot worse off than that. He tossed the *Illustrated History of Scotland* onto the bed.

"If I may, Corporal," McAllen asked as they headed downhill back to town, "why are we pursuing this? The man was rumbled in an alley. The miscreants are bound to be long gone, hiding out or gone to the Creeks. Stewart's name or that he was from Scotland or what fairy he used isn't going to help us find them." Fairy, Sterling knew, was a word for the prostitutes who plied their trade out of the cribs on the stretch of street called Paradise Alley. His father would have considered the name of the street to be pure blasphemy.

"Because I don't think, although some might disagree, that this was any street brawl or attempted robbery gone wrong," Sterling said. "This isn't Seattle or Chicago or even Toronto or Winnipeg. I don't know the last time a man was set upon by thugs in an alley. Nothing similar has happened since, which surely it would have if we had a thief in town. No, this was personal. And to find out why, we have to find out who this Stewart was. And why he had enemies."

* * *

"Ray," I said to my business partner, "do you know much about the history of Scotland?"

"What kinda question's that?" he replied.

"Just wondering." I fluttered my fingers in the air. Ray looked at me through narrowed eyes.

"I went to school. All Scottish children go to school, you know that, Fee."

"Yes, but we didn't learn much about Scotland."

"No. I can name the Kings and Queens of England though."

"My governess hated Scotland with a passion. Her opinion was only strengthened shortly after her arrival when she decided to venture forth because it was warm and sunny. A storm blew up in a matter of minutes. Cold, wet, drenching rain. She got lost and spent many hours wandering the barren hills." I smiled at the memory. "The earl sent every one of the male staff out on the search. My father found her, a wet, miserable, weeping mess. She'd lost her hat. She never forgave Scotland for that. Miss Wheatley retired to her room for the remainder of the week, and Euila and I were excused attendance in the schoolroom. I don't believe Miss Wheatley ever dared leave the house again. I miss Scotland, sometimes, Ray. The hills, the heather."

"Your father was a servant? I always figured your parents for gentlefolk." Trust Ray to pick out the only damaging bit in my entire story.

"I meant the male staff and the houseguests, of course."

"All I remember o' Scotland, Fee, was the poverty. The dirt. The hunger when my dad was out of work. The landlord at the door, and Mum making excuses for why she couldn'a pay the rent. Begging to be allowed a wee bit more time. No, I don't miss any of it."

Ray and I were partners. We trusted each other with our livelihood. But we were not friends. We rarely, if ever, discussed our pasts or hopes for the future. Even during the long cold nights on the trail from Skagway to Dawson City, we talked about little other than plans for our saloon and dance hall. Even here, in Canada, we couldn't entirely avoid the social gap. I was well-spoken, educated. He, barely literate, rough of manner and appearance.

Outside of the business, we were not confidants. I'd darn well better remember that. What was I doing, reminiscing fondly about my childhood to someone bound to know the social stratification at an earl's country estate?

"We did," he said, "sometimes get a teacher who told us a wee bit o' Scottish history. Why da ye ask, Fee?"

"Have you heard of anyone in town named MacGillivray? Anyone other than Angus and me, I mean."

He shook his head.

I'd finished doing the day's accounts and was on my way to the bank. About ten men were in the bar, the norm considering it was not yet noon. Not-Murray was serving. I heard the roulette wheel spin: at least one customer was in the gambling room. Ray was coming in as I was heading for the door, and I asked him the question on my mind. I hadn't been able to stop thinking all morning about Angus's theory. That the dead man was telling me *his* name, not gasping out mine.

I turned to the assembled drinkers. I never could have a private conversation in this town. Everyone always leaned closer to listen in, not using any artifice to disguise their eavesdropping either.

"Have any of you gentlemen encountered such a person?"

They shrugged in unison.

"There's a couple o' MacDonalds," one grizzled old sourdough said, trying to be helpful.

"A fellow name of McNamara works at the Horseshoe," offered a man, missing the end of his nose. To frostbite, most likely, as he was also missing three fingers.

"Isn't there a Mrs. MacDonald what owns a ladies dress shop on Front Street?"

"That's right. And Mary McKay works for Joey Leblanc."

I refrained from sighing. No doubt before long someone would arrive, pretending to be one Mr. MacGillivray, hoping to get into my good books.

"Mrs. MacGillivray," said Ray, who didn't have to be charming to the customers, "wasn't askin' about every blasted Scotsman or woman in town, ye ken."

I tightened my grip on the burlap bag containing the day's banking. "Gentlemen," I said, "enjoy your drinks." I headed for the door. Ray accompanied me. We stood outside for a moment in the warm sunshine watching the passing parade.

"Ye didn'a tell me why ye were asking about Scotland."

"Nothing. Forget it. Something Angus said got me thinking."

"Wanting ta know his history, is he?"

"Yes. That's it."

"Can't help ye there, Fee. The old county's best forgotten to my way of thinking. New world. New life. New problems are enough for one man."

Best forgotten. I decided that would be good advice for me. The death of that unfortunate man was none of my business and I would think of it no longer.

Chapter Thirteen

Angus worked in the shop all morning, hurried home to change his clothes and clean up a bit, wolfed down the packed lunch Mrs. Mann had prepared for him, and arrived at Miss Jennings' photography studio precisely on time for his first day of employment. He'd spent the last fifteen minutes circling the streets. She'd said two o'clock, and he didn't want to appear too eager.

"Heavens," she said, looking up from a photograph she held in her hand. "Right on time. You are eager. As you're here, tell me what you think of this?"

She offered him the paper and he took it. It showed the stage of the Savoy, the dancers gathered. The faces of Maxie and Betsy, at the back, were blurred. No doubt because they'd been trying to subtly press their way forward when the picture was taken. Irene, in the front, looked far more beautiful than she was in real life, with her head lifted and her chin thrust forward. The girl beside her, whose name Angus didn't know, smiled demurely, a nice contrast to Irene's air of glamorous self-importance. The rest of the dancers flared out around the two in the centre as if they were nothing but gaily-dressed props. Irene and the woman beside her were what the camera had captured.

"It's grand, Miss Jennings," Angus said. "My mother will be so pleased."

"Not bad, I suppose," she sighed. "I'd prefer it if those stupid girls in the back had stood still, but there isn't much one can do in a group picture. At least Miss Davidson looks lovely."

"My mother says Miss Davidson's worth her weight in gold," Angus said. "She's the most popular dancer in town. The men love her."

"Is that so?" Miss Jennings picked up another photograph. "Is your mother also ... fond of Miss Davidson?" She handed him the picture.

It wasn't as good. This time several of the dancers were blurred, and Irene had turned her head slightly making her nose appear too prominent. "I guess she likes her okay." He handed the picture back to Miss Jennings. A small smile touched the edges of her lips. "This one isn't as good," he said.

She studied it. "I wish people wouldn't insist on smiling for the camera. It distorts their features so."

"What are we, I mean you, going to photograph today?"

"Nothing."

"Nothing?"

"I'd like to get a feel for the town and the people. Once I have done that, I'll take the camera out. I'm thinking of beginning with the police. Your Mounties look quite handsome in their red tunics, don't they? It's unfortunate the photograph can't capture the colour."

He puffed up his chest. "I help the police a lot, you know. I'm going to be a Mountie someday."

"Do you now? Why don't you take me to the fort, then. It's an imposing edifice, and will photograph well."

Imposing wasn't exactly the word Angus would use for the handful of wooden buildings built around a muddy parade square. It didn't even have a fence, much less a palisade. But Miss Jennings was an American; she probably didn't know what an imposing building looked like. He dimly remembered his mother showing him Buckingham Palace and a day's outing to Windsor Castle to picnic on the grass.

"We'll stop at the Savoy to show your mother the picture. What time would be best?"

"She's usually there in the afternoon. Then she goes home for supper and to change into evening clothes and gets back around seven."

"Miss Davidson? What time's she come in?"

"Just before the show begins at eight. Ma — I mean, Mother — says Miss Davidson usually stays all night for the dancing, although as the headliner she doesn't have to."

"It will be your job, Angus, to record my observations. As I discover places that might be good to photograph, I'll want you to write them down. There's a pencil and a notebook on the table. Use that."

He picked them up, pleased with his new responsibilities.

Miss Jennings placed her hat on her head and collected her reticule. She opened the door and came face to face with Graham Donohue, hand raised as if to knock. He jumped back, startled. "Miss Jennings. How nice to find you in."

"I'm on my way out," she said, not sounding too polite. "Are you here to make an appointment?"

"An appointment? Oh, you mean to have my photograph taken. No. I'm a newspaperman. I report on the news. I don't feature in it. Consider this a social call. Perhaps I can walk with you."

"I have my assistant, thank you."

"Your assistant?" He peered into the room and noticed Angus, standing slightly behind the door. "Oh, it's you."

"Yes, sir. Miss Jennings and I are going to check out photographic opportunities."

"An excellent idea."

Miss Jennings held the door for Angus. She locked it behind him and they stepped into the street. Graham Donohue fell in beside her. "The real story of the rush is to be found up at the Creeks. It's an amazing sight. Right, Angus?"

"That it is."

"Hundreds of miles of useless wilderness have simply disappeared. Stripped down to the bare essence of rock and soil. And beneath. Shafts dug into the frozen ground, rivers diverted, miles upon miles of sluices built to bring water to where it's needed. New mountains, this time mountains of mine tailings, thrown up. Modern man's ingenuity in all its glory and power. The face, Miss Jennings, of the twentieth century."

Angus refrained from saying he hoped there'd be some place left in the twentieth century for trees and streams, bears and wolves.

Miss Jennings stopped walking and looked up at Donohue, a spark of interest in her eyes. "To whom, sir, do you believe this twentieth century will belong?"

"To the brave. To the adventurous. To the man... or woman... who can capture it."

"We stand on the verge of great things."

"Exactly. And right here, in the Klondike, the twentieth century, the time of America's glory, has already begun."

"Yet this territory belongs to Canada."

"For now."

Miss Jennings smiled. And then she set off at a pace that had Angus and Donohue hurrying to catch up.

Fort Herchmer had been here, at the meeting of the Klondike and Yukon Rivers, before there was a town to speak of. Not very well positioned, it had flooded so badly in the spring men paddled canoes to get from one building to another.

The day was warm and still, but as they approached the fort the flag at the top of the tall pole in the centre of the parade square caught a gust of wind and snapped open. The Union Jack soared above them.

Miss Jennings stopped walking and stood looking around her. The breeze ruffled her hair and blond strands blew across her face. "Perhaps the officials would like a group portrait of their men," she said. "Angus, write that down. Do you know any of the senior officers here?"

"Inspector McKnight. He comes to the Savoy sometimes, right Mr. Donohue?"

"McKnight fancies Irene Davidson."

"Does he indeed? Can you arrange an introduction, Angus?"

"Sure."

"A collection of men in uniform standing in the square would make an impressive photograph."

Angus scribbled. They watched the Mounties go about their business. Men crossed the square, went in and out of offices and barracks. No one paid them any attention.

A man came out of one of the buildings. He began to walk away, spotted them, and changed direction. Miss Jennings broke into a smile.

Richard Sterling touched the brim of his hat. "Good afternoon. What brings you folks out here?"

"I'm showing Miss Jennings around," Angus said. "She's looking for places to photograph."

"That's right, Corporal. Perhaps you could put in a good word for me with your superiors. I'd love to take pictures of the men as they go about their duties."

"I'm sure I can do that."

They smiled at each other. Graham Donohue shifted his feet and cleared his throat. "Now that's settled, don't you have business to conduct, Sterling? Wasn't there someone murdered in our town a few days ago? How's that investigation going?"

"It's going smoothly," Sterling said. "We'll be making an arrest shortly."

"My mother'll be pleased to hear that," Angus said. "It's been bothering her."

"How about right now?" Miss Jennings said.

"What right now?"

"An introduction to your commanding officer. I've heard so much about the famous Sam Steele, I'm anxious to meet him. I'm sure he would be delighted to have his photograph taken, and I could tell him my suggestion. A formal portrait of the men assembled in the square and additional pictures of a more casual nature."

Sterling smiled at her. "Ma'am, I'm afraid the superintendent isn't in the territory at the moment. Inspector Starnes is in charge. But whoever's in command, I'm not in a position to knock on his office door in the middle of the day and introduce him to my friends."

She pouted prettily. "We'll need more roundabout methods then. Inspector Starnes will have to do. Mr. Donohue, do you have the acquaintance of that gentleman?"

"We've met. But not under the, uh … best of circumstances. The authorities are not always well disposed toward the press, you know. Let's say, I don't expect the inspector will be granting this American newspaperman favours any time soon."

She turned to Angus. "Your mother?"

Angus blinked.

"Never mind. I'll find a way. I am a determined woman, gentlemen. You had best learn that immediately." Her eyes sparked. "Angus, continue with the tour. I'd like to see this Paradise Alley I've heard about."

Angus gulped. "Miss Jennings, I cannot take a lady there."

"I'm not a lady. I'm a photographer. I intend to tell the story of the Klondike though photographs. Mr. Donohue, do you know any of the ladies who work there that you could introduce me to?"

Donohue's face flushed a brilliant red. Angus almost laughed. Graham Donohue knew the inhabitants of the Paradise Alley cribs quite well. A fact that he lived in fear of Fiona MacGillivray discovering. "I, uh ... certainly not," he stammered.

"I'll leave you to it," Sterling said. "Miss Jennings, I must inform you that Angus, as a minor, cannot go everywhere, nor can a respectable lady unaccompanied. If you want to visit the cribs, Donohue here will be an excellent guide."

Donohue began to sputter a protest, but Sterling talked over his objections. "If you'd like to visit one of the other dance halls one evening, for pure research purposes of course, might I have the honour of escorting you?"

Angus blinked again. Was Corporal Sterling offering to step out with Miss Jennings?

The edges of her mouth lifted in a gentle smile. Her blue eyes opened wide. "I'd like that very much. Thank you."

"I'm off duty tomorrow. Shall I come to your studio at eight o'clock?"

"You may."

Sterling touched the brim of his hat in farewell and turned and headed back to the row of offices lining the square.

A few moments passed before Angus was aware that Miss Jennings was retracing their steps back to town. He hurried to catch up with her.

"You said Inspector McKnight comes to the Savoy some evenings," Miss Jennings said over her shoulder.

"Yes."

"I don't suppose you know what evenings?"

"No."

"Then I will simply have to lie in wait. What would be the best time?"

"Promptly at eight o'clock, I'd say," Donohue said. "He likes to get a seat at the front. He doesn't usually stay long. Look, Miss Jennings, when Sterling implied I know my way around Paradise Alley he was naturally referring to the fact that in my role as a newspaperman I have had occasion to interview the women in their … uh … place of business."

"I understood perfectly."

Donohue peeked at Angus out of the corner of his eyes. "Glad to hear that."

It hadn't rained in a couple of days, but the streets never seemed to dry up. Many a man had lost a boot in the muck, which consisted of more than mud as horses and carts and dogs regularly passed by. Going was slow as the small group trailing in Miss Jennings' wake confined themselves to the crowded board-walks. At the corner of Harper Street, they almost collided with a well-dressed gentlemen who stepped into their path.

He swept off his hat and gave a slight bow. "Miss Jennings, the photographer. What a stroke of good fortune. I was planning to stop by your studio later in the day."

"Count Nicholas. Good day."

"Call me Nicky, please, madam. There is no use for archaic titles and privileged nobility in the New World."

"We are of like mind, sir," Miss Jennings said.

Nicky, as he liked to be called, took Miss Jennings's arm. Angus and Donohue fell in behind. The Russian began talking about his hopes to go big-game hunting one day. He would like to shoot a bear, a wolf perhaps. Would Miss Jennings care to accompany him, and photograph the expedition?

Donohue glanced at Angus and drew a circle around his ear with his finger.

"I say, Angus," said a voice from behind. Roland the Magnificent, also out for a walk. "Nice day, isn't it?"

There wasn't much to do in Dawson, other than drink or gamble or visit the cribs. Everyone seemed to spend a good part of their day walking up the muddy streets and then walking down again. Three people could not walk abreast on the narrow boardwalk unless one of them stepped into the mud. Angus dropped back.

"Strange town, this," Roland said.

"That it is."

They never did make it to Paradise Alley. Too many of them, perhaps. Miss Jennings led the way down Front Street, studying everyone and everything, with Roland the Magnificent, Count Nicholas Ivanovich Prozorovsky, Graham Donohue, and Angus MacGillivray trailing in her wake, along with a couple of percentage girls from one of the less respectable dancehalls, two young cheechakos, Angus's friend Dave, and a stray dog. Occasionally Miss Jennings would stop, lift her hands to her face, make a square of them, and peer intently into the distance. Her entourage leaned forward, trying to see what she saw. She snapped out commands to Angus, and he made notes in the book she'd provided. She was interested in the shops of Bowery Street, clustered along the waterfront where boats of all shapes and sizes and varying degrees of seaworthiness or lack thereof had been tied up.

Angus's lunch was but a fond memory and he was trying to remember what was planned for dinner when at last Miss Jennings pronounced herself satisfied with the day. The percentage girls had disappeared long ago, the cheechakos got distracted by one of their friends, Dave headed home for supper, the count stepped in a puddle, soaking his pant leg, and returned to his lodgings to change, and Graham Donohue remembered that he had a story to write if it was going to leave on tomorrow's boat.

Only Angus, Roland the Magnificent, and the dog remained.

"Did you get many ideas?" Angus asked.

"Most certainly. A good day's work, young man."

"I wrote everything down that you told me to."

"Good boy."

The dog lifted a half-chewed-off ear.

Like Angus's mother, Miss Jennings wore a watch pinned to the waistband of her dress. She pulled it out, flipped open the lid, and consulted it. "I'm going to head home and put my feet up for a short while. I intend to be at the Savoy at eight o'clock. Will I see you there, Angus?"

"Uh …"

"I'll be there," Roland said. "In fact, I have to be there as I am the opening act. You seem to have misplaced something, young man." He pulled Angus's pencil out from behind his ear.

Miss Jennings laughed.

*   *   *

We were almost finished the evening meal before Angus stumbled in. He mouthed apologies for his tardiness, but his expression indicated he wasn't at all sorry.

Tonight we were dining on corned beef and cabbage. I detest corned beef almost as much as I detest boiled cabbage. Mr. Mann was complaining about a neighbouring shop trying to undercut his trade in pickaxes, and Mrs. Mann was muttering words of sympathy. I was remembering a meal of Dover sole I'd had in the Savoy — the original Savoy in London. The fish had been prepared perfectly with a trace of lemon, served with bright green peas and tiny boiled potatoes drenched in butter and sprinkled with parsley. I'd been in the company of Lord Alveron. Or was it the Honourable Randolph Greenhaugh?

Never mind. The fish had been followed by a light lemon sorbet and then a Bakewell tart, the crust cooked to perfection. The name of the wine has escaped me.

Wine. Dover sole. Lemon.

As I recall, after the meal he, yes it had been Randolph, had presented me with a gift of pearl earrings. The pearls, I knew, belonged to his grandmother, the dowager duchess. They were intended to match a necklace of uncompromising quality that had been presented to the duchess by no less a personage than the Duke of Wellington himself, in exchange for some favour or other her husband had performed. (That was the official family story. Less officially it was whispered that the dowager duchess herself had been the one providing favours for the Iron Duke.) Randolph had taken the less valuable earrings, but had not had the nerve to sneak the necklace out of his grandmother's jewellery box. I managed that myself one night when the family, meaning Randolph, his wife, and the dotty old lady, were at a ball to which I had not been invited.

Good times.

"Isn't that so, Fiona?" said Mrs. Mann.

"Quite so," I replied with no idea as to what I was agreeing.

Angus returned from the temporary house and slipped into his seat at the table. Mrs. Mann got up to prepare his plate, and he dug in with enthusiasm and a hearty appetite.

"Are you going to tell us what prompted this tardiness?" I asked. Not that any of us, particularly me, kept to a rigid schedule. Still, I did try to maintain some standards.

"I was helping Miss Jennings. It's grand seeing things through a photographer's eyes." Still gripping his fork, he held his hands in a square in front of his face and studied me. I swatted at them.

"She has the photograph she took at the Savoy to show you. I think you'll be pleased. She's going to drop by this evening."

"I hope she's not going to become a nuisance. Everyone," I included the Manns in that statement, "becomes a positive fool when a camera shows up. I don't know why anyone bothered to invent the dratted thing in the first place."

"I'm going to make an appointment," Mrs. Mann said. "I'd like a photograph of Jürgen and me to send to my family back east. To show them how well we're prospering."

Mr. Mann grunted his disapproval. I had no doubt he'd be spick and span when the time came.

"She's going to take some pictures down at the waterfront," Angus said. "We were scouting out locations today. That's a technical term, Mother, meaning looking for good places to photograph. Perhaps she could photograph the shop."

"Not proper," Mr. Mann said around a mouthful of corned beef and cabbage. "A lady going into dance halls. Men's homes. Places of business. Not proper."

"It's a new world, dear." Mrs. Mann beamed at me. "Why look at Fiona. A businesswoman!"

That Mrs. Mann herself was a woman of business, running a boarding house and a busy laundry, probably hadn't occurred to her husband.

I dabbed my lips with my napkin. "I must go and dress." I began to get to my feet but stopped as Angus slapped his forehead. "Oh, no. I forgot."

"What did you forget?"

"My theory about the man who died, Mother. What I told you this morning. I meant to tell Corporal Sterling when I saw him earlier. I guess I was confused about what he said to Miss Jennings."

"What did he say to Miss Jennings?"

My son's eyes slid away from my face. "Uh ... uh ... I don't remember."

"Angus, what did Corporal Sterling say to Miss Jennings that was so shocking you forgot about a man murdered almost in front of you?"

He gave me a sickly smile. "Nothing important, Mother. He offered to accompany her some evenings, one evening I mean, to the dance halls. Not the Savoy, the other ones. The other one. One of the other ones. To help her with her photography business. As part of his job. Yes, that's it. To give her a police escort." He shovelled cabbage into his mouth so fast he began to choke.

I went to my room to dress for the evening. I had no claim on Corporal Sterling, none whatsoever. I had suspected he was fond of me, but really, that wasn't a unique experience. I had offered him nothing in the way of encouragement. I thought we were friends. Yes, friends. We were friends. If Richard wanted to court Miss Jennings, who was after all a most attractive unattached woman, I would be happy for him. For the both of them. Very happy.

I ripped the length of fake pearls off my neck and threw them across the room.

Chapter Fourteen

Richard Sterling was finishing up some paperwork in the detachment office when Angus MacGillivray knocked on the door.

Sterling leaned back and rubbed his eyes, happy at the interruption. Paperwork never had been his strong suit.

Angus stood stiffly in front of the desk. Almost at attention. Sterling hid a grin.

"You have something to report, Mr. MacGillivray?"

"Gee, how'd you know that?"

"Policeman's intuition. Take a seat."

"I had an idea, about the man. The one who was murdered."

"Go ahead."

Angus explained his theory that the man might not have been saying his mother's name, but telling her his. Or even the name of his attacker.

It was a good point, and Sterling kicked himself for not thinking of it himself. Mrs. MacGillivray had assumed the man — Jim Stewart — was addressing her. Sterling had not stopped to consider that her assumption might not have been correct.

"Smart thinking, Angus. But we know he wasn't telling your mother his name. We found him. Jim Stewart. Mean anything to you?"

Angus thought. "No. Common enough name, I guess."

"He might have been naming someone else, though. His attacker. The name of his boyhood dog. Men say strange things, so I've been told, when they're about to die." Sterling gestured to the pile of papers on his desk. "This can wait until tomorrow. I like your idea, Angus."

The boy sat a bit straighter in his chair.

"Jim Stewart's a common name, as you said, but MacGillivray isn't. I don't think I ever met a MacGillivray until I met you and your mother. Do you know of any others?"

"I've never met a MacGillivray either. My mother says it's a well-known name in Scotland. MacGillivrays fought at Culloden."

"Where's that?"

"It was a really big battle. In 1745. The real king of Scotland was some guy named James, but the English had taken over Scotland and sent King James into exile to France. When James's son Charles, who they called Bonnie Prince Charlie, and his army tried to retake Scotland, the people rose up to throw out the English. It was a terrible battle; my mother says they remember it in Scotland to this day. The English soldiers won and they destroyed the Highland clans."

"I saw something about that in a book Stewart had among his possessions. Men in kilts with swords against solders with firearms."

Angus nodded.

"Why does your mother know so much about it? I thought she was English, although her married name's Scottish."

"I guess my father told her. He was a proud Scotsman. Well, I think he was a proud Scotsman. My mother doesn't talk about him much." Angus fell silent. Richard Sterling couldn't remember a day he and his father weren't at loggerheads. He assumed his father was still alive because his sisters hadn't written to say he'd died.

Hard on a boy, though, never to know his father.

Hard on a woman, to raise a boy to be a man — a good man — without his father. Particularly in a rough-and-tumble town like this one, where prostitutes plied their trade openly, the gambling halls were open day and night, and the liquor never stopped flowing.

"Did you ask your mother if any other MacGillivrays are in Dawson?"

"She said no one she's heard of."

Half the men in town wanted to get into Fiona MacGillivray's favour. If anyone could claim to be a long-lost relative of her late husband, chances were he'd be quick enough to come forward.

"I guess I haven't helped much then, have I, sir?"

"You've helped a great deal. Reminded me not to take what witnesses assume as gospel truth for one thing."

Once he'd found the identity of the murdered man, Sterling had figured he'd be well on the way to apprehending the person or persons responsible. But that didn't seem to be happening. The man didn't have a job, not one they could find. McAllen said Stewart wasn't known to the ladies who plied their trade in the cribs of Paradise Alley, and it was unlikely any of the higher level of prostitute would come forward to voluntarily claim a relationship.

McKnight was pressing for an arrest. Any arrest. The citizens, he informed Sterling, were not happy at having a murderer on the loose. Sterling wasn't happy about it either, but he refrained from telling the inspector so. McKnight wanted to see an American arrested, remind the newcomers flooding over the border exactly who was in charge here. He stopped barely short of ordering Sterling to find a suitable American, any suitable American, to haul in front of a judge.

"I'm going to get another copy of the man's photograph made," Sterling said. "You're trotting around town after Miss Jennings, perhaps you can show the picture at the same time."

"That would be grand, sir. But do you think Miss Jennings would want me showing that picture — of a dead man — to her potential customers?"

"I'll have a word with her myself. Remind her that in the Dominion everyone is expected to co-operate with the police. Didn't she say she was planning to go to the Savoy this evening?"

"Yeah."

Sterling got to his feet. He took his hat down off the shelf.

"Uh, sir." Angus shifted in his seat. The boy looked most uncomfortable.

"Angus?"

"Do you think the Savoy's the best place to ... to uh ... go in search of Miss Jennings?"

"Why not? If she's there."

"My mother's there also."

"So I would expect."

"Sir, Miss Jennings is a nice lady and all. But ... but ..."

"Spit it out, son. Is there a problem with Miss Jennings?"

Angus jumped to his feet. "No, sir. It's just ... I thought you and my mother ... someday." He fled. The outer door slammed shut behind him.

Sterling let out a long sigh. He could guess what Angus was thinking. He didn't want to hurt the boy. But some things couldn't be helped.

He set off for the Savoy. Any opportunity to be in the company of the charming and pretty Eleanor Jennings.

*   *   *

I studied the contents of my wardrobe. Pathetic. A handful of day dresses that would never do for evening. The impractical white muslin was clean and pressed, buttons replaced, shoved to the very back. I wasn't yet ready to wear it again.

The red silk gown I was tired of already, I'd worn it so often. I took out a green skirt and blouse ensemble and studied it. The bodice was rather nice, although a mite loose as I'd lost weight over the long winter of near starvation. It had an abundance of sequins and the shoulders were trimmed with ribbon in a darker shade of green. I'd recently been told I should never wear green as it didn't suit me. Tonight, it would have to do.

Tomorrow, I would go in search of a dressmaker and order a new gown. Blue would be nice. I didn't own much that was blue. Other people, Miss Jennings for example, might think it suitable to wear practical garb at all hours of the day or night. I did not. Having to manage without a lady's maid since leaving Toronto, I'd had to reduce my standards somewhat and make some adjustments to my wardrobe. No hooks down the back, minimal number of buttons on the sleeves.

Grumbling to myself I began to dress for the evening.

I arrived at the Savoy in high dudgeon. I had politely stepped to the side of the boardwalk to allow an older woman to pass, and one of Joey LeBlanc's wretched whores had "accidently" shoved me off. Directly into a puddle that contained, I feared, more than good Yukon mud. There had been, as I recalled, a dead dog lying in that section of the street this morning. My boot was caked in muck, the hem of my dress filthy, and I sensed a somewhat acrid odour following me as I continued on my journey.

I was late and the musicians were coming outside as I arrived. They, except for the piano player for obvious reasons, carried their instruments. The banjo player strummed an opening cord, and the trumpeter bellowed into his trumpet. The caller cleared his throat. Men stopped their restless wandering to watch.

I plastered a radiant smile onto my face and sailed through the doors. No matter what sort of foul mood I might be in, the sight of my place — my own empire — never failed to lift my heart. The saloon was packed and Ray and his men were fully occupied pouring drinks and weighing gold dust. Patrons streamed through the doors into the back, heading for the dance hall. A good many of them wouldn't manage to make it all the way and would end up spending the evening in the gambling room, dropping money into our coffers.

Eleanor Jennings had arrived before me. She stood against the wall beside the water barrel, surrounded by men. The musicians finished and strode back into the building, heading for their places at the side of the stage. They would play a brief song to warm up the audience. The audience, many of whom came every night, didn't need warming up, but I thought we needed some sort of an introduction to the evening's festivities.

"There you are, Fiona," Miss Jennings said, catching sight of me and breaking away from her circle of admirers. "May I call you Fiona?"

I considered saying no, but decided there was no need to antagonize the woman. These North Americans could be scandalously informal at times.

As was her dress. Anyone might take her for a percentage girl were it not for the way her eyes were always moving, showing an interest in everything around her. For a moment I found myself almost liking her, thinking perhaps we could be friends.

I remembered Angus telling me Richard Sterling was paying attention to her. Not that I minded in any way if Corporal Sterling found a lady attractive. Absolutely none of my business. It lessened my regard for Miss Jennings to discover that she, like all the others, was only in Dawson to find a man to marry.

That was it. We could not be friends if I did not respect her.

I smiled at the lady. "My son tells me he had a most enjoyable day being your assistant."

"Angus is a remarkable young man. Intelligent, capable, and also kind. You must be very proud."

Perhaps we could be friends after all.

"I'm here to ask a favour of you, Fiona. But first, I thought you'd like to see the photographs I took."

She carried a large flat leather case. The assembled men pressed forward to get a better look. Eleanor pulled two sheets of stiff paper out of the bag. I found myself leaning closer also.

The photograph was a mite dark, but still excellent. Irene looked enticing, and the contrast with the innocent-looking young Colleen was striking. The other dancers almost faded into the background, yet they were still there, functioning as accessories, props. A little something for those who weren't lucky enough to get a turn on the dance floor with the main attraction.

"This is absolutely splendid!" I said, not even trying to hide my enthusiasm. "It will make a perfect advertisement. Ray! Ray, do come and have a look at this." The men sifted aside to create a narrow corridor so Ray could squeeze through. Count Nicky, in his immaculate suit, clinging to his glass of whisky, managed to follow before the gap again snapped closed.

"That is good," my partner said. "Irene looks …" He was simply lost for words. Not that Ray ever had many to spare in any event.

"You took another picture?" I asked.

She showed it to me, saying, "Not quite as good, I fear."

It was an adequate portrait, but nothing as special as the first. "May I keep these?" I asked.

She nodded. "If you approve, I'll print a few more, which you can hang in various places around town. I'll charge my regular fee. The negatives belong to me."

I didn't know what negatives were, but they didn't sound worth much. "The girls will be very pleased. You might get some further business out of this, Miss Jennings."

"Please, call me Eleanor."

"Eleanor."

She looked at the crowd of men, straining to get a glimpse of the photograph. "I'll be available in the mornings for private appointments. Should any of you gentlemen wish a portrait to send to your loved ones, you will find my rates very reasonable."

More than one of the onlookers told his friend he was thinking of doing so.

"Bar's still open," Ray reminded the audience. "Sounds like the show's starting."

The men began to drift away. Empty glasses needed filling and seats awaited them in the dance hall, from where came a roar of laughter. I hoped the audience was laughing at the antics of Roland the Magnificent, not because some drunk had cracked his head open trying to mount the stage. Count Nicky bowed stiffly to us and made his way to the gambling tables.

"I'll develop the pictures tomorrow," Eleanor said to me. "They'll be ready for someone to pick up on Sunday."

I shook my head. "Monday. No one will risk a fine or worse by going to your place of business on Sunday."

She lifted one eyebrow. "The law's that strict?"

"Most certainly."

"This really is a foreign country."

"You said you need a favour?" The majority of our audience had departed leaving us with some semblance of privacy.

"I'd like to meet Inspector McKnight. I understand he comes here some evenings to watch the show."

"He does. Why do you want to meet him?"

"I've a mind to photograph the fort and the men. I suspect I need official permission."

I lifted my hand and snapped my fingers. Joe Hamilton hustled over.

"Ma'am?"

"Is Inspector McKnight in the audience tonight, Joe?"

"Yes, ma'am, he is. Front row centre, like usual."

"Thank you." Joe beamed at me with the usual scent of rotting meat emitting from his mouth before heading back to his duties.

"The show will go on until midnight," I said to Eleanor. "The inspector doesn't usually stay until the end, but he might on occasion. I'll alert you to him when he leaves, but I won't interrupt the show. You're welcome to find a seat yourself, although the company might be a bit too close for comfort." Some of the men, I didn't need to say, did not always conform to strict standards of hygiene. I'd sometimes been unfortunate enough to observe fleas leaping from one unwashed head to another.

"Do you wager, Miss Jennings?" I turned quickly. A man had come up behind me and I hadn't heard him. I don't like to be caught unawares.

"No," she said. "My mother's brother made his living as a poker player. Perhaps I should say he attempted to make his living. Thus I know better than to take part in a game of chance. But I enjoy watching a good game of cards."

"I'm here for a game myself, and heard you ladies talking. If you're wanting someplace to spend a while, why not join me? You can give me some luck. John Turner's the name."

This gentleman didn't look any too sanitary himself. He obviously spent some of his time around horses. It was the man who'd almost gotten into a fight with Richard Sterling the night previous.

He grinned at Eleanor and then turned to me. His gaze was open, appraising, bordering on insolent. "Mrs. MacGillivray." He held out his hand. The cuticles were torn, yellow nails broken, dirt trapped in the folds and crevices. I did not accept it, and he shrugged. He might have been good-looking, if he cut his hair and cleaned himself up. And let some warmth into his eyes.

"I hope we won't have any more trouble tonight," I said.

"Trouble? I don't cause trouble. Don't turn away from it, though." His eyes were very dark. He stared into my face without blinking. I found myself breaking the glance.

"Don't care to have the Yellow Stripes looking over my shoulder." A grin played at the edges of Turner's mouth. His lips were plump, moist, and pink. He knew he was making me uncomfortable. He liked making me uncomfortable.

"Plenty of other gambling halls," I said.

"True. But this place isn't worse than any of the others in town. They're all infested." I assumed he wasn't referring to fleas.

Silence hung between us for a moment. I was very cold all of a sudden, as if someone had opened the door to find winter had unexpectedly arrived. Then Turner turned his attention back to Eleanor. "I hear tell you're a photographer. Might want to have my picture taken some day."

"I'm taking appointments."

"Good. Now, let's go play poker. You I'll let look over my shoulder."

They walked away without excusing themselves. I gave my head a mental shake. Plenty of unpleasant men in this town; no need to let one spook me.

I'd looked away when he was being insolent. I'd shown weakness. That, well I knew, was a mistake.

Chapter Fifteen

The orange and yellow glow of the world's greatest city filled the sky as I approached. I'd walked for two days and nights.

I was thirteen years old. I'd been living with a family of Travellers for the past two years, since the murder of my parents. The family patriarch, who protected me as a source of income, had died and his son demanded I move into his tent, using the end of his fist as incentive. It was, I decided, time to take my leave.

I owned a beautiful hand-embroidered lace handkerchief, the shoes on my feet, the dress I was wearing, and the knife stuck through my belt, hidden by the folds of the dress.

Not much with which to begin a new life in London.

I had two things to my advantage: I spoke extremely well, having been educated in the big house alongside Euila, the only daughter among the earl's twelve children, on the estate where my father was gamekeeper. And I had inherited my mother's startling beauty.

Fortunately the weather had turned warm for November and the rain stayed away. I ate nothing but windfall apples for two days and drank from slow-moving streams while uninterested sheep observed me. I spent the first night in a churchyard, curled up on a patch of soft grass beside a large tombstone.

I have never feared the dead — it was the living I had to be on my guard against.

I walked into the city with a sense of awe. The din was so loud I wondered that anyone could hear themselves think. People shouted and laughed and hurled abuse, horses' hooves pounded on cobblestones, tack jangled, wagon wheels clattered, merchants shouted out the attractions of their wares and begged potential customers to come closer and sample. No one paid any attention to one wide-eyed country girl. Intent on their own business, they pushed around me as though I were a boulder in their stream. Men tapped canes or walking sticks impatiently on the sidewalks and women kept their noses in the air.

I'd been raised on the Island of Skye, walking the barren hills alongside my father. The Travellers always pitched their tents far from cities where they were not welcome except to work. I'd been to Oxford, where I'd stood on a street corner begging for pennies with my cut-glass accent, working dress (one of Euila's mother's cast-offs), and the tragic story of my penniless, abandoned, invalid (although well-bred) mother. But we always returned to the Traveller's camp outside the city at night.

I had made a great deal of money begging for my gypsy family, and my plan was to support myself by doing much the same in London. I did not happen to be wearing the good dress when I fled, but I still had the accent, the looks, and could relate the sad story. I also had the knife stuck through my belt, and knew well how to use it.

I set myself up on a corner in a street of neat homes surrounding a lovely park, stark in the November afternoon. Nannies came and went, pushing baby carriages or leading children in sailor suits and stiffly starched pinafores. Carriages pulled by exquisitely groomed horses rattled down the road. Ladies and the occasional gentleman regarded me with disdain. Servants hurried by intent on their business.

The only person who approached me was a policeman. He was tall, imposing, and scowling. He lifted his fist and shouted, "Be off with you, you little wretch. Don't let me catch you hanging about here again."

I fled.

My first night in London was spent in the alley behind a pub, curled into a dark corner. The place stank. All night men staggered down the alley, often stopping to relieve themselves into the dirt a few feet from where I huddled. I fingered the blade of my knife, and knew I couldn't survive alone. I also knew that my hair, face, and hands were getting so dirty it wouldn't be long before no one would be impressed by my looks.

I did not cry. I have not cried since the day my parents died.

The second day I had eaten the last of the apples, and the water in the city gutters didn't look fit for a beast to drink. I found myself in a rabbit-warren of buildings, crowded, dirty, reeking. It was, I later found out, Seven Dials, one of London's worst slums.

"Hoi, there. What you doin'?" a voice said.

I looked down. A girl, younger than me, very small, little more than yellowing skin stretched over a bag of bones. She sat on the pavement outside a three-storey brick building that advertised itself as a livery stable. Her face was thick with grime, her nose ran, and her left eye was weeping.

"I am taking a look around," I replied. Her eyebrows lifted when I spoke.

"You're not from 'ere?" At least that's what I thought she said. Her accent was exceedingly thick and not familiar to me.

"I'm new to town."

"Get off my patch."

"Your patch?"

"This is my corner, and I don't need you scaring the punters away. Mr. Jones'll tan my hide if I have another bad day."

"Sorry," I said. I knew all about one's corner. We Travellers were careful about not setting ourselves up to beg or sell trinkets anywhere near a spot which another gypsy had claimed.

I began to walk away. Then I turned back, desperate perhaps for a bit of human contact. "My name's Fiona. I'm from Scotland."

The girl studied me. "Maise. I'm from down the street. What's Scotland like?"

"Beautiful. Cold. Wet."

"Sounds like London. Except London ain't ever beautiful. You talk like a lady, but you don't look like one."

"I have fallen upon difficult times."

"Where's your mum and da?"

"Dead."

Maise nodded. "Mine too. Least ways my mum is. Don't know about my da." She struggled to her feet. One leg was badly twisted making her lean considerably to one side. She used a crooked length of wood to pull herself upright. "I like you, Fiona. Will you be my friend?"

A friend. I had only ever had one friend. Euila. I wondered what Euila was doing now. Did she think about me? Did she wonder what had happened to me? Where I'd gone? Had her brother Alistair been made to pay for the death of my parents?

The answer to that last question was obvious. *Of course not.* He was the earl's son.

"I'm not making any money. Mr. Jones said he'll throw me out soon. I ain't worth nothing to him. Maybe if I bring you to him, he'll be happy with me. Do you want to meet Mr. Jones, Fiona?"

I did not. However, I realized I had little choice. I could wander the crooked streets of London until I starved, wrapped in my independence and pride. Or I could meet Mr. Jones. I felt my knife, secure in the depths of my clothing and said, "I'd like that, Maise."

We didn't have far to go. Maise couldn't have walked far at any rate. She leaned heavily on her stick and alternately hobbled and hopped down the street. We turned into an alley. It was full daylight, and somewhere above the smoke of the city the sun was shining, but the alley was so dim it might have been the onset of a storm. The air smelled of piss and vomit and rotting meat. A naked black tail slithered between crumbling bricks at our approach, and I shuddered. We rounded the building, and Maise opened the back door. I peered into the gloom. A set of stairs led sharply upward. I smelled old cooking and fresh urine and a sharp acrid odour I could not identify.

I hesitated. The stairs disappeared into darkness.

"It'll be all right, Fiona." Maise said. "Mr. Jones isn't a bad man. And it's too early for him to have been drinking yet."

I decided to trust her. If I did not care for this Mr. Jones I could simply leave.

We climbed three flights of stairs, Maise labouring to move slowly and painfully.

In later years I had occasion to read the works of Mr. Charles Dickens. Although *Oliver Twist* was written many years before my time with Mr. Jones, that man might well have served as the inspiration for the character of Fagan.

Mr. Jones ran a pack of children. Beggars and thieves. The children went out begging. They handed their pathetic earnings over to Mr. Jones at the end of the day. In turn, he fed them and let them sleep in one of his flea-infested blankets on the floor of the building I now entered. In some nod to propriety, the boys and girls had separate rooms.

The first two floors of the building served as a brothel, also owned by Mr. Jones.

When the girls reached a suitable age, if they were unmarked and moderately pretty, they were cleaned up, given an unpatched dress, and sent downstairs to work in the brothel. The boys were kicked back out into the streets from whence they had come. I never did decide which group had it better. In the second year of my residence, Mr. Jones took delight in telling us that Tommy, a lad who'd recently left us, was going to be hanged for killing a boy in a scrap over some spilled coins. If public hangings hadn't recently been banned, I am sure Mr. Jones would have taken us on an outing to watch the event. Instead he tut-tutted and said, "Let that be a lesson to you, boys and girls, of what happens without my tutorialage."

He liked to use big words, and usually employed them incorrectly. After the first blow to the side of my head, I never again corrected him.

But I'm getting ahead of my story. On the day I met Maise, Mr. Jones was seated in the main room, which he used as an office of sorts and where the children ate. He sat at a table, scarred and pitted (the table as well as Mr. Jones's face), counting coins and sorting them into piles.

He had heard Maise's stick on the stairs and was staring at the door, his face a mask of fury when we entered. "What the hell are you doing, you stupid cripple, come here at this time of day?"

"I ..." the girl's voice broke. "I brought you someone, Mr. Jones. This girl. She needs work. I thought ..."

"I've enough bloody girls," he growled. He got to his feet. Maise cowered against the door.

I stepped forward, and the weak light that penetrated the grime of the window fell on my face. "I am Fiona MacGillivray, and I am pleased to make your acquaintance, sir."

His jaw dropped open.

"I have recently arrived in London and am looking for accommodation and employment." I had learned to speak properly from Euila's governess, the formidable Miss Wheatley. Miss Wheatley was a member of the minor aristocracy, forced to earn her own living when her father drank and gambled (so Euila whispered to me) the family's money away prior to taking the coward's way out and putting a bullet into his brain. Miss Wheatley could be counted on to order me to hold out my hand for a beating should I let slip with a "wee" or "ye ken" or speak in any way like my parents. The Travellers recognized that my accent had as much worth as a sack of gold, and punishment would be dealt out should I forget myself. I had become accustomed to using my accent as a weapon. It could be relied on to have men like Mr. Jones giving me respect I did not deserve any more than poor crippled Maise did.

He walked up to me. I was aware of Maise holding her breath. Mr. Jones smelled of clothes that were rarely washed and cheap gin drunk too often. He studied my face for a long time. I did not blink.

"Untie your hair."

I lifted my arms and pulled out the red ribbon. Long, thick black tresses fell around my shoulders and down my back. I ran my fingers through it. My hair was dirty, as was I. But I was a good bit cleaner than anyone else in this room. Or on the street outside.

"You'll get an extra slice of meat tonight, Maise," he said. "Now, get back to your corner."

"I would like her to stay," I said. I liked Maise, but I wasn't about to protect her. However, I had to establish my place here and now. Let Mr. Jones know I was not going to cower against the wall, as grateful for an extra piece of meat as a starving dog. "I need her to show me around. To help me settle in."

Maise sucked in a breath. For a moment I thought Mr. Jones would strike me. If he had, I would have had my knife in hand and be backing out the door before the blow landed. Instead he threw back his head and laughed. His teeth were surprisingly good. "You've a mouth on you, girl. I like that. Come on in, sit yourself down. Maise, you can stay. For a while."

He took the room's only chair. The carpet was stained and worn almost through. I gathered my skirts around me and lowered myself to the floor. I kept a distance from Mr. Jones's foot and my eyes on his face.

He grinned. He knew I did not trust him.

He liked that. He lifted a stick off his desk and rapped the floor three times. Then he settled back in his chair and said, "What brings you here, Fiona?"

"I propose a business relationship," I said, trying to sound as though it really didn't matter much one way or another what happened. Inside, my heart was pounding; my palms were damp with sweat. I kept my breathing level, focused my eyes on his face, and struggled not to wipe my hands on my dress.

Heavy footsteps on the stairs, the door opened, and a woman entered. Substantially overweight with small black eyes that peered malevolently at the world from within a face the colour and texture of pudding. Her chins wobbled, and breasts the size of melons drooped toward the floor. She was barefooted, with toenails like yellow claws, but her dress was surprisingly fashionable and well-fitting, and delicate gold hoops were in her ears. She looked at Maise as if she were something found underfoot, at Mr. Jones with downcast eyes, and at me with instant hostility.

"Mrs. Hancock," Jones said, "bring some bread and dripping for my fledgling guest."

The woman's expression changed. From antagonism to curiosity.

"And be quick about it," he said.

She growled something incomprehensible in response and went back to her lair. The stairs shook at her tread.

"Thank you, sir," I said. "A small luncheon would be acceptable."

"I bet it would," he replied. "So, while we're waiting for your *luncheon*, tell me what you can do for me, girl."

I rose to my feet. I folded my hands neatly in front of me, and cast my eyes downward. "Good sir," I said, "I wonder if I might ask you to be so kind as to grant me a small favour. My mother has taken ill. Hers is a sad story that I will not weary you with, but I'm afraid I've been robbed of the coins she gave me to buy her medicine. I dare not return home to disappoint her. I need only a few shillings."

He gaped at me. Then he burst out laughing. "You are good. I almost reached into my pocket myself. But, my sweet young thing, you won't be able to use that story in Seven Dials."

"There are better places, I am sure. With a young man to watch my back and a nice clean dress ..."

"It might well work. And work well. Okay, my girl, we'll give you a try."

Footsteps on the stairs once again. Mrs. Hancock lumbered in, bearing a plate on which sat the heel of a loaf of bread and a spoonful of greasy dripping. Mr. Jones nodded and she put the food on the table. "Help yourself," he said to me.

I refrained from leaping forward and stuffing my mouth as fast as possible. "Maise," I said, "would you care to join me?"

"I'm not feeding that runt in the middle of the day," Mrs. Hancock yelped.

"Be quiet," Jones said. "Let Maise eat." The girl crept forward. When she realized this was no trick and no one would leap out and smack her, she ripped off a hunk of bread, swiped it through the dripping, and retreated as fast as her twisted leg could move to her corner. I took the plate and settled back on the floor, the food on my lap. I ate. It was dreadful, even the Travellers ate better than this. But it was food and I needed it.

"Find a dress for the girl," Jones said.

"Why?"

"Never you mind why. A neat dress, clean. Decent. One of the whores must have something she can wear, even if you have to alter it a mite."

Mrs. Hancock studied me. My skin pricked under her unblinking black eyes. I looked into her face and did not look away first.

"I'll see what I can do," she said.

"Thank you for the meal. It was delicious."

Jones laughed.

I lived in the small room above the brothel in Seven Dials for two years. Mrs. Hancock might be a miserable old bag and a whore mistress, but she was a good seamstress. She altered a dress to fit me and used the extra fabric to make it decent and even pretty. The original owner of the dress complained loudly, and slaps and cries drifted up the staircase.

I wore that dress standing on street corners, looking quite lost and somewhat confused and frightened. I sniffed into my embroidered handkerchief and told my sad story, altered when I considered it appropriate, and a good number of men and women pressed money into my hand with kind words for my poor abandoned mother.

Mr. Jones was highly pleased with me and I rose in rank through the levels of his band of street urchins. With improved status came more and better food and I was awarded an extra blanket after one particularly successful day. I did what I could to share with Maise, who as she grew older became less pathetic and less able to earn her income begging.

They were a rough bunch of children, living on their wits and what speed they had to get out of the way of Mr. Jones's fist. When he swung out at one child, sometimes for no reason, he didn't much care if the primary object ducked and another one took the blow. I watched the boys dodging Mr. Jones and fighting amongst themselves. On several occasions a neighbouring gang pounced on us. Jones's boys could defend themselves with their feet and fists, and I found myself imitating them and sometimes even joining in the battle. I learned to fight like a boy on the streets of Seven Dials.

I kept my knife close, under my clothes, at all times. I slept with Maise, on a thin blanket under the window where we caught the cold winter winds and the damp mist. I know she saw the knife, but she never said anything to me, and I did not talk about it. One of the boys, a nice young lad named Alfie with warm brown eyes and a bad stutter, was badly beaten by the biggest of the boys, the one named Nigel who Mr. Jones used to keep the children in line when they were outside the house. I could have helped Alfie, I could have pulled out the knife and defended him. But I did not. If I revealed it, they'd take it away. I would use it to save my life, nothing less.

I practised sometimes, when I could snatch a bit of privacy in a dark alley. Using the knife the way the gypsy boy had taught me. Keeping myself, and the weapon, sharp and ready.

It was, truth be told, a miserable life. Mr. Jones and Nigel kept the children in line with kicks and punches and, worst of all, withholding of food. Each child was expected to earn a certain amount per day, and if they were short, then they would not eat. There was no reward for earning extra, but Mr. Jones might (just might) not punish the culprit too severely if they were short the following day. The boys were expected to supplement their income by picking pockets. If they were caught — well, you could be sure Mr. Jones wouldn't be rushing to their defence. They were usually never seen again. Lessons in the art of picking a man's pocket or relieving a lady of her reticule were given in the upstairs room. I earned enough money by begging that I didn't need to be a thief. But I was eager to learn, nonetheless, and eventually I could snatch a few coins out of even Mr. Jones's pockets.

I was quickly earning more than most of the other girls combined. That did not make me friends. The girls, numbering between six and nine in the time I lived there, were jealous and hostile. I might have helped them out, on occasion, if they had shown the slightest kindness. But they did not, and so I left them to their own devices. I began to accumulate a few nice things from the "ladies" downstairs. Hair combs, ribbons, cast-off dresses and undergarments, a small amount of rouge. Not because they had gifts to spare, most certainly not, but because Mr. Jones realized that the better I dressed, the more believable my story and the better the money I was able to earn. The other upstairs girls were madly jealous. They excluded me from their circle, they snatched food off my plate, they tripped me and snuck in the occasional surprise blow to my stomach or kidneys. But they knew better to take any of my things or do anything that might mark my face. That Mr. Jones would not tolerate.

I tried, when I could, to keep Maise close. The girls resented her for bringing me in. Her they could harm. And she had little capacity to defend herself.

Mr. Jones allowed absolutely no familiarity between the boys and the girls. He probably could have made a nice income from a pregnant begging girl, but he had a strange concept of morality. Couldn't have any romantic relationships between the unmarried children under his care. He ran a whorehouse, but that was business.

A few times, I thought of leaving Mr. Jones, his hard fist, his cold drafty rooms, his cruel band of children. But where else could I go? I was still a child myself and there were worse masters than Mr. Jones.

I did, however, provide for my own future. And for Maise, who I'd decided to take with me when the time came. I found a wallet in an alley behind the pub one day, when I'd not been in London long. It was empty, of course. But it was good tough

leather and waterproof. The wall behind the farriers where I'd
first met Maise had a loose brick. I dug the brick out and created
a space behind, put my wallet inside, and replaced the brick.
Most days, I'd slip a few small coins into my knife pouch while I
worked. On a couple of memorable occasions, even a pound and
once a half-crown. A boy, Nigel usually, had the job of watching
over me. It was easy enough to do a slight-of-hand and keep him
from seeing how much money I was actually being given. I had a
secondary hiding place underneath a loose floorboard in the girls'
room. I knew better than to keep all of my money in one spot.

My friends, such as they were, were the unfortunate women
who lived and worked downstairs. The whores. Mr. Jones and
Mrs. Hancock ran a brothel that catered to men with money
and exceptionally low standards. I was, despite witnessing the
murder of my parents and begging on the streets, somewhat of
an innocent when I arrived. That didn't last long.

The women who lived and worked on the bottom floors
were a sad bunch. Beaten down by life, they took me under their
wing. I suspect now they liked my innocence, such as it still was,
and my looks provided a bit of beauty in their sad lives. I was
almost a plaything to them. They would pinch my cheeks and
comb my hair and paint my face so I looked like a baby whore.
Each girl had a small room of her own where she slept and enter-
tained clients. At least they had real beds with sheets and didn't
have to sleep on the floor with only a discarded blanket for cover.

A large parlour, gaudily decorated in wallpaper of royal blue
and gold, had lamps with fringed shades, a piano, well-uphol-
stered chairs and sofas, and a beautiful clean carpet. Framed
paintings of pastoral country scenes hung on the walls. Glasses
and fine china were kept in the sideboard and there was a handsome wooden table on which to prepare drinks. The women
didn't eat any better than we did upstairs, but cheeses and bread

and cakes were kept under lock and key in case the customers desired a snack to recover from their exertions.

As time passed, I began to notice a plethora of bruises and black eyes on the whores. Fine one day, they would be walking stiffly and with obvious pain the next. One of the younger girls, fifteen-year-old Alice who'd recently come down from the girls' room upstairs, appeared one afternoon with a savage welt across her cheek, running from the corner of her eye down though her lips. She looked as if she'd been struck by a whip. The welt healed badly, leaving an ugly scar. Alice grew bitter as her worth declined. One day she was simply gone, and I was told she'd been kicked out.

A woman by the name of Annie took me under her wing. She was older than the rest — probably in her thirties — but the years weighed her down. Alice taught me a few things about dealing with men. Like how to recognize trouble in time to get out of the way. How to knee them in the crotch or to drive a foot into their knee and execute a grab-and-choke hold. From Annie, I learned to fight like a woman.

When business was slow at the brothel, the girls would be sent out into the streets, to ply their trade in the pubs and back alleys of Seven Dials. I shuddered, thinking of the rain-slicked streets and the piles of garbage. Annie said she didn't mind. Rather a rough-spoken working man who fancied a quick tumble and would pay for the privilege than the toffs who descended into Seven Dials with their posh accents and fancy clothes and money to do things that would cause their well-bred wives to recoil in horror.

Carriages ratted over loose and broken cobblestones and dragged through the filth to reach our front door. Well-dressed men, with diamond stick pins, gold watches, emerald cufflinks, starched shirt collars, and accents as good as mine, would disembark and head inside. Some bold and brazen, some clinging to the shadows, some tittering with embarrassment.

I had been in residence for about six months when I developed a bad cough. As a child raised walking the hills of Skye, and later living with Travellers as they moved about the countryside, the air in London came as a shock to my poor lungs. I stood on street corners, hacking and spitting phlegm into my lovely handkerchief and took in even more money than when I was well. I couldn't sleep, however, and was often up, just looking out the window at the activity on the streets below and trying to remember the colour of heather on the hills, the sound my father made when he laughed, the way my mother's fingers moved when she sewed.

It was getting on toward morning, and a weak sun was trying to break through the smoke and gloom of the city. For a brief moment all was quiet, the night over, the day not yet begun.

Below me, a man came out the front door. His carriage was waiting — an impressive thing with a shiny gold crest on the doors, pulled by high-stepping black horses. He carried a sturdy walking stick, and was dressed in formal evening wear. His face was hidden by his hat as he turned and pulled out his billfold. He counted money and slapped it into Mrs. Harrison's waiting palm. She said, "Do not come here again, sir," and he replied, "Have no fear of that. You've a cheap quality of whore." He climbed into the carriage, the driver whipped the horses, and they were off. A few minutes later, the front door opened again.

At first I thought Mrs. Harrison and Mr. Jones were discarding a soiled carpet. They carried a weight between them, him at one end, her at the other. They crossed the street and tossed their burden into the gutter. It rolled up against the wall and I could see it was no carpet. It was a woman.

I slipped downstairs and out the back. I crept around the house, where a few lights were still on and women laughed fake laughs and someone played, badly, the untuned piano. I crossed the street. It had rained. Mud was thick in the streets, and the gutters ran with rainwater and filth. I knelt down and touched the woman. She groaned and one eye opened.

Annie. She had failed to protect herself.

I gasped and fell back. Her face was a mass of blood and torn skin. Blood stained the bottom of her dress so thickly it might have been a crimson gown, and her right arm was twisted into an unnatural angle. She opened her mouth and spat blood through a mouthful of broken teeth.

She looked at me. I believe she knew I was with her.

More blood gushed from her mouth, and she lay still. I knew she was dead.

I went back inside, climbed the stairs, passed over sleeping girls, settled by the snoring Maise, and tried to get some rest. In the morning the body was gone. Only a patch of drying blood marked the spot where Annie had lain. I wondered, for a short while, why Mr. Jones had dared discard the dying woman outside his door. Then I realized that no one would much care. Another dead whore found in the morning. If the police did come knocking, and that in itself would be a shock, he would simply deny the woman worked for him. Certainly he wouldn't identify her killer, and none of the other whores would dare to step forward.

Bad for business, I'd expect.

I had been with them for two years and my fifteenth birthday had passed unremarked. I returned late one evening from my begging job. I'd handed Nigel a coin and suggested he stop at the pub on the way home. Too stupid and greedy to question why I'd give him anything, he took the money quickly enough. I went to my hiding place behind the farriers and secured the excess of my day's earnings. I hadn't taken a penny out in two years and the sum was accumulating nicely. Whenever I got the opportunity to be alone, I moved money from beneath the loose floorboards to this spot, recognizing the possibility of Mr. Jones or one of the other children uncovering my hiding place.

I wore a cast-off dress of green satin with clean lace around the collar and cuffs and stiffly starched petticoats. A matching ribbon held back my hair and small cheap earrings were in my ears. I had been given a belt to match the dress, but had left it behind because it would be difficult to wear with the knife belt beneath. My looks were important to my earning potential, so I was kept supplied with soap for washing and even given a brush for my hair and one with which to clean my teeth. Unparalleled favours. The other children stayed dirty and if their faces broke into spots and their teeth were stained and darkened and their eyes wept with infection, it would only make them look more deserving of charity.

No wonder the rest of the begging girls hated me.

A man was stepping out of a hired cab when I arrived at the house. His eyebrows lifted at the sight of me. I nodded politely and went around the building, to the back entrance. I felt his eyes following me. It was the end of a warm sunny day, a treat in London in mid-November, but I shivered.

We ate our supper, sausages tonight, which was an indulgence, prior to the other children being sent back out for the evening trade. I didn't work at night. According to my story, I did not have the sort of mother who would allow me to walk alone on the streets after dark.

I had managed to gain possession of a couple of books. About a month previous, an elderly man walked past the corner on which I stood looking sad and frightened. He'd asked if I were lost, and when I repeated my story of the theft of my mother's money, he'd shaken his head regretfully.

"I've not a penny on me, my dear. So I can do little to help your mother. But books are of value beyond compare." He thrust a battered satchel into my arms. "I'm sure your mother would enjoy listening to you read to her when she is unwell." He walked away. I opened the bag. Mr. Currer Bell and Miss Jane Austin were among the treasures within.

Nigel had wanted to take the books to the rag-and-bone man, but I'd held them close and refused to give them up. He didn't dare strike me: he knew by now I'd fight back.

It was difficult, sometimes impossible, to read in the light of the single poor candle Mr. Jones allowed to be lit in the upstairs rooms. But read I did when I could and for a while at least I was taken beyond the confines of Seven Dials, back to the hedgerows and sunny fields of England.

Mr. Jones mounted the stairs. I looked up from the depth of the book and got to my feet.

"I've a job for you," he said.

"Yes?"

"Downstairs. There's a man wants to meet you. Be nice to him and I'll give you an extra shilling to buy whatever you like."

I put the book down, and rose to my feet. "No."

"No? You can't say no. Go and brush your hair. Put on the dress you wore this afternoon."

I held my back straight, my arms loose at my sides. I felt the weight of my knife belt around my waist. "I am not a whore."

"I didn't say nothing about whoring."

"I know the man you mean and I can guess what he wants. I will not go downstairs and I will not let him touch me."

"Two shillings then."

"No."

We faced each other. I stared into his face and did not blink or turn away. That would be to show a weakness. I kept my voice calm. I judged the distance to the door. Mr. Jones was used to smacking around disobedient children. I should be able to knock him aside and get out before he gathered his wits enough to react.

"I can get a lot for you, you know. It's almost time you start working for Mrs. Hancock anyway. You're a virgin, I'll bet. You do a good job and I'll split some of the proceeds with you. Don't tell the others or Mrs. Hancock. Don't want them thinking I've gone soft." He tried to laugh.

"I will not whore for you. Now or at any time. Do you understand?"

He lifted his fist and took a step toward me. I didn't move. "Strike me and I'll never work for you again. Not in any capacity. I said, do you understand?"

He stopped. I don't know what might have happened had Mrs. Hancock or the other children been watching. He probably would have beaten me and dragged me downstairs to be raped by the waiting man. He would have tried at any rate.

But no one was watching. I saw the moment the fight left his face. "You're a tough one, Fiona. I'll give you that."

"I've been meaning to discuss business with you. This seems like an appropriate time. I'm earning a good deal more money for you than you're spending on us. I think meat for supper an extra two times a week. Good meat, too. Enough for everyone. You can afford it."

He stared at me, speechless.

"I'd like you to find another job for Maise. It's not doing her any good sitting out in the cold and rain."

"Maise ..."

"Time for a more equal partnership," I said, full of fifteen-year-old bravado.

He burst out laughing. "I never heard such a thing."

I picked up my copy of *Jane Eyre*. I would be like Jane. Strong and confident. "One more thing. It's time for new bedding. You can start with providing for Maise and me and then the other children. Pillows would be nice. Soft feather pillows."

"Take care you don't go too far, Miss Fiona. You've airs above your station and a mouth on you I don't like. I'm not buying pillows for the likes of Maise. She's lucky to have a roof over her head. She'd starve without me. All of them would."

"You'd starve without them out on the streets every day."

"You can't keep begging forever. You're growing up." He ran his eyes down my body. It was beginning to change, becoming softer, rounder. I was taller than him now. Taller than most of the other children, even the boys.

"When the time comes I am not making money, I will reconsider my options. But be advised, Mr. Jones. I will not be whoring." I resumed my seat and opened the book. I pretended to read. I flipped a page. He stood against the wall, watching me. And then he left.

The months crawled past. Winter turned to spring. Children came and went. The downstairs business continued to be busy. I was still making money, but I knew the time was coming when things would have to change. I couldn't stand in the same places more than once. Not telling the same story about the sick mother. Men were beginning to approach me. And not in a way I wanted. More than a few men said they'd give me money. After I took them back to my rooms. Maise fell ill, and I could hear her throughout the night, coughing. She got progressively weaker and soon her stick was barely adequate to enable her to limp around. Mr. Jones did allow her to move to a better spot for begging. A nice corner under the eaves of a not-too-disrespectable pub. She made less money there (not that she made much in her old patch). I knew Mr. Jones would have thrown her out, was I not watching out for her.

Things came to a head in May. I was heading for the house after an unsuccessful day. I was getting too old for this. My child-like innocence and sweet charm were long gone and with my recent height increase and the maturing of my body, I couldn't even pretend any longer. I was too often being mistaken for a prostitute rather than an upper-class girl down on her luck.

I walked, deep in thought. Too deep in thought. I had neglected to pay attention to my surroundings. A carriage fell into step beside me, and I paid it no mind. I turned into a quiet street. The carriage turned with me.

Who knows what might have happened had not a pub door opened abruptly, bringing me up short and making me aware of my surroundings. Three men spilled out of the pub, loud and drunk, spoiling for a fight.

The publican stood in the doorway, slapping a billy club into his meaty palm. "I'll not see the likes of you in my house again," he roared. The men scrambled all over each other to get out of his reach. They ran across the street, frightening the horses pulling the carriage. The publican noticed me and touched the brim of his cap, "Beggin' your pardon, miss. Some folks." He went back inside, with a shake of his head and a final slap of the club.

It took the driver a moment to settle his horses. Then he climbed down from his seat, and the carriage door opened. I glanced from one man to the other. The driver was large and heavily muscled. His passenger was slight and well-dressed. He might have been handsome, except for the blackness behind his eyes and the cruel twist to his plump lips.

The very man who had approached me at the brothel some months ago.

The driver held a blanket. He stepped toward me. "Come for a ride, girlie," he said.

I backed up. I felt the wall of the public house behind me. The street, normally so busy, was quiet. I heard laughter from inside the pub. The carriage driver approached me with a smile so false it turned my blood cold. His employer remained behind, staying with the carriage, watching, saying nothing.

I pressed my back up against the wall. "Please, sir," I said, my voice quavering. "I don't want to go."

"Nothing to be afraid of. Come along and you'll be nice and warm. You'll like that, won't you, dearie? A bit of supper too."

"No. Go away. Please."

He leapt toward me, the blanket extended. He intended to wrap it around my upper body and bundle me into the carriage. I dodged to the right; he stumbled past me still reaching for where I had been.

I spun on my left foot and extended my right leg. Brought it hard into the side of his knee. He yelled in pain and surprise and fell forward, crashing into the wall. I danced back, taking myself out of reach. He whirled around, breathing hard. The smile was gone from his face. I flexed my fingers and balanced on the balls of my feet. He came at me with a roar, still holding the blanket. Still not understanding that I was prepared to fight him.

I feigned to the right with a frightened squeal. He closed in. I slipped my hand into the folds of my dress and brought out my knife. I slashed at his arm, tearing the sleeve, opening up a thin line of blood.

He stared at his arm, as if not understanding what had happened. Then he yelled, "You bitch." He threw the useless blanket to the ground. More used to street brawls than a stand-up fight, probably accustomed to hitting women who didn't fight back, he charged me. His hands were clenched into meaty fists. If he got anywhere within striking range, I didn't have a chance. I squeaked, once more, and half turned as if to run. Instead I ducked and his punch passed my face by a wide margin. I spun around and drove the knife directly into his soft belly. He fell to the ground, mouth open but making no sound. He touched his stomach and his fingers came away soaked with blood.

I took a step backward. Then another. For the first time, I dared take a look at the man standing beside the carriage. He hadn't moved, but the edges of his mouth turned up in a cruel smile.

He licked his lips. "I'll enjoy taming you."

I ran across the street and ducked into an alley that I knew opened onto a main road. I ran for a long time. People looked at me inquisitively; one or two men began to ask if I was in need of assistance. I kept running.

Gradually my panic began to ebb. I slowed to a walk. I kept looking over my shoulder. No one was after me.

Now.

But he would be back. I had absolutely no doubt about that.

I dared not return to the rooms above the brothel to collect what few possessions I owned. Almost certainly Mr. Jones had sold me to the man. He wouldn't be happy to hear he wasn't going to get his money.

I briefly wondered how much I was worth.

I walked for a long time. I slipped back to Seven Dials under the cover of night. I found my wallet behind the loose brick. It contained enough money that I should be able to rent a room in a slightly more reputable area for a couple of months and buy some respectable clothes. The money hidden under the loose floorboards would have to be abandoned.

Enough of begging on street corners for pennies. Enough of handing over my earnings to a man in exchange for a scrap of meat and a tattered blanket on a cold floor.

Time to strike out on my own.

I had absolutely no idea what I could do to earn my living. But I had no doubt I'd think of something.

My only regret was leaving Maise. I'd promised myself I'd take her with me. But I didn't dare return to either Mr. Jones's house or Maise's corner. He knew we were close. He'd be watching her, hoping to catch me.

I gathered my courage around me. Lifted my head high. And walked into the London night.

Chapter Sixteen

It wasn't long before Eleanor began yawning in the company of Mr. Turner. The man had taken a seat at a poker table and she sat slightly behind him. To Turner's obvious displeasure, the other players weren't interested in high stakes. It was too early: the big games didn't usually begin until much later. After the stage show, when bottles of Champagne had been drunk in the private boxes and men were made bold by drink or anxious to impress their favourite percentage girl. Often both. The occasional professional gambler passed through our doors, but mostly the clientele were miners with more money than they knew what to do with or cheechakos fresh off the boat with more time than they knew what do to with. Real gamblers, the sort of men I'd seen in the backrooms of private London clubs, were unlikely to be the sort to brave the rigours of the Chilkoot or the lengthy journey by sea and river north to the near-Arctic. Count Nicky had chosen to play roulette for a change. He was losing steadily. That was not a change.

Fortunately for Eleanor the night was still young. Irene had only sung one song when Inspector McKnight made his way through the rows of benches and mud-encrusted boots and out of the dance hall.

"Leaving us early, Inspector?" I said.

"Regretfully, I must, madam. There is a murderer and a madman loose on our streets. I cannot rest until we have him behind bars."

I fluttered my eyelashes and smiled my appreciation. McKnight was straitlaced and narrow-minded, but he was no fool and, regretfully, as honest as they came. I'd once hoped to be able to bribe him with Irene's favours, but he resisted nobly.

Eleanor jumped out of her seat and came to stand with us. I made the introductions and slipped away. It was time for the first play to begin and I wanted to make sure the performers were behaving themselves tonight. But first I'd check the saloon to get an idea of how many patrons we had. We hadn't yet had a riot in the dance hall as men fought for a good seat or for a turn with their favourite girl, but I lived in fear of such an event.

I entered the front room as Richard Sterling came through the doors. He was in uniform, so this was not a social call or a night out on the town.

He saw me watching and something tightened across his face. He said a word to Ray, who was explaining to an excessively inebriated young gentleman that if he didn't leave immediately he would not be leaving under his own power. Ray shook his head, indicating he didn't need assistance. Richard pushed through the crowd toward me.

"Good evening, Mrs. MacGillivray," he said, sounding quite formal. "Looks as if all's well tonight."

"No worse than normal. Richard, I wonder if we might have supper tomorrow evening. I'm quite ridiculously tired of Mrs. Mann's corned beef and would enjoy a restaurant meal." I blurted out the words without thinking. Pure horror immediately followed. *Had I asked a man to take me to dinner?* I knew what a Mountie made — a dollar and a quarter a day for a constable. A corporal probably earned a bit more, but still! In a town where a one-minute dance and drink with a percentage girl cost a dollar, and a steak could set a man back eight dollars or more.

I couldn't snatch the words back, so I added, "Perhaps something light, rather. Or an evening stroll along the river."

Richard looked about as horrified as I felt. "That would be very nice, Fiona. Unfortunately, I have a previous engagement tomorrow. Another time?"

"Another time. If I can find the opportunity."

We were saved from any more dreadfully awkward moments by the arrival of Eleanor Jennings and Inspector McKnight. The inspector had his hand on her arm and was escorting her from the gambling hall. Clearly, the meeting had been a success.

"Richard," Eleanor said with something approaching delight. "I wasn't expecting to see you again until tomorrow evening."

I felt as if I'd swallowed a lemon. And not a thin slice of delicate citrus laid across a perfectly cooked piece of Dover sole either. "I believe I'm needed elsewhere," I choked out. "Excuse me." I bolted for the back.

In all my years, I have never been so embarrassed. Or so humiliated.

I glanced around the gambling hall, looking for someone to tear a strip off.

Turner was watching me, a smile on his fleshy lips. Merely a coincidence, I'm sure, that he happened to look toward the door the moment I arrived. He closed one eye in a long slow wink before turning his attention back to his cards.

* * *

"This is boring."

"Shush."

"I'm not gonna shush. I'm bored."

"Go home then."

"Suppose something happens?"

"Nothing's going to happen if you keep talking."

In Toronto, Angus and his friends would slip out of their dorm rooms and clamber down the ivy to the ground. Then a dash across dark lawns and into the woods where they could get into all sorts of trouble. Not that they had much trouble to get into, or any desire to do so. It was enough to know they'd escaped the bounds of supervision. They usually sat under the ancient oaks and told ghost stories for an hour or so before creeping back to bed.

Here, in Dawson, almost at the Arctic Circle, it didn't get dark enough in summer to provide any sort of cover, and he was reduced to dashing from one street corner or shop doorway to another.

He never should have brought Dave along.

Angus had brooded all afternoon and made his plans at the last minute. His mother had never told him she had feelings for Corporal Sterling, but Angus had read her thoughts in her face. Particularly on Gold Mountain, when he and Sterling had rescued her from a fate worse than death. He'd almost expected them to kiss. Instead they'd greeted each other as if meeting at a garden party.

But Angus knew.

He hadn't lived close to his mother much. Boys of his class didn't. In London he'd had a nanny and then a governess; in Toronto he'd gone to boarding school, often spending the holidays with his friends at their summer cottages. She'd never introduced him to gentlemen friends or anyone attempting to court her. Some of his schoolmates had mothers or fathers who'd died. They all had step-parents. He'd heard it was natural for those who'd lost their husband or wife to seek out another.

Then again, his mother wasn't exactly like other women. Some of the things she knew…. Angus didn't know much about women, but he didn't think other boy's mothers carried a knife in the top of their stockings (as he'd seen on the Chilkoot Trail) or could pick a lock with a hatpin as fast as he could blink (the day they'd been accidently locked out of the house).

Still, she was just a woman, and it was Angus's responsibility as her only male relative to protect her. If she had feelings for Corporal Sterling, feelings Angus had believed — hoped? — were reciprocated, then it was no more than Angus's duty to ensure she was warned if Sterling was involved with another woman.

It was Saturday night, thankfully, and everything would shut down at midnight. They had dinner at six and then his mother went to dress for the evening. Angus had come in as she was arranging her hair. She looked almost vulnerable, with the long black tresses falling across her shoulders, the pearl earrings in her ears, the folds of silk draped around the chair.

He waited until she was out of sight before leaving the house in time to be in position at Miss Jennings', well before eight. He ran into his friend Dave, heading his way.

Angus didn't want a companion tonight, but then again it might be useful if he needed to watch two doors at the same time. He informed Dave he was on a secret assignment and they had to stay quiet.

The boys went to the photography studio. Miss Jennings lived in the rooms above, where a lamp was lit, indicating they weren't too late. Angus and Dave crept into the shadows of the bakery opposite. Fortunately, the shop was closed. Dave tried to talk but Angus hushed him. Secrecy, he whispered, was of the essence.

Smack on time, Corporal Sterling arrived and knocked on the studio door. Upstairs the lamp was extinguished, and a few seconds later the door opened. Miss Jennings hadn't bothered to dress up for the evening, Angus noticed with relief. She wore a plum-coloured dress that fell in simple lines to the ground, with an unadorned belt wrapped tightly around her thin waist. Her hat was a square straw thing plopped on top of her head. A few blond curls peeked out to fall around her face. She locked the door behind her. Sterling, dressed in a tweed suit, held out his arm. She accepted it.

They walked downhill, heading toward Front Street and the dance halls, unaware of two shadows silently following.

First stop was the Horseshoe. Angus positioned himself across the street, behind a boulder. He assigned Dave the closer spot, near the door.

The streets were busy. Saturday night and everyone knew the dance halls would be closing in a few hours. A light rain began to fall. More than a few people gave the boy couched in the lee of the boulder an odd look, but no one stopped to ask what he was doing. No doubt they figured he was waiting for his father.

Not more than half an hour passed before Sterling and Miss Jennings reappeared. They strolled down the boardwalk, chatting, laughing, and Angus and Dave fell into step behind them. It was good that the street was crowded. If Sterling should happen to stop and look back, the boys would be hidden by the throng. The Monte Carlo, the Savoy's strongest competition, was next. A portrait of the Queen hung over the front door and the name of the establishment was mounted above the second-floor windows. Like the Savoy, it was nothing more than a wooden shack with pretentions.

The rain was falling harder now. A couple of people brought out umbrellas but most walked on, heedless of the wet. Angus and Dave couched behind a sign advertising the Dawson Headquarters of the *Post Intelligencer*. They had no cover and before long cold rain water was leaking through his jacket and dripping down the back of his neck.

"I'm bored," Dave complained and Angus shushed him.

A few minutes passed.

"I'm getting wet," Dave said.

Angus rolled his eyes. Some people simply weren't cut out for a life of adventure and danger.

"What are we doing anyway?" Dave asked. "I know that guy. He's a Mountie. I don't think the police'll like it much if you're sneaking around after them."

"We're watching the lady. She mustn't know we're here."

"Why?" Dave repeated.

"Does a soldier question his orders? Does a Mountie put up his hand and ask, 'Superintended Steele what are we doing this for?' No. They do what they're told."

"We're not soldiers or police," Dave said, perfectly sensibly. "Don't tell me the Mounties have called you in for special duty, Angus. They don't use boys."

"You can go home if you want."

"I'll stick around a bit. You're watching them because you think the Mountie's sweet on that lady and he has an understanding with your ma, right?"

"Don't be ridiculous," Angus said.

The rain continued to fall. A mangy dog came to investigate. Angus held out his hand and the dog growled, showing a row of teeth, yellow but still sharp. Angus snatched his hand back. He took out his watch. Only ten o'clock.

"Here they come," Dave said.

Angus cursed himself. He'd almost missed them. Sterling and Miss Jennings were once again on the move. The boys melted into the crowd.

Their quarry went into a much less prominent establishment this time. "You wait here," Angus told Dave. "I'm going to have a look." Heart pounding, he walked down the boardwalk, keeping to the inside. He glanced through the window as he passed. The room was small and dark and appeared to be nothing more than a bar. There weren't many customers. Miss Jennings was speaking to the man behind the counter, while Sterling stood at her elbow. The corporal glanced around. Angus dropped to his haunches. He duck-walked the rest of the way past the building.

"Are you hurt, Angus?" a man asked. "Do you need me to fetch your ma?" Angus had no idea who this was, but he looked pleased at the idea of running to fetch Fiona.

"No. Just playing a game. Me and my friend over there. A game." He waved to Dave.

"There you are," Dave said, shouting so loudly heads turned. "Isn't this a fun game we are having?"

The man walked off, shaking his head.

"Keep your voice down," Angus hissed. He grabbed Dave's sleeve and they darted into a space between the buildings protected by a narrow overhang. "We can see from here and stay out of the rain."

"There he is again," Dave said, peering around the corner.

"Who?"

"That man over there. He's been everywhere we have. At first I figured it was a coincidence. He was checking out the Horseshoe and the Monte Carlo. But he doesn't go inside."

The crowd was thinning. Everyone inside having a last drink or heading home. A man stood on the other side of the street, smoking and watching the entrance to the bar. He wore drab clothes with his tie tucked between the buttons of his shirt. His hat was pulled low over his face. His hands were flat and broad.

"Do you know him?" Dave asked.

"No."

The man tossed the end of his cigar into the mud and stepped back, into the dark entranceway of a store advertising fine candies. Angus had been in the store, pockets jingling with his wages from Mr. Mann, his hopes high. He'd left disappointed: they didn't have any sweets, just the usual canned fruit.

Sterling and Miss Jennings strolled past the alley. Angus muttered under his breath. He hadn't seen them come out of the bar. If they'd gone in the other direction, he would have lost them.

Dave took a step forward, as if to follow. Angus placed his arm across his friend's chest, held his finger to his lips, and pressed them both against the side of the building. In a moment the man, the one who'd been watching, passed.

Angus counted off a few seconds and then, pulling Dave behind him, fell into step.

He could see Sterling up ahead, hat bobbing above the press of men all around him. The much shorter Miss Jennings had disappeared. The unknown man kept his distance but matched their pace.

Saloon doors flew open and all of a sudden they were surrounded by laughing, shoving, drunken men. Midnight.

Angus lost sight of Sterling. The unknown man used his elbows to push his way through the crowd. "Hey, watch where you're going," someone said. He stepped back and collided with Angus. Angus staggered off the boardwalk and felt his boot sink into the mud of the road. Dave grabbed his sleeve or he would have fallen.

"Sorry about that, young fellow."

Angus said something about being okay. He'd lost sight of his quarry — old as well as new.

"What do we do now?" Dave asked.

"I hope I know. Come on." Angus broke into a run. It wasn't easy going, with the press of men heading in all directions. Everything was closing, no place for Sterling and Miss Jennings to go except home. It was light out, so they might go for a walk, but the rain was falling harder now.

He rounded the corner into York Street. The throng thinned a fraction and up ahead the unknown man was calmly strolling along.

When they came in sight of Miss Jennings' studio, Angus once more retreated to the shadows, pulling Dave behind him.

Sterling and Miss Jennings stopped at her door. The man walked past, not glancing to the side. Miss Jennings stood very close to Constable Sterling, looking up at him. She said a few words and he smiled. During the evening much of her hair had escaped the confines of its pins and soft yellow strands fell across her face. She lifted her hand and tucked a piece behind her ear. She pulled her key out of the depths of her bag and unlocked the door. Miss Jennings hesitated for a moment before kissing Sterling lightly on the cheek. Then she ran inside, shutting the door behind her. Leaving the Mountie standing on the stoop.

Sterling turned and headed up the street.

The door of the house in which Angus had taken shelter opened suddenly. A man filled the doorway, dressed in his underclothes, dirty shirt, once-white long johns.

"What do you think you're doing?" he bellowed. "Get off with you or I'll call the Mounties."

Angus and Dave ran. Fortunately Corporal Sterling did not look back.

Chapter Seventeen

Monday morning, I was pleased to see the first of the photographs of the dancers appearing around town. I had instructed Murray to collect the copies from Miss Jennings and place them in prominent places. The most prominent being the front window of the Savoy. When I left, heading for the bank, a group of men were standing in front of it, studying the picture.

"Hey." One of them hailed me as I passed.

"I beg your pardon?" He was much taller than I, at well over six feet, but I managed to look down my nose at him.

"You work here?"

"As a matter of fact, I do. May I be of assistance?"

He took off his cap and scratched his head. I tried to ignore the insects scurrying for cover. "That lady in that there picture, she dances here?"

"Every night of the week, save Sunday. The show begins at eight o'clock." Our advertisement was working already!

"I might come and see it then," he said. "Right pretty lady."

"That is Lady Irénée, the most popular dancer in the Yukon. The seats fill up quickly, so do come in good time."

"What's the name of the older one then?"

"The older one?" I peered at the photograph. The man was missing the first joint of his index finger. He used the stub to tap at the image of Irene, dead centre.

"Yeah, this one. She looks like she has a few miles on her. Might do for my pa there." He indicated the oldest of the men, who stood grinning at me through a wad of chewing tobacco.

Good heavens, he'd been attracted, not by Irene, but by Colleen, standing to the right of centre. Colleen, merely a chorus dancer and percentage girl.

I walked off without answering the man's question. Colleen hadn't shown much in the way of talent, but that was no reason to not have a stage career in Dawson. Few of the performers in any of the dance halls did. I might move Colleen forward for a couple of the dances, perhaps ask her if she could sing. See how the men reacted. If they liked her, maybe she could have a solo.

I completed my banking and, rather than going home for my morning nap, headed up the hill. I needed a new gown. I knew where the best-quality fabric in town was to be found.

I also knew that, for me, the price would be astronomical.

Being Monday morning, I figured Irene was likely to be awake. The girls danced every night until six a.m. so naturally they slept during the day. Sunday the Savoy was closed, as was everything else, so they often slept right around the clock. She might, of course, not be in. Monday was the best day for dancers and performers, and me, to do household tasks, shopping and the like. It was unfortunate we did not have the use of a telephone in Dawson. It would make life most convenient, I thought as I trudged through the streets on what might be a useless trip, if one could telephone in advance to ascertain if one would be received. If Irene was not in her lodgings, I would have wasted my time.

Not entirely wasted though, it was a pleasant day. The sun was large and hot, the sky a soft blue with fluffy clouds in the distance. The colours gave me an idea for my new gown.

Irene had lodgings on Fifth Avenue. Only one room in a women's boarding house, but the house was nicer than most.

The rent was high, and thus the rooms were occupied by head-liners at the other dancehalls and one or two of the town's more successful independent businesswomen. I lifted my skirts to step around a pile of recently deposited, judging by the smell, dog dirt, and knocked on the front door. It opened almost immediately. I stated my business to the landlady and entered.

I had been to Irene's room before and did not need to be shown it. I knocked loudly.

"Who's there?"

"It is I. Mrs. MacGillivray."

Irene peeked out. Her hair was dishevelled, her eyes heavy with sleep. She wore a loose white nightdress, all crisp cotton and excessive amounts of lace and ribbons. "What do you want?" she said, displaying a shocking lack of courtesy.

I dearly hoped I would not find my business partner luxuriating in her bed.

"I'd like to purchase some fabric. I've a mind to have a new dress made. The yellow satin would be nice." I smiled at her. I was here to beg a favour, after all.

Irene had been close friends with a dressmaker of rough manners but unparalleled skill. My delight on finding her, the dressmaker, had been beyond bounds. Unfortunately, she met an untimely demise before completing my order. Irene had the presence of mind to rush to the shop and grab the most valuable of the fabrics. She kept them in a trunk in her room and charged exorbitant rates.

"The yellow's still left. Come on in."

I stepped forward and the door shut behind me. To my considerable surprise Miss Eleanor Jennings was seated at the small round table in the centre of the room, a cup of coffee at her elbow. She, at least, was dressed. She wore her habitual plum and green costume, and her feet were bare. Her shoes were on the floor, her stockings tossed across the — unmade — bed, and her bonnet onto a shelf.

"Good afternoon, Eleanor," I said.

"Fiona. This is an unexpected pleasure." Her tone implied that it was no pleasure at all.

"The yellow." I turned to Irene. "And the navy blue velvet, if you have some. Maggie told me I should always wear strong colours."

Irene stared into my face. A long moment passed. "Sure," she said at last. "Let's have a look." She threw open the lid of the trunk and knelt in front of it. Eleanor Jennings rose to get a better look.

The trunk was about half empty. Irene had taken only the best — the silks, satins, and velvets — leaving poor-quality cotton, felt, and homespun behind in the dead woman's shop. She pulled out the bolt of satin. It was a brilliant yellow. A highly unfashionable colour, but I knew it would look spectacular against my black hair and dark complexion. I would set a fashion of my own. "Do you want the whole bolt?" Irene asked.

I nodded. She shoved it into my arms. "And the blue velvet?"

"All of it."

The bolt of navy blue joined its fellow.

"And three yards of white lace if you still have some."

"There's a bit left. Pass me those scissors, will you, El?"

Eleanor Jennings leaned behind her, found the seamstress's scissors on the shelf, and passed them over. Irene measured using her arms and sliced through the fabric. She piled the white lace, as heart-breakingly delicate as a pattern of fresh frost on a windowpane, on top of the others. I could barely see her over the top.

I should have brought Angus to carry it all home.

Irene named an outrageous sum. I swallowed. I came here knowing I'd have to pay. If I wanted to haggle, Irene would tell

me she'd find other customers. She could have disposed of all the
fabric by now if she wanted. She kept the best of it, waiting for
me to come begging.

"Let me hold that for you," Eleanor Jennings said sweetly,
"so you can get out the money." She relieved me of my burden.

I dug into my reticule. "This is all I have on me. I'll pay you
the remainder this evening when you come to work."

Irene grinned as she accepted the payment. "I guess you're
good for it."

Eleanor gave me back the cloth. I hoisted it in my arms as if
I were a laundry maid carrying sheets to the linen cupboard and
said my goodbyes.

So, Irene had taken up with Eleanor Jennings. It was none
of my business (funny how I kept thinking that lately) but poor
Ray if he ever found out. Poor me, if everyone else found out.

Irene was a Sapphist. A lover of women. Only I knew that
she had been the lady friend of the late, much lamented, seamstress, Maggie. Irene's entire value, to herself as a dance hall
performer, not to mention to me as my best girl, rested on her
sexual allure. If the men found out she showed signs of such a
shocking degree of mental aberration, Irene would be ruined.
When I lived in the slums of Seven Dials, I'd known women
who sought love with other women. It never seemed as if they
were mentally ill to me, although the doctors considered them
to be so. After all, I'd seen some of the men those same women
had to pretend to love.

Pretend to love.

Not only Sapphists had to pretend to love the men they
married, whether for family expectations or to provide themselves with financial security. But why, if Eleanor Jennings was
attracted to Irene Davidson, was she apparently interested in
Richard Sterling? Plenty of richer men in town.

Was it possible she was attracted to Richard as well as to Irene? Did that happen?

I knew normal women did not have sexual desires. I had myself been abnormal in that department. I received enormous pleasure from sexual relations with Angus's father, a man I had deeply loved. His betrayal had made me fear he'd considered my craving for intimacy and the joy found therein to be shameful. Sometimes, when I've been close to Richard, I've felt those strange, wonderful stirrings I'd thought long dead.

If Richard was attracted to Eleanor, and if he believed her feelings were returned, was it my duty as his friend to inform him of her aberration?

So bothered was I by these thoughts, I was scarcely paying attention as I made my way west on Fifth Street heading home. I couldn't see where I was placing my feet with the bolts of cloth I carried. I could only hope I wouldn't encounter the product of another passing dog. Or worse — its remains.

Most days I could scarcely set foot onto the street without a gaggle of men clamouring to be of assistance. Today, when I could have used assistance, not a soul of my acquaintance was to be seen. I'd been so embarrassed, first at having to go to Irene for what I needed, and then at finding her in dishabille in the company of Eleanor Jennings, that I'd forgotten to so much as demand Irene wrap the cloth in paper and string. This was not a street in which it was wise not to be able to see where one placed one's foot. The boardwalks were tilting in all directions, cracked and pitted with holes. The duckboards, placed across the street to provide passage over the mud, fared no better. Puddles were full of water so thick and opaque one couldn't estimate if one was likely to dampen the bottom of one's shoe or plunge to perdition. Or trod on a dead beast. I reached the corner of King Street, only two blocks from home. I felt with the toe of my boot for the edge of the boardwalk. As I was a few blocks uphill from the river, the street wasn't too dreadfully muddy, and by stretching my neck and peering around my burden I estimated I could safely cross without encountering rotting livestock or dangerous depressions.

I stepped into the road.

A woman screamed and a man yelled. I heard hoof beats, coming fast in my direction. To my left, I saw a man leap to the safety of the boardwalk. He struck the wood with his toe and went down, arms and legs flailing, hat rolling. A woman held her hands to her face, wide eyed with horror. Instead of also jumping out of the way, I stupidly thought that I mustn't drop the precious fabric into the mud. The hoofbeats got closer. I stood in the road, frozen into indecision, unable to see where I should go.

Something struck me, hard, on my left side, and I fell into the roadway. Fabric scattered. I looked up, directly into the underbelly of an underfed and out-of-control horse.

Chapter Eighteen

Angus kept his hands firmly behind his back as he studied the jars and equipment spread out on the tables in Miss Jennings' studio. It was an impressive array of stuff. The lady herself had finished developing plates moments before Angus's arrival, and an air of bitter chemicals floated around her like a strange perfume. She wore a long white apron over her dress and her thick braid was scraped back into a coil. She usually wore gloves and now that she wasn't, Angus could see that her fingers were stained black and covered with small marks, old burns probably. She held up her left hand. "Photography chemicals are harsh. Took me a few wrong moves to learn that. Silver nitrate turns the flesh black."

He blushed to have been caught staring.

"How did you learn, ma'am? Is there a school of photography in Chicago?"

"My father taught himself and then he taught me. I grew up around exploding plates, flashes of light, black boxes. He was a lawyer; photography was his passion. My parents had five children, of whom I am the youngest, and the only one, to his great disappointment, who showed any interest in his hobby. Father would rush home from the office, kiss Mother on the cheek, and head downstairs to his darkroom. I followed on my wobbly little legs and watched." She smiled to herself. "Eventually he ceased even kissing Mother when he came in the door, such was his haste to get to his one true love. His camera room. I guess that's why I am the youngest child." She gasped. "Oh, Angus, pardon me. Such an indelicacy."

He tried not to blush. "I understand," he said, as heat tore across his face.

"I've had a productive morning," she said, untying her apron. "Two clients for sittings: a wealthy businessman wanting a photograph to send to his mother, and one of the ladies from the Savoy. The young one who looks so good in the photograph I took of the group. Her father was so pleased with it, he wanted a personal photograph of the both of them."

"Word's spreading," Angus said.

She smiled. "I developed the batch I took over the weekend. Most satisfactory. I haven't heard from Inspector McKnight about my request, but seeing as to how I now have his acquaintance, we're going to call on his office this afternoon. I'm going upstairs to change. If you like, you can have a look at the pictures drying in the darkroom. Don't touch anything."

"I won't," he promised.

Miss Jennings had a small room built against one wall of her studio. The door was open now, and the kerosene lamp lit. Angus slipped in. A red cloth was draped over the small window, casting the room in an eerie red glow. A drying rack held six glass plates, and when Angus bent to look he could see the image in reverse. Black was white and white was black. Paper was laid on the countertop, the photographs drying, a roll of blotting paper to one side. He studied the pictures. He recognized Betsy from the dance hall, posing in her bloomers and shift, peeking coyly from behind an opened fan. Rather, she was trying to peek coyly. Even Angus, young as he was, knew there was nothing at all alluring about the sturdy farm girl.

Two men posed stiffly, arms straight at their sides, hats equally straight on their heads, staring at the camera, eyes held wide open, expressions frozen. Angus leaned closer and he fancied he could see defeat in their faces. The brows were heavy, skin lined, eyes empty. What an amazing thing this photography was! It showed people as they were, not as they wanted to be, which is what you saw in paintings.

He smelled chemicals, heard fabric rustle, and turned to see Miss Jennings standing in the open door. "Like them?" she asked. Her head was tilted to one side as she also studied the pictures.

"Yes." No further words were needed.

"I'm anxious to do your mother."

Angus shook his head. "She won't agree."

"How about if you propose a portrait of the both of you? A memory of your youth. She won't be able to resist that."

Angus hesitated, and Miss Jennings laughed. "Never mind. I don't want to pressure you into doing anything you'd rather not. Plenty of other subjects in this town."

She turned at a knock. The door to the street opened. "Put out that lamp, will you, Angus? Mr. Donohue, what a pleasant surprise."

The American newspaperman held his hat in his hand. "I was passing and thought I'd drop in. Oh, Angus, you're here."

"Yup," Angus said, smiling.

Miss Jennings gathered up her hat and gloves. "We're off to the fort to pay a call on Inspector McKnight. Why don't you come with us, Graham?"

"Don't mind if I do."

"Angus, I've changed my mind. Rather than try to make an appointment to photograph the police, I'm going to take the camera with me. Present them with a *fait accompli*, so to speak. Bring it, will you."

Angus gathered up the camera case. Before they could leave, the door opened once again. This time it was the Russian count. He doffed his hat and bowed stiffly to Miss Jennings. "I hope I am not interrupting anything of importance."

"We're on our way out, but I can spare a minute. Are you here to make an appointment? Angus, get out the book."

"Yes, I will do that. But, as Mr. Donohue is here, I have a request."

"Yeah?"

"You are a newspaperman, correct?"

"Chief correspondent for the *San Francisco Standard*. Do you have a story, Count?"

"Please, please, call me Nicky. It is the American way, correct?"

"Yeah. We don't hold with titles or royalty or such. What's on your mind, Nicky?"

The count glanced around the room. "Is it just we three here?" he said.

Angus should be offended at not being considered worth counting, but he was more interested in what this fellow thought was so secretive. He remained silent.

"There's no one hiding in the back rooms, if that's what you're asking," Miss Jennings said, her tone harsh.

"It never harms one to be sure." Nicky leaned forward. Donohue and Miss Jennings instinctively followed, as did Angus, from the other side of the table. "I would like," Nicky whispered in conspiratorial tones, "for you to arrange a meeting for me with the American consul."

"What?" Donohue whispered. He shook his head, straightened up, and continued in his normal voice. "Well, Nicky, I'm afraid we aren't quite that equal even in America. I don't happen to know Mr. McCook, and the one time I did try to interview him he refused to see me. He's none too fond of the press, I've heard."

Nicky appeared confused. "Miss Jennings?"

"Don't look at me. I wouldn't know the fellow if he ran down the street naked whistling Dixie."

"I beg your pardon?"

"She means," Donohue said, "she can't help you either. What do you want to talk to him about anyway?"

"It is a matter of vital importance. The very destiny of North America hangs in the balance."

"Is that so?" Donohue said. "You can tell me, pal. When I know what's up, I'll help you get in to see McCook."

Miss Jennings smiled encouragement. Nicky looked uncertain. He glanced behind him. The door was closed, but they could hear people and wagons passing on the street outside. A man shouted and another answered.

Donohue lifted his eyebrows in Angus's direction and pulled a face. He was all smiles and serious interest when Nicky's attention returned.

The count stepped further into the room. Donohue and Miss Jennings followed.

"This might not be suitable for your ears, Miss Jennings." He gave her another bow. "I am here to discuss ... politics."

"Oh, for heaven's sake. If you insist." She turned her back and made a show of arranging the papers on her desk. Angus's mother had told him many times that men believe women possess a certain intuition, when they merely know how to listen without appearing to do so.

"Mr. Donohue, you are an American, correct?" Count Nicky said lowering his voice once again.

"Yes."

"You are therefore naturally interested in seeing the disputed border between Canada and the United States settled in your country's favour?"

"Well, yeah, I guess I would. What's this about?"

"I have an offer to make to the American authorities."

"Will you look at the time?" Donohue said. "We'd best be off, Eleanor, or you'll miss your appointment."

"Alaska," Nicky shouted, "in exchange for the Yukon."

"Well, as nice an offer as that is, Count, you don't exactly own Alaska. And we don't own the Yukon. Even in Dawson, man can't bet what he doesn't own against another man for something he doesn't own." Donohue's laugh was not friendly.

"Hear me out, sir. Russia is in decline. Trapped in a feudal society, falling further and further behind the other great powers every day that passes. Nicholas is a know-nothing fool, totally unable to manage affairs of state. Yet he is determined to maintain the absolute authority of his father. The rest of the world changes, yet the leadership in Russia, a weak collection of aging aristocrats determined at all costs to keep their own privilege, will not, indeed cannot, change with it. Or even see the need for change."

"As fascinating as that is," Donohue said, "I fail to see how I can help you."

"Myself, and a group of like-minded, progressive ..."

Miss Jennings snorted.

"... members of the aristocracy, have decided it is too late to save Russia. Therefore ..." he paused for effect, "... we wish to move it. To start anew, so to speak. A new Russia. In a new world."

"If you and your friends want to come to America, just say so," Miss Jennings said, forgetting that her simple woman's mind was not to be bothered about such things. "Our doors are open to all comers."

"You misunderstand me, madam. I am not surprised you fail to grasp the larger implications. We do not want to become Americans. We are proud Russians. We wish to create a separate Russia. A new Russia. I have like-minded friends, ready to come with their servants and peasants. We wish to settle in Alaska. Our county made a mistake selling Alaska to the United States, and we would like it back."

"Sure," Donohue said, "help yourself. Ready, Eleanor?"

"Do not mock me, sir." Nicky stretched himself to his full height and puffed up his chest. His eyes glowed with fever. "This is not a laughing matter. Allow me to finish my proposal. In exchange for Alaska, the boundaries still to be determined, my compatriots and I will provide an army to take the Yukon and hand it over to the United States. You will surely agree this is the more valuable territory."

"May I ask where these compatriots are? I don't hear rumours of a Russian army massing on the borders."

"I am merely the advance guard," Nicky replied with a sniff. "They wait in Russia for my orders."

"Next time I'm talking to President McKinley, I'll mention your plan," Donohue said.

Nicky smiled broadly. "You have that gentleman's acquaintance? Excellent."

"Count Nicholas," Miss Jennings said, "I'd be thrilled to hear more about this delightful plan." Angus wondered if something was wrong with her voice. It had lifted a couple of octaves and was almost dripping with honey. "I know people who can help you. Make an appointment with Angus to have your photograph taken and we can talk at that time. We don't want the Canadian authorities to catch word of what you have in mind, now do we. I can act as an intermediary. A messenger."

"An excellent plan. Tomorrow morning?"

"Miss Jennings is free at nine," Angus said, consulting the appointment book.

She crossed the room and held open the door. "Until tomorrow."

Nicky bowed deeply, put on his hat, and left.

When Miss Jennings had shut the door behind the Russian, Donohue burst out laughing. "The man's as mad as a hatter."

"I can't wait to tell my mother about this," Angus said, also laughing. "I can see his army of Russian peasants armed with pitchforks attacking Dawson now."

"One look at the dance halls, and they'll be deserting en mass."

"Don't say anything to your mother, Angus," Miss Jennings said. She had not joined in the laughter.

"Why not? It's funny."

"Madness is rarely funny. Although in this case I have no doubt his ambition considerably exceeds his reach. Poor man, searching for a past that will never come again. I doubt our count has any intention of forming his peasants into a voting democracy. Get them out of decaying Russia and under his control more likely. He plans to set himself up as czar of all the Alaskas, I suspect. Nevertheless, you know how rumour spreads. We don't want news going around that the Russian army is preparing to attack the town, now do we?"

"You're right," Donohue said reluctantly. "Better to keep it to ourselves. Why did you agree to meet with the man, Eleanor? You should have sent him off with a flea in his ear."

"I think it wise to get rid of him. Although it's none of my business, and he certainly isn't interested in my opinion. I'll hand him a letter addressed to the president at the White House and tell him it's an introduction. I suspect that'll be enough to have him scurrying south on the next boat."

"That's a grand idea, Miss Jennings," Angus said. "We don't need trouble of that sort here, where the Mounties don't have the resources to deal with it."

She smiled. "Precisely what I was thinking."

Chapter Nineteen

The air moved as the horse leapt over me. The world went dark. Men yelled and footsteps pounded. I felt hands on my body and a woman said, "Stand back, you fools. Don't move her."

I opened my eyes, which I'd snapped shut in order not to see the horse's feet crashing down into my face. A sea of faces, full of concern, gazed down at me. A large, plainly dressed woman crouched beside me, her hands moving across my chest. "Stay still," she ordered.

I breathed and nothing hurt. I wiggled my toes and then my fingers. "I'm all right. Help me up."

The woman rose and held out her arm. I rolled to one side and realized that a man lay close to me. A couple of men got behind me and, with a suck of mud, I was levered ungraciously to my feet. Others helped the fallen man rise. He winced with pain and held his arm across his chest.

Roland the Magnificent. "A close call, madam," he said through gritted teeth.

"What on earth happened?"

"That horse was heading straight for you," the woman said. "This gentleman was nearby. You're darned lucky he was here and fast on his feet. If you're not hurt, Mrs. MacGillivray, I suspect he needs attending to."

Roland's face had turned the colour of my fine lace. "My

arm," he said, "doesn't seem to be responding to instructions."

"I'm a nurse. Let me see." She took the offending limb tenderly in large capable hands. He sucked in a breath.

A crowd was gathering.

"You woulda been killed, if that man hadn't pushed you outta the way," someone yelled.

Men began to murmur. Hands reached out to slap Ronald on the back. He cowered in terror, protecting his arm, and the nurse growled at them to stay back.

"Is that true?" I asked Roland.

He shrugged. "Horse came out of nowhere, out of control. I saw it heading straight for you, and did what I could to assist."

"Thank you," I said.

"Come on. Better get you to the doctor. I suspect your shoulder's been dislocated," the nurse said.

"It can't be. I can't perform stunning feats of magic with a bad shoulder." His tone was light, but his face showed a great deal of pain.

"Come to the Savoy when you're released from the hospital. We'll make an arrangement."

He nodded, and allowed the nurse to lead him away. The crowd respectfully stepped aside to let them pass.

"Here you go, miss." A boy handed me my bolts of fabric. The yellow was cheerful and sunny no more, and the white lace would do for a vampire's wedding dress. Protected to some degree by being in the middle, the blue velvet didn't look too bad. I took the pile.

The cloth was disgusting, but it was only mud (and whatever filth was mixed in there) so Mrs. Mann should be able to get it clean.

I had almost lost my life because I was too stubborn to throw the fabric aside and flee.

The crowd shifted again and a Mountie came through. Young Constable McAllen. "Mrs. MacGillivray, are you all right? I heard something about a horse?"

"I'm fine, Constable, thank you. I seemed to have survived." I shivered, despite the heat of the sun, and clutched the bolts of fabric to my chest. "My rescuer didn't fare so well, and he's been taken to the doctor."

"Let me see you home, ma'am. You," he addressed a boy, "carry Mrs. MacGillivray's shopping."

"Someone needs to stop that horse," I said.

"Constable FitzHenry's gone after it."

I handed my package to the lad indicated. I'd intended to go directly to Mrs. MacDonald, the dressmaker on Front Street, but aside from the condition of the fabric, I didn't trust my own condition. My legs were wobbly, my head spinning, and an ache was beginning to spread through my bottom. I needed to get home, sit down, and have a cup of tea.

McAllen held out his arm. I took it gratefully.

He walked me home, slowly, while about a hundred men followed and a dirty-faced boy carried my bolts of cloth. A lame dog brought up the rear.

Mrs. Mann screamed at the sight of me. Alerted, no doubt, by the noise of the procession, she'd been standing in the patch of dirt and weeds that passed for a front yard when we rounded the corner. She ran forward and grabbed my free arm. Her hands were still hot from the laundry she'd been doing in the shed. "What on earth have you done this time?"

"Mrs. MacGillivray's unharmed," Constable McAllen said, "but she needs to lie down. An incident with a runaway horse. Nothing serious, fortunately."

I nodded. McAllen led me toward the front door.

"My cloth!" I shouted over my shoulder. "Helga, get that fabric."

*   *   *

Richard Sterling headed down Queen Street back to the detachment office. He was thinking about his evening escorting Eleanor Jennings around the various dance halls when he heard a commotion up ahead. A stream of men came east on Fifth Avenue, chattering excitedly. A crowd could form in this town for pretty much anything, so aimless was the pack of men, and he didn't pay undue attention. Whatever had happened, the show was over. He fell in behind a dusty group. The boardwalks were crowded so they walked down the centre of the road.

"Saw it all," one man said. "She woulda been killed, I tell you. Killed. 'Course I tried to reach her myself but she were too far away."

"Pull the other one, Danny," his companion said with a sneer.

"Man aughta get a medal," a third fellow said. "Can't imagine this town without Mrs. MacGillivray."

Sterling groaned. He had never met a woman, a person, who could get themselves into so much trouble. What had she done now? He lengthened his stride and came up beside the men. "Excuse me. Couldn't help overhearing. What happened back there?"

"Mrs. MacGillivray, what owns the Savoy, almost got her pretty self killed, that's what happened." The man spat a lump of tobacco into the roadway.

"Woulda too, if'n that English fellow hadn't been right there."

"I repeat," Sterling said, "what happened?"

"Outta control horse. Almost ran her down. The English fellow who does magic tricks pulled her out of the way in the nick of time."

"Where is she now? Was she taken to the doctor?"

"Nah. The Englishman was hurt, but Mrs. MacGillivray went home. Young constable escorted her."

"Can't wait ta see what she makes outa that yellow cloth."
The men smiled at the thought.

Sterling changed his mind and headed west on Fourth
Avenue. He encountered Constable McAllen coming in the
opposite direction.

"What's this I hear about a horse and Mrs. MacGillivray?"

McAllen told him the story. It didn't take long. "She's shook
up, but not hurt."

"And the horse?"

"FitzHenry went after it."

"I'm going back to the office. When you see FitzHenry tell
him to report in."

Sterling had taken only a few steps when McAllen shouted.
He turned back to see FitzHenry heading their way, leading a
severely emaciated brown horse by its bridle. The animal's flanks,
so thin Sterling could count every rib, heaved. Its neck was
soaked with sweat and white foam bubbled around its mouth.

"Crying shame," McAllen said, shaking his head. "See an
animal looking like that."

FitzHenry was grinning wildly. "Got it," he said, unneces-
sarily. "It ran out of steam up the street a bit and stopped to try
to get its head through the fence around a plot of vegetables."

"Do you know who this animal belongs to?"

They turned at a shout.

"Probably that fellow there," McAllen said.

A red-faced, round-bellied man was walking quickly
toward them. "Miserable wretch," he snarled. "Aughta sell it
for dog meat."

"You own this creature?" Sterling asked.

"For all that's worth."

"You need to keep it tied up better. Someone could have
been hurt."

"I know how to look after horses, friend. None better. That horse was tied up just fine. I'd unhitched the wagon earlier and left the horse tied to a rail outside the cigar store. Weren't gone more than a couple minutes and I came out to find the horse gone."

More than a couple of minutes had obviously passed. Sterling let it go. Most cigar stores were owned by independent businesswomen and provided services that had nothing to do with sales of tobacco products.

McAllen had taken hold of the bridle, and he was stroking the long powerful neck, making soothing sounds. "If you fed him now and again, he wouldn't have to run off looking for something to eat."

The horse owner bristled. "You find me hay, son, and I'll be happy to give it to him." He reached for the rope attached to the bridle. Sterling put out a hand and stopped him.

"What?"

Sterling took the rope, and held it up. The rope was in no better condition than the horse. Stiff with dried mud and years of horse sweat, frayed all along its length. It was bound to snap soon.

But it hadn't snapped today.

It had been cut.

A clean fresh cut made by a sharp knife.

Sterling showed the end of the rope to the owner. "Can you account for this?"

The man blinked at first, not understanding. Then his eyes widened. "Son of a bitch. Someone stole my damned horse."

"Watch your language," McAllen snapped.

"Freed it from the rail, at any rate," Sterling said. "Although theft might not have been the intention."

"Someone looking to make trouble," FitzHenry offered. "A spot of mischief to liven up the day."

"Perhaps." Sterling handed the rope to McAllen and walked around the horse. He ran his hands over the sides and belly, feeling every rib. It hadn't felt the touch of a brush in a long time, if ever. The animal shied away from the probing hands. McAllen stoked the nose, soft as velvet, stared into the liquid brown eyes, and spoke softly. The horse began to settle. Sterling reached the hindquarters and let out a long breath. "McAllen, come here."

The constable handed the rope to the owner with a scowl and joined Sterling.

"What do you see there?"

McAllen reached out a finger and lightly touched the spot at the left rear leg Sterling indicated. The animal shuddered. McAllen lifted his finger. A drop of red liquid shone in the sunlight.

The two men exchanged glances. The horse stamped his feet and tried to move away. The owner swore at it and jerked on the rope. McAllen laid his hands on the animal's quivering skin and leaned closer. "There," he said.

A cut, a long one, so fresh it was still bleeding. About an inch from the root of the animal's long ragged tail.

"Mighta run into a fence post," McAllen said.

"In the rear?"

"Backed up and panicked. Horses panic easy."

"FitzHenry said he was trying to get at some vegetables. Can't do that with his rear end."

"No."

"This cut was made by a knife." Sterling kept his voice low. McAllen nodded.

"Okay," Sterling said, louder. "You can go. Look after this horse, will you. Though I don't think you were neglectful in tying it up."

The man spat one more time, grabbed the bridle, and yanked. With a last, long sad look at Constable McAllen, the horse let himself be led away.

Chapter Twenty

I stood at the back of the hall, watching the show. My entire body ached, particularly the nether regions. I'd landed hard on my rear end. By the time I'd arrived home it had been aching something dreadful. I'd peeked at myself in the mirror to see a massive bruise forming.

Not only had I not gone to the dressmaker, I'd crawled into bed and slept through the afternoon. I rose on wobbly legs and as I arranged my hair my hands began to shake. Until then I hadn't really comprehended what had happened. What had almost happened.

I could have been killed. Trampled to death by a horse run amok, all in the pursuit of a new gown.

I have a knife cut running from the base of my throat to the swell of my breasts. The scar is healing well, but will probably always be with me. The men find it quite enticing. I ran my index finger down its length. How ironic it would be, after all I've endured, to meet my doom in a street accident.

I'd dressed and gone to work, trying hard to keep my quivering limbs under control.

It was approaching midnight and the climax was building. Every one of the dancers, except Irene, was on stage, dancing the hugely popular cancan. The girls high-stepped across the stage, lifting their skirts, kicking up their legs, giant smiles on their faces, while the orchestra struggled to play the accompanying music from *Orpheus in the Underworld*. The audience roared their approval; the higher the skirts were held the better. The line retreated to the rear of the stage while Maxie took her moment in the limelight. She lifted one leg as high as her head, gripped the ankle in her hand, and danced in a circle. That was Maxie's only trick, and it alone was worth keeping her on. The men bellowed so loudly the ceiling shook.

Colleen was keeping herself to the back and sides. The girls provided their own costumes, and hers wasn't particularly good. I'd seen kitchen maids more exotically dressed. But her petticoats were fluffy and her stockings clean, which is more than I can say for some of them. Her neckline was higher than the norm and her skirts a bit longer. She wore a single black feather in her hair and a length of black ribbon around her neck. Her kicks were high although her smile was a mite too tight.

Roland the Magnificent came to stand beside me. He'd staggered into the Savoy moments before eight. He was as white as the dusting of snow on the distant mountains, but he managed to give me a wan smile. A black sling cradled his right arm. He told me, with a shudder, that the doctor had unceremoniously wrenched his shoulder into place. A few days rest and it would be back to normal.

I told him he'd be paid for the days off.

It was hardly my practice to pay sick time, but what else could I do? The man had been injured in the act of saving my life.

The story of his heroism spread through town like wildfire (miners loved gossip even more than dowager duchesses). Men pressed forward, anxious to buy the hero of the day a drink. He humbly accepted, and I'd gone to the dressing room to check on the girls.

"Having a break?" I asked now, keeping my eyes on the stage. He'd spent the previous hours at the poker table.

"I'm out. Lost last night's winnings."

"What do you think of the dark-haired girl in the back?" I asked. "The tall one in the pink dress."

"Why do you ask?"

"Just wanting a male opinion."

"She's good. Doesn't look like she's enjoying it much though."

"She's somewhat shy." I tried to remember what Colleen had told me when she'd come looking for a job. It didn't matter to me if she'd danced professionally before. All I really needed on the stage were female bodies. She was young and healthy and not ugly, so I hired her.

"The men like her," Roland said.

"You think so?"

"I know so. I heard a couple talking earlier at the bar. They asked Ray when the new girl in the picture was going to be on."

"What did he say?"

"He said she'd be here all night."

Good for Ray. He didn't know, nor care, what went on in the back room. He simply told the customers what he figured they wanted to hear.

The lively song ended and the girls pranced off. Ellie, the oldest and most experienced, brought up the rear. She paused at the edge of the stage, looked over her shoulder, winked, and kicked back one leg. She disappeared to a round of applause. Ellie knew how to play to the crowd.

Time for the big climax. Irene and her dance of the seven veils. The piano player ran his fingers across the keys; the men whispered to each other in excitement.

I left Ronald and went through the saloon into the kitchen cum storage closet at the back. When I slipped into Helen's domain, she was washing glasses in a bucket of dirty water. Jake sat on a stool, puffing on his pipe, enjoying a break. The room was crowded with the three of us in it.

"How's it going?" I asked the head croupier.

"Good."

"I've been wanting to ask you about Roland, the magician. He's at the poker table every night. Losing much?"

"He's losing more than you're paying him, I'd say, Mrs. Mac, but no more than most."

"Working here is amounting to a net loss then?"

Jake dusted cigar ash off the front of his shirt. He dressed the part — starched white shirt, stiff wing collar, crisp cuffs, buttoned vest, gold watch chain, imitation-diamond stick pin, black jacket, black hat, striped pants. "Maybe he works here to be close to the table. I'd say if he wasn't working, he'd still be playing. He's a good player, Mrs. Mac, but luck doesn't run his way most of the time. He likes the social part of it too. Can't be a big winner if you're chatting and being friendly. We've got a regular table going now. That Russian guy — now he knows how to lose money. Can't play worth a hill of beans, has a face as expressive as my four-year-old nephew. Keeps upping the stakes though."

"What about Mr. Turner, who almost threw a punch at Constable Sterling the other night?" When I walked through I'd noticed Count Nicky and Turner still at it. A couple of other men had joined their game.

"He plays with them most hands."

"Keep an eye on him. He's trouble."

"Thanks for the tip, Mrs. Mac. Never would of thought of that by myself." He dropped the end of his cigar to the floor and ground it out under his foot.

I laughed. "Helen, I came in to talk to you. I'm going up to my office. Will you please go to the ladies' dressing room once the show's finished and ask Colleen to come and speak with me."

"Which one's Colleen?"

"Ask one of the girls. Oh, and get the violin player too." I waved my hand in the air. "Tom something or other. Tell him to bring his violin."

I was standing behind my desk looking out the window when I heard footsteps on the stairs. I'd assumed a properly authoritative pose to face my employees. I was not sitting because when I had attempted to do so, I had been most unpleasantly reminded of the recent trauma to my bottom.

I rarely drink liquor — I've seen too much of where that road can lead — but I'd asked Murray to pour me a glass of whisky. I sipped at it. My legs were still weak and my wrist was aching where I'd fallen on it.

Six more hours to go.

Midnight, but full daylight outside. Below the crowd surged back and forth, from one dance hall to another.

"You wanted to see us, Mrs. MacGillivray?" Colleen asked.

I let a couple of heartbeats pass and then turned. She didn't look particularly worried, as she should, at having been singled out to come to the boss's office. The violin player, now he quaked in his boots.

"Do you like working here, Colleen?"

Her shoulders shifted. "It's fine."

I would have appreciated a bit more enthusiasm.

"I've been thinking of making a few changes to the show. Rearrange the lineup. Can you sing, Colleen?"

The violin player stopped quaking.

"Yes," Colleen said.

"Sing something for me."

"What?"

"I don't know what. Anything. Tom will give you accompaniment if you need it." He placed the instrument under his chin and held his bow at the ready.

Colleen thought for a few seconds. "Do you know 'Break the News to Mother'?" she asked him.

He did. Ellie sang it every night.

He plucked the opening notes, and Colleen began to sing. Her voice was good, young and clear. The tune filled the room. I myself am totally tone deaf. It is, I hasten to point out, my only flaw.

She quivered to a halt. Tom stretched out the last note.

"Thank you," I said to him. "That will be all."

"Ma'am." He left.

"Would you like to sing as part of the show?" I said. "Not that song, it's Ellie's. Come up with something new. I'm thinking a ballad of some sort. Something melancholy. The men like that, reminds them of home."

I smiled at her, waiting for gratitude.

She shrugged again. "Okay."

"What do you mean, okay? I'm taking you out of the line and giving you a solo song. Are you not pleased?" I peered at her. Was the girl stupid?

"I'm pleased, ma'am. Thank you. I'll practise hard."

"Good. I'm not offering an increase in pay until I hear the song performed. You'll have to talk to the gentlemen in the orchestra and be sure they can accompany you. Today is Monday; you can practice on Tuesday and begin on Wednesday. You will sing your song at ten o'clock. If it's satisfactory, I'll increase your pay by ten dollars a week. If it's more than satisfactory, I'll consider giving you another increase and a speaking role in the play. Do you know MacDuff's lines?"

"Yes."

"That's settled then." I began to turn back to the window, indicating she was dismissed.

"I'll have to talk to my dad."

"You have to ask your father if you can be paid more?"

"He might not want me putting myself forward."

"You won't be putting yourself forward, I will be. Colleen, I think you can be an asset to the show. I'm offering you an opportunity to make more money and start moving ahead. Regardless of your father's sentiment, the choice is up to you. How old are you?"

"Twenty-two."

"Old enough to make your own decisions, wouldn't you agree?"

"My father's all I have. My mother died when I was young, my brother and sister with her. Scarlet fever." Her eyes glistened with unshed tears. "My father brought me to the Klondike because he couldn't bear to be parted from me. He doesn't want me to be on the stage, thinks it isn't proper. But he's had trouble finding work." Her voice trailed off.

I figured he should have considered that "bad back" before coming all the way to a frontier mining town. "What's your last name?"

"Sullivan."

"Well, Colleen Sullivan. You have a song to practise before Wednesday night. If you think it would help if I speak to your father, he may call on me tomorrow morning between the hours of ten and twelve, here in my office. I believe you're needed downstairs. The dancing seems to have begun."

"Thank you, ma'am," she said. She slipped away so softly I didn't hear the tread of her feet on the loose floorboards in the hallway.

I picked up my glass and studied the bronze liquid. The liquor was making me soft. I should have told Colleen to forget it and left her to slink back to the chorus. Plenty of girls would kill to get a shot at a solo on the stage of the Savoy. I did not need complications with controlling fathers.

I threw back the rest of the whisky. It burned its way down my throat leaving a warm tingling sensation. Now, to tell Irene I was cutting one of her songs.

I might need another drink before doing that.

* * *

Mr. Sullivan was waiting for me precisely at ten o'clock the following morning when I arrived at the Savoy. Not-Murray had unlocked the door a moment before, and aside from Mr. Sullivan we had only one customer. Colleen's father was a large man, muscle gone to fat, balding and red faced. His eyes were the same light shade of blue as his daughter's, attractive on her, somewhat creepy, I thought, on him, trapped as they were in weighty black bags and criss-crossed with red lines. He had a lush, full beard, mostly grey with a few strands of what must at one time have been a startling red. His clothes were cheap, practical, many times mended but reasonably clean.

He was leaning against the bar, a glass of freshly poured whisky in hand. "Mrs. MacGillivray," he called as I entered, "a moment of your time."

"Sir?" I said.

Helen was behind the bar, running a rag across the counter. No need to wipe off the bottles — they didn't sit there long enough to gather dust. As soon as she saw me, she took her cloth into the back room. She'd put the kettle on and bring a cup of tea upstairs.

"Gerry Sullivan," the man said. "Colleen's dad."

"Mr. Sullivan."

"My girl tells me you want her to sing in your show."

"I believe she has potential. If she does a respectable job tomorrow I'll add her to the programme."

Not-Murray stopped in the act of stacking clean glasses to listen in.

Mr. Sullivan stroked his beard, deep in thought. I wasn't going to stand here all morning waiting for him to speak. "A pleasure to meet you, Mr. Sullivan." I half-turned.

"Not sure about that," he said. "I don't want my girl putting on airs."

How I hated negotiating with husbands and fathers. "There will be an increase in her wages. If she does get the spot that is."

His blue eyes glittered. Or it might have been the flicker from the kerosene lamp on the wall opposite. "I don't want my girl going onto the stage. Ain't respectable. Won't say we can't use the money, though." He shook his head.

"Be that as it may, Colleen is on the stage. I'm simply offering her an opportunity for advancement. The decision, I believe, should be left up to her. She's old enough. Now, if you'll excuse me."

Not-Murray had put down the glass and wasn't bothering to pretend he wasn't interested in our conversation.

"English are you?" Sullivan said, apropos of nothing.

"Most certainly not. My late husband's name, as you know, is MacGillivray. I myself was born in the Highlands."

"I guess that's okay then," Sullivan said. What my being English or not had to do with the employment of his daughter, I did not know. But men were always looking for excuses to do what they wanted to do in the first place. He drained his glass and handed it to Not-Murray who dutifully topped it up.

"Colleen will be a great asset to the show," Not-Murray said.

I glared at him. He did not take the hint and return to his chores.

Mr. Sullivan grunted. "Long as she doesn't have to sing 'God Save the Queen,' though. I won't have that."

Personally, I didn't give a flying fig what Mr. Sullivan would have or not. "Good day," I repeated. I headed for my office. Not-Murray followed.

"Mrs. MacGillivray," he cornered me at the bottom of the stairs, "is that true? You're offering Colleen a song?"

"If I said it, young man, then it is true."

He coloured. "Sorry, ma'am, I didn't mean ..."

"What did you mean?"

"That's real smart of you. Colleen'll do a great job. The customers like her. I've had a couple of fellows come in and want to meet the girl in the picture." He pointed to the window, where our advertisement photograph was displayed.

I studied Not-Murray. His name, I'd finally learned, was Edward. Eddie, the other employees called him. I continued to think of him as Not-Murray simply because that was how I'd first identified him. I took little interest in the male employees, which was Ray's domain. Not-Murray, Eddie, was young, probably not much out of his teens. His face was shiny and scrubbed, his hair neatly combed, his eyes wide and clear, and his multitude of teeth were in good condition.

I hid a smile. Clearly Colleen had one admirer. "Thank you for your advice."

The door flew open and a pack of men stumbled in. Long-haired, wild-eyed, foul-smelling, they had the look of desperation which indicated they'd only just stumbled off the boat.

"You had best attend to your duties," I said to Not-Murray.

Chapter Twenty-One

A week had passed since the killing of Jim Stewart outside the Savoy, and the investigation was going nowhere. Despite McKnight's entreaties to find someone to blame, Sterling hadn't been able to come up with any suspects at all. Jim Stewart had arrived in town on Saturday, found lodging in a men's boarding house, kept himself to himself, and died in a back alley on Tuesday evening. A week was a long time in Dawson. In seven days a substantial portion of the town's population turned over, businesses rose to great prominence and crumbled to insignificance, shops and bars changed hands, fortunes were found and squandered.

The person who'd murdered Stewart was most likely long gone. No doubt he, or they, had planned on robbing the man and things had taken a wrong turn. Shocked by what they'd done, they would have been on the next boat out. With no telephone or telegraph at his disposal, Sterling had no way of contacting the departing boats even if he did have a suspect.

Still, he'd keep looking, keep asking questions.

Fiona MacGillivray knew more than she was saying, and he couldn't imagine why. But she was a woman in control of herself, and if she didn't want to talk then she wouldn't. Angus, however, was another matter.

Every Tuesday, Angus took boxing lessons from Sergeant Lancaster. Lancaster had set up a ring behind the kennels, where he instructed not only Angus but any of the younger Mounties who might be interested. Lancaster had, according to him, been a championship fighter in his youth. That may or may not be true, but he did know how to throw a punch, how to block one, and how to move his feet. Indecisive, incompetent, overweight Sergeant Lancaster wasn't of much worth to the police these days, but he was respected for his past service and the boxing allowed him to retain some dignity, a reason to think he still had a contribution to make.

When Sterling arrived at the makeshift ring he was surprised to see not only Angus, Lancaster, and the odd Mountie who might wander over to watch, but also Graham Donohue, Miss Jennings, and Inspector McKnight. Angus was setting up the camera equipment in a patch of dirt. Inspector McKnight observed the scene, while Miss Jennings arranged the sergeant, dressed not in his casual clothes but full dress uniform, against the rope surrounding the ring. His chest was puffed up so high Sterling feared they were in danger of getting a flying button in the eye. Lancaster had waxed his moustache to stiff points and poured about a week's worth of oil into what remained of his hair.

"Not much boxing today, I gather," Sterling said to Donohue.

"Man's pants won't stand the strain if he has to lean over." Sergeant Lancaster had put on a considerable amount of weight since he'd been fitted for his dress uniform.

"I assume you have the inspector's permission to photograph here."

"Eleanor called on him yesterday. Had him melting into her little hand. She can be most persuasive."

At that moment the woman under discussion turned. Catching sight of Sterling she broke into a wide smile and gave him a cheerful wave. He waved back. Angus scowled.

She went to stand behind the camera. More Mounties were gathering. Dogs barked.

"Step forward ever so slightly, sir," Miss Jennings called. "Lift your head a bit. No, no that's too much. Don't forget to breathe."

Lancaster stared off into the distance; his face set in lines of grim determination, his eyes resolute and focused. A general surveying his troops before battle.

Sterling chuckled. "That instrument turns everyone into a blasted fool."

"Not that Lancaster needs encouragement in that department," Donohue said. "Starnes would agree with you. McKnight told Eleanor she can take pictures of the men going about their duties, but Starnes put a stop to the idea of a full-dress parade. He said his men don't have time for that sort of foolishness."

"Excellent," Eleanor called from under her black cloth. She turned the plate around. "Now why don't we take a shot full on? Turn and face me, sir."

"Anything happening with the Stewart murder?" Donohue asked.

"Our investigation continues."

"Nothing, eh?"

"Our investigation continues."

"Tomorrow's my regular day to send my copy to the paper. Be nice if I could follow up the story with a satisfactory conclusion."

"In that case I'll get onto it right away."

"Richard. This is a pleasure. I hope you've come to allow me to take your picture. No charge." Eleanor Jennings had finished with Sergeant Lancaster and left Angus to gather up the gear. A couple of Mounties were examining the equipment and asking questions. Angus chatted happily, explaining how it all worked. Lancaster remained by the rope, as if fastened into place.

"No thank you, Eleanor. I've no interest in having my picture taken." Out of the corner of his eye Sterling saw Donohue's eyebrows rise at the use of her first name.

"I've got permission to poke about the fort a bit, as long as I don't go into any buildings. I'd enjoy your company, if you can spare the time." She looked up at him, eyes sparkling.

He smiled down at her. "I'd be delighted."

Donohue coughed. "About my offer to escort you to the Creeks?"

"That'll have to wait. I've so much I can do here." She kept her eyes fixed on Sterling although she addressed Graham Donohue. "I hear dogs barking. Is that the kennels behind us?"

"We use dog sleds in winter, pack dogs in summer," Sterling said.

"Do you have horses?"

"A few for pulling larger wagons, but not many. Horses aren't good in deep snow, and it's hard to feed them over the winter."

"I'd love to photograph the dogs. Angus, what do you think? We could get pictures of some of the fellows working with the dogs." The young Mounties broke into smiles and straightened their backs.

"When you've finished with that critically important business, perhaps you can find time to track down whoever killed a man on the streets in broad daylight," Donohue muttered. Sterling let the remark pass without comment.

"Well," Donohue drew out the word, "some of us have work to do, so I'll be off. Unless you need me for anything, Eleanor?"

"Bye," she said. "The light's good right here. Do you think you could bring the dogs out, Richard? Oh, uh, Sergeant, you can relax now. I'm finished with you."

*   *   *

I looked up from my ledger at a knock on the office door. I'd been so wrapped up in the numbers on the page I hadn't heard footsteps coming my way. Graham Donohue stood in the open door, smiling.

I put down my pen, glad of the interruption. My rear end was still tender (not to mention colourful), and I'd placed a cushion on my chair. "Good afternoon, Graham. To what do I owe the honour of this visit? You don't often call in the afternoon."

He walked into the room, kicking the door shut behind him. He did not take a seat. "I've come from the fort. Angus is there, helping Miss Jennings with her photography."

"He's quite keen to learn. He's muttering something about becoming a photographer himself."

"It's good for a lad to have ambitions, Fiona. I suspect photography has a bright future. She causes quite a fuss wherever she goes, Eleanor I mean. Men fall all over themselves to stand in front of her camera."

"Women too. The girls here are talking about nothing else. They're all wanting to pose."

"I've seen some of the pictures she's done of them. They're good. You should have your photograph taken, Fiona. Although I fear the radiance of your beauty would set the camera aflame."

Blatant flattery. I never tire of hearing it.

"Richard Sterling's showing her around," Graham said.

"That's nice of him."

A badly sprung horsehair couch decorated in fading shades of sage and peach sits in one corner of my office. A soft oatmeal-coloured cashmere blanket is tossed over the back in the event of cool weather. Graham sat down. He sunk further than he might have expected and struggled to remain upright. He patted the place beside him, inviting me to join him. I remained behind my desk.

"They seem quite fond of each other."

"Who?" I asked sharply.

"Sterling and Eleanor. I would have thought he'd be busy, with that murder still outstanding, but a man can always find time for the things he wants to do, wouldn't you agree, Fiona?"

"I'm sure he was ordered to be polite," I said, my voice sounding sharp in my own ears. "The NWMP wants to put on a friendly face to our American visitors."

"No one ever bothered to put on a friendly face for me." He leaned back, crossed one ankle over his knee, and spread his arms across the back of the couch.

"I have work to do," I said. My shoulders were tight and I rolled them to get some relief. I had not intended the action to be a hint, but Graham was on his feet instantly. He came behind me and placed his hands on my shoulders. His fingers began to move, finding all the sore stiff spots. Despite myself, I let out a contented sigh and leaned back into the pressure.

The numbers on the page before me blurred, and the clamour of the constant passing of men, horses, and dogs on the street below and the shouts and chatter of drinkers coming from the saloon under our feet retreated. I sighed. It had been a long time indeed since I'd felt the loving touch of a man (not counting my son).

Graham's fingers moved up and began rubbing the back of my neck. Sheer pleasure. "You have the most beautiful hair," he murmured. "I'd love to see it flowing free." He threw pins onto my desk. I felt the weight of hair falling down my back. Graham ran his hands through it, massaging my scalp.

Then his hands were on my arms and he was lifting me to my feet, turning me to face him. He is the same height as I. I looked into warm brown eyes, half-closed. His breathing came in short spirits.

"Fiona," he said, in a low deep voice. "Ever since the moment I first saw you ..."

I do not know what would have happened next. Fortunately I did not have to find out. We both leapt out of our skins at a sharp rap on the door. It flew open and Ray Walker stood there.

"Fee, we need ye downstairs. There's been an accident." Only then did he notice Graham behind my desk, my hair in disarray, how close we were standing. "Sorry ta bother ye."

"You're not interrupting anything, Ray. What's happened?"

"Helen's fallen. She mighta broken something."

I fumbled for hair pins and followed Ray downstairs at a rapid clip.

* * *

One of the boards on the stage had given way as Helen was sweeping. Her right leg had fallen through. By the time I arrived, men were trying to lever her out of the hole, and she was yelling to beat the band. Not in pain, fortunately, but in sheer anger.

"Get me out of here," she screeched. "Save me."

Two fellows had her by the shoulders, tugging, another was reaching through the broken boards, pawing at her leg, while several others milled about, shouting instructions. Her skirts were pulled up past her knees, showing black stockings topped by a band of flabby white flesh. Her bucket had tipped and dark water spread across the stage.

"Hold on," one of the helpers, peering into the hole, called. "Her shoe's caught on somethin'." Hands reached in and felt about. Helen bellowed. The men at her top end continued to tug.

"Stop pulling at her." No one paid any attention to me. Such was the level of distress.

I clambered up onto the stage. "Stop that," I said to the would-be rescuers. "You're going to rip her leg off."

Helen screeched all the louder. I took a moment to be thankful this hadn't happened during a performance. With the stage full of women in various stages of undress and the room packed with wild miners, we would have had a riot on our hands.

"Got it," the man at her foot called. Helen yanked, and her leg came free. A gash ran down the calf, blood dripping. It mixed with the spilled cleaning water, and a pink stain formed a slow stream, leaking through the cracks between the boards.

"Save me," she yelled.

"Doctor's coming," Ray said.

"I can't afford the doctor."

"It's only a cut," I said. The leg had moved as Helen did and it was not lying at a bad angle. Not broken. Not even too serious a cut, I suspected. "Lie down a moment and rest." I knelt beside her and pushed lightly on her chest. She dropped back against the boards of the stage. "You," I ordered the pair of legs standing nearest, "give me your jacket."

"Huh."

"For a pillow." I rearranged Helen's skirts to try to conceal her legs.

He tore his garment off, rolled it into a ball and, crouching down, lifted Helen's head gently and tucked the jacket beneath. Gerry Sullivan.

"Murray, run up to my office and get a blanket. There's one on the couch." The crowd pressed closer, everyone wanting to get a look. More down my cleavage, I suspected, than at the injured woman. "The situation seems to be under control. Thank you, gentlemen."

"Bar's open," Ray reminded them.

One at a time the men drifted away.

Murray came back, bearing the cashmere blanket. He handed it to me. "Can you try to get up?" I asked Helen. She nodded, and so I instructed Murray and Gerry Sullivan to support her.

They lifted a wobbly Helen to her feet. I slipped the blanket around her shoulders. She was led to a bench and dropped heavily onto it. She was pale and her breathing ragged, but she had been able to put some small amount of weight on the leg. The bleeding had almost stopped.

The doctor arrived.

"The emergency's passed," I told him. "Although she's somewhat shook up."

He took Helen's hand and looked into her eyes.

I left them to join Ray standing at the back of the room. "Could have been a lot worse."

"Aye."

"We'll have to get that board replaced immediately. I'd suggest you check out the rest of them. Can't have a dancer falling through and bringing the whole line in with her."

"Murray," Ray called, "get over to that carpenter fellow and tell him we have a rush job. We'll be paying through the nose for it," he muttered to me in an aside.

I did not glance at Graham Donohue as I slipped out of the room.

Chapter Twenty-Two

Richard Sterling showed Eleanor Jennings and Angus around
the fort. Not that there was much to see other than a handful
of wooden buildings only fractionally better constructed than
most of the others in town. The outside of the men's barracks,
the mess hall, the officers' quarters, and the offices. She wanted
to see the jail, but conscious of the fact that Inspector Starnes
had said she wasn't to be allowed into any buildings, they had to
stand outside and hope a prisoner would come to the window.
Seeing as to how it was the middle of the day, and thus the
prisoners were out chopping wood, Miss Jennings pronounced
herself disappointed.

Eleanor handed her card to anyone who showed an interest
(which was just about everyone they met), and Angus recorded
appointments in the book he carried for that purpose. The boy
was clearly fascinated by this photography thing, and he sent a
constant stream of questions Eleanor's way. She answered with
equal enthusiasm. Sterling felt like a child trailing behind his
elders, not quite sure what they were talking about.

Eleanor was a good businesswoman, no doubt about that.
She wasn't the first photographer to set up in Dawson, but her
enthusiasm for her business and the obvious passion she had for
the art attracted people who'd not seriously thought about posing for a photograph before.

It didn't hurt that she was very pretty and her tiny delicacy made men feel large and powerful.

He walked Eleanor and Angus back to the road. She thanked him for his help. Angus hoisted the camera box and stood in the dirt of the road. Sterling's tongue felt too big in his mouth. He cleared his throat. "If you, ah, need any further assistance, feel free to call upon me."

"How kind of you," she said, blue eyes wide. "Mr. Donohue has been suggesting I visit the Creeks. Do you think that would be wise, Richard?"

"It's an interesting place."

"I'm not sure about having Mr. Donohue as my escort." She crinkled her pert little nose in thought. "I've an idea! Could you, perhaps, see your way to accompanying me?"

Sterling shifted his boots and avoided Angus's grunt of disapproval. He wasn't quite sure what had come over the lad the last couple of days. Angus had never been sullen before. Onset of puberty, perhaps. "I have my duties here, in town. But I might be able to be excused."

"You have an appointment at four o'clock," Angus interrupted. "We'd better be going."

"Plenty of time," Eleanor said. Her eyes remained fixed on Sterling's face.

"Yeah, well, I have to get home," Angus mumbled.

"Until later, Richard," Eleanor said in a soft voice. She turned and walked away. Angus threw Sterling a filthy look and followed, kicking up clumps of dirt.

Sterling rubbed his face and watched until they rounded the corner.

When he got back to town detachment, Constable McAllen was waiting. He had a man with him, a dirt-encrusted, heavily bearded miner who looked like he'd been living in the bush for years. As he might well have. His right cheek bulged so much he resembled a chipmunk collecting nuts in anticipation of a hard winter.

"This is Lou Redfern." McAllen made the introductions. "He knows something about that Stewart fellow."

"Glad to hear it. Come on in. Constable, bring Mr. Redfern a chair."

The three men crowded into Sterling's office. He'd never had an office before, and was rather proud of this one. Until he had to hold a meeting in it.

Sterling sat behind his desk. Redfern took the chair McAllen brought in, and the young constable took his place up against the wall, arms crossed over his chest. He looked rather pleased with himself.

"Tell me," Sterling said.

Redfern spat a lump of tobacco onto the floor. He cleared his throat. When he spoke it sounded like the instrument didn't get used often. "I recognized the picture you've been showing around. Not a good likeness, mind, but good enough. Stewart. A cheechako. Green as the grass on my father's grave. He had an accent so strong it was hard to understand him sometimes. But my old granny on my mother's side, bless her, was from the Highlands, so I could make out most of what he said."

"What was it he said?"

"Not a lot. Asked questions mostly. Listened a lot."

"Where was this? Where did you meet him?"

"The Yankee Doodle."

The Yankee Doodle was a bar in Klondike City, a rough, makeshift settlement on the other side of the Klondike River, which gloried in the nickname of Louse Town. The bar, as its name suggested, was frequented almost exclusively by Americans. A strange place for a Scotsman who'd been in town for less than three days to find himself.

"Where are you from, Mr. Redfern?" Sterling asked.

"Toronto, once. Left twenty or more years ago. Been prospecting ever since."

"Had much luck?" Not if you judged by the man's appearance, he hadn't. But these old timers didn't change if they did strike it rich. They spent their money on women and drink, not on improving themselves.

Redfern shrugged. "Enough."

Sterling glanced over the man's shoulder. McAllen was rubbing his thumb and index finger together.

The miner might have money, but he clearly wasn't interested in spending it on laundry or baths.

"You're wondering what I'm doing in the Yankee," Redfern said in answer to Sterling's unspoken question. "I don't go there for the company. There's a lady works there I'm fond of. They call her The Stallion."

McAllen made a sign to indicate a female of substantial proportions.

"I see," Sterling said, keeping his face neutral. He'd seen the woman around. She occupied the bottom rung of Dawson's prostitution ladder. Must weigh three hundred pounds. He couldn't imagine how she got all that bulk over the Chilkoot Trail.

"Anyway, I came in from my claim on Monday. Went to the Yankee Doodle straight away. The Stallion was busy so I had a drink or two while waiting. All the talk was about duties, as it usually is."

Sterling nodded. The Americans complained constantly and vociferously about having to pay a tax of 10 percent on the gold they dug out of the frozen Canadian ground. The remaining 90 percent they spent as they liked or sent to their families or banks back in the U.S. They didn't bother to consider that if the shoe was on the other foot — if the gold was in the States — other nationalities weren't even allowed to claim it.

Redfern pulled a tin of tobacco out of his jacket pocket and tossed a wad into his mouth. His teeth, what few remained, were stained brown. He chewed thoughtfully. "I didn't think much of it at first. Usual talk, usual moaning and groaning about how hard done by they are. Poor babies. They talk a good talk, mind, when they're in their cups, but they go back to their claims happy enough once they've had a couple of drinks, a good meal, and the services of a good whore. Or a not so good one." He laughed uproariously at his own joke, tobacco juice spraying across his shirt front. And Sterling's desk.

"I was minding my own business, mind, drinking their lousy liquor. Then I realized one guy was there what didn't belong. No American this, sounded like my dear old granny. Hard as nails she was, tougher than any man I ever met." He paused for a moment. "Raised me, she did. My mother was a drunk; my dad scarpered long before I was born. If my mother even knew who he was.

"But you aren't interested in all that. This Scottish guy was talking to the Americans, egging them on, I thought. Asking why they weren't doing something about it. He asked them why they were handing over ten percent of what they worked darned hard for to a foreign government. Now it seems to me they're the foreigners, not the Canadian government. But I've got no interest in politics, so I didn't say anything." He chuckled. "Besides, if I had, I'd have been lucky to escape with my scalp. The Americans were getting mighty riled up. Your Stewart had money to spend; he was buying rounds. Even bought one for me. It was a busy night. Had to wait a long time till The Stallion was free." He grinned at Sterling. "And well worth the wait it was."

Sterling kept his face impassive. "Did anyone seem particularly interested in Stewart?"

"Aside from getting their free drinks? Not that I noticed. The talk was all about taking the Yukon for the Americans, pushing out the Yellow Stripes and their laws. A couple of fellows started talking about forming a miner's meeting."

Sterling groaned. Miner's meetings were what passed for authority in the gold camps of Alaska. A group of miners who set themselves up as the law and passed judgement as and when they liked. Precisely the sort of vigilante justice the NWMP was in the Yukon to prevent.

"It's all talk," Redfern said. "That bunch isn't gonna organize themselves. They come to town to get drunk and to buy supplies and then head back to their claims. They're not going to start a rebellion for ten percent."

Sterling wasn't so sure. The boundary between the Yukon and Alaska wasn't settled. The Americans complained, but by and large they weren't going to stop working on their digs to get involved in politics. Add a political agitator to the mix? Who knew where that would lead?

"Did Stewart leave with anyone?" Sterling asked.

Redfern shook his head. "Didn't see. He was still there when my lady came in. Later on, he wasn't."

"Thank you for taking the time to tell me about this. I appreciate it. If you can remember anything more, let us know will you."

"Happy to. I'm making good money now. Men start causing trouble, getting all political, does no one any good." He grinned. "I'm getting married."

"Is that so?"

"Yup. The Stallion's coming to my claim. I'm going to make an honest woman out of her. Winters have been getting mighty cold last couple of years. It'll be nice to have something to keep me warm at night." He smiled. It made him look almost human.

"Congratulations," Sterling said, meaning it. "What's the lady's name?"

Redfern looked puzzled. "Do you know, I never asked."

* * *

Helen had been led away, limping but whole, her leg heavily bandaged, complaining she couldn't afford the time off work. Ray had instructed one of his men to see her home. The carpenter had arrived at a fast clip, dollar signs dancing in his eyes.

For the remainder of the afternoon, the front rooms of the Savoy shook with the sound of hammer and saw. Ray had sent Murray to give the carpenter a hand and worked the bar by himself, his scowls getting deeper and darker with every hammer blow.

I remained downstairs, chatting with the men, until Graham Donohue took his leave, muttering something about a story to write.

When the door swung behind him, I let out a long deep breath. The man standing next to me swallowed and tossed back a full glass of whisky. He was young, shiny faced, and perhaps not used to consuming such a prodigious quantity all at once. He broke out in a round of coughing. I left Barney to slap him on the back and bellow for water.

The door opened once again. Angus. He caught sight of me, and we met in the centre of the room. "I've finished with Miss Jennings for the day, and thought I'd walk you home for supper, Mother. If you're ready?"

"What a nice idea." I slipped my arm though his. He was only twelve years old but already reaching my height of five feet eight inches. His father had been very tall. I pushed that thought aside. It was replaced by Graham's description of Eleanor Jennings and Richard Sterling.

Fond was the word he had used.

"What's all that noise?" Angus asked.

"Helen put her foot through a board on the stage. We have to get it repaired and the others checked out before show time. Ray's not happy at the cost. I'll be a couple of minutes. Go and have a look, if you want."

Angus wandered off. I couldn't imagine anything less interesting than watching boards being checked in the back room of a dance hall, but everything fascinated Angus.

It was a trait I hoped he'd keep for a long time.

The Savoy was beginning to fill up. Barney sat in his usual stool, regaling, as usual, a crowd of eager cheechakos with the story, considerably embellished, of the discovery of gold at Bonanza Creek. At another end of the bar, Gerry Sullivan was recounting the saga of Helen Saunderson's mishap in the back room. I caught enough of the story to learn that her leg had almost been sliced right through and only the rapid intervention of he himself had saved the unfortunate lady.

Roland was in the gambling hall, waiting for a poker game to begin. Count Nicky arrived, dressed to impress as always. He took off his hat and approached me. "Madam. Good afternoon."

"Here for a game of cards?" I asked.

"Most certainly. Our English friend wants to get in a hand or two before he's needed on the stage." He looked around the room, studying the men and activity. He indicated the portrait of Queen Victoria behind the bar, clearly disapproving of everything she saw. "You hang an American flag."

"A proper hostess makes all her guests feel welcome."

"The stripes on their flag are effective," His voice drifted off. "A Russian eagle in the corner perhaps, where the stars are. The joining of two great nations. Do you think that would be impressive, madam?"

"What? Oh, yes. Most impressive." Whatever it was supposed to be. "If you'll excuse me …"

"Most of these people are Americans, no?"

"Yes. Here searching for gold."

"Will they stay, do you think?"

"Stay? You mean in the Yukon? Heavens no. They're leaving already, many of them. The best claims are taken, not many new ones being found. These aren't settlers, Nicky. Only a few brought families with them. No gold, no reason to stay."

"But surely there is gold? Much of it. Nuggets the size of apples, lying openly on the ground."

Far be it from me to disabuse anyone of their dreams. "I'm afraid I don't know much about gold mining, sir. I'm just a dance hall hostess."

"Pardon me. Such a topic is not suitable for a lady's ears. Ah, here he comes now. Let the game begin."

John Turner crossed the room. "Afternoon, Count. Ready to lose some money?" He turned to me, but he did not smile. His eyes dropped, with no attempt at subtlety, to the front of my dress. "Miss." He addressed my bosom.

I sniffed and walked away, the feel of his eyes burning into my back. That man made my skin crawl. I've encountered plenty of unpleasant men in my life. Some merely impolite, some obnoxious, a few down-right dangerous. I feared Mr. Turner fell into the latter category.

I've learned the hard way never to ignore my instincts.

I'd have a quiet word with Richard. See if the authorities had any reason to expel the man from the territory.

Richard. Was he truly *fond* of Eleanor Jennings?

Angus returned. He'd only been gone for a couple of minutes, but his face was troubled.

"What's the matter?"

"What makes you think something's the matter, Mother?" he answered, very quickly.

"Your face is as readable as a book." I peered closer. "What is it?"

Taking hold of my arm, he steered me toward the door. He dragged me down Front Street at such a rapid pace I couldn't say another word.

Which, I am sure, was the intent.

Chapter Twenty-Three

Angus scarcely tasted his dinner. His mother kept throwing worried glances his way. When he gave her what he thought was a cheerful smile, her expression became even more concerned.

At last the meal ended, and she went to her room to dress. Mrs. Mann poured hot water into the bucket on the counter to wash the dishes while Mr. Mann leaned back with a contented sigh and took out pipe and tobacco.

Angus remained at the table, lost in a sea of indecision.

He hung around the Savoy, visiting his mother, scrounging meals off kind-hearted Mrs. Saunderson, chatting to Ray Walker. The staff knew him and never chased him out. The women wanted to pinch his cheeks and fuss over him. The men wanted to show him pictures of their own children.

So no one minded when he'd slipped behind the faro table and watched the man who'd entered the gambling hall as Angus walked through from the back. The man had gone straight to a waiting poker game. He sat down with Roland the Magnificent and the strange Russian. Two other men joined them. Jackets were unbuttoned, cigars and pipes taken out, money and gold dust and chips laid on the table. The dealer shuffled cards.

The poker player was the man Angus had seen following Corporal Sterling and Miss Jennings. Who Angus and Dave had also been following.

He should find Corporal Sterling immediately and tell him.

But how could he say he'd seen someone spying on them without letting on that he, Angus, had also been spying?

Perhaps the man hadn't been following Sterling, but Miss Jennings? A woman alone. No man to protect her.

Did he have unnatural designs on Miss Jennings?

In that case he could be dangerous. It was Angus's duty to tell the police what he had seen. But he figured he'd be in more trouble for snooping than in anyone's good books for reporting a non-existent crime.

He couldn't warn Miss Jennings, not without her asking how he knew this.

If the man was intent on Miss Jennings, then it was Angus's responsibility as her employee, albeit part-time, to look out for her.

The man frequented the Savoy. Was he at the Savoy only to play poker? Did Angus have to worry about his mother, also? Surely his first duty was the protection of his mother, not a woman he scarcely knew.

His head hurt.

"Are you not feeling well, dear?" Mrs. Mann asked.

He opened his mouth to say he was fine. Behind her he could see the biscuit tin. "I'm a little tired," he said instead. "Do you have anything that would give me some energy?"

She got down the tin. "I made these for your lunches, but I'm sure it wouldn't hurt to have one now." The battered tin was stuffed full of cookies. The cookies were stuffed full of raisins.

He took one. Then he took another. "Thanks, Mrs. Mann. You always know what I need."

She preened.

"I'm off." Fiona's head came around the door. Tonight she was going out without a hat. Her long black hair was tied with a red satin ribbon into a loose knot at her neck. From there it cas-caded down her back. Even in Dawson a woman never went out in public without a hat, not unless she was of the commonest sort. But Fiona always seemed to be able to get away with more than other women could.

Angus jumped to his feet. "I'll walk with you, Mother."

"How nice."

He grabbed another cookie, barely avoiding having the lid snap down on his fingers.

Angus enjoyed escorting his mother through town. Many of the men they passed knew her and quite a few of the women as well. Those who didn't know her sometimes stopped and stared. Men whispered her name to their companions and women tugged at their husbands' arms to get them moving. Tonight, her unbound hair was a sensation. She'd told him a few things about her life in London — the parties and dances, the dinners, the theatre or opera, late suppers in the Savoy Hotel. Tonight she looked every bit as regal as if she were off to Buckingham Palace to attend a ball. Except that the skirts of her scarlet gown were tucked into the belt to keep from dragging through the mud, her footwear — shockingly exposed — was sturdy prac-tical boots, her jewellery was fake, and a dead dog lay in the middle of the road.

"I keep meaning," she said, as they skirted the dog, "to call on the dressmaker. I've bought all that fabric and it's sitting at home doing nothing."

She'd told him about yesterday's near-accident with the run-away horse. Hard not to as she was walking gingerly and pro-tecting her side. Today she seemed so much better he'd almost forgotten about it. Until now.

He stopped in his tracks.

Was it an accident?

The poker player had been following Miss Jennings. He'd been hanging around the Savoy.

A man had been murdered behind the Savoy.

Was Fiona in danger?

"What's the matter?" she said.

"Nothing!"

"Come along then. You've been acting quite strange this evening, Angus."

He gripped his mother's arm tighter and picked up his pace.

After he deposited her at the Savoy, and she went to the back to supervise preparations for the entertainment, Angus slipped into the gambling hall.

The poker game was still in progress. The man he was interested in had a generous pile of chips stacked in front of him. Count Nicky was almost out. Roland checked his watch. "Time for me to go, chaps."

The unnamed man growled. "Can't quit now."

"Duty calls." Roland gathered up his small pile of chips. "I'll be back later if you want to stick around, Turner."

Turner. Angus had a name.

Roland spotted Angus watching them. "Hello, my lad. I haven't seen you around much these last few days. What have you been up to?" He slapped Angus heartily on the back. The boy almost pitched forward into the faro table.

"I'm working for Miss Jennings, the photographer, in the afternoons," he said, once he'd recovered his balance.

"Good boy. Keep busy. Help your mother support the family."

They stepped aside as the members of the orchestra walked through, lugging their instruments. "Showtime," Roland said. "Time to regale the citizens of this fair town with feats of stunning derring-do and acts of spectacular magic." He laughed heartily. "And then, I'll go on. Come and watch the show, why don't you?"

Angus muttered something non-committal.

"Interested in cards, are you?"

"No. I mean, why do you ask?"

"Because you keep glancing over at the game." Roland dropped his voice. "The Russian can't play to save his life. The guy on his right's not half-bad but he's not as good as he thinks he is. It's all in the cards anyway. Don't fall into it, my boy. The only winner is your mother and the house."

"Why do you play then?" Angus asked, genuinely interested.

"Because I'm a sucker. I'm finished on stage by nine; if you're still around, why don't we go next door for a waffle?"

"Okay."

"I'm on again at ten-thirty, but that'll give us time." Roland slapped Angus's back again. This time he was ready and managed to keep his footing.

Ellie and Betsy sashayed through the room, wiggling their hips, tossing their hair, greeting men they knew. They made their way, slowly, into the saloon to remind those few who were so deaf they couldn't hear the band in the street and the caller announcing the delights to be found within that the show was about to begin.

When Angus turned his attention back to the poker table, the man, Turner, had half-turned in his seat. He was staring at Angus openly. He kept his cold dark eyes fixed on Angus's face until, embarrassed, the boy dropped his head.

* * *

Undeterred, Angus remained in the gambling room. He pretended to be interested in the other tables, roulette, faro, another poker game, but kept his attention on the main table. No matter how much the Russian fellow lost, he kept playing. And drinking. He kept the waiter well-tipped for providing a constant supply of whisky.

Angus had almost forgotten about the Russian and his crazy plan to capture the Yukon and trade it for Alaska. He wondered if he should alert someone in authority to the plan, but decided that if Count Nicky was spending all of his time, and money, playing poker and drinking he wasn't too much of a threat to this remote section of Her Majesty's Dominion. Miss Jennings told him the count had arrived for his appointment this morning. She'd taken his photograph and told him she was still composing an introductory letter to the president of the United States.

Men parted as if they were the Red Sea and Angus's mother were Moses. She walked into the gambling hall, all smiles and charm.

"What are you doing here?" she said, catching sight of Angus trying to disappear behind a fat, cigar chomping man.

"I'm interested in the psychology of gambling," he said the lines he'd prepared in expectation of such a question.

"What does that mean?"

"Psychology is a new form of medicine, Mother. The study of the mind."

"Pooh."

"Really. It's very interesting. The mind can express itself without a person even being aware of it. That's called the subconscious."

"Humph."

"How's the stage?" He changed the subject. His mother didn't mind him coming to the Savoy during the day, but she chased him out at night. It would be hard for him to protect her if he wasn't allowed to be near her.

"Seems to be satisfactory. The hole was fixed and some less-trustworthy boards replaced and new nails put in to be sure.

Then Ray and the men jumped up and down on it. Everything seemed to hold. I can only hope …" Her voice trailed off.

She was staring at the poker table. Turner had leaned back in his chair and was openly studying her. His look was insolent and not at all friendly.

"Who's that man, Mother?"

"I don't know. But I know I don't like him. Isn't it time you were off home?"

"I'm having a waffle with Roland when he finishes."

"That's nice. It's time I had a word with Ray." She walked away, and Angus let out a long breath.

A chorus of cheers and stomping feet announced that Roland the Magnificent had reached the end of his act and the women were coming on stage.

Roland took Angus next door to the so-called bakery run by the Vanderhaege sisters. They only thing they baked was waffles, which they sold for twenty-five cents each, but they did a roaring trade late in the evening (early morning rather) when custom in the dance halls began to trail off. This early there was no line. Roland went up to the plank laid in front of the open door that served as a counter. The shop had burned down not long ago, but the sisters had rebuilt quickly. The interior of the bakery was festooned with flags, most prominently the Union Jack and the red-white-and-blue of Holland along with colourful orange banners. The Stars and Stripes were only slightly less noticeable than the Union Jack. Anike, who'd suffered minor burns in the fire, greeted Angus with a wide smile.

"Two of your best waffles, please," Roland said, digging into the pocket of his waistcoat. "I'll have a coffee also. Angus?"

"No thanks, sir."

Roland passed over some coins, and Anike placed hot, steaming waffles into their hands. Later in the night, when the women were rushed off their feet and many of the customers too drunk to care, the waffles would be cold and either undercooked or burned.

Angus and Roland leaned against the shop front and watched the passing parade, munching in contentment.

"Your mother and Ray Walker are partners in the Savoy?" Roland asked.

"Yup."

"More than partners?"

"What do you…? Oh. No. They own the Savoy together and that's all."

"I thought so. They seem an unlikely couple, even just as business partners."

"Mother says neither one of them could make a success of it on their own. She's a woman, so would have trouble being the boss of men, and the Mounties might not let her anyway. Ray doesn't have a head for business, so Mother handles the money."

"Knew each other in the old country did they?"

"No. They met in Skagway. Mother planned to stay in Alaska, but that didn't work out. Ray was coming to the Yukon, but he was ready to believe what anyone told him. He would have had trouble making it this far ahead of the crowd. They teamed up and here we are." Angus tossed the last bite of waffle into his mouth and wiped his hands on the seat of his trousers.

"Another?" Roland asked.

"Sure."

Roland handed Angus a quarter. "I guess it helped, both of them being Scottish."

Angus shrugged. Anike called to her sister in the back for another waffle. "My mom's not really Scottish. She was born on Skye, but she moved to England when she was a girl. She never went back. Ray's Scottish though. From Glasgow."

"Did your mother like England?"

Angus bit into his waffle. "Well enough, I guess. I don't remember England much. I remember seeing a castle once. And a park with big trees. We came to Canada when I was four."

"Why?"

"Better opportunities, she said. You might have noticed, sir, that my mother is somewhat unconventional."

Roland smiled. "I did notice. Is this unconventional mother of yours interested in politics? She ever talk about the ownership of the Yukon, say, or the situation in Canada?"

"She didn't like Skagway. Alaska's too lawless. She says people need a stable government and a belief in law and order to be able to do business successfully."

"That's good to hear."

"She thinks women should be allowed to vote. She says they can't make much worse decisions than men make."

Roland chuckled. "She's probably right about that. Tell me about Walker. He ever talk about Scotland?"

"Told me once it was not the place for a poor man like him."

"Is that so?"

"Why are you asking?"

"Just making conversation."

"He'd like to go back some day. Visit his sisters, see his nieces and nephews again. Show them all that Ray Walker had made something of himself."

"Resentful is he?"

"I don't know about that. Everyone comes to the Klondike expecting to make it rich. We came over the Chilkoot together. Plenty of nights sitting around the campfire, talking about our dreams." He didn't mention that he and Ray talked while Fiona nursed her sore feet, melted snow to wash in, attempted to mend her tattered skirts, and swore she would never set foot outside a city again.

"Does Walker have many Scottish friends?"

"Gee, I don't know. I don't think he has many friends of any sort."

"Get a lot of Scottish people in the Savoy?"

Angus thought while he chewed. Everyone came into the Savoy. His mother had once said she wouldn't be surprised to one day see a Hottentot or the king of the Zulus walk through the doors. Some men came in who spoke with the same accent as Ray. He always seemed glad to see them. "Quite a few, yeah. They put their heads together and talk about Scotland." Angus didn't know what they talked about. But if Roland wanted to make conversation, Angus thought it would be polite to make conversation back. He remembered something he could tell Roland. "Scotland would be a fit place for a Scot to live, Ray says, if the English would leave."

Roland drained the last of his coffee. He made a face. "Disgusting."

Chapter Twenty-Four

After doing the banking Wednesday morning, I took my bolts of cloth to the dressmaker, who oohed and aahed over the quality of the fabric. We had a consultation, and I was poked and prodded and measured. I'd decided to get two gowns. Extravagant, certainly. I excused the expense on the grounds that I hadn't made the final payment on the dress left unfinished when the previous dressmaker died.

New gowns naturally require new hats. New jewellery would be nice also, but I drew the line there. Besides, not much of quality could be found in Dawson. Those dance hall girls who'd been favoured by newly rich miners sported belts or necklaces made of gold nuggets strung together.

Valuable to be sure, but dreadfully tacky.

My rear end was still badly bruised — the colour of an approaching thunderstorm — but the soreness was fading and my limbs were no longer quite so stiff.

I returned home via York Street, slowing as I approached Miss Jennings' photography studio. I wondered what I would look like in a photograph. It wouldn't hurt, surely, to have one taken. I would wear one of my new dresses. The navy blue perhaps. With a lovely hat. I would insist on posing against a plain backdrop — I needed no distracting props.

Perhaps I could have Angus with me. Something for him to

cherish as he grew up, for me to look back on in my later years.

One photograph, for my own purposes. It would never get to London or Toronto where there might still be men searching for me.

Although she had said she could make copies. Could I trust Eleanor to destroy the original?

As I stood kitty-corner to the studio contemplating the wisdom of surrendering to vanity, the front door opened. Irene came out, followed by Eleanor herself. Eleanor wore her usual skirt and blouse, but Irene was dressed in the red-and-black gown she wore most evenings for the dancing.

At six o'clock this morning, as the Savoy was closing, Ray Walker suggested Irene join him for breakfast. She'd batted her stubby eyelashes, said she had a terrible headache and would he mind if, just this once, she declined.

He'd offered to walk her home, whereupon she'd said she needed a quiet time to enjoy the cool air. Alone.

Clearly she had not exactly meant alone. Probably not quiet time either.

Irene set off down the street, heading away from me. Eleanor glanced over and saw me watching. She didn't smile or wave, simply stood looking at me, her hands folded across her stomach. A horse came between us, pulling a cart, straining against the mud. When it passed Eleanor had gone back inside and closed her door.

I decided not to get my photograph taken today.

A small boy collided with me. "Sorry, miss," he mumbled, darting around my skirts. He bolted across the street. I glanced around, hoping to see his mother following him.

Instead I saw John Turner leaning against a shop front, smoking. He made no effort to pretend he wasn't watching me; his gaze was open and impertinent.

I hiked up my skirts and, after checking for oncoming runaway horses, waded into the street. Turner tossed his cigar onto the boardwalk and crushed it with his heel. He stood his ground and watched me approach.

"You, sir. I demand that you stop following me."

"Following you, ma'am?" he said, in a voice so lazy it bordered on insolence. "Now why would you think I'd be doing that?"

"I've seen you watching me, and I do not care for it."

"Seems to me if you don't like it, ma'am, you shouldn't dress to attract attention. Shouldn't frequent a dance hall either."

"As you are well aware, I own a dance hall."

"My mamma always told me, you aren't gonna find a *lady* in a saloon."

I bristled. Clearly I had been insulted. I wasn't exactly unaccustomed to men looking at me. And I hadn't actually seen Turner *following* me. I'd turned around and there he was, standing on a street corner. Had he been standing on that street corner all along?

I knew better than to let the slightest doubt cross my face. "If I see you watching me again, I'll have the police on you."

"Yellow Stripes lock up every man in town who looks at you, ma'am, there won't be many left to drink in your bar."

That might have been a compliment. I did not take it as such.

"You have been warned." I lifted my head and sailed off.

I rounded the corner walking fast, not looking back. I kept walking, in case he truly was following me.

That encounter had been a mistake. If Turner had not been following me, I'd made myself look like a fool. A lot of people passed through this town, but it wasn't all that large. I ran into plenty of people I knew every time I set foot out the door.

On the other hand, if he was following me, then I'd let him know I was aware of it. Would that discourage him, or make him bolder?

I remembered Eleanor at her door, bidding Irene a fond good-bye.

Was it possible Turner had not been following me, but watching Eleanor and Irene?

*   *   *

I scheduled Colleen to perform her solo song at ten o'clock. While I'd been home having my afternoon nap, she and the musicians gathered in the back to rehearse. I didn't bother to listen in. It would be acceptable or it would not. If not — meaning only if the audience didn't like it — I'd drop it. I'd asked Angus to write a sign to place beside the photograph of the girls with a big arrow pointing to Colleen that said: "Solo performance tonight!"

Irene was in a black funk. As expected, she hadn't been the least bit pleased when I informed her we were giving Colleen the ten o'clock song. Irene was accustomed to singing a cheerful ditty that had the miners clapping and stamping their feet. She'd tried to argue, but I wasn't having any of that and went on my way, daggers piercing my back.

It didn't hurt, occasionally, to remind the employees exactly who was boss here.

Angus had walked me to the Savoy again this evening. Two nights in a row. An unprecedented occurrence. Something was on his mind, and I wondered if it had anything to do with the killing we had witnessed.

I'd heard nothing about that incident for a few days, and had largely forgotten about it with all the other things going on. My mind wandered to that unfortunate man, and how his last words had been my name. And *Culloden*. Richard had told me the fellow's name — Jim Stewart. Common enough.

I watched Roland the Magnificent do his act. Toward the end, he always hauled someone out of the audience to poke fun at. The men at the front leaned forward, in anticipation of that moment. No one seemed to mind being made to look a fool, not if they were at centre stage.

We had more than a full house tonight. Men were lined up against the walls and crammed onto the benches with scarcely enough room for a flea to squeeze between. I stood at the back, watching, my elbows stuck out at right angles clearing me some space. Every now and again someone (usually a newcomer) tried to "accidently" press up against me. A jab in the ribs or stomp on the foot tended to correct this enthusiasm.

Above, the boxes were full. Men lined the stairs, shoving against each other in a struggle for the best viewpoint. Murray came through carrying two bottles of Champagne. He bellowed at men to get out of his way.

An unprecedented three Mounties were in the building. One in the saloon, two more watching the show. They should have been watching the audience, but one's attention did tend to wander.

Roland sent the hapless cheechako back to his seat. The fellow was flushed red with embarrassment and grinning from ear to ear. I thought it would be an excellent idea if I could arrange to have his photograph taken as Roland was removing coloured scarves from his ear. I was sure his friends, if not he himself, would cherish a memento of the occasion. Unfortunately it would not be possible to squeeze Miss Jennings, her camera, and all of her secondary equipment into the room. Never mind the possibility of her flash power exploding in the crowded room.

Just as well. No telling how much damage impromptu photography could do to one's reputation and legacy.

"We're not letting any more men in," Richard Sterling said into my ear. "What have you done this time?"

I smiled at him. "Simply running the very best dance hall in town."

He grinned. "Don't tell me all these people are here to see him." He gestured toward the front, where Roland was taking extravagant bows. The men began booing at him to get off the stage. The boos turned into a roar as musicians struck up "There'll be a Hot Time in the Old Town Tonight" and the girls pranced out.

Richard and I were quiet for a few moments. No point in trying to talk over the din.

I noticed Irene climbing the stairs. A peacock in her scarlet-trimmed gown amongst the men, almost uniformly dressed in dull brown or dirty black. When not on stage, the women were expected to be available for those well-heeled customers who might like company in their box. Along with said company, the men were expected to purchase a bottle of Champagne with which to entertain their favourite. Irene never went into the boxes during the show. She was paid enough that she could enjoy the luxury of taking a rest when she wasn't performing. Tonight she joined a miner (who looked to be only slightly younger than Methuselah) at his table. Smiling broadly, he hailed the passing Murray, after ensuring everyone noticed his companion. I'd seen Irene paying him attention before. I didn't have time to wonder if that meant anything.

I nodded toward the door. Richard understood and went first. It was only slightly less noisy in the gambling room. We went through into the bar. I made my way to the tiny alcove beneath the stairs where the crowd was fractionally less dense.

"I suspect," I said, when I thought I could be heard, "they're here for Colleen."

"What?" He put his hand behind his right ear.

"Colleen," I bellowed in the manner of a fishmonger in Covent Garden. "They're here for Colleen's new song."

He nodded.

This was impossible. I pointed upstairs. His eyebrows lifted.

The noise faded to a dull roar as we ascended the stairs. "A man can't hear himself think," Richard said. "I figured you might need a hand, so I've posted extra men in the Savoy. I can't allow any more in, Fiona. Someone's likely to get crushed in the throng."

"I'm surprised myself." I led the way to my office and unlocked the door. The lamps were unlit and the remains of the northern daylight cast long shadows. "I assume they're here to see Colleen sing her song, but I don't know how everyone knew about that."

Richard gave me his old smile, the one that lifted my heart. I wondered if he smiled that smile at Miss Eleanor Jennings. I myself stopped smiling.

"Her father's been showing that picture all around town. Telling everyone they'll see something tonight that will, in his words, blow their socks off."

"He is?"

"Do you know what this something is?"

"No. I told her to perform a melancholy ballad. Her voice is good but nothing special."

"I suspect her voice is not what they're here to see. I have to warn you, Fiona. Anything improper and I'll have to shut the show down."

I didn't bother to argue. The smile had gone and his face had turned serious. I knew the law as well as anyone. We, like all the saloon and dance-hall operators, skirted it occasionally, and the Mounties turned a blind eye. But they'd never stand for outright flaunting.

"I'll have a word with her," I said in my meekest voice.

"Good idea."

"I'm surprised at her father though. I got the impression he didn't like her being on the stage."

"He's a practical man, perhaps. He doesn't have to like it, but if it's going to happen he'll make the best of it."

"I did notice he's found a good seat." Gerry Sullivan had arrived early and plopped himself front and centre.

Silence fell between us. Richard looked at the window. I studied the crack running in a jagged streak down the wall. Surely it was longer than it had been yesterday.

"Fiona."

"Yes, Richard?"

"Fiona, I …" He stepped toward me

"There you are! Murray said you'd gone upstairs. Hi, Corporal Sterling. I'm not interrupting anything, am I?"

"No, Angus, you're not. What's up?" Richard retreated.

"Did you know Joe Hamilton's guarding the door? Not letting anyone in. Why's it so crowded?"

"A new singer tonight. There seems to be some … expectation around her," I said.

"I heard a couple of guys talking about it this afternoon, when Miss Jennings and I were photographing the waterfront. They said it's gonna be a dance that was banned in the East."

I groaned. If Colleen danced this banned dance, the police would shut us down. If she didn't, the men would riot. If the police tried to stop her, they'd riot at that.

"Perhaps we need more men," Richard said. "Angus get to the fort. Tell McKnight I'm expecting trouble."

"Yes, sir." Angus loved to be of assistance to the police. Then he eyed me. "Perhaps you should remain here, Mother."

"Remain where?"

"Here. In your office."

"Why on earth would I do that?"

"In case of trouble."

"I'll look out for your mother," Richard said. "Hurry now."

Angus ran out the door.

"Let's go and have a word with this singer of yours."

As we hurried down the stairs, I glanced at my watch. Nine forty-five. Joe Hamilton was standing behind the door to the street, hands on hips, feet planted. Faces were pushed up against the windows, trying to peer inside. Ray had taken himself off bar duty to pace back and forth across the room. He slapped his billy club into his hand as he walked.

The bar wasn't as busy as it had been earlier. Only a few hardcore drinkers remained. The gamblers, however, were busy at it: not much could interrupt their game. Roland had joined Count Nicky and John Turner at the poker table. Jake was dealing tonight, but his mind didn't seem on it. He kept glancing over his shoulder to the dance hall. I fancied the walls themselves were bulging under the strain.

I remembered why I'd tried to speak privately to Richard. I wanted to have a word with him about Turner. Too late now.

We entered the dance hall. Ruby was alone on stage singing a cheerful ditty.

We stuck to the walls, our progress impeded by the press of men. Richard went first, pushing and shoving to clear a path for me. At the sight of the uniformed Mountie, heading backstage, they began to murmur. And not in a friendly way.

We reached the entrance to the backstage area, guarded by one of Ray's men. I glanced at Richard. "You can't come in." Heaven knows what state of undress the ladies might be in. They would be getting ready for the performance of *Macbeth* scheduled to follow Colleen.

"I'll wait here."

An air of expectation hung over the dressing room. None of the usual chatter as the women changed costume. They'd done *Macbeth* a hundred times before, most of them never gave it a second thought. Tonight all eyes were on Colleen.

Irene wasn't here, I noticed. Probably still upstairs sulking and quaffing Champagne.

Colleen stood alone at the back of the room. She was breathing deeply and rhythmically, sweeping her arms in a pattern, down at her sides, then up to touch her chest and down again. Her eyes were closed, her face calm. She wore a blue dressing gown. Threads hung from the hem and elbows, one sleeve was ripped. It had been patched in several places.

Wide-eyed girls stepped aside. I walked up the middle of the room until I stood in front of Colleen. "Is that what you plan to wear on stage?"

She opened her eyes. They darted around the room and did not look into my face. "No."

"Take it off."

Her fingers shook as she untied the belt and dropped the dressing gown. The girls gasped.

Colleen wore black stockings and a short black lacy skirt. So short it barely covered her knees, so lacy I could see the outline of her upper legs. Her pink blouse — if you could call it that — covered little more than her plump breasts. The neckline was deeply scooped, a row of tassels sewn to the bottom of the blouse. Her bellybutton was exposed as well as the top of her hips. Arms and shoulders were bare.

"Are you out of your mind?" I screeched as my composure broke.

She lifted her chin and looked directly at me. A trace of defiance flared momentarily. Then it died, and she dropped her eyes.

"Ellie," I called.

"Mrs. Mac?" Ellie, as the oldest of the girls, was the only one permitted to use the short form of my name.

"In the absence of Irene," curse her wounded pride, "you'll have to do the next song."

"Me?"

"No, not you, the other Ellie. Of course you."

"What shall I sing?"

"I don't damned well care. Get the hell on that stage and sing your heart out. Make it a cappella if you have to. Maxie and Betsy, you'll dance behind her. Make something up, but make it good."

"What's a cappella?" Maxie asked.

"Get out there the second Ruby comes off. I want no breaks in the performance. We'll go to the witches' scene immediately after. And where the hell is Irene!"

"Here."

I whirled around. Irene stood in the doorway. Her hands were crossed demurely in front of her, her head was high, and the edges of her mouth turned up. "The audience has noticed an unusual number of Mounties in the hall. Inspector McKnight's chewing his pipe just about in half and not looking at all pleased. As I don't have a song at this here time," she sniffed, "I was enjoying a glass of Champagne in the boxes. But then I figured you might be in need of assistance. I had to pass Corporal Sterling himself to get into the dressing room." Her eyes glittered with self-satisfaction and malice. When Irene attempted to put on airs, she tried to imitate an upper-class accent. My accent. It made my hair curl.

"Do your regular song," I said through gritted teeth.

The other girls might not have been in the room. Irene and I stared at each other through a tunnel of silk and cotton, feathers and baubles.

"What's it worth?"

"Your job."

"You wouldn't dare."

My mind raced. If I offered Irene an increase in salary now, when everyone could see I was desperate, I'd be exposing a vulnerability. If I refused, she might walk away.

"I believe Ruby is about to finish. I want someone on stage in one minute. Irene, do it. Or leave. Ellie, be ready to move."

Irene's face hardened. If she hadn't been on the far side of the room, she might well have struck out at me. Instead she let out the breath she was holding. "Yes, Mrs. MacGillivray," she said.

I didn't let my relief show. Irene was practical and sensible. She wouldn't walk out on this job, not without the guarantee of another. She was possibly the best-paid dancer in all of Dawson. A position she would protect at all costs.

I'd gambled and won. For now.

I turned back to Colleen. "Your costume is highly inappropriate. Are you aware of that, Colleen?"

"No, ma'am. I'm sorry, ma'am. My dad wanted me to have fun with it, that's all. He said it would be popular." She looked about ready to cry.

Popular all right. I didn't bother to address the fact that her father (her father!) suggested she appear in public in that attire. Did the man not know it would likely get her a night in jail? "What song did you intend to perform, may I ask?"

"The Hootchy-Kootchy."

The girls gasped. "Spare us," someone cried.

"Are you insane!" The Hootchy-Kootchy was considered so degenerate it would surely have Colleen arrested, daring costume or no. Along with me for allowing it to be performed, the orchestra for playing the music, Ray for being the proprietor of the establishment where such an offence occurred. Possibly the other dancers simply for being in the company.

That explained the costume. I'd heard rumours that various females from Egypt or Algeria were performing their native dances in New York and Chicago, causing some not-inconsiderable degree of scandal.

Colleen began to cry. Fat tears rolled down her cheeks. "Does that mean I can't sing?"

I wondered if she was simple. I turned to face the watching women. "Finish getting ready. We'll continue with the programme as normal." Onstage, Irene's voice lifted as she began to sing. I wondered how long I had before the men would notice that the woman they'd come to hear was not performing. Fortunately we had not put the time of her song on the sign. They might not even realize she hadn't appeared until the show was over and the dancing had begun.

Or not.

Back to Colleen. She'd pulled the tattered dressing gown over her shoulders. "The orchestra was okay with you doing this dance?"

She shrugged. "They didn't say anything."

The dance itself needn't have been provocative. Not if she simply moved around the stage to the music. It was the costume, and whatever she intended (heaven help us!) to do with it.

"I thought I told you I wanted something melancholy." My fault, I was beginning to realize, for not speaking to the orchestra leader and not attending the rehearsal.

"My father said this would be better."

"Your father approved of this?"

"It was his idea."

That set me back on my heels.

"The men are here because they would like to hear you sing. Do you know any *suitable* songs?"

She thought. "I can sing 'Wild Irish Rose.'"

"That should do. You will go on at the conclusion of the last scene in *Macbeth*. You will sing that one song, dressed in your street clothes." I refrained from telling her she would never sing in the Savoy again. Regardless of whether the girl was simple or simply an obedient daughter to a greedy or degenerate father, I didn't need trouble. No matter how appealing she was in the photograph.

"I'll tell the musicians to be ready with 'Wild Irish Rose.' If they don't know it, you'll have to sing without accompaniment. You will sing your song, take your bows, and leave the stage. Understood?"

"Yes, ma'am."

Once more I passed through the line of watching women. Disaster averted, my heart struggled mightily to settle back into its regular rhythm as I left the dressing room.

Richard lifted his eyebrows in question. I nodded to indicate all was well. Some of the tension drained from his handsome face.

The musicians, fortunately, told me they knew the music to Colleen's new song. They didn't question the change in plans, which made me suspect they'd been hoping she would do something scandalous.

Richard and I headed for the back as the men applauded Irene. She took a long time indeed over her bows. When the enthusiastic applause was dying down, rather than leaving the stage, she strolled lazily to the front of it, hips swaying. She stood there a moment, waiting, as the music ground to a halt.

I stopped walking. "Oh, no."

She ran her eyes over the room, sweeping the audience, pausing now and again to fix on someone and centre him out. Almost every man sat straighter. Murray paused on his way up the stairs, Champagne bottles in hand. The waiter coming down, bearing the empties, stopped with one leg hanging in the air. Irene lifted her head and surveyed the boxes. The miner she'd been entertaining was almost hanging over the railing to get a better look. No one moved. No one breathed.

Inspector McKnight tugged at his shirt front. Ray was beside him, not looking happy. It couldn't be easy knowing your loved one was desired by a good number of men.

And that, as I knew, wasn't the half of it.

Richard muttered something under his breath. We were near the back of the hall. Too far away to intervene.

I had never heard the room so quiet when it was so full.

Abruptly Irene leaned over. She scooped a gold nugget off the floor. Most nights she was showered in nuggets and other tokens of the men's appreciation. Tonight, although we were full to bursting, the haul was down. I suspected they were holding back to see what Colleen had to offer.

Irene held the nugget in her hands. It wasn't very big. She turned it over and examined it for a long time. I fancied I could hear the mice moving in the walls. At last Irene again studied the audience. She placed one hand on her hip and cocked her head to the side. The silence stretched.

"Now, tell me, boys," she said in a good loud voice, "is this the best you can do?"

They roared. A blizzard of gold began. The men threw nuggets onto the stage. The ones at the back pressed forward, to get a better aim. One fellow up in the boxes began waving his Champagne bottle. I dearly hoped he wasn't going to throw it.

Irene looked directly at me as gold and jewellery fell around her feet.

When the storm had ebbed, she lifted one hand. "Thank you, one and all," she said. "I will be making an announcement at the end of the evening." Whereupon she began gathering up her loot. A couple of the girls ran out to help her pick it all up.

"Spare me," I said.

"Do you know what this announcement is, Fiona?" Richard asked.

"I live in fear. Don't excuse your men just yet."

There's usually an ebb and flow through the dance hall all night. Men sit for part of the performance, watching their favourite bits, and then they might wander into the bar for a drink or a chat with their friends, or into the gambling hall for a turn at the tables. Back to the hall for another skit.

Tonight, no one moved. Men who hadn't found seats or a place along the wall crowded the stairs or pushed and shoved at the door. I worried about the state of the men's bladders. No one was being allowed into the Savoy, therefore those already inside couldn't leave to relieve themselves in the alley without giving up their place.

The night crawled on. Richard huddled in corners with Inspector McKnight and various Mounties. Ray Walker patrolled the rooms slapping his billy club into his hand. The waiters struggled to serve their customers. The girls onstage had less bounce in their step and less range in their voice. Everyone was waiting … for what no one knew.

I could see Mr. Sullivan, Colleen's father, sitting in the front row. I edged my way toward him. He was an American, newly arrived in town. Was he so unaware of the laws and norms of the territory that he'd thought his daughter would be able to perform such a dance in such a costume? She'd told me he didn't like her to put herself forward.

Tonight, I was finding that hard to believe.

He was chomping on a fat cigar and not paying much attention to the show. He shifted in his seat constantly — earning him more than a few sour looks from his bench mates — glancing around the room, eyeing the police, checking his watch. As the time came and went for Colleen's aborted dance, he began to twitch.

Oh, yes. He'd known the fuss she was going to cause.

I stood against the wall, having evicted the previous place-holder, and watched everything.

I had not seen Angus again since he'd been sent to fetch Inspector McKnight. I doubted he had meekly gone on home.

The three witches scene from *Macbeth* is always popular. The girls, dressed in their dance costumes, sit around a kerosene lamp and shout the immortal lines in loud piercing voices meant to resemble cackles. Ellie then comes out, playing the Thane of Cawdor, dressed in her bloomers. The bloomers are, of course, part of her costume, as she is supposedly wearing trousers. On such a flimsy pretext the police allow bloomers on stage.

I decided not to venture backstage to confront Irene about the nature of this announcement of hers. No doubt she'd refuse to tell me, ensuring the girls all heard her, and I'd look as if I didn't know what was going on.

I didn't, but I'd never admit it.

Roland was up again once the *Macbeth* scene ended. He saw me watching as he climbed the stage — the booing even louder than normal — and I pulled my finger across my throat. Cut it short. I wanted to get this night over with.

He did a couple of weak card tricks, pulled a white rabbit out of his hat. And then he scampered off. He appeared to be pleased to do so.

I grabbed Maxie as she headed backstage after doing the rounds of the boxes. "I want to finish early tonight. Tell the girls to drop Ellie's song and the *Macbeth* fight scene. Colleen can sing her song, then we'll have the cancan, and Irene can wrap it up."

"Why?"

I glared at her. She got the hint and slunk off. If she messed up my instructions, I'd sack her.

Irene wandered onto the stage, dressed in a nightgown — a white cotton garment, high of neckline and long of sleeve, unadorned. Not the fancy one she wore to entertain Eleanor (and Ray?). I shuddered at the image that brought to mind. Time for the dramatic hand-washing scene. Mr. William Shakespeare would be rising from his grave in righteous indignation if Irene ever set foot onto a stage in London. Acting was not, shall we say, one of her talents. She moaned and collapsed to her knees and wiped at the red cloth between her hands intended to represent blood only she could see. "Out darned spot," she cried. Yes, I am well aware that the line is *damned spot*. But we didn't want to see Irene dragged off to jail for the use of vile language.

I glanced toward the back of the room. A couple of taller men shifted and I caught a flash of clear tanned skin and pale hair. Angus. I should have known.

I hesitated. I didn't want him here. Particularly not tonight when trouble itself hung heavily in the air. But Colleen would be going on at the conclusion of Irene's scene and I needed to ensure she knew I was here, watching.

Irene croaked out the last line, staggered to her feet, curtsied low so the audience could get a glimpse down the front of her shirt, and vacated the stage.

It was as though everyone knew something was about to happen. The men leaned forward in their seats. Even the poker players — Turner, the count, Roland — had abandoned their game to stand in the non-existent space at the back of the hall. The stage was empty for a moment, we all breathed, and then Colleen stepped out. She was, as instructed, dressed in her street clothes. She looked very small alone on the stage. She walked to the front, clasped her hands in front of her. She might have been about to recite bible verses to the congregation. Her eyes darted about the room, found me, moved away, and settled on her father seated in pride of place, front row centre. The piano player tinkled the keys and they began to play. Colleen waited for a few notes, opened her mouth and sang.

Her voice was nicer than I'd heard upstairs in my office. It had a sweet melancholy to it, and she could project to the back of the hall.

The men smiled and nodded. A couple whispered to their companions. More than a few closed their eyes to enjoy the music. The Mounties standing at the back relaxed.

I let out a long breath.

Disaster averted.

The music came to an end. Colleen, now smiling, curtsied as the men hooted their approval. A couple of gold nuggets fell at her feet and she scooped them up. She appeared pleased with herself, and I was pleased with her.

I had started to turn, to head for my son and order him to go home, when a shout broke over the trailing end of the applause.

"You! You jealous witch. You silenced her!" To my considerable surprise the voice was directed at me. It was Gerry Sullivan and he was on his feet. His blotchy red face bulged with indignation. He pointed a scarred and yellow-nailed finger at me. He surveyed the audience. "Are you going to stand for that? My girl was going to do a dance that would have been the talk of the town for years to come. But she — they — silenced her. She — they — wouldn't let you see it. Are you going to stand for that? Are you American men or Canadian mice?"

"Shut up, old man," someone yelled. A chorus joined him. They'd been given a song by their new favourite, and they'd enjoyed it. Now they wanted to see the rest of the show. Richard Sterling was heading toward me, relaxed no longer. I lost sight of Angus.

"Sit down," a sensible voice called.

"Let the girl dance," some fool suggested. A couple of men took up the call. "Let the girl dance." Feet began to stomp in chorus. I saw Constable McAllen grab a collar and drag a man backward out of the room. Joe Hamilton arrived at a run.

"Outta the way, you fat old fart. I wanna see the dancing," the man seated directly behind Sullivan shouted.

I gestured to the orchestra to start the music for the cancan. That should settle the men down. I could only hope there would be someone backstage with presence of mind to realize I wanted the lively dance to begin *now*.

The music began to have the desired effect. Some of the protesters settled down. Joe Hamilton could find no one to expel, and the end of Ray's billy club remained in his hand.

The man seated behind Sullivan, who'd told him to get out of the way, lumbered to his feet. He lifted his arms in triumph and half-turned, to ensure his friends had seen him exercising authority. Sullivan hit him full in his exposed side. Followed by a punch to the face. The man dropped to the benches in a tumble of arms and legs. Blood streamed from his nose.

His friends leapt to their feet.

"English cowards," Sullivan roared. He leapt over the bench and stood with his back to the stage, fists up.

"Protect the American!" someone yelled.

And the fight was on. The "Infernal Galop" ended in mid-note.

As no one was dressed in their country's colours, I doubt any national pride lay behind the brawl. But all it takes is one punch and every man in a room seems to think he should be involved. Three or four men rushed to Sullivan's defence. Benches toppled, glasses broke, musicians grabbed their instruments and attempted to flee. Blood flew and bones snapped. Dancers screamed and either yelled at men to stop or egged them on.

Richard Sterling waded into the thick of it, grabbing men and tossing them behind him to waiting Mounties. Ray cracked heads, and Joe Hamilton struggled to subdue swinging patrons.

A secondary fight broke out in the back of the hall, impeding the efforts of those few sensible folk attempting to get out of the way. Two men were exchanging blows on the stairs leading to the boxes while one of the waiters cowered against the railing, clutching thirty-dollar bottles of Champagne to his chest.

Angus. I had to get to the spot where I'd seen my son last. I slunk along the wall, keeping my back against it. I'd taken no more than a couple of steps when a hand grabbed my arm and swung me around, pulling me off balance. Dirty fingers pawed at the front of my gown and fat wet lips slobbered on my cheek, searching for my mouth. I screamed and attempted to pull myself free.

He wrapped his arms around me and thrust his knee between my legs. I lifted my foot and raked it down his instep. His boots were thick and high and I made little impact. He fumbled for my breast. I grabbed his head. I felt through strands of greasy hair for his ear. I gripped it and twisted. He grunted and his hold on me relaxed.

Not much, but enough.

I raised my knee and drove it into his crotch. He staggered back, instinctively bending over to protect the precious family jewels. I gripped the shoulders of his jacket in both fists, pulled him close, and squeezed my arms together. His face bulged as air began to be choked off. His eyes stared at me, round and black and full of shock.

I let go and stepped back. I held my hands up and bounced on the balls of my feet. I breathed consciously, deep and slow. "Do not," I said, "touch me again."

He leapt over a broken bench, skirted two men rolling on the floor, and fled, never to be seen again.

Richard Sterling was frozen in the act of coming to my rescue, his mouth a round *O* of surprise, his eyes wide. He shook his head and went back to breaking up fighters.

Chapter Twenty-Five

A fight. At last Angus was in a fight. He braced himself the way Sergeant Lancaster had taught him. Feet planted lightly on the ground, knees slightly bent, fists raised. He was ready. But no one was coming toward him having also assumed the correct stance. Instead the room was a melee of flying bodies, swinging fists and feet, spraying blood and spittle, and a whole lot of yelling.

His mother. He couldn't see his mother. He leaped onto a bench. Over the mass of men, he spotted her, the scarlet of her dress shining like a beacon amongst the drab men's clothes. She was heading to the rear of the room, keeping her back against the wall. A man followed. Angus didn't care for the look in the fellow's eyes. He reached out and grabbed her arm, pulled her around to face him. Angus opened his mouth to shout.

A body crashed into his legs. He swung his arms, trying to keep his balance. The bench collapsed and Angus jumped. Into the middle of a brawl. A fist streaked past his cheek. He raised his hands to protect his face and danced backward, taking himself out of the way. All around him men were yelling and women screaming. He felt a hand on his shoulder and began to turn. A man stood there, frozen in the act of swinging a punch.

"Beggin' your pardon, young Angus. Didn't recognize you there for a moment. Your ma know you're here? She won't like it."

"That's okay, Mr. Jordan."

Jordan leapt back into the fray. Roland the Magnificent made his way through the room, stepping carefully, avoiding bodies. He carried a full glass of whisky. "Rather a to-do, old boy, wouldn't you say." Turner, the gambler, clocked a dirt-encrusted sourdough with a beard reaching halfway to his belt who was yelling something about Yankee honour. The miner crashed into the wall and slid slowly downward, where he sat with his legs outstretched shaking his head.

Count Nicky studied the fallen creature at his feet with a sniff.

More Mounties were arriving and miscreants either being hauled away or deciding it would be wise to take their leave. A couple of fierce brawls were still going on, but otherwise the room was beginning to settle down.

Angus looked again for his mother. She was heading his way now, and the man who'd been following her was nowhere to be seen.

Richard Sterling was holding out a hand to pull a young fellow, blood pouring from his nose, up from the floor. Inspector McKnight had lost his hat. He was breathing heavily and looking highly pleased with himself as he rubbed his knuckles. McAllen was marching a man out the door, arm twisted behind his back. Mounties broke up the last fighters. A group of women had ventured onto the stage, where they stood watching.

Benches were scattered across the floor, some broken. Hats and jackets lay abandoned. Judging by the smell, and the wet sawdust on the floor, more than one man had lost control of his overfull bladder. Angus crushed a cigar, still burning, out with his foot.

"I wonder if I might put in for danger pay," Roland said.

Four or five men began straightening benches. Once that was done, they took their seats and waited calmly for the show to resume. The oldest of them lit his pipe and tossed the match onto the floor.

Inspector McKnight and Richard Sterling met in the centre of the room. Angus's mother joined them.

"… an unpardonable fuss," McKnight was saying. The knuckles of his right hand were beginning to swell.

Fiona sniffed. "You understand, of course, that was absolutely none of our doing."

"You led the men to believe a scandalous display would be on offer, madam."

"I most certainly did not. You cannot hold me responsible for rumours spread by others about my establishment. You saw it yourself. Colleen's song was nothing but totally proper. Subdued even." Colour was high in Fiona's face and her shoulders were set.

McKnight hesitated, then he turned to Sterling. "What about the man who started the fight? Have we apprehended him?"

"He got away. We shouldn't have any trouble finding him."

"I want that man in jail. Cursed Americans, always making trouble. He deliberately attempted to cause a riot. He'll spend a month chopping wood and then get a blue ticket."

"Do you know him, Mrs. MacGillivray?" Sterling asked.

Some of the tension left Fiona's face as the focus of the police attention shifted. She'd been worried, Angus guessed, that they'd shut the Savoy down. "His name's Gerry Sullivan. He's the father of the singer."

"Get the girl," McKnight said. "I want her to …"

The men who'd taken seats near the stage began clapping. Others joined them, hooting and stomping their feet. Men began drifting back into the dance hall. Benches were righted and pulled into place and the room began to fill up once again.

Fiona groaned.

"Mrs. MacGillivray," McKnight said. "There will be no more performances here tonight. We've all had enough excitement for one evening."

"I'm inclined to agree with you," she said. "I'll announce that the dancing will begin early. Angus, on your way home, tell Ray the show will not be continuing."

"But ..."

"No buts. I don't know why you're here this late. Don't make it a habit."

Angus slunk away. Sterling gave him a slap on the back as he passed. He shrugged the Mountie off.

* * *

I never appear on the stage. Tonight, as I climbed the stairs, the faces in the audience lit up with expectation. Everyone leaned a bit closer. Only a few Mounties remained in the room, the rest of them were taking the fighters unlucky enough to be nabbed off to jail. Behind me I heard the excited whispering of the girls, speculating as to what I was up to.

I stood patiently until the chatter died down and I had everyone's attention. It didn't take long.

The musicians had resumed their places; the performers waited in the wings. I lifted one hand.

"Gentlemen, we will be opening the floor for the dancing early. I am sure you all understand that some of the ladies are so distressed by tonight's events they won't be able to perform to their best."

"I wanna see the cancan," a man called.

I glared at him. "Then you may return tomorrow."

The men grumbled, but they didn't seem too upset. Most of them didn't much care what we did. Stage show or the dancing, it was all the same to them. They came here to spend some time with women, to drink, to brag about their exploits out on the Creeks.

I lifted my skirts and descended the stage. The waiters began moving the benches, shoving them to the sides of the room to clear the floor. The orchestra started up; the percentage girls sashayed into the crowd.

"Colleen." I spotted the cause of all our troubles trying to blend in.

She glanced around, looking as though she were hoping a knight in shining armour would swoop down and cart her away. When none did so, she approached me. Somewhat as a mouse might approach a waiting cat.

"Ma'am?"

"You're fired."

Her eyes filled with tears. "Please, ma'am, no. I need this job."

"Do you expect me to do anything else? If your plan had been permitted to succeed we would have been shut down. Perhaps permanently. Then we'd all be out of a job. As it was, your father almost caused a riot. Just as well the police were here in force, or who knows what might have happened. I notice your father has conveniently disappeared."

"I'll tell him to stay away from now on."

"Too late, Colleen. I don't need trouble and your father seems intent upon causing it. One way or another."

Fat tears rolled down her pink cheeks. "My father's a good man, Mrs. MacGillivray."

That I doubted. But it was neither here nor there. Men were pressing closer to us. "Dance, miss?" one scruffy fellow asked Colleen. Heavens, if we continued with this conversation in public I might well have another riot on my hands.

"I'm sorry, sir," I said to the would-be dancer partner. "The Mounties have some questions for Miss Sullivan regarding her father. Later perhaps."

He nodded politely but made no move to leave us, simply stood smiling stupidly at Colleen.

Inspector McKnight came over. "Is this the lady?" he asked me.

"Miss Sullivan," I replied.

"Do you have someplace we can speak privately?" he said with a glance at the listening men.

"My office. You know the way."

McKnight stood aside, gesturing for Colleen to precede him. She hesitated. I felt a shiver of tension spread through the watching men. Oh, dear. If it looked as though she were being arrested, they might try to do something to stop it.

Betsy passed by, looking for a mark … I mean a dance partner. I called her name and waved her over. "This gentleman would like a dance."

Betsy simpered. The man didn't look too terribly impressed.

"On the house," I said.

"Wow. Thanks, ma'am." He grabbed Betsy around the waist and hauled her away much in the fashion that he might once have collared cattle for branding. The remaining men grinned and the small crowd broke up.

McKnight seemed to have something wrong with his eye: he was looking at me with something approaching approval. He said, "After you, Miss Sullivan."

I debated going upstairs with them. It was hardly proper to allow the girl to be interrogated without a female companion. But I didn't dare leave the floor. Tension was as thick in the air as tinder ready to burn and wouldn't take much of a spark to ignite it.

"Mrs. MacGillivray!"

Irene descended upon me. Her black eyes blazed like burning coal, her jaw was clenched tight, and a vein pulsed in her neck. "You," she declared. "You did that on purpose."

"You didn't honestly expect we could continue with the show, did you? In any event it wasn't my doing. Inspector McKnight ordered it."

She spoke over my protestations of innocence. "You closed the show early to keep me from making my announcement."

"Oh. That." I'd honestly forgotten all about her theatrical pronouncement. More important matters had been occupying my mind. "It'll have to wait for another time. I don't suppose you want to tell me what your grand proclamation is?"

She sniffed. "You'll find out in due time."

"I'm satisfied to wait." I turned and walked away, leaving her fuming.

I went through the gambling hall. Turner, Roland, and the count were back at the poker table, concentrating on the cards in their hands. The roulette wheel spun to a halt, the croupier said, "Twelve," and someone cheered.

"It seems I've missed all the excitement," Graham Donohue said.

"Have you just arrived?"

"I was researching an article I'm writing when I heard word a riot had broken out in the Savoy. By the time I made my way here, it was to find a troop of Mounties carting a pack of sad-sacks off to the fort. What happened?"

"I scarcely know. I stopped one of my dancers from doing something indecent and her father took offence to that."

"Her father? Her father wanted her to do an indecent performance?"

"Seems strange, doesn't it? Particularly as I got the impression she's a somewhat shy and reserved girl."

"Takes all kinds, I guess."

"That it does." I drifted away, thinking. It wasn't unheard of for a father to get a perverse sort of titillating pleasure out of his daughter. But perhaps Mr. Sullivan wasn't Colleen's father? Rather her much older husband? No reason for subterfuge. A good number of the percentage girls were married, as were some of the headliners and chorus performers at the other dance halls. Maybe he liked watching her perform for other men. I glanced up, toward the ceiling. When the police were finished questioning her, I'd send her packing.

Not my problem any longer.

Chapter Twenty-Six

To Angus's disappointment Mr. and Mrs. Mann had gone to bed before he got home. He had to wait until morning to tell them about the previous night's excitement. He acted out the highlights of the fight in great detail, dancing around the kitchen while Mrs. Mann attempted to start breakfast, blocking and parrying and jabbing at the air in front of his face.

Mr. Mann wanted to hear every detail. Mrs. Mann wanted to cook bacon.

Angus didn't mention that he, himself, hadn't actually taken or laid any blows. Finally, he dropped into his chair, exhilarated.

Mr. Mann punched the air, happily reliving fights of his youth.

"Men," Mrs. Mann huffed, flipping bacon.

All morning, working at the shop, Angus played the brawl in his mind. His own part began to grow. That man had been following his mother, intent on who-knows-what mischief. Clearly he'd been frightened off by Angus's steely-eyed stare. He ducked an incoming blow and responded with a fast right hook. A lady shopping for a laundry bucket eyed him suspiciously. "Are you having a fit, young man? Should I fetch a doctor?"

He blushed. "Sorry, ma'am. That'll be ten cents."

She handed over the money and walked off with the bucket under her arm, head shaking.

Too bad he'd arranged to help Miss Jennings as soon as he finished at the store. He'd like to find Dave, tell him about the fight.

Miss Jennings would be interested in hearing the story. After all, she was always asking him questions about life and people in Dawson.

She'd left the front door unlocked in expectation of his arrival and was in the developing room when Angus arrived. He called, and she shouted that she'd be finished in a few minutes. When he first started working for her, Miss Jennings had explained that he absolutely mustn't open the door. Even a sliver of light would ruin the undeveloped plates. He flipped through the photographs on the table. Some good ones of the police going about their business, boats on the busy waterfront, Front Street festooned with banners. Dancers peeked from behind fans or ostrich feathers, and men posed stiffly with pick axes and shovels. Count Nicky, with one foot up on a wooden crate, his neck stretched, chin thrust forward, face as firmly set as that of Napoleon in David's portrait.

The developing room door opened.

"You've been busy," Angus said.

Miss Jennings smiled. "Business is good." She took off her apron. "Today I've a mind to finally go to Paradise Alley."

"Why?"

"Because the women who work there aren't coming to me. Therefore I must go to them."

Angus hesitated. "I don't know, Miss Jennings. My ma won't be pleased she hears I took you there."

"I won't tell her if you don't." She put her hands on her hips and studied him. "We won't be going inside anyone's room, Angus. I'd like to see the street, that's all. You can come, or not, as you like. I'll be photographing outside and it's a sunny day, so I won't need the flash powder." She found her bonnet amongst

her stack of papers and plopped it onto her head, tying the ribbon under her chin.

Angus picked up the camera case. They left, Miss Jennings
locking the door behind her as she always did.

Some of the women who lived and worked in the muddy
stretch of street known as Paradise Alley shied away as the photographer and her assistant approached. But a good number
came out for a peek. Business was slow early in the afternoon.
More than a few men slunk into the shadows at the sight of
the determined Miss Jennings followed by Angus carrying the
bulky camera box.

"Good afternoon," Miss Jennings said, projecting her voice
to be heard. "I'm going to take a picture of the street. Anyone
who wants to be in the photograph is welcome."

She instructed Angus to set up the camera. He found a place
on a moderately stable section of the boardwalk. The street was
narrow. A row of tiny, hastily constructed buildings ran down
each side of the road. Only a few feet wide, each had a single
window and a door that opened directly onto the boardwalk.
In some cases, the resident's name was painted above the door.

A few of the ladies wandered over. They watched Angus
unfolding and adjusting the tripod and fastening the camera
into place. Their dresses were plain, undecorated, and well-
worn. They smelled of unwashed clothes, cheap perfume, and a
sharp bitter scent Angus couldn't identify.

Miss Jennings studied the street, head cocked to one side.

Two men rounded the corner. Their faces were hard under
rough beards, their clothes dirty. The women shied back as they
approached. "Are you lost, lady?" one of them asked.

"No."

"What you got there, sonny?"

"It's a camera."

"I can see that." The larger of the two men stepped in front of Miss Jennings. The other put his back to the camera. He waved at the women as if shooing flies away. They retreated. Some went inside, the bolder of them stood on the opposite boardwalk.

"Excuse me," Miss Jennings said, "you're blocking my view."

"There's nothing for you to take pictures of here."

"I'll be the judge of that."

"You're chasing away the customers. Men who come here looking for a bit of entertainment don't like to think a nice lady such as yourself is watching them. Interfering where she shouldn't."

"It's a public street." Her voice was calm and smooth. She made a square of her hands and held them up to her face, peering around the man. He moved to block her.

"Angus," she said, "you might need to run and fetch the police."

He was hardly going to leave her here alone, but he didn't say so. He knew who these men were. Employees of Joey LeBlanc, the madam who owned, in a literal sense, many of the prostitutes on this street. Joey and Fiona were bitter enemies. He wouldn't tell his mother he'd been involved in a confrontation with Joey's men.

"We don't need no yellow stripes."

"Glad to hear it. If you'll step aside and allow me to take my pictures, we'll be on our way as soon as I've finished."

The men glanced at each other. Their boss was nowhere around and they didn't quite know what to do now. Miss Jennings stepped behind the camera. Angus held the black cloth. "I've got a splendid idea," she said cheerfully. "You, sir, remain where you are. It will make a lovely photograph. A souvenir for you to send home to your mother, with the street in the background."

He leapt aside. Miss Jennings bent over and Angus tossed the cloth over her head. She made a few adjustments, then removed the cap from the lens and quickly replaced it. "Another, I think. Sure you don't want to be in the photograph, sir?"

The men grumbled to each other. One woman, older than the rest, lifted her skirts high and crossed the street. She grinned. She didn't have a tooth in her mouth and her scarred scalp, pitted with scabs, showed through thinning hair. "I'll be in your picture," she said.

The man growled at her and lifted a hand.

"Don't you threaten me, Mr. Black. Ain't gonna do no harm. Give the lady what she wants and she'll be on her way. Stand here arguing all day, ain't none of us gonna get no business." She put a hand on a scrawny hip, tilted her head to one side, and smiled.

Miss Jennings took the picture and tossed the black cloth to Angus. He packed up the equipment. The men stood in the street watching until they'd turned the corner.

Angus let out a long breath. Miss Jennings laughed. "That was fun. I don't know if I can do much with the portrait of the hideous old cow, but I got most of the street in the background. What a wretched place that was."

"Where to next?"

"That's enough excitement for today. Good work, Angus. You kept your cool."

"They wouldn't have done anything," he said, pleased with the praise but trying to be modest. "Mounties are waiting for the chance to give those two a blue ticket."

They made their way back to the photography studio. Miss Jennings pulled the key out of her pocket as they approached. She came to a halt so suddenly, Angus bumped into her. He peered over her shoulder.

The wood around the door handle was smashed and splintered, the lock dislodged. They exchanged glances. Angus put the camera equipment on the ground, and Miss Jennings slowly reached out and pushed on the door. It swung open on unoiled hinges.

At first glance they could see nothing out of the ordinary. The darkroom door stood open, everything resting where it had been left. The photographs on the table were untouched, props and photography equipment still in place.

Miss Jennings let out a long breath. The building was quiet. Empty. "Oh, dear." She touched his arm. "Angus, you didn't move the flash powders did you?"

"No. You said we wouldn't need it."

"They're gone."

Chapter Twenty-Seven

Gerry Sullivan had disappeared. Colleen, shaking and close to tears, had taken Sterling and McKnight to the tent in which they lived. Her father had not been there.

The Sullivans were living in the tent camp high above town. Sterling returned this morning. The girl, showing signs of a sleepless night and plenty of tears, said she hadn't seen him.

He wasn't too concerned. Hopefully the man had skipped town on the first boat out. Which was all the Mounties were going to do to him at any rate. Too bad about the girl, if her father had abandoned her.

"You will let us know if you hear from him," Sterling said.

She nodded.

"Does your father get into trouble much?"

She shook her head. "He wanted me to sing, that's all."

"But you did sing. I heard you. It was nice."

"What am I doing to do, sir? I don't have a job any longer. I can't support myself if my father goes to jail."

"I'm sorry," he said. He started to walk away. She stood watching, her hand on the tent flap. "Miss Sullivan. About that ... uh ... aborted dance. Did your father tell you why he wanted you to do it?"

"He said this stuffy British town needed some livening up."

"Why have you come here, Miss Sullivan, if your father dislikes it so much? He isn't mining, is he?"

Her eyes filled with more tears. "For the Brotherhood. It's always for the Brotherhood." She ducked and shut the tent flap behind her without making a sound.

Sterling walked downhill, heading back to the detachment office, deep in thought.

When he reached Second Avenue, rather than turning left he kept on going, heading east to cross the rickety bridge over the Klondike River to Louse Town.

The Yankee Doodle was nothing but a wooden shack with a hand-painted sign in a muddy row of equally unimpressive establishments. An American flag hung prominently over the door. Feeling highly conspicuous in his uniform, thinking it might have been a better idea to come in mufti, Sterling pushed open the door and walked in.

Conversation stopped. Only one small, very dirty window graced the room and no lamps had been lit. Not many men were in the establishment in the middle of the morning. Ghostly shapes in the gloom. A red fire glowed as someone sucked on his pipe. The bartender, a long-bearded, long-haired fellow with a scar running though his upper and lower lips, stared at the Mountie.

"Lost, are you?" he said at last.

"No. This is the place."

Sterling's eyes began to accustom themselves to the light. Three men, aside from the bartender. A door led off the back of the main room, probably to where The Stallion plied her trade prior to her marriage.

"I've heard talk," Sterling said, "of miners' meetings. You men aren't planning anything like that here, are you?"

Heads shook.

"Glad to hear it. I'm looking for a man by the name of Sullivan. I've also heard talk he drinks here sometimes."

Heads shook again. Sterling had, in fact, heard no such thing. But it was possible, if the man was an American agitator, he'd find his way to the Yankee Doodle. It was also possible he'd gone to any one of a number of bars Sterling had never heard of.

"What's he done?" someone asked.

"Don't need to have done nothing," his tablemate answered, "for the Fly Bull to be after him."

"Conspiring to start a riot," Sterling said, peering through the gloom at the man who'd spoken last. Something familiar there. "Participating in a riot."

"Tsk tsk." The bartender shook his head sadly. "Can't have that, now can we?"

Coming here was a mistake. No one would tell him anything. Even if they knew anything. "If Gerry Sullivan happens to come around," he said, "tell him his daughter needs him."

The men shifted uncomfortably. They might be hostile to the law, but talk of daughters was another matter entirely.

"Sure," the bartender said.

"You," Sterling said to the man he'd recognized as having wanted to buy a rifle from Mr. Mann the other day. "Keeping yourself out of trouble, are you?"

The man spat a wad of chewing tobacco onto the floor. "Always."

"Glad to hear it." Sterling headed for the door. Waste of time.

"Hear there's going to be some explosive excitement on Front Street tonight," a man said in a loud voice. "Might be worth finding a spot on the river to watch."

Laughter followed Sterling into the street.

A cigar store — a real cigar store — was situated across the street from the Yankee Doodle. Remembering that he was almost out of pipe tobacco, Sterling slipped inside before heading back to the office. He chatted with the woman behind the counter for a few minutes while she weighed his purchase and counted out change.

"That place across the street," he said. "See many men coming and going?"

"A low-life bar. Like any other. I'm pretty sure they're running prostitutes out of the back room."

He pulled the photograph of Jim Stewart from his tunic pocket. It had been shown all over town and was beginning to look rather the worse for wear. "Have you seen this man there?"

He knew from Lou Redfern that Stewart had been to the Yankee. Never hurt to have it confirmed, though.

She studied the picture, head cocked in thought. "I might have. I don't pay much attention, mind. I run my business, I let them run theirs."

He took the small package of tobacco. "Thanks anyway."

"You're welcome."

He stepped into the street, tucking the package into his tunic. Then he leapt back into the store.

"Forget something?" the shopkeeper asked.

"Shush."

A man Sterling definitely recognized was walking through the doors of the Yankee Doodle. He had not hesitated in the road, or stopped to read the sign. Just pushed the door open and entered, as if he'd been here many times before.

Roland the Magnificent.

* * *

I didn't know what grand announcement Irene planned to make, but I figured it would do me no good. I cornered Ray the moment he came through the doors that afternoon.

He shrugged and said he had no idea what Irene was up to. "Tell ye the truth, Fee, I'm beginning to think you were right. She's not the woman for me."

I refrained from shouting "Hallelujah!" and instead settled my face into thoughtful, concerned lines and said, "Why's that?"

His ugly face twisted. "I love her, Fee. I really do. But I don't see nothing being returned. Oh, yes, she can be sweet and attentive. Make me feel like the centre of the universe she does. Then I see her here, laughing and being charming with men who've paid a dollar to get the same attention."

"That's her job. It's why she's so popular. It's all an act."

"Is it an act with me too, Fee? I sometimes think she's hiding something, using me as a front, ye ken?"

I patted his arm, and he went behind the bar, small and sad.

Count Nicky was listening to Barney talk about the old days (which in Dawson means last year). The count stroked his chin. "Know your way around the territory, do you?" he asked.

"None better." Barney lifted his empty glass to his lips. He tilted his head far back and gave the glass a shake. Then he lowered it and ran his index finger around the inside.

"Have you been up the river? All the way to the ocean? Near to Russia?"

"Ocean's downriver." Barney sucked on his finger. "And I've been there, many times."

"I might be in need of a guide." Count Nicky dropped his voice. Curious, I slid closer. "I might be bringing a substantial number of men and supplies down the river."

"Up the river you mean. Anyway, glad to be of help, my good man. Will you look at that? My glass is empty."

Count Nicky sipped his own whisky. "When does the river freeze up?"

"Mid-September usually."

"Probably too late for this year, then. I am leaving for Washington shortly."

"Washington, eh? I have a sister what lives in Seattle. Least ways she used to live in Seattle. When did I hear from her last?" He crinkled his face in thought. "'Seventy-seven, I think. Or was it seventy-eight? I remember better with a drink in my hand."

"Not Washington State," Nicky said, "but the city on the east coast. I have business to conduct there. A letter of introduction to *important* people."

"Sure. When you get back look me up, will you? I'll be here. Unless I've died of thirst in the meanwhile."

"Why would you do that? This is not the desert."

"He's wanting you to buy him a drink, Count." John Turner appeared out of nowhere. I hadn't even realized he, like me, was eavesdropping.

"Isn't that a fine idea," Barney exclaimed. He held up his glass. "Don't mind if I do. Walker, I'll have a drink on my friend here."

"Going to Washington are ye?" Ray asked, pouring the drink. As if suddenly aware that a good number of people were party to his private conversation, Nicky blanched. He grabbed his glass and took a hearty swig.

"If you're going," Turner said, "Best be on your way. Wouldn't want you to be delayed on your important business." He looked at me and then at Ray. His eyes were cold and angry. "Seems to me more than a few folks would do worse than to be heading off back to where they belong." He swallowed his drink. "The count'll get it," he told Ray. He walked out. Ray shrugged. I had no idea what all that was about.

"Been a while since I did a spot of guiding," Barney said. "I'm sure I haven't lost the knack. How many fellows you planning to bring, Count?"

But Count Nicholas Ivanovich Prozorovsky had clammed up.

*　*　*

It didn't take long for Miss Jennings and Angus to search the photography studio and the upstairs rooms. Nothing but the powder used for illumination appeared to be missing.

Miss Jennings rested her right hip against the table. "If not for the broken door, I might not have even noticed someone's been in here."

"But they had. And they don't seem to mind that you noticed. I'll go for the Mounties."

"No."

"Why not? I have to tell them. You've been robbed."

"They didn't take much."

"Perhaps we frightened them off. In that case there may have been two of them. One to watch out for you returning. We came back earlier than usual, and they had to run before taking anything more."

"I'm not entirely sure I left the flash powders there. Now that I think of it, I used the last of that portion yesterday."

"It was there. I saw it myself."

"I don't want to bother the police with this."

"I don't understand. You've been robbed, Miss Jennings. It doesn't matter that they didn't take much."

"Leave it." She threw her hat onto the table. "I insist."

"If that's what you want."

"It is. Now, I need you to run and fetch someone to fix that door and put on a new lock. Then I think you're ready to help me in the darkroom. You have to keep your mind fully on the task at hand, Angus. One slip, one sliver of light, even for less than a second, and the image will be ruined. Once gone, it cannot be brought back. A photograph is as much a picture of a time as of a place or a person."

Chapter Twenty-Eight

I made it my business to know what was going on at the other dance halls. The Savoy might be the most popular today, but popularity in this town swung as wildly as a rumour of a new gold discovery. I paid a bartender at the Monte Carlo and a musician at the Horseshoe to keep me informed of the news. No doubt several of my employees were making a little something on the side as well.

I was leaving the dressmaker the afternoon after the near-riot, highly pleased with myself. The navy blue gown needed but a few tucks and adjustments to be finished and the yellow was coming along nicely. A man in his forties, who always dressed as if he were about to go grouse hunting on a Scottish estate, slid up to me. His Harris tweed jacket was immaculate, matching trousers tucked into high brown boots polished to a brilliant shine. He wore a cloth cap and carried a stout walking stick with a gold tip. "Heard you had some trouble last night, Mrs. MacGillivray."

"Nothing we couldn't handle."

"Heard that also. The men liked that new girl you have. The young one. Pretty they say. She sang a new song."

"Yes." I paid for information going in one direction only. I wasn't about to tell him I'd sacked Colleen.

"New act at the Monte Carlo tonight," he said. "A couple of twins. Real lookers, too. Young."

"Is that so?"

"Yup. I heard 'em rehearsing just now. Can't sing worth a hill of beans, but that don't matter much, does it, Mrs. MacGillivray?"

"Apparently not."

He touched his cap and strolled away, stick swinging.

Twins, eh? Men loved twins. These girls might be twins, or they might not. Might not even be sisters. All they had to do was say they were and the men would come to see them. I was not entirely displeased at the news. I did not want a repeat of last night's fiasco, and I suspected the Savoy audience would not be happy when Colleen failed to put in an appearance. The more men who went to the Monte Carlo to see the twins, the better.

As long as they eventually drifted back to the Savoy.

* * *

"Are you not feeling well, Angus?" Mrs. Mann asked.

Angus was sitting at the supper table, pushing moose steak around on his plate. The meat was tough but flavourful, and the gravy thick and good. He didn't have much of an appetite.

"I'm fine, ma'am," he said. "Not hungry."

"Not hungry! That's a new one."

Angus's mother wasn't at dinner tonight. She'd gone to the dressmaker and was running late, so would eat in her office.

"Mrs. Mann," Angus said, drawing out the word, "if something's happened to someone and you know it's wrong, but that someone doesn't want you to tell the authorities, should you?"

"What?"

"I mean if you know a crime's been committed, but the victim doesn't want to tell the police, is your duty to your friend or to the police?"

"Police," Mr. Mann growled around a mouthful of moose. "Always. Your duty." He helped himself to another ladleful of mashed potatoes.

"It depends." Mrs. Mann leaned back in her chair and studied Angus's face. "Did your friend …"

"A theoretical friend."

"This theoretical friend. Did he or she commit a crime?"

"No."

"They're the victim of it?"

"Yes."

"Then the decision is up to them, Angus." She cut a small piece of meat.

"Thanks Mrs. Mann. That's a help."

"Unless …" She studied her fork.

"Unless?"

"Unless the person who committed the crime is a danger to others. A man who's attacking women, for example. Understandably the woman in question won't want to go to the police, but suppose they could catch him? And thus prevent him attacking another woman?"

"It's not like that."

"You'll do what's right, Angus. I know you will."

Angus wasn't so sure. He didn't know what was right. Someone had broken into Miss Jennings' studio. Did it matter that they hadn't stolen anything of value, or damaged anything? It was still a crime, right? She'd told him not to worry about it. It was a minor matter, not worth bothering the police.

He was finishing dinner when a knock sounded on the back door and Dave came in. "Hi, Mr. and Mrs. Mann. Hi, Angus. Want to go fishing?" Dave was carrying the pole his father had made for him.

"Sure."

"Sit down," Mrs. Mann said. "We haven't finished our dinner. I have made a strudel for dessert. Apple. Would you like some?"

"Would I?" Dave dropped his fishing pole and lunged for Fiona's empty chair.

There's nothing like fishing for making a man think. When they lived in Toronto, Angus spent part of the school vacations at the cottages of his friends. When the boys' fathers came up to join the family on the weekend, they'd often go fishing and sometimes catch enough to provide the fish course at dinner. The cook would drench it in a rich creamy sauce or serve the fish plain and unadorned and everyone would exclaim that it was the best fish they'd ever tasted. The boys would preen, proud at providing food for their families.

Even if they didn't catch anything worth eating, Angus remembered one father saying, "It's not the fish. It's the fishing."

He and Dave walked along the banks of the Yukon River past the tents and the roughly constructed shacks to where there could still be found a trace of peace on the river.

They put worms onto hooks, dangled their legs over the edge, and tossed the ends of their lines into the water. Angus had a fishing pole one of his mother's admirers had made for him in an attempt to get into Fiona's good books. It wasn't anything like the sturdy factory-constructed and store-bought poles they used on Stoney Lake, but he liked this one — string with a weight at the end and a worm for bait — better. It felt good and right in his hands. He let out a bit more line.

"You been following that Mountie and the lady anymore?" Dave asked.

"No. Didn't seem any point to it."

A flock of geese flew high overhead, their honks of encouragement loud in the quiet evening.

Reasonably quiet at any rate. The boys could still hear the commotion from town. People talking, men laughing, wagons rolling, hammers and saws.

"I wonder," Angus said, "how long it will be before all this is gone?"

"All what?"

"Geese. Fish. Quiet."

Dave shrugged, not much caring.

They knew it was eight o'clock when the town erupted in noise. The dance halls sending their callers out into the street to attract custom. Angus thought of Roland. He'd promised to teach Angus a couple of easy tricks to impress his friends, but that hadn't happened. Perhaps Roland also was just pretending to befriend Angus to get closer to Fiona.

No matter.

Although, Roland didn't look at Fiona the way men who liked her in that way did — with a stupid simpering smile on their faces. When he thought no one was watching, Roland looked at Fiona almost as if he didn't like her much.

There'd been a lot of strange people in the Savoy lately. Sometimes it seemed as if Dawson was populated by nothing but strange people.

Count Nicky, who wanted to get Alaska back in order to create a New Russia. Miss Jennings had written a nice formal letter introducing him to the American president. That President McKinley had not the slightest idea who Eleanor Jennings was, she said with a laugh, wouldn't become apparent to the count until he was refused entry to the White House. If he even got as far as Washington. She had a feeling, she told Angus, Count Nicky was easily distracted.

And how about John Turner, who was always playing poker at the Savoy, and who'd also been following Miss Jennings?

The boys fished. They didn't have much luck. Dave caught a couple of small grayling, but Angus came up empty.

What, Angus thought, *would anyone want with a small amount of magnesium?* If you needed light, kerosene was easily available, along with lamps in which to use it. Wood made a longer-lasting fire. The only real need for the magnesium powders Miss Jennings used was to create a sudden brilliant flash, so she could take her photographs indoors.

A jerk on his line and the pole was almost pulled out of his hands. "Hey," Dave shouted, "you've got a big one."

Angus threw the fishing pole to the ground. "I've gotta go. You take it."

He jumped to his feet and ran. The pole was pulled down into the cold waters of the Yukon River. Dave grabbed his own, scrambled to his feet, and took off after Angus.

*   *   *

Eleanor Jennings stood in the faint light coming from the room behind her. Between the buildings long shadows still lingered in the near-Arctic night. "I'm sorry I'm late," Sterling said. "Something came up at the detachment."

"Gave me a chance to catch up," she said. "I've spent the time writing a letter to my father."

Sterling thought she looked nice, in an evening gown of green taffeta with a salmon-coloured over-dress. The neckline was scooped, the bodice tightly fitted, the waist pouched, the sleeves short. A black collar dotted with pearls was cinched around her neck. She pulled on her gloves.

"I walked past the Savoy on my way here," he said, taking her arm after she'd locked the door behind them. "The crowd seems manageable tonight."

"I need not fear being trampled to death then?" Her laugh as light as chimes in a soft wind.

"Not tonight." Any place else it would be scandalous, escorting a lady to an evening at a dance hall. Even in Dawson, Sterling expected to get more than a few raised eyebrows. But Miss Jennings didn't seem to be at all concerned with respectability. He'd offered to take her to dinner, and she'd asked if, instead, they could go to the Savoy. She was fascinated, she said, by the place. All those undercurrents of humanity. She was hoping to meet more of the customers and hand out her cards.

He ruefully reflected that she seemed more interested in making business contacts than in the pleasure of his company.

Word had spread that twin sisters would be performing at the Monte Carlo. Thus the custom at the Savoy was down considerably tonight. He didn't know how they'd be able to manage if it had gone *up*. It had been a close call last night. Good thing the police had been on their guard and expecting trouble. A riot could travel through town with the speed of a wildfire. Or a rumour.

Ray Walker did a double take when Sterling and Eleanor Jennings came through the doors.

She left Sterling to order drinks — whisky for him, lemonade for her — and joined the group of men gathered around Barney's customary stool.

"Gentlemen, good evening."

They touched hats and caps. Barney grinned through tobacco-stained and broken teeth. "I'm still wanting to take your photograph, sir," she said to the sourdough, wagging her finger like a displeased schoolmarm. "You promised to sit for me."

"Can't imagine what you want with this ugly mug. I figure my face might break your camera."

"You have a truly original face."

"You can say that again," a man snorted.

Sterling handed her the drink. He sipped his whisky. A rare indulgence. Not bad stuff at all.

"I'm surprised to see you here this evening, Nicky," Eleanor said. "I thought you were leaving town."

"In due course. In due course. Couldn't leave without a last evening with my new friends."

"Didn't know you had friends," John Turner said.

The man never smiled, at least never when Richard Sterling had been around to witness.

"You are my friend," Nicky replied, not realizing he'd been insulted. "We play together, no?"

"If you call giving me all your money every night playing, then I guess you could say we're friends."

"Excellent. Now, time for a game, I believe. Our English friend should be completing his second round of performances shortly."

The two men ordered a refill of their drinks, and then went through to the gambling hall.

Eleanor Jennings drifted around the room, chatting to men, handing business cards to those she had not yet met. Sterling watched her. She smiled and held her head to one side and listened in total attention. She had a way of making the speaker think he was a person of incomparable interest.

She reminded him, he realized, of Fiona.

Chapter Twenty-Nine

As I'd expected custom was less than normal tonight. I was glad of it, yet hoping this wouldn't be the start of a downward spiral into bankruptcy and, worse, insignificance.

Ridiculous. I still employed the most popular dance hall girl in the territory, had the best lineup of performers, the most enthusiastic chorus line. The audience would tire of the twins soon enough and be once again streaming through our doors.

Irene was tense tonight. So tense I could almost smell it. The big announcement was coming. I doubted very much that I'd like it. But there wasn't much I could do other than take her off the stage. And that would do nothing for our custom.

Tension, however, served to make her bold. Bolder than usual, that is. Her gestures were more extravagant, her voice louder, her dancing more daring. She smiled widely, kicked her legs with abandon, sang as if her heart were breaking. And I do believe when she shouted "out darned spot" there might have been a tear in her eye. Even the audience, most of whom were here in hopes of catching a glimpse of a dancer's knee or maybe even — if fortune's face was shining — her knickers, and didn't care about the quality of the performance any more than they cared about the quality of the mud they waded through to get here, seemed to be impressed. They sat a bit straighter, were a fraction quieter, and now and again nudged their fellows in admiration rather than amusement or lechery.

Ray Walker stood at the back, watching the show, something he didn't usually do. He stared at Irene, his face long and sad and wanting.

If Irene's big announcement was that she was leaving the Savoy for another dance hall, I would have no choice but to up her already considerable salary.

I detest feeling as though I'm at someone's mercy.

The three poker players were hard at it when Ray I walked through the hall. Roland focused all his attention on his cards, John Turner scowled at everyone, and Count Nicky was performing to the few uninterested folk who'd stopped to watch the game.

Eleanor Jennings was in the saloon, sitting at the big round table in the centre, surrounded by men. She had a stack of her cards in front of her and was explaining the principles of photography. To my surprise, Richard Sterling stood against the bar. His boot was on the footrest and he held a glass of whisky in his hand. I had a fraction of a moment before he realized I'd arrived in which to observe him. He was watching Eleanor Jennings with an unreadable expression on his face.

He looked up, saw me. His eyes opened in what I took to be pleasure and then his face closed so abruptly someone might have brought down the shutters.

I turned away and went back into the dance hall, stomach churning.

Chapter Thirty

I didn't make it.

"Mother!" a voice shouted across the room. Angus was striding rapidly toward me. Richard moved away from the bar and Angus turned and spoke to him. I couldn't hear the words but my son's tone was sharp and his face anxious.

I crossed the room at an unladylike clip. Men stopped in midsentence and turned to watch. Eleanor Jennings rose to her feet.

"What on earth?" I began. "Has something happened? What's the matter?"

"Magnesium. It's explosive."

"What's magnesium?" I asked.

"A powder. When combined with other chemicals it's used to create a sudden bright light for the taking of photography," Richard answered. "The mixture is explosive. What about it, Angus?"

"Stolen. From Miss Jennings."

"When?"

"An explosion," someone said. "There's going to be an explosion? Where? When?"

The word passed though the room as fast as though someone had offered to pay for a round.

"Upstairs," Richard ordered.

"I don't know if we have time," Angus said.

"Time for what?" I asked.

"Angus, I expressly told you not to talk about this to the police." Eleanor had come to join us. Her blue eyes as dark as a storm-tossed sea.

"I'm sorry, Miss Jennings, but I can't keep it secret. I have a duty to the people of this town. Someone stole a quantity of the powders used to create a flash from Miss Jennings' studio this afternoon, sir."

"What else was taken?"

"Nothing."

"You're sure they were stolen, not simply misplaced?"

"They were stolen, all right," Eleanor said. "I do not misplace my supplies or equipment. I didn't want to create a fuss, which is precisely what seems to be happening now."

"I believe it's up to the police to decide if a fuss needs to be taken, madam."

"Oh, Richard," she said, though wide eyes and thick lashes, "don't be angry with me." The corners of her mouth turned into a pout but the storm still raged.

"Explosives?" one of the onlookers repeated. "Someone's stolen explosives?"

"Nothing to be concerned about," Richard said, "simply misplaced, that's all."

"But the lady here said …"

"And *I* said there's nothing to be concerned about. Now, George O'Reilly, if you haven't spent enough time on the woodpile …"

"Guess I heard wrong," O'Reilly said. "Nothing to worry about, folks. Bartender, pour me another." He slipped away, heading for the safety of the far end of the counter.

"This isn't the first time today I've heard word of an explosion," Richard said. "I thought someone was talking about fireworks and didn't pay them any mind. Let's go upstairs and talk about this."

"There isn't time," Angus said. "I think it's here. The …"

"Keep your voice down, for heaven's sake."

"The ... object ... is here."

As one we all turned to study the room, looking for a pile of magnesium powder. Like me, most of the others wouldn't know such a thing unless it had a sign prominently displayed.

"Angus," Richard said, "what makes you think it's here? It could be anywhere. It could have been taken by someone wanting it for other purposes. Mining for example."

"It's not strong enough to blast rock."

"I know that, but the thief might not."

"Mr. Sullivan has it. I'm sure of it. He tried to cause trouble here before. What better trouble than a bomb? He was at your studio the other day, right Miss Jennings? For a photograph of him and his daughter. If the picture was taken indoors, you would have used the flash powder. That means he saw it, saw where you kept it, and how to use it."

I might be prepared to dismiss my son's protestations as the immature histrionics of a child. But aside from the fact that Angus was never one to have histrionics, he clearly wasn't looking for attention, and he wasn't creating a bother. He was speaking slowly, calmly, and his face was set into determined lines. Richard seemed to think the same.

"Fiona, has Sullivan been in the Savoy tonight? He must know the police are looking for him, with orders to arrest him on sight for instigating a riot."

"I haven't seen him. A great many people come through our doors and I don't necessarily spot them all. Ray?"

"Nae a sign of him."

"I'm going to have a look around. Do you want to close the Savoy, Fiona? Walker? Get everyone out of here?"

Ray and I exchanged glances.

"Won't that cause a panic?" I asked.

"Quite possibly. I would, for that reason, advise against it.

"Walker, you and Joe check upstairs. I'm going to have a look in the dance hall. Angus, go to the fort. Get reinforcements."

"I'd rather not, sir. I know what the powder looks like, remember. You need me here."

"I'll send one of the girls," I said. It was approaching midnight and two of the percentage girls wandered in as we talked. I waved them over and told them to run to the fort and ask for several officers to come to the Savoy.

"Why?" they chorused.

"Because I said so," I replied. Hadn't I said that to Angus when he was small?

"But ..."

"But if you aren't back, with the police in tow, in ten minutes, you're both fired."

They fled.

We'd been trying to keep our voices low, but there was no keeping secrets in the Savoy. A couple of the drinkers whispered among themselves, before slipping out. (They did not fail to finish their drinks first.) Barney's chatter ground to a halt as he realized no one was left for him to regal with his stories.

"What can I do?" Eleanor asked.

"Like Angus, see if you can locate this stuff. How much are we talking about, anyway?"

"A couple of spoonfuls," Angus said.

Sterling refrained from groaning. A man could hide a couple of spoons full of any sort of powder in his pockets.

"Fiona," Richard said, "start looking for Sullivan. Don't approach him if you see him, come and get me or one of the other Mounties. Walker, get searching. Angus and Eleanor, you too."

I strolled — well, I tried to stroll — into the back rooms. The gambling hall was packed. As well as the three regulars, two other players had joined the poker game. Jake was behind the roulette table, and I pulled him aside. I told him to watch out for anyone acting suspiciously. He regarded me as if I'd told him I was turning the Savoy into a nunnery. Watching for those "acting suspiciously" was the primary job description for the head croupier in a dance hall.

I headed for the back. Time for the penultimate act, the cancan, followed by Irene's dance of the seven veils. Something caught my attention. I stopped and turned. One of the poker players I hadn't seen before. He had a heavy beard, round thick spectacles, bushy black eyelashes, and long hair that hadn't felt the touch of soap and water for a very long time. His right eyebrow was drooping downwards at a highly unnatural angle.

Something rather familiar about him.

Gerry Sullivan. I was sure of it. Heavily disguised, but him none the less.

I hurried back into the saloon. It was practically empty. Everyone had run off to do as Richard had ordered.

I caught Barney in the act of attempting to crawl across the bar to reach the bottles on the back shelf. For a moment I forgot we were in deadly danger and shouted, "Stop right where you are."

He didn't look the least bit apologetic. Merely settled back onto his stool with an air of offended dignity.

I lifted my skirts to unseemly heights and galloped up the stairs. Voices at the end of the hall. "Ray," I bellowed, "I've found him."

"Found who?" Ray asked as his head popped around a corner.

"Sullivan. He's here."

Back down the stairs with my partner at my heels. Through the salon, this time ignoring Barney casually pouring himself a drink, into the gambling hall.

The man with the beard wasn't there.

Into the dance hall. The men were on their feet now, cheering the cancan. On stage legs and petticoats flashed, women smiled. The orchestra played. Maxie moved to centre stage; she lifted her leg and grabbed her ankle. The men howled and hooted.

"There!" I grabbed Ray's arm. "It's him."

The bearded man was on the far side of the room, standing at the bottom of the steps.

Angus, my precious son, was between us. He'd recognized Sullivan and was heading in that direction. I ran, pushing and shoving men out of my way. I knew Ray was behind me. I didn't see Richard anywhere.

Sullivan wasn't yet aware of us. He had a cigar in his mouth. He pulled a box of matches out of his shirt pocket, took one out, and struck the tip. He held the flame to his cigar and puffed. Over the music and the shouting and the thunder of women's feet, I heard Angus cry, "You there! You're under arrest."

Saints preserve us. My son thought he was a Mountie.

"Angus," I yelled. "Stop."

My son charged Sullivan, somewhat in the manner of a scrawny bull charging a matador. The man glanced around. His eyes widened when he saw Angus, followed by Ray and me, approaching. He dropped the match to the floor.

"No," Angus yelled.

A black boot came out of the crowd. It stepped on the match, ground it into the sawdust. Extinguished it. "Gerry Sullivan, you've changed since yesterday," Richard Sterling said, grabbing the man's arm. "You're under arrest."

Angus dropped to the floor. I feared he was having a stroke, shocked by events. He scrabbled through the sawdust at men's feet. "Got it," he said.

He scrambled to his feet and slowly opened his hand. Grey powder.

Chapter Thirty-One

The percentage girls arrived with two Mounties in time to escort Gerry Sullivan to the fort. He didn't go without a fuss. Much yelling about the glory of Ireland and the cursed British oppressors and damning of our beloved queen.

What blowing up a saloon in the Yukon had to do with the fate of Ireland was beyond my capacity to understand. Perhaps some things truly are men's business.

Eleanor Jennings had screamed at Angus to put the powder mixture down, instantly. Apparently it could go off accidently if exposed to flame. Ray grabbed an unfinished glass of whisky from the nearest customer and Angus dropped the powder into the liquid. The man was so shocked by this behaviour he didn't object to having his drink ruined.

The clientele of the Savoy are, as was displayed the previous evening, not averse to leaping into a fight on any pretext. They might not much care about the political situation in Ireland vis-à-vis their British overlords, or like to hear a fat, matronly old lady cursed, but anything to do with the oppressive British would normally have the Americans rallying to the cause.

Tonight, however, the expected fight did not materialize. Whispers about explosions, attempts to blow up the Savoy, accompanied by "slaughter us all in our beds," and enough dynamite to blow the whole town sky high, took the wind out of a prospective fighter's sails. They might be happy enough to swing a fist in any direction, regardless of the cause involved (or lack thereof), but Sullivan had threatened their favourite watering hole, not to mention life and limb of anyone in the vicinity.

"How much damage might that have done?" I asked.

"Enough to blow off a careless photographer's arm," Eleanor said. "Which has been known to happen. The danger here would have been if it ignited the floor and the fire spread. Plus the panic the initial explosion would have caused."

"What on earth could the man have been thinking?"

"Not thinking at all, I suspect. After all, he was the closest one to the powder and the match. His foot would have been the first to go."

Richard Sterling slapped Angus on the back. "Well done, lad. Good thinking and fast action."

Angus beamed. I did not like that beam. He was getting altogether overconfident for my liking.

John Turner, Roland the Magnificent, and Count Nicky stood at the door, watching.

The cancan and accompanying music had drifted to a halt when everyone became aware of the commotion at the back. Now that Sullivan was gone, escorted out by two burley Mounties, the girls milled about on the stage, unsure of what to do. The audience had stood up, straining their necks to get a better view. Impromptu show over, they began to take their seats. Soon the hooting and thumping began. Someone might have attempted to blow up the Savoy, to wreak havoc and destruction in our midst, but enough was enough and it was time to get on with the show.

The orchestra didn't seem inclined to start up where they'd left off with the "Infernal Galop" and the girls gradually drifted off the stage.

Time for Irene's big dance.

But the air of anticipation in the room had departed along with Gerry Sullivan and his police escort. The men at the front were still enthused, but many others had lost interest and a few of those who'd gone out to the street to watch Sullivan being taken away had not returned. Irene went through her dance by rote, her face barely cracking a smile, discarding the lengths of chiffon as if leaving them for the maid.

I had had the presence of mind to order Angus to leave rather than risk him witnessing the sensuous dance. Which was turning out to be about as sensuous as Mrs. Mann labouring in the laundry shed.

Irene finished the dance, wrapped in the last length of chiffon, and took a desultory bow. Only a scattering of small nuggets fell at her feet. She gathered them up and stomped off the stage with a scowl.

The caller laboured to his feet and bellowed at the customers to "grab your partners for that long, dreamy, juicy waltz," while the benches were shoved aside and the percentage girls either sauntered or careened onto the floor.

When I returned to the saloon, Richard Sterling was waiting for me.

"Where's Angus?"

"I sent him home. Told him he'd done a good job, but if I found him on the streets tonight he'd be arrested for breaking curfew."

"There's a curfew?"

"For Angus, there is."

I laughed.

"He takes your safety seriously, Fiona. He thinks himself your protector, and it bothers him a great deal that he's too young to do much about guarding you."

"Perish the thought. My son following me day and night? I suspect he'd get bored fairly quickly."

"He's been spending some time with Roland, he tells me. Roland's been asking questions about the clientele here. I don't like to see the men taking advantage of Angus."

"I agree. But as you pointed out, it's hard for me to keep the boy away for long." I changed the subject. "Where's Eleanor? Don't tell me there's a curfew on her too?"

He shifted his feet. "No. But I suggested she could do nothing more here. She should have told us about the disappearance of the magnesium. Or at least let Angus do so."

I chastised myself, a little bit, for the frisson of pleasure I felt at hearing Richard criticize Eleanor. Still enjoyed it, though.

"We had a narrow escape."

"That we did. I'm going to the fort now. McKnight will want to question Sullivan about the murder the other day. The one you witnessed."

"You think he was responsible?"

"It's a possibility. I believe he and Stewart may have visited the same bar in Louse Town. I don't know what they could have argued about in the short time Stewart was in town, but perhaps Sullivan will tell us. Good night, Fiona."

"Good night, Richard."

As the door swung behind him, three fresh-faced young cheechakos pushed their way in.

I forced my face into a smile. "Good evening, gentlemen. Welcome to the Savoy."

One of them leered at me, one blew the fumes of near-poisonous liquor into my face, and one belched. "We're here to see the Lady Irénée," the leerer said, addressing my décolletage. "Are you her, sweetie?"

"I am not. Neither am I your sweetie. The dancing, however, has begun. You'd better hurry."

They did so, pushing each other aside in their haste.

"I'm glad that's over," I said to Ray a few minutes later when he passed me after having ejected an argumentative alcoholic.

"What's over?"

"That nasty murder business. Gerry Sullivan killed that man in the alley last week and he'll hang for it. Poor Colleen. I wonder what will happen to her now."

Ray peered at me. "You aren't getting sentimental over the lass, are ye, Fee?"

"Good heavens, no. Merely speculating aloud." Colleen would find herself alone in a harsh world. She'd survive.

I had.

Chapter Thirty-Two

Unlike Fiona MacGillivray, Richard Sterling wasn't so sure it was over.

Gerry Sullivan was loud and argumentative. He denounced British imperialism, sang the phrases of Ireland, vowed revenge for centuries of abuse. He proudly pronounced himself a member of the Brotherhood. He was, as Sterling had suspected, a Fenian.

The man had probably never been to Ireland in his life, and would no doubt be seriously disappointed if he had, but reality was rarely an impediment to a man with a vision. The Fenians were finished. They'd made a nuisance of themselves for a few years over the sixties and seventies, having some idea that they could capture Canada for the Americans and thus avenge the British control of Ireland. But their dream — illusion more likely — had died, and eventually even the Americans turned against them. Gerry Sullivan, loud and proud, and very stupid, was the last to realize the cause was finished.

They had no trouble getting him to confess to attempting to start a riot in the Savoy. He'd thought of the idea all by himself, he claimed proudly. Initially he wasn't pleased that his daughter Colleen had to resort to pounding the boards of the stage in a dance hall, but when she was promoted he recognized the opportunity immediately. She would dance a seductive, illegal dance, stirring men's passions. When the police tried to shut the dance hall down, as they were sure to, the audience would riot in objection. Sullivan was confident that once their dander had been roused, the Americans could be spurred to a full-scale revolt ending in the eviction of the Canadian presence. The Yukon, at least, would be freed from the crushing yoke that was British imperialism.

It was, Sterling thought, one of the dumbest revolutionary ideas he'd ever heard. The Americans might be quite happy to see the territory become a possession of the United States, but few of them would countenance any disruption of their single-minded pursuit of finding gold and spending it as quickly as possible.

"Jim Stewart," McKnight said, cutting Sullivan off in the midst of an explanation of the noble aims of the noble Fenian brotherhood.

"Who?"

"Jim Stewart. Tell us about Jim Stewart."

Sullivan scratched his chin. The fake beard had been discarded along with the rest of the disguise. It had been a mighty poor disguise. In better light and without being able to hide in a crush of people, Sullivan would have been spotted almost immediately. "Never heard of him."

McKnight said, "Why'd you kill him? Opposed to the aims of your brotherhood, was he?"

Sullivan did look confused, Sterling had to admit. "I didn't kill no one."

"You did. And we have you now. Tuesday evening before last. A man was knifed in the alley behind the Savoy. Judge'll think better of you if you confess."

Sullivan shook his head. "Nothing to confess. Hey! You aren't going to pin that on me." He tried to get out of his chair, but Constable FitzHenry slapped him, none too gently, back down.

"I didn't kill no one, I tell you. I don't even know anyone name of Stewart."

"A Scottish fellow. About five feet seven, light build. You were seen in his presence in the Yankee Doodle," Sterling offered. "Trying to drum up trouble, I suspect." It was a wild guess, but it hit its mark.

"Okay, okay. Now I remember him. I met a fellow by that name a couple days ago. Yeah. Stewart. I figured that for his first name. I've a cousin by marriage name of Stuart." He spelled it out. "Same name as the would-be king. I didn't kill him, though."

"You expect us to believe ..." McKnight said.

"What was he doing in the Yankee Doodle?" Sterling interrupted. "An unlikely place for a Scotsman fresh off the boat to find himself."

"I figured he figured the Yankee'd be a good place to find like-minded folk."

"Like-minded? In what way?"

"Men wanting to free the Yukon."

"Yes, yes," McKnight said, "from the yoke of British Imperialism. Whether we want to be freed or not. I've had enough for one night. Constable, take the prisoner to his cell."

FitzHenry pulled Sullivan to his feet.

"You don't have to be so god damned rough. I'm coming," Sullivan said.

"Any more language like that," McKnight said, "and I'll add to the charges."

"Give me a blue ticket and let me get the hell out of here. I'll collect my daughter and we'll be gone."

"Oh, no, Mr. Sullivan. There's no blue ticket for murder. You'll be our guest on the woodpile until next time the judge is in town. And once your trial's over, you'll hang."

* * *

Once again Irene didn't make her grand announcement. I assumed she was waiting until the time was right, and she had the audience's attention cradled in the palm of her hand. She didn't have to stay for the remainder of the evening's entertainment, although she usually did. Tonight she stalked out shortly after the floor was cleared and the bumpy gallop they called dancing began.

Just as well, as her scowl would put the toughest sourdough off his stride.

It was approaching closing time; the dancers were asleep on their feet, smiles frozen into place; the violinist had forgotten how to make a tune and was dragging his bow across the strings without rhyme or reason. Murray wiped the counter, and wiped the counter, and continued to wipe the counter, his strokes so rhythmic they were lulling him to sleep. Most of the customers had left, but a few hearty souls possessed of limitless energy danced on. And drank on.

My feet were aching, and I dared be so bold as to rest my backside against the arm of an unoccupied chair. My eyelids fluttered shut. "Tired, Fiona?" said a soft voice.

My eyes few open and I jerked myself upright. "Certainly not." I pulled my watch out of my pocket and flipped it open. The hands had scarcely moved since the last time I'd checked. I refrained from shaking it to see if it were still working. "Good heavens, is it that late already? Almost closing time. Is Mr. Sullivan tucked in for the night?"

"He is," Richard said. "He'll be charged in the morning with the murder of James Stewart."

"Good." I didn't ask why he'd done it. It was largely irrelevant. As long as it didn't have anything to do with me.

"I'm not so sure. That's why I've come back. To talk to you. Fiona, are you sure Stewart said nothing more before he died? Perhaps even something that didn't make any sense at the time?"

I glanced around the room. Murray was wiping the counter. Barney had left long ago and his stool had not been claimed. Ray was pouring drinks and chatting to the customers. Ray never looked tired. He'd tried to follow Irene out when she left, but she gave him an angry growl, and he retreated back to his post. I could hear the roulette wheel spinning, Jake calling for last bets. I could smell cigar smoke, damp sawdust, and the acrid odour of a man losing far more money than he could afford.

I shook my head. The lie so ingrained I could not now take it back. Besides, it made no difference.

"What was the name of the last king of Scotland?"

The change of topic was somewhat abrupt. "What?"

"The last king of Scotland. Angus told me about Bonnie Prince Charlie and some big battle for the throne."

"James. James VII was Charlie's grandfather. James was deposed, sent to exile in France. His son, also named James, should have been king on his death."

"Did these Jameses have a last name?"

I nodded slowly. "Yes, they did. Stuart."

"James Stuart. Jim Stewart. I wonder if that means anything?"

I was prevented from answering when a man sitting on a stool at one end of the bar fell off it. He crashed to the floor, glass and whisky flying. He lay where he fell, blinking. Then he rolled over and tucked his hands underneath his head to make a pillow.

Ray lifted his eyes to the ceiling. Richard went to give him a hand. If the man wanted to sleep, he'd find the mud of the street nice and soft.

Chapter Thirty-Three

As I feared, Angus was rather full of himself, having prevented the destruction of the Savoy (or at least a section of the floorboards). He was describing his thought process in great detail to Mr. Mann when I came into the kitchen the next morning. Judging by the expression on Mr. Mann's face, this was not the first time he'd heard the story. Probably not the first time today, either.

"You're up early, Fiona," Mrs. Mann said.

"I wanted to catch Angus before he left for the shop. I have important news. I'll have a coffee, please." I sat down. I hadn't dressed yet and wore my scarlet dressing gown, the one with the gold dragon streaking across the back, my hair tucked into a rough knot at my neck.

I waited until I was sure I had everyone's attention. And a cup of coffee. No cream again today. Drat.

"Mr. Sullivan has been charged with the killing of that unfortunate man outside the Savoy last week."

"He has?"

"The judge has been sent for and there will be a trial as soon as he's able to arrive."

Mr. Mann nodded with satisfaction. "Good. Then he will hang. Trouble us no longer."

Angus didn't look as pleased at the news as I expected.

"Are you sure, Mother?"

"Yes, I'm sure. Why do you ask?"

"I don't see it myself. Mr. Sullivan wanted to create a big explosion, attract lots of attention. He wasn't even all that concerned at getting caught. He could have put the magnesium into a cigar, hidden it under a table with a long, slow fuse. He could have done something so he'd be well away before it went off. But he didn't. He waited around. He wanted to be there. He wanted to use the commotion to start his so-called revolution. That's not the work of a man who stabs anyone in a back alley."

I didn't want to know how my son managed to become so intimately acquainted with the workings of the criminal mind. "Perhaps this Mr. Stewart became aware of Mr. Sullivan's nefarious plot and had to be silenced." I myself am quite acquainted with the workings of the criminal mind. A fact I try not to advertise.

"But Mr. Sullivan didn't have a nefarious plot, Mother, not when Stewart was alive. He didn't see Miss Jennings' flash powders, and thus come up with the idea, until a few days ago." Angus shook his head thoughtfully. I attempted to distract him.

"What do you have on today?"

"Work at the store. Then meeting Sergeant Lancaster."

"Why on earth would you be meeting Sergeant Lancaster?"

All the blood rose into his face before draining rapidly away. He gaped at me and struggled to find words. "Because he … uh … he wants to … I mean I want to …"

"Continue with the boxing lessons," I said, sipping overly strong coffee.

"You know about that?"

"I know about everything, my dear. Now, time to be off. Are you assisting Miss Jennings later?"

"Yes. She's teaching me how to develop the plates. It's really interesting. Red light doesn't destroy the image, but other light does, so you have to work in this really low red light."

"I do believe I said it's time to be off. Mr. Mann has gone in search of his hat."

Mrs. Mann handed Angus his lunch packet and he stumbled all over his big feet in the effort to get out the door. I drank coffee, quite pleased with myself. I had not known Angus was taking boxing lessons from Sergeant Lancaster. However, I knew the sergeant offered such lessons (I doubt there is anyone in town not informed that he was once the champion of Winnipeg). I had, on occasion, seen a bruise or two on Angus's face and noticed chapped knuckles, which I'd believed to be the result of overly enthusiastic boyish antics. When Angus mentioned a meeting with the sergeant, with whom he had absolutely nothing in common, I simply put the facts together.

The police would do well to employ women as detectives. I might suggest that to them someday.

* * *

I stood in front of the windows of the Savoy. The advertisement was still on display, still with a notice indicating Colleen would be performing tonight. I'd seen several other photographs and notices to that effect around town. We should probably have them taken down.

One of our regulars accosted me when I came through the doors. He wanted to know when the "sweet young thing" would be back. "I was very disappointed, Mrs. MacGillivray, not to hear her last night. I enjoyed her song very much, I did." The men within earshot all nodded.

I babbled something nonsensical and headed to the back to check on progress in the ladies' changing room. The twins at the Monte Carlo had been a dud. The performers were "No more twins," I'd overheard one fellow complain, "than me and my aunt Fanny." Tonight I could expect custom at the Savoy to be back to regular levels — meaning bursting at the seams.

Which, I reminded myself happily, would mean that when I went to the bank tomorrow morning, the sack I carried would also be bursting at the seams.

Irene normally had little to do with the other women, performers or percentage girls. She kept herself to herself as befitting her lofty status as headliner. Tonight, she was even more aloof. She sat on a chair in the corner, wrapped in her own thoughts, while all around her women dressed, made themselves up, and chatted. She seemed so sad, so lonely, I actually leaned over and asked in a low voice, "Is everything all right, Irene?"

She looked at me through dark and angry eyes. I took a step backward. "Right as rain, Mrs. Mac. Absolutely peachy keen. Why wouldn't they be?"

The words themselves were such a contrast to the hiss with which she spoke them, I didn't even bother to reprimand her for the familiar use of my name. "Glad to hear it. Carry on." I scurried away. She'd had a fight, no doubt, with her lover. With Eleanor. Did female lovers fight? Presumably they did. They were still human, after all.

The girls had stopped their preparations and their gossip to watch the exchange. I snarled something about a show to put on, and left them to it.

Roland was climbing the stage when I came out. The men booed and hissed in their friendly manner. He took a deep bow in acknowledgement.

I entered the saloon in time to see Count Nicky arrive. He was particularly well dressed tonight in a long-tailed black frock coat, crisp white shirt, and grey cravat. Diamond stickpin at his throat and stout gold-tipped walking stick in hand.

The count paused in the entrance. He lifted his stick.

"Gentlemen. Friends." He spotted me. "Distinguished lady." He paused, waiting, presumably for everyone's attention. As a pronouncement of that sort usually preceded the buying of drinks for all present, the men obliged.

John Turner accepted a glass of whisky from Not-Murray. Barney paused mid-story. Helen Saunderson came out of the closet behind the bar, carrying a clattering mop and sloshing pail. The count glared at her. She ignored him.

He raised his hand. The jewel in his ring glittered red in the weak kerosene light. "I will be departing on the morrow. I have important business to conduct in Washington."

"Didn't he tell us that already?" Barney muttered.

"I will, I hope, be back with news of critical importance. Thank you all." He lowered his hand.

The men waited.

Count Nicky headed for the back. One more round of poker, no doubt.

"It's customary," Barney shouted, "for a fellow what's leaving town to buy a round for his friends."

The men muttered agreement.

"You have to do it, Nicky," I said. "You can't stand there looking important and leave the men with empty glasses."

"Very well," he said with a martyred sigh, "I suppose I must become familiar with your customs. Bartender, a drink for my friends."

The stampede began. Word that free drinks were on offer spread through a dancehall faster than news of an out-of-wedlock pregnancy through a duchess's garden party.

John Turner moved in the other direction, away from the press surging toward the bar. He stood alone, studying the count with a serious expression. He turned, saw me watching, and came over, habitual frown firmly in place.

"Think he's finally leaving?"

"He does seem to enjoy telling everyone he has important business in Washington."

Turner studied me for a long time. Then he gave me a slight nod and walked away. I felt he had told me something. But I had absolutely no idea what that might be.

Eleanor Jennings, my son trailing in her wake, came in as the free round was ending and the men were heading back to the gambling tables or benches in the dance hall. "I thought I might enjoy the show this evening, Fiona," she said. "I haven't seen it before, you know."

"I'll ensure you find a good seat. But Angus cannot watch."

He pouted, not surprised. Even if I were inclined to let him in, which I most certainly was not, the police wouldn't allow it. Something about corrupting the morals of a minor.

"I've never heard Irene sing," Eleanor said, her tone wistful. "I'd like to. This may be my last chance."

"You're leaving?" I said, warm with pleasure.

She blinked. "Me? No, I have no plans to leave."

"Oh. Angus, go home."

"Ah, Mother, it's still early."

"Find something entertaining to do then. You should be playing with your friends, not hanging around a dance hall."

Eleanor touched his arm. "She's right. You've proved to be a wonderful assistant, but you need to have fun also. I'll see you on Monday. Oh, there's Richard. How lovely." She turned the full strength of her smile onto the new arrival and fluttered her gloved fingers at him. A blond ringlet bounced as she cocked her head to one side.

I ground my teeth.

"Richard," Eleanor said, "you're just in time. I'm going to watch the show. Won't you join me?"

"Another time, perhaps." He glanced around the room. "Where's Roland?"

"Still on stage," I said. "He'll be finished in a few minutes. Why do you ask?"

"No reason. Why's the count all gussied up?"

"He's saying his farewells. You can probably still get a free drink out of him."

"Won't be sorry to see him leave," Richard said. Probably the only man in the place who'd ignore my suggestion of a free drink. He wasn't in uniform, meaning he wasn't on duty, so he should be able to unwind and enjoy himself. But he wasn't looking the least bit relaxed.

"He says he has business in Washington. I wonder if he's a Russian diplomat of some sort."

"Of some sort," Eleanor said.

Angus laughed.

"What does that mean?" Richard asked her, his voice surprisingly sharp.

"Nothing."

Angus laughed again.

I felt as though I were in the midst of a play for which I had studied the wrong script.

Nicky freed himself from a pack of enthusiastic well-wishers and headed toward us. Behind me a glass fell to the floor. I turned at the sound and saw John Turner standing against the wall. He watched our small group with a steady, unblinking stare. Helen was heading for the broken glass and spilled liquor, mop held high.

Boos and catcalls sounded the end of the magic act. Cheers and hooting announced the arrival of the dancers.

"Where's Walker?" Richard asked me.

I glanced around. My partner was nowhere to be seen. He paid little attention to what went on in the gambling hall, trusting Jake to keep control, and rarely watched the stage performance although he sometimes showed up for Irene's closing dance. He customarily spent the long hours behind the bar, serving liquor and watching for trouble. "He was here earlier. Probably taking a break."

"One last game, no?" Count Nicky said to John Turner.

"Sure. Where do you suppose our friend has gotten to?"

Richard didn't bother to excuse himself. He pushed his way through the crowd in the direction of the dance hall. Angus watched him go.

Then he followed.

I couldn't allow that. I had told my son he was to go home. I set off in pursuit.

I was waylaid before I'd gone three feet. "Mrs. MacGillivray, another lovely evening in your fine establishment."

Habit took control. "So nice to see you, sir. It's been a while, I believe, since you were here last."

He smiled at me. "Making my fortune, my dear. Making my fortune. And now I'm back to spend it. Let me buy you a drink."

"No thank you, sir. Enjoy your evening."

I hurried through the gambling room. The room was full but the poker table in the centre was unoccupied. Waiting, presumably, for the big money game.

The man who accosted me next wasn't quite as friendly as the previous fellow. "You're a handsome filly." He belched rotting meat and cheap cigar smoke into my face. "Let's have a little squeeze, eh?" A filthy hand reached for my left breast. I backhanded him without so much as breaking stride.

When I arrived in the dance hall, I could see Richard's head moving through the row of men lining the walls, Angus's shorter one bobbing along behind. They stopped by the stairs to the boxes. Richard spoke to Murray, carrying a tray of empty glasses and discarded bottles. Murray looked around and shook his head. Richard and Angus pressed on.

I felt a niggling touch of worry low in my stomach. Something was wrong. I had absolutely no idea what, but it was enough to have me concerned. Ellie was on centre stage, singing a lively song while the chorus line cavorted behind her. The audience looked pleased. Richard was heading for the rear of the building now. Very strange.

I ploughed on, alternately accepting greetings from well-wishers and growling at pests to get out of my way.

The Savoy has one back entrance, leading out into the alley. The door was normally kept locked. Richard reached it. He turned and said something to Angus. Angus replied, Richard opened the door, and they stepped outside. I ran across the few empty feet and made it before the door closed behind them. The light was still good.

Good enough to see two men grappling on the ground. Good enough to reveal the flash of a knife blade. The man on top had the weapon, the other one cried out as the knife fell, but he had strength enough to grip the wrist, trying to keep the blade from striking again.

Richard shouted. Angus yelled. I do believe I might have screamed. Richard crossed the few feet of the alley at a run. He reached down and grabbed the man on top, the one with the knife, by the shoulder. He pulled. The man leapt to his feet with a roar, arm extended, knife held out.

Roland.

I glanced at the man on the ground. Ray, breathing heavily. Blood poured from his left arm.

Roland and Richard faced each other. Roland moved to his right, and Richard did also.

I laid my hand against Angus's back.

"Put the knife down," Richard said, voice calm and steady, eyes focused on Roland's hand.

"Stay out of this, Yellow Stripe. This is big boy's business."

"In this town it's the business of the North-West Mounted Police. Put the knife down."

Ray scrambled backwards on his rear end, taking himself out of range. Then he pushed himself to his feet. He glanced toward Angus and me, gave us a sharp nod.

"I'll have you up on charges, Sterling," Roland said. "Get the hell out of here, and take that interfering bitch and her whelp with you."

"You're making a serious mistake. Ray Walker is no more interested in the cause of Scottish independence than I am. Put the knife down and we can talk it out."

Scottish independence?

"Please, Mr. Roland," Angus said, "This isn't right."

Roland and Richard circled, facing each other. Richard held his hands up; Roland slashed empty air with the blade. Their breath came in deep spurts. Music drifted through the walls of the Savoy. A dog barked into the night.

When Roland's back was to us, Angus charged. He hit the magician full on before I could so much as order him to stop. Roland spun around, the knife slicing downward. I screamed. But Angus had danced back, taking himself out of range. Richard leapt forward, grabbed Roland's wrist. He twisted. The magician snarled, teeth exposed like a rabid dog. The men grappled and then, with a grunt of pain, the knife clattered to the ground. Roland punched Richard in the stomach and spun around searching for the weapon.

Angus stepped forward and slugged him, a right fist of the sort that would do a former champion of Winnipeg proud, full into the magician's face.

Roland, magnificent no longer, fell hard.

I kicked the knife into the shadows.

Chapter Thirty-Four

Richard dropped to the ground beside Roland. He put his knee into the man's back and pulled his arms up. He shouted at Angus to fetch one of the bouncers. I ran to Ray.

"I'm all right, Fee," my partner said through ragged breaths. His left sleeve was sliced open, leaking blood. I ripped the cloth and rolled it back. The cut didn't look too large and the blood was just a thin trickle. He struggled to sit up. I put my arm around him and helped him stagger to his feet.

"Took me by surprise. Would nae a happened in the old days."

Joe Hamilton burst through the doors, Angus hot on his heels.

"Let's get him up," Richard said. "We'll take him to the fort."

"I'll help," Angus said.

"No!" I shouted.

"No," Richard said. "Stay with your mother. I'll come back later."

Eleanor Jennings stood in the doorway. John Turner beside her.

"Mrs. MacGillivray," Richard said, "will you please get back inside, and take these people with you."

"I'll give you a hand," Turner said, stepping forward.

"I don't need ..." Richard said.

"I'll give you a hand," Turner repeated, firmly.

Richard looked at him, something unsaid passed between them, and he nodded.

The two of them, with the help of Joe, wrestled Roland to his feet. "You'll be sorry about this, Corporal," the magician shouted. "I'll see you hanged for interfering in this. And you. I don't know who the hell you are, but I can guess. You'll be busted down to latrine-cleaner."

"Hey," someone shouted from inside the Savoy, "what's going on out there?"

Men's heads began popping up, trying to peer over Eleanor's shoulder into the alley. I decided that Richard did not need further assistance. "Angus, get inside and shut that door. Then find Helen." Among food supplies and cleaning equipment, she had a small supply of bandages in the storage closet. I kept my arm around Ray. He was able to stand, but I feared shock would be settling in soon. "We'll go around the front. I don't dare walk through the dance hall like this."

Eleanor stepped aside as Angus slipped past her. "Everything's okay," I heard him say as the door closed behind him. "Mr. Walker had a fall. My mother's with him."

Eleanor took Ray's other arm.

"I don't need any help," I snapped.

"But I'd like to give it," she said. "If you'll let me."

"I can walk perfectly fine, ye ken," Ray said. He took a step forward and his knees wobbled. We grabbed him and supported him around the building and through the front doors of the Savoy Saloon and Dance Hall.

Chapter Thirty-Five

After all that excitement, I could do nothing but let the evening progress as it normally did. Helen pulled out bandages and clean cloths and tidied Ray up. Fortunately the wound was not deep. Angus found a shirt in one of the upstairs rooms to replace the blood-stained, torn one. Ray rested for a few minutes while Helen fussed, changed his shirt, and then announced he was needed behind the bar.

I am not his mother, nor his boss, so I didn't try to stop him from going back to work.

Few of the patrons realized anything was wrong, and those who had were satisfied that Ray had taken a tumble in the alley. Count Nicky complained loudly that his poker companions had disappeared on him. And just when he was beginning to win.

But, he reminded us all, he would be leaving soon with important business to conduct in Washington.

Eleanor Jennings went into the dance hall to hear Irene sing. She left immediately after the song, saying nothing to me. She blinked rapidly, refusing to allow the tears to fall.

Richard had told us he'd be back after settling Roland into jail, so I allowed Angus to wait upstairs in my office. He deserved to know what was going on.

I asked Ray, while Helen was tending to his wounds. He shook his head. "I've nae a clue, Fee. Roland said he wanted ta talk ta me after his act. I figured he had an offer for a job — him or me. No harm in listening to what he had to say, even though I'm not looking for a job and you do the hiring. I went out ta the alley with him, and he pulled a knife on me. Do ye figure he's the one killed Jim Stewart?"

"I can't imagine two knife-wielding maniacs are wandering around town."

Richard returned to the Savoy about an hour later. He hadn't changed, and his suit jacket was dusty and rumpled. His eyes were sad. He stroked his chin. "Shall we go upstairs?"

Ray came with us. His colour was not looking all that good, but I figured he was able to take care of himself. Nevertheless, I ensured he took a seat on the sofa.

Richard stood at the window, looking out, twisting his hat in his hands. Angus gave me a look and I indicated he was to keep quiet. Let the man think.

Richard turned and faced us.

"Roland is here, in Canada, to investigate suspicions of a Scottish Independence movement showing an interest in the Yukon."

"You mean Jim Stewart," I said.

"Probably not his real name. He assumed the *nom de guerre* of his hero, James Stuart. Stewart was known as a Scottish agitator. Whether he was here to drum up anti-British sentiment wherever he could find it, I don't know. I suspect he was, thus the visit to the restless Americans down at the Yankee Doodle. Ray, did Stewart approach you?"

Ray shook his head. "Never seen the fellow before he ended up dead. If he'd talked ta me about freeing Scotland I would have laughed in his face. The old country's problems are none o' mine. Fee, you know anything about that?"

"Nothing at all. It is possible, I suppose, that he was coming here. To meet with us."

"MacGillivray and Walker," Richard said. "He might have suspected he'd find sympathetic ears at the Savoy."

"What made you realize it was Roland who'd killed him, sir?" Angus asked.

"Soon as I heard about James Stuart, the uncrowned King of Scotland, I wondered at the coincidence of the names. I came across a book in Stewart's room. An *Illustrated History of Scotland*. The pages to do with the Jacobite Rebellion that ended with the Battle of Culloden were heavily used."

I shifted in my seat.

"You know something about that, Mrs. MacGillivray?"

"Nope."

Richard gave me a long look before continuing. I folded my hands politely in my lap.

"When Angus told me Roland had been asking about Scottish people hanging around the Savoy, I began thinking. I didn't suspect Roland of having anything to do with the death of Stewart until I saw him entering the Yankee Doodle, a place he, if he was who he said he was, would have no reason to frequent. When I did, I began realizing that Walker, and even you, Mrs. MacGillivray, might be in some danger."

I kept my face impassive, but inside I shuddered. So, this Jim Stewart had been coming to meet me. Expecting, no doubt, to find me, a MacGillivray, eager to avenge *Culloden*. He would have been sadly disappointed to meet a woman with the queen's own accent and not the slightest interest in men and their armies and their fantasies of revenge for one-hundred-fifty-year-old battles.

"Good thing," Ray said with a grimace. "Man must be daft."

"What was all that about having you charged?" Angus asked. "Who is Roland?"

"Real name, as he was in a rush to inform us, is Roland Montague-Smythe. Major, British Army."

Ray blew out a puff of air.

"Major Montague-Smythe is here on Her Majesty's business, looking into rumours of dissent in the territory."

"There are always rumours of dissent," I said. "Gossip and complaining are the life blood of this town. No one means anything by it."

"Some do," Richard said. "Look at Gerry Sullivan and his pathetic remnants of the Fenian so-called Brotherhood. I suspect that might have been some inspiration to Stewart. The Fenians planned to capture Canada and hand it back to Britain in exchange for Ireland. As you may know, that was a prime inspiration for the creation of the Dominion back in sixty-seven. I guess the Fenians didn't notice, or think it mattered, that Canada is no longer a British possession. Same plan for Scotland? Perhaps. Angus, what are you wanting to say?"

"Count Nicky. He's … uh … planning to march a Russian army into Dawson to capture it and trade it to the Americans in exchange for Alaska, which he'll call New Russia, with him as the head."

"How do you know this?" I asked.

"He told Miss Jennings and Mr. Donovan. I was there."

"You didn't think to inform the authorities?"

"Miss Jennings told me not to. She said she'd give him a letter to the president and he'd be on his way with no harm done."

"Miss Jennings again," I said. "Angus, you can't keep things secret simply because that woman tells you to. It's none of her business, anyway."

"Actually," Richard said, "in a way it is. She's here to keep an unobtrusive eye on potential American discontent. With the specific intention of keeping a lid on it. With trouble brewing in the Philippines, the U.S. government has no interest in a bunch of Americans agitating for taking the Yukon. Not at this time, at any rate."

"You're telling us that Miss Jennings is ..."

"An American spy. The photographer cover gave her ample excuse to wander around town. Taking pictures of the fort, the police, the waterfront. I've known that all along." Richard looked into my face. "I was instructed to ... uh ... become friends with her. Inspector Starnes wanted to be kept privately appraised of her movements. Eleanor will be leaving the territory tomorrow. Better make sure you get wages owed, Angus."

"Is anyone in this place who's what they seem?" Ray asked.

"John Turner isn't," Angus said.

"No. John Turner is a Mountie. What we call a plainclothes detective, Angus. His job's to keep an eye on troublemakers."

"You knew this?"

Richard shook his head. "No. I assumed he was a general layabout like so many others. He was, in fact, also interested in Count Nicky and his rather strange plans. The count, Turner told me, is the one person in all this who is precisely what he says he is. A Russian aristocrat who has some muddled idea of installing a group of serfs in Alaska in a sort of democracy. He, of course, plans to be head of that democracy. He doesn't entirely understand the concept."

"Lunacy," I said.

"Madness certainly. But madness unchecked can have a way of bringing about unexpected consequences. Nicky has enough money to buy influence."

"Rather a clever idea on Eleanor's part," I said, grudgingly. "It'll take him a couple of months to make his way to Washington and be refused admittance to the White House. By then he might well be distracted by another brilliant idea."

"We can only hope. John Turner, as part of his cover, played the obnoxious gambler. I think, Fiona, when you next see him you'll find him more amiable."

"Turner was watching Miss Jennings, also," Angus said. "He must have suspected her of being more than she appeared."

"How do you know that?"

"Uh ... just a guess. What will happen to Roland? Will there be a trial?"

"Probably not, I'm sorry to say. He'll be sent home with a flea in his superiors' ear. He'll claim he acted to protect the country and no one will want the details to become public."

"I must admit," I said slowly, "that I can't be too sorry to see Roland let off. Yes, he tried to kill you, Ray, but he didn't, did he? He saved me from that runaway horse, and was injured in the process. You have your suspicions about that, Richard. I can see it in your face. That wasn't an accident, was it?"

"No. We arrested one of Joey LeBlanc's enforcers for knocking around a girl badly enough to put her in the hospital. He let us know, before receiving his blue ticket, that Joey had a way of trying to deal with her enemies. He didn't come out and say it, but it was implied that he saw the opportunity and took it in expectation of a nice reward if you'd been injured. Roland was probably watching you, Fiona — he suspected you of being a secret Scottish agitator, remember — and intervened instinctively when he saw the impending accident."

"Gerry Sullivan?" I asked, filing away the information about Joey LeBlanc. I'd deal with her, in my own way and my own time.

"He'll be freed from the charge of killing Stewart, and given a blue ticket. Probably tomorrow. I have to be getting back. We've left Roland to stew for a bit, but Turner wants to start questioning him soon."

Ray struggled to get out of the clutches of the bad-springed sofa. Angus leaned over and gave him a hand. "Perhaps you should go home and rest," he said.

Ray laughed. "Where I come from, my lad, the night would have only just begun with a brawl like that one."

I refrained from mentioning that Ray was a considerable amount older than that young man punching his way through the slums of Glasgow. Instead, I checked my watch. "Getting on to midnight. Angus, go home."

He didn't argue. He was lucky to be able to stay to hear Richard's report, and he knew it.

"I'll walk you downstairs, Mr. Walker," Angus said.

They left. Angus shut the door quietly behind him.

Richard twisted his hat in his hand. I smoothed down the fabric of my dress. "Fiona," he said at last.

"Yes?"

"Miss Jennings is ..." he coughed "... a lovely lady and all."

"That she is." One with more depth than even I had seen.

"But, she ... I mean, I was ordered to escort her around town."

Not exactly an arduous duty, I managed to refrain from pointing out. "Yes."

He took a deep breath, threw his hat onto the desk, and crossed the room. He put his hands on my shoulders. My heart pounded. His brown eyes were liquid pools, dark and deep, in his chiselled face. He hadn't shaved for some time and the stubble on his chin was black. Curls were forming at the back of his neck. "There is," he said, his voice catching, "only one woman in all the world for me."

"And that would be...?" I whispered.

He bent his head.

The door crashed open. "Mrs. MacGillivray, you have to come right quick. Irene's going to make her announcement tonight and she sent me to fetch you. She says you'll want to hear it." Betsy stood there, chest heaving with exertion and excitement.

From where I stood I could hear the buzz rising from below. It was, as I'd observed, approaching midnight. Time for Irene's big dance. Unlikely I was the only one being summoned for tonight's command performance. Irene would want to be sure everyone had been rounded up from the bar and the gambling tables.

"I have to be going," Richard said. "You can tell me about this announcement tomorrow." He scooped up his hat, plopped it on his head, and walked out the door. Betsy stood aside to let him pass. She kept her expression neutral, but I suspect I saw a malicious smirk touching the edges of her over-painted mouth.

Chapter Thirty-Six

Irene danced the dance of the seven veils with glorious abandon. The audience was in fine fettle and they accompanied the discarding of every bit of cloth with ribald enthusiasm. I stood at the back, watching, not happy. Whatever this big announcement was, I doubted it meant me any good.

Gold rained down upon her at the conclusion. She stood on the stage, a colourful cloud of chiffon at her bare feet, beaming, accepting the adulation. She picked up some of the larger nuggets and left the other girls to run out from backstage and scoop up the rest. When the booty was gathered, Irene stepped to the front and held up her hands. The hoots that served as applause died down. The men leaned forward in their seats or where they stood. Beside me, I felt Ray stir. He was no happier than I. I put my hand on his uninjured arm and gave him an encouraging smile. He did not return it.

A born performer, Irene stood on the stage, arms held out, waiting until every foot was still and every eye on her. Girls crowded the wings, all of them eager to hear the news.

"I have some hard news for you," Irene said. She paused. No one breathed. "I will be leaving the Savoy, effective tonight."

Men shouted, "No!"

I groaned. "The Horseshoe, I'll bet," I said to Ray. "They're losing customers every night because of that pack of mules they call dancers." I did calculations in my head. How much more could I offer Irene to entice her to stay? Rather a cheap trick on her part, to announce to her crowd of admirers that she was leaving, preparatory to demanding an increase in pay.

"I am," she said, "getting married."

Ray choked.

"Come on up, George, and say hi to the boys," Irene shouted.

The short old miner, the one I'd noticed her paying an excessive amount of attention to, lumbered onto the stage. He smiled proudly, the effect spoiled by the fact that he didn't have a single tooth in his mouth. He stretched onto his tiptoes and planted a kiss firmly on Irene's cheek.

The men sat in stunned silence. I saw them exchanging glances, looking for clues as to how to react.

I gave it to them. I didn't want to chance another brawl breaking out. I applauded, while gritting my teeth. Ray growled at me.

The audience broke into scattered applause. George preened. Irene curtsied. In the wings, the dancers were looking highly pleased at this turn of events. Once again, Irene lifted a hand. The applause died down. "Leastways," she said, "'till spring. I'll be back, boys."

They leapt to their feet and roared.

Temporary marriages were not uncommon. A woman needed money, particularly over the long, cold winter when the dancehalls were largely empty, everyone huddled in their cabins out on the Creeks. A man needed female companionship. A business transaction. George would have paid a great deal for a temporary arrangement with the most popular dancer in the territory. I looked at him, short and ugly. All I felt was sorry for her.

Show over, Irene shooed her prospective husband off the stage and went to change. Benches were pushed aside, the musicians picked up their instruments, and the caller announced that the floor was open for dancing.

I waited for Irene outside the dressing room.

"I won't say your job will be waiting," I said once she emerged. "Who knows what the situation will be like next year. But you can come and ask."

"Thanks, Mrs. MacGillivray."

"Is it going to be worth it?"

"Probably not. He's promised me a lot of money, if I last till spring. I was raised on a farm with ten younger brothers and sisters and a mother who was sickly more often than not. I can cook and clean. Mend his socks. Do whatever else he wants, which likely won't amount to much. But you know what, Mrs. MacGillivray? I'll feel a lot cleaner with George. We both know what we're getting and so does everyone else. He wants a house-keeper and a companion. I want money. I won't be living a lie, pretending, like with Ray. And I won't be hiding in the shadows. Like with Eleanor."

I held out my hand. "I wish you luck, Irene."

We shook, and she walked away, head high. George was waiting to escort her to their new life. She did not say anything to Ray Walker as they left.

Chapter Thirty-Seven

I needed a new headliner. And fast.

Fortunately I had someone in mind.

"You've a good voice, and a nice stage presence. The men seem to like you. Do you want the job? Seventy-five dollars a week. An increase in a month if I decide it's earned."

Colleen Sullivan tilted her head to one side in thought.

We were taking tea at the Richmond Hotel. The sandwiches were fish paste, which I detest, and the tea had been stewed in a tin pot. The milk was powdered and lemon was nothing but the colour of some of the china. The delicate cup had a crack in the rim and the saucer didn't match. The waiter scratched his belly and burped as he asked if we wanted more.

I'd invited Colleen to tea to make my proposal. Her father had been expelled from the territory. If she wanted to leave with him, fine, but I'd extend the offer. I still had a stack of Eleanor Jennings' photographs to use as advertisements. I could scrawl something across Irene's face but the picture would be pretty much useless with the two central women gone.

Eleanor Jennings had left the territory yesterday, expelled. I had not gone to see her off, but Angus had. As she supervised the loading of her photography equipment onto the steamship, she handed my son a gift, in thanks for his friendship. A book on the new science and art of taking photographs. I arrived home to find him pouring over it.

Count Nicky, Angus told me, had boarded the same boat. Miss Jennings hoped she'd be able to avoid him. Fortunately for her, he'd have Roland the Magnificent to play poker with. As Richard had suspected, Roland had been ordered to leave the territory quietly. No doubt a strongly worded letter would be sent to his superiors.

Colleen nibbled on a fish-paste sandwich. "My father's been given a week on the woodpile," she said, "and then he's to leave the territory and never return. He told me to be ready to go soon as he gets out of jail. Ever since I was a little girl, it's been Ireland. Always Ireland. My dad was born in New York. He's never even been to Ireland. I hear it's a poor, ignorant, dirty place, but there's no telling him that. The Fenians are finished, they abandoned the cause a long time ago, but for my father that only proves the importance of remaining faithful.

"It will be nice to be free of all that. Thank you, Mrs. MacGillivray. I'll accept your offer. When do I begin?"

I consulted my watch. "In four hours. I trust you know *Macbeth*. If you need to brush up on the lines, Angus has a book you can borrow. And please, we will not have the hoochie koochie, thank you very much."

Chapter Thirty-Eight

Angus kicked a rock aside. Back to working at Mr. Mann's shop. He'd been down to the ship to see Miss Jennings off.

"I wish I'd had a chance to take your photograph, Angus," she said, as the porter carried her trunks aboard the steamship bound for St. Michael. "Not only would you make an interesting subject, but you'd have a memento of my visit. Nevertheless, here is a little something to thank you for your help." She pressed a book into his hands.

He'd thanked her and waved goodbye as she boarded. Her tiny blond head and neat brown bonnet were instantly absorbed by the crowd.

It was beginning to look as though he'd be stuck working in Mr. Mann's shop for the rest of his life. He flicked through the book. No, he had no further interest in being a photographer. It would be nice to have a camera, to take pictures of things of interest, but not to make a living from it. After the events of the past weeks he was more determined than ever to become a Mountie. Not only were the police required to track down murderers and pickpockets and patrol the cribs and the gambling halls, to be on guard against the use of vile language and loose morality, but they had to watch out for spies and foreign agitators too.

Roland was leaning up against a building when Angus rounded the corner. "Afternoon, my boy," the magician said.

"Thought you'd been evicted," Angus said.

"Decided my work here is done. Time to take my leave. My boat's leaving shortly."

"You said you wanted to be my friend. But you only wanted to hurt my mother and Mr. Walker." Angus walked away.

Roland fell into step beside him. "I misjudged. The Savoy wasn't a centre of the Scottish independence movement. No harm done."

"No harm! A man is dead. And no one will ever be held accountable."

"You mean Stewart. His real name, by the way, was the somewhat mundane John Green. We live in perilous times, son. Perilous times call for bold action. The Americans are growing in strength. About to go to war with Spain. They'll have their eye on Canada next and after that, what? The British colonies in the Caribbean that's what. What would you have us do? Put Green in jail for thirty days? Expel him from the territory? The Mounties here, they have no strength."

"Not kill him," Angus sputtered. "And everyone who might be associated with him."

"Say goodbye to your mother for me. I did enjoy working at her place."

Angus walked away. Behind him, Roland called out, "You forgot something."

The magician was holding a quarter between his thumb and forefinger, grinning.

Angus headed back to Mr. Mann's shop.

Author's Note

I have attempted wherever possible to keep the historical details of the Klondike Gold Rush, and the town of Dawson, Yukon Territory, accurate. Occasionally, however, it is necessary to stretch the truth in the interests of a good story. A few historical personages make cameos in the book, but all dramatic characters and incidents are the product of my imagination.

Information on photography of the time was provided during a fascinating visit to the George Eastman House: International Museum of Photography and Film, Rochester New York. I'd like to thank Jared Case and Todd Gustovson for taking the time to show me around and talk about old cameras.

The reader who is interested in learning more about the Klondike Gold Rush is advised to begin with the definitive book on the subject *Klondike: The Last Great Gold Rush 1896–1899* by Pierre Berton. Also by Berton, *The Klondike Quest: A Photographic Essay 1897–1899*.

OTHER READING:
- *Gamblers and Dreamers: Women, Men and Community in the Klondike*, Charlene Porsild
- *Gold Diggers: Striking it Rich in the Klondike*, Charlotte Gray
- *Good Time Girls of the Alaska-Yukon Gold Rush*, Lael Morgan

- *The Klondike Gold Rush: Photographs from 1896–1899*, Graham Wilson
- *The Klondike Stampede*, Tappan Adney.
- *The Last Great Gold Rush: A Klondike Reader*, edited by Graham Wilson
- *The Real Klondike Kate*, T. Ann Brennan
- *Women of the Klondike*, Francis Backhouse

FOR INFORMATION ABOUT THE NWMP:
- *The NWMP and Law Enforcement 1873–1905*, R.C. Macleod
- *Sam Steele: Lion of the Frontier*, R. Stewart
- *Showing the Flag: The Mounted Police and Canadian Sovereignty in the North, 1894–1925*, W.R. Morrison
- *They Got Their Man: On Patrol with the North West Mounted*, P.H. Godsell

Vicki Delany is a prolific and varied crime writer whose work includes standalone novels of gothic suspense, the Smith & Winters series, and the light-hearted Klondike Mysteries: *Gold Mountain*, *Gold Digger*, and *Gold Fever*. She lives in Picton, Ontario, and can be found online at *www.vickidelany.com*.

From the Same Series

Gold Mountain
A Klondike Mystery
Vicki Delany
978-1-459701892
$17.99

In the summer of 1897, Fiona MacGillivray and her eleven-year-old son, Angus, arrive in Vancouver in time to hear the news of gold discovered in the Klondike! Fiona immediately sets off for Skagway, Alaska, intent on opening a theatre. After one encounter with infamous gangster Soapy Smith and his henchman Paul Sheridan, she decides to pursue her ambitions on the other side of the border, in Dawson City. As a dying man breathes his last, he passes on to Sheridan a map pointing due north to the fabled Gold Mountain, where hills of gold keep the heat from hot springs contained in a valley as warm as California.

Sheridan is determined to become the king of Gold Mountain and to marry Fiona and make her his queen. Fiona, of course, wants no part of these mad plans. When Sheridan refuses to take no for an answer, Fiona must rely on Corporal Sterling of the North-West Mounted Police, young Angus, and a headstrong assortment of townsfolk to help thwart his scheme.

Gold Digger
A Klondike Mystery
Vicki Delany
978-1-894917803
$18.95

It's the spring of 1898, and Dawson, Yukon Territory, is the most exciting town in North America. The great Klondike Gold Rush is in full swing and Fiona MacGillivray has crawled over the Chilkoot Pass determined to make her fortune as the owner of the Savoy dance hall. Provided, that is, that her twelve-year-old son, growing up much too fast for her liking; the former Glasgow street fighter who's now her business partner; a stern, handsome NWMP constable; an aging, love-struck ex-boxing champion; a wild assortment of headstrong dancers, croupiers, gamblers, madams without hearts of gold, bar hangers-on, cheechakos, and sourdoughs; and Fiona's own nimble-fingered past don't get to her first. And then there's the dead body on centre stage.